ALL THE GIRLS IN TOWN

A NOVEL

STACI GREASON

ALL THE GIRLS IN TOWN

A NOVEL

STACI GREASON

Relax. Read. Repeat.

ALL THE GIRLS IN TOWN
Staci Greason
Published by TouchPoint Press
Brookland, AR 72417
www.touchpointpress.com

ISBN-13: 978-1-956851-12-0

Editor: Kelly Esparza
Cover Design: David Ter-Avanesyan/Ter33Design
Cover images: Shutterstock and iStock (licenses on file)
Author Photo: Sela Shiloni

Visit the author's website at www.stacigreason.com

 @staci.greason @stacigreason @staciwrites

First Edition

Printed in the United States of America.

For Larry, the best guy in every town

JUST-DESERTS.COM

At three a.m., I gripped the wheel and maneuvered the Taurus through scattered taillights on the 134, praying that the crunch under my bald tires was loose gravel. Putting the car in park on the shoulder of the freeway, I took a deep breath, wiped my palms on my jeans, and turned to Steve who was staring in silent defiance through the windshield. The fluorescence from a street light cast eerie shadows across the chiseled contours of his handsome brown face, making him look more like a villain in a superhero movie than just another cheating husband with a band.

"Is it Vasha?"

Steve snorted with disgust. "Vash isn't the one you need to worry about."

"Who then?" Hysteria rose in my throat. "Who am I supposed to be worried about *now*?"

A big rig passed, shaking the car.

"This is really dangerous." Steve hit the hazard button on the dash. Yellow staccato flashed around our car. "I don't know who gave it to me. Okay?"

Okay? Tomorrow, I would need to get tested for the venereal disease of the 21st century, or risk dying of cervical cancer because my husband couldn't keep his dick in his pants. "Sleeping with my own husband is more dangerous than sitting on the side of the freeway." I laughed until my fists found his body, and I hit until he grabbed my wrists, pulling me toward him in a hard kiss. I bit his lip. He yelped and pulled away.

"This relationship is toxic." Steve wiped a spot of blood from his mouth. "Everybody says so."

"Everybody in your band? Or just everybody you're fucking?"

He shook his head. "You're crazy."

And then, I opened the glove box, pulled out the .32 caliber and shot him. Dead.

DANI

Satisfied, Dani hit "publish" and took a swig of her Diet Coke. God, she missed smoking. And Ding Dongs.

It was Karyn, her OA sponsor, who'd politely suggested that Dani try journaling, as a way to fix some unresolved issues from her marriage and fill her God-shaped hole with something other than screaming resentment, sorrow, and sugar products. A soft-spoken, irritatingly sweet person, new to sponsoring, Karyn took her Overeaters Anonymous duties very seriously. Eager not to be the one to discourage her fresh out of the gate, Dani had gone to Michael's Art Supply and purchased a hardcover sketch book with blank pages, plus a few black pens, because she didn't like writing on lines or in blue ink. At the time, it had seemed like a futile exercise to write about how much her ex-husband had hurt her during their five-year marriage, and even more so after, but Dani was tired of crying herself to sleep covered in powdered sugar dust. And her boyfriend, Barney, was, too.

With three pages in, her ex was already dead. Bad potato salad at a family picnic. It was surprising, exhilarating, life-affirming. Dani had danced around her apartment singing, "Ding dong the dick is dead. Which old dick? My dirty old ex-dick." And she didn't even like dancing. The next morning, Peter, was hit by a truck. When Dani wrote, "His perfect body cracked the semi's windshield in a bloody sunburst," she achieved poetic justice.

Each morning, Dani awoke, heart fluttering, eager to stab, shoot, or poison Peter. She filled the blank pages of journals with the flames of her revenge fantasies until they caught fire and exploded into her blog, "Just Deserts," with (currently) sixty-one avid followers @just-deserts. Of course, once she went online, Dani changed everyone's names. Peter, her ex, was Steve on the blog. Sasha, the backup singer, became Vasha. And his real-life band, The Disasters, were The Calamities. It suited them. They could all fuck off.

Shortly after the divorce, Peter & The Disasters had released "Crazy Girl, Crazy Boy, Love." Dani first heard her lyrics playing on KROQ 106.7 one morning while driving to a shitty temp job. Shaking with fury, she ran a red light, hired a blood-thirsty attorney, and sued for half of the rights. The lawsuit went to trial, six brutal, violating months, which had increased the band's visibility into a record deal, but decreased Dani's bank balance to zero. "Crazy ex-wife sues over 'Crazy Love' song." A tabloid feeding frenzy. Without documentation, email or paper trail, there was no way to prove she'd written the song. Peter won. A week after the trial, Dani received a check for ten thousand dollars with "God!ess! We wish you peace," written in a feminine scrawl in the memo section.

"Does God!ess know you're fucking my husband, Sasha?" she'd shouted.

Then, Dani cashed the check, hired a couple of guys outside of Home Depot to help carry her away from their married apartment full of roaches and sorrow in Van Nuys, and moved into a sunny two-bedroom in lovely green Pasadena.

She told herself she was starting over but spent the next few months cramming treats down her gullet until, thirty pounds later, her younger sister, Monica, a turnstile twelve-stepper, suggested Overeaters Anonymous. For once in her miserable life, Monica had been right.

Researching and devising creative ways to kill Peter was filling Dani's God-shaped hole, not in the way mortified Karyn had hoped, but at least she wasn't shoveling baked goods into her pain. Ten pounds shed, and a reason to get out of bed. Who could have imagined that Danielle Desi Smith, crossing over the hump of thirty-five, earning fifteen an hour as a shitty temp, was born to be a literary assassin?

"Okay," Karyn had waxed and warned philosophic. "When God closes a door, he always opens a window. Without your ex-husband's infidelities and emotional abuse, you might never have discovered your writing talent. You should take a screenwriting class and move away from this kind of dangerous fantasy thinking."

Killing Peter didn't make Dani feel bad. She didn't want to write screenplays. She appreciated her sponsor's support, but Karyn wore on Dani's nerves. She had beaten on a closed door until smashing her fist through a window. She had the ugly scars to prove it. She wouldn't quit killing him now. It felt too good, almost better than sugar. She was hooked on revenge, a race car speeding toward a cliff, eager to see how close she could get to the edge.

RED

Highway 395 curved like a razor scar through the sharp rock incline of the Mojave desert. The gray sky overhead offered a false promise of rain. Red rolled down the window, letting the cold air hit her hot tears, and turned up the volume. *Take it. Take another little piece of my heart now*, Janis defied. "I want you to come on, come on, come on, come on and take it, Take it! Take another little piece of my heart now, baby! Oh, oh, break it!" Red screamed, banging her fist on the wheel.

The hurt was sharp like the tip of a blade in the center of her chest. What in the hell was wrong with her? The first time Peter had broken her heart was twenty years ago. Back then, she was a virgin, a Christian, a college junior. Now, she was a jaded, wary agnostic, a women's crisis counselor, of all things. Hadn't she learned anything?

The horizon darkened as the car sped through the flats of the Morongo Valley, trailer parks, pottery, an Italian restaurant with a faux-Western facade, then up the grade with cactus, stumps of old Joshua Trees, an abandoned yoga studio, and down into JT as shadows spread across the desert floor. She shivered, wiping away tears with her sleeve, turning left on Old Woman Springs Road. A wave of nausea, a small cramp. She'd given him her heart, and he'd smashed it into pieces. Again. Why?

Peter was a master at the art of seduction, talented at reconciliation, skilled at playing regret without any apologies. He had that infamous hangdog look with those dark brown puppy eyes, pretending he was warm and that he meant true love—that he was more than an actor. He'd worked his way back into her heart to get what he needed, and when she'd refused, he'd broken it harder than the first time.

She was the girl who fell on the knife.

The property was a ten-minute drive up the road from Pappy & Harriet's bar through Nature Conservancy land. No wires, no plumbing, no lights, few humans. "HERE," read a cardboard sign on the padlocked gate. It was forty acres owned by Carlos, a metal artist, who was dating her close friend, Matt, an eternal-romantic. Matt worked for a human rights group that hosted fundraising events for organizations like Planned Parenthood. He was a smart guy when it came to work, and a supportive friend with a great sense of humor. But when it came to love, Matt's choices were as skewed as Red's. This had cemented their friendship. She hoped Carlos, a real Renaissance guy, was a positive choice for her friend. Carlos was generous. He planned to build a house on the land with his own hands. Until then, he offered the land as a nature retreat for friends. She entered the padlock's combination and swung the wide gate open. A weekend to herself.

Red drove up the steep hill, parked, and climbed out, dust settling around her feet. She dragged her camping gear up the small hill. Mice, rats, a stray dog or maybe a coyote sparkled across the desert floor. There was nobody around for miles. After pitching her tent under the lone pine tree, Red started a fire in Carlos's makeshift cooking barrel. While she waited for her chili to heat, Red twisted off a Pacifico cap, flipped it into the night, and took a swig. And then another. She hit repeat on the button on her iPhone and turned up Janis. She knew she would dance this song out—this rage and this sorrow—all weekend, barefoot and alone under the desert stars, unwinding memories until she purged everything about him.

They met in a college class. "Hey, Red?" Peter had called, chasing her out of the classroom one sunny afternoon.

She'd turned. "My name is Rebecca."

His gaze moved to her breastbone, which was bare in a summer dress. Her heart beat a little faster. She smiled and bit her lip. Caught, Peter had looked up, face flushed. "You have the most beautiful hair I've ever seen. The way it catches the light. It's like fire, or a sunset."

"Oh. Thanks." Her stomach fluttered under his soulful gaze, but she had a boyfriend. Brad. He went to school in Tulsa. They were waiting to consummate.

Peter offered her a promo flyer. Open mic at a coffee house in North Hollywood. "I'm playing there this weekend." The color rose in his cheeks. "It's no big deal. I just do cover stuff. But it would be cool to see you."

She took the flyer from his outstretched hand, well-muscled, strong. A shiver crept up her spine, like the ones she'd heard about in movies. "My boyfriend, Brad, is in town this weekend. I'll see if he wants to come."

Peter didn't hide his disappointment. "My loss."

If only Brad hadn't come down with a bad cold and cancelled his trip. If only her roommate, Savannah, hadn't commandeered their living room for a Trivial Pursuit party with Jell-O shots. If only curiosity and loneliness hadn't driven her across the San Fernando Valley to that gig.

The coffee house was rustic Western themed, with scuffed wood floors powdered in sawdust and old, black-and-white photographs of cowboys tacked to faux-log walls. A small plastic tree flashing cheerfully in the front window reminded her that it was almost Christmas again. It was Rebecca's most dreaded holiday. Soon, a festive card would arrive from her parents, happily playing volunteers for orphans on another continent, while Rebecca anxiously found ways to stay busy until the new year, when classes resumed and her loneliness would recede.

After paying the mohawked waitress for an overpriced, frothy peppermint drink, Rebecca had found an open seat at a large wagon wheel table and waited, feeling like a sore thumb in the hip crowd.

When Peter finally jumped up on stage, her heartbeat quickened. There was no way to ignore it; he was devastatingly handsome, and she had a crush. Those dark, long lashes, the strong chin. Full lips. Dressed in a button-down, short-sleeved cotton shirt and worn jeans, Peter had moved easily in his lean frame. Carrying a small amp to the front, the sinewy muscles of his arms engaged, and Rebecca's whole body blushed to life. It was a new feeling, to physically yearn for a person just by looking at him. She'd never felt that attraction for Brad.

It was a sin—forbidden, but delicious.

Peter grabbed his guitar and straddled the wooden stool. Leaning over to tune, a thick wave of dark hair fell across his face, and he pulled it into a ponytail. Rebecca desperately wanted to clutch fistfuls of his thick locks.

"One, two, three." His deep voice into the microphone tested the sound levels. He strummed, tuning slightly, and Rebecca took a sip of her sweet drink, hoping no one could read her improper thoughts.

"Woo!" a guy's voice from the back of the room belted.

A young woman's voice called out, "Go, Peter."

Rebecca turned in the direction of the female voice to discover a pretty woman with short, cropped hair and big eyes staring up adoringly at Peter. A small violin case rested on the table near the woman's arm. Suddenly, Rebecca regretted giving up piano lessons in eleventh grade.

Peter looked out into the room, and their eyes met. He clasped his hands together at his heart, as if Rebecca took his breath away. She blushed with hormones and possibility.

Please, let him kiss me, she caught herself thinking, forgetting about God completely.

Peter cleared his throat and leaned back into the microphone, never taking his gaze from hers. "Hey, everybody. Thanks for coming," he said, his voice quiet, almost humble. "I'd like to dedicate this song to a new friend. I hope she'll stick around." He winked at Rebecca.

She squirmed, feeling the flow of heat below and crossed her legs.

He strummed a few chords and started to sing, "*Just before our love got lost, you said, I am as constant as a northern star.*"

His raw, masculine voice dripped with honey, with the sincerity of a man who'd felt love and loss. Rebecca hadn't a clue about Joni Mitchell, or any kind of secular music except country, but the melancholy sound, the poetry of loving something, someone so wrong, rang true.

In later years, she'd wonder if falling in love with Peter had been Joni's fault. The depth of a soul, looking into her soul. Someone who understood loneliness and pain.

Constantly in the darkness, where's that at? If you want me, I'll be in the bar.

Peter drew her in with Joni's words. Making Joni's melancholy their own. "*I could drink a case of you darlin' and I would still be on my feet. I would still be on my feet.*"

Her body hummed with music. The sound of his soothing voice was a communion, an invitation, to join with his energy. She drifted into the vibration with Peter. Was this the way real love felt? Her heart opened, and for the first time, she wasn't alone. She and Peter rode this current together.

"Love is touching souls. Surely you touched mine. Part of you pours out of me in these lines from time to time."

Later, in Peter's apartment in Van Nuys, candles lit and jazz softly playing, Rebecca had willingly given her virginity to Peter and been reborn as Red. The sex was slightly painful, but not frightening. It was slow, tender, and exciting, full of sweet words and promises, caresses that were freeing, opening and healing. "You are not alone. You are not alone. You are not alone."

Afterwards, lying naked and sweaty, together as one, on the hard futon, Peter had wrapped his strong arms around her shaking shoulders and whispered, "I see you," caressing her hair. "I see you." His eyes filled with tears of love.

Peter made her feel like she was the only woman in the world.

The next day, she broke up with Brad and moved into Peter's shitty apartment.

It was pure bliss.

Love doesn't come with a warning sign. A woman will fight for years to get back the first hit of bliss. The memory, the pictures and feelings, are vivid. She can lose her compass and get lost in what-was, unable to see what is—the dead end getting closer, right in front of her.

Peter finished college and got a graphic design job to support them, while Red worked that last year to finish her BA in psychology. They made candlelight dinners, went to the movies, drank Chianti, had great sex, and Red started singing backup for Peter at the coffee house.

She had never been happier in her life.

Finally, after much love and cajoling, Peter decided to be brave and play his first original song on stage. Because it was a friendly place, people loved him, and Red had promised to sing backup.

"Mi madre, mi madre el ángel," he'd sung, his buttery voice honest and raw. *The stars are like your eyes when I look up at them. . . .*

Yes, Red had cringed a little over the lyrics. They were clunky, but it was his first. And to fail at first meant that Peter had been trying. She hadn't wanted to discourage creativity. "Madre, so lonely so lost," she'd quietly sung backup beside him.

"Mi madre el ángel," they'd sung in unison. "You are an angel up in heaven."

Suddenly, a man's voice had called out, "Dude, go back to covers," followed by a smattering of uncomfortable laughter.

Peter immediately stopped strumming. Red had looked out across the warm, dim room. Maybe ten people were seated with coffees, watching in silence, not a big enough crowd to humiliate. She spotted a tall guy wearing a Dodgers cap by the bar. A friend of Peter's. She'd shaken her head, shooting daggers at him.

"Hey," the guy called out. "I was only kidding. How about some Van Halen?"

The small group had laughed.

Peter stood then and walked silently off stage with his guitar, leaving Red to grab the small amplifier and chase after him to their car in the parking lot.

For the next two years, Red watched Peter watch TV, smoke pot, drink beer, go to bed, get up, go to work, repeat. Avoiding Woody, his guitar. Avoiding her. Refusing to talk about that one ridiculous bad moment, to recover, to climb back on the horse.

Peter's wounded ego turned their lives into an emotional roller coaster.

There were days of tender and harsh words, nights filled with kisses and fights, a weekend of laughter, followed by an unkept promise, suspicious behavior, ignored red flags. Their love made her happy, made her terrified, left her feeling crazy, but she clung to it fiercely, certain that one day the good times would return.

Red went on a big job interview for a regional coordinator position at Planned Parenthood, and Peter fucked Prisha, an Indian immigrant he'd met at the laundromat.

Red got the Planned Parenthood job. Peter took her to dinner to celebrate. Over the tiramisu, he broke the news about Prisha.

"Why?" Red had sobbed.

"Sometimes, a guy wants something different." Peter had shrugged.

After Peter had carried his last box to the car and driven away to Prisha, Red walked to the Liquor Mart at the corner and bought a bottle of Chianti for seven dollars. That night, she laid on the couch and drank the whole thing, listening to Joni. If the neighbors heard her sobs, she didn't care. She woke up in a fetal position on the floor at four a.m. and threw up what little remained in her stomach. That afternoon, she bought another bottle. She called in sick to work for a week, eyes swollen from crying, head pounding, stomach aching from alcohol and sorrow. She never slept in their bed again. She took kitchen shears to the red locks he'd loved, burned the lyrics he'd written her in the kitchen sink, and stomped on every Joni album until they were shards of plastic. A month later, she donated what little furniture they'd shared to Goodwill and moved into a studio apartment across the Valley. But she never gave up the wine. Wine was the only thing that dulled the hurt.

A year later, she heard that Peter had kicked out Prisha to marry an ordinary, dumpy white girl named Danielle. Life was all gray.

Twenty years later, she was drinking Mai Tais with Matt at La Cita downtown, and suddenly, there stood Peter. Still handsome. His dark eyes lit with warm recognition. She'd smiled, nodding her head.

"Girl, be careful," Matt had warned placing a hand on her arm.

A few more Mai Tais and an impromptu set on stage drove the girls crazy. Peter's eyes bore into her soul from the stage. There was chemistry, intimacy, and yes, understanding, *I see you*, and *you see me for who I really am*. She'd felt the connection as strong as ever. He was singing original material. It was fucking good. His voice was rock solid real. He was famous, for God's sake. He'd overcome his fears.

Twenty years erased like a day.

How to explain a relationship out of time in the real world? How to make sense of a recognition for another soul? He felt like a member of her family, a twin, brother or husband, returning from another lifetime.

Sure, she'd glanced for a while at the tabloid covers in line at the grocery store. The divorce and subsequent legal battle over rights for his first hit, the song that had skyrocketed The Disasters from playing KROQ's Weenie Roast to Coachella. Peter's charisma had propelled the band to the top of the charts. Red didn't own a TV, but even she'd heard he was living with the beautiful backup singer in his band.

"Tabloid rumors," Peter said, promised even. He'd been unhappy in his marriage for a while. "Sasha let me crash at her pad when Dani kicked me out. She's cool, more like a sister. I don't even think she's that pretty. Not like you. You . . . ." He'd clasped his hands to his heart in that familiar gesture, and Red had instantly fallen for him all over again.

She ignored Matt's vocal warnings, "I'm watching the red flags as they sail on by."

God, she'd missed this, the insatiable hunger—yes, to be desired completely by this man. She continued to ignore the red flags. She swatted away Matt's whispers and pleas until he left the bar.

Drinking made it easier to forget, to forgive—whatever it was that alcohol did for her.

Yes, yes, smell, taste, all of it. All of the mistakes, yes, he'd agreed. Mistakes made for wisdom, he'd repeated, "You're really different. I like it."

Another red flag unfurled and sailed into the wind as Red surrendered, inviting him to her home and into her bed before three a.m.

Years of cognitive behavioral therapy, self-help book groups, several fairly healthy, very boring boyfriends, a supportive girlfriend, Al-Anon and spiritual study, and true love had returned to Red. Peter was weary of his animal ways and ready to be a better human.

That's the story Red told herself. She had changed her bad love karma, and love had returned a changed man, ready to make up for his mistakes.

For ten blissful, sex-filled days, they'd hidden from the world in her small blue house in Echo Park, a sliver of greenish pond viewable from the bathroom window. Peter, anxious to stay far away from paparazzi, said, "No, let's stay in," ordering takeout or making pasta, drinking Chianti, making love on the living room couch, on a chair in the kitchen, the bathtub, on the floor of her bedroom next to the golden eyes of the curious cat. Red wanted to drink in every bit of him before The Disasters left on the first leg of their North American tour.

She'd think of those late nights, naked in the bath, curled against his body, glistening in the candlelight, so tender and intimate. *I could drink a case of you, and I would still be on my feet.*

I would still be on my feet, she sung in reply, completely forgetting that she'd grown to hate the melancholy of Joni Mitchell.

"I always thought you had the most beautiful voice," Peter whispered, stroking her hair, winding his finger around a strand. "I wish you were singing backup on my tour. Come with me?"

"I have a job, silly." She splashed warm water at him. "I can't just drop everything for months."

"I'm kinda nervous," he confessed. "I'd be all right with you by my side."

This should have been the biggest flaring red flag.

Like a drag on a cigarette after years without, the brain remembered *yes* binding to synapses, *yes*, this was coming home chemistry. Be mine, baby. Baby, be mine. *Yes*, she'd cried into his shoulder. Red and Peter, *love is touching souls because surely you touched mine.*

Red had used all of her sick days and vacation time at the clinic to reconnect.

Standing together on the sidewalk outside of her house that last morning, she'd wrapped her arms around him, smelling the clean, soapy scent of his neck, winding her fingers through his luxurious locks, feeling like her heart might burst.

Peter bent down, tenderness in his eyes and kissed her again.

"I'll miss you," she'd repeated.

A black town car pulled to the curb.

Peter offered a distracted smile. "Oh, yeah. Talk to you soon, babe." Climbing into the backseat, he said hello to the driver and shut the door without looking back, as another red flag sailed past.

The town car disappeared around the corner. Red walked back inside and shut the door, the high still lingering but the house quiet. She hit The Disasters on Apple Music, humming to his vocals on the new hit, "Postal Blues," while she picked up sticky, half-finished cartons of Chinese food, empty wine bottles, even a pair of his dirty socks, carrying the trash bags out to the street. She folded the greasy pizza boxes and put them in the recycling bin. A slight breeze rustled the bamboo leaves lining the front yard, a quiet hum in her body still warm in oxytocin and melancholy. She'd shielded her eyes from the bright, midday light and looked across her yard at the boxed garden of carefully tended vegetables and herbs. Once vibrant and alive, they were now tinged with burn, limp and abandoned, almost dead.

A whisper of fear spread through her chest.

For several hours, Red had apologized to the withered plants, pulling weeds, until a small rain shower drove her back indoors with the cat to finish the last bottle of Chianti, convincing herself that it was old stuff, PTSD. Peter was different. The small house was too quiet, and when she knew his plane must have landed in Chattanooga, the first stop, she sent a text.

RED: Miss you! xo

And waited. She finished the wine, while raindrops pounded the sidewalk, the cat slept, and the world pulled away again.

That night, after several more unanswered texts and a voice message, Red finally went online, in a frenzy, to The Disasters' Instagram, driven by an unsettling dread. There were a lot of pictures of him with several pretty girls pouting out their lips and hanging onto his body. She scrolled deeper, moving away from the current successes and into older posts and band gigs until she found her—the girl he said he loved like a sister, onstage with the band in a small gig. The young woman he said wasn't even that pretty. Like a sister. No, Sasha wasn't pretty. She was luminous, curvy with dark, voluminous hair, big dark eyes, and light brown skin.

Her beauty hit like a bullet. Sasha was much different from Red's pasty, freckled face.

Two days later, somewhere outside of New Orleans, Peter tried to ease her anxieties during a phone call. "Red, babe, listen. Sash isn't on tour. Remember, I wanted you to come? I really needed you. We have twenty cities. A total gruel. When we're not onstage, we're sleeping."

The Disasters' pages told a different story: an orgy of late-night parties, bodies of drunken bandmates with fans and selfies of groupies, women half-dressed, laughter, crazy late-night stoned or drunk, heavy-lidded. Peter, red-eyed, tired or high. Both? She hated that he got high—that it relaxed his nerves before a show, only to put him down after. In truth, Red knew that as long as Peter was awake, he had to be using something—alcohol, drugs, women. He couldn't live his truth sober.

While counseling women at her job at The East Valley Women's Center, whether it was pregnancy or sexually transmitted diseases, listening to women who'd been battered, abused, or raped, women who were addicted, anorexic, or bulimic, victims of hate crimes, cancer survivors, rich or poor, Red's thoughts were elsewhere. She became obsessed that Peter was cheating or lying again to her. She worried like a needle on the groove, heart pounding to the music of anxiety. The shortness of breath, feeling of panic tight against her ribs. The images of him having sex with other women invaded her at work, at the grocery store. Even while pumping gas, she had to fight to keep the demon of jealousy at bay. She needed to get a grip. She was a therapist for Christ's sake. She had gone back to college to get the Ph.D. to prove it and then landed a better position. Peter became her drug again; she drank him night and day, fed off the anxiety, the release, the lies that kept her digging harder for the truth.

Six weeks later and no period, Red was forced to take real action when the test came back positive. She had to stop being the victim, waiting, looking at his social media pages, and do something to ease her suffering besides drinking red wine. "I'm flying out to see you," she said through an announcement on his voicemail. "I've got exciting news." It might have been a false positive, but her body told her differently. She booked a ticket. "I'll be at the Oklahoma City show on Thursday. I love you." A pit in her stomach. When he didn't call back the next day, she'd sent a text. She must have sent over fifty without any reply.

On the day of her flight, she sat in her parked car in Burbank Airport's long-term lot and texted him.

RED: I'm pregnant. (baby emoji)

Her cell rang.

"You work at Planned Parenthood."

Her chest tightened. "I haven't worked there in ten years." She took a deep breath. "What's going on?"

"Babe." His voice softened. "Sash and I were secretly married six months ago in Bali. It's all cool. She doesn't care about other women. I wanted you on the road singing with me. I miss that, us together onstage. We work. But, this baby shit, I really can't handle it. You have no idea."

She opened the car door and vomited onto the asphalt.

What a fucking idiot she'd been.

Red tossed the empty beer bottle into the desert night, hearing it land with a soft clank on the earth. What kind of man acted like that? A sick man, a bad guy. A man who liked to hurt women because he could. A man who was selfish, who only saw love as a transaction and nothing more. Man, she hated it—needing him, like a drug. She danced, around the oil drum, screaming like a hyena. She was like a wounded animal, pounding her fists on her chest, swinging her red hair, like a circle of fire catching, unwinding her pain counter-clockwise, stomping back the last few months, the last twenty years, that one night, one man, who hadn't cared. Peter again had unraveled her. She had to weave herself back together.

All day long she counseled women, girls, those who didn't want another child, a runaway hiding from an abusive parent, or those who were impregnated by a deadbeat boyfriend who didn't like condoms. Was there a choice? Whose choice was it? The woman. The woman. The woman. The woman got to choose, had to make the choice, to be in charge. It was all right to be a single mother, or to choose to be one later.

"For now, it's legal, safe, and available," she'd tell a terrified or defiant pregnant woman seated across from her.

I want to finish my law degree.

I want it.

I can't afford it.

He hits me.

We don't have the money for another baby.

I won't make it. My diabetes.

It's a baby.

It isn't a baby.

It's tissue.

It's God.

It isn't his.

It can be reincarnated.

I don't feel anything for it.

What happens to it?

I always thought I'd want a baby.

I want to put her up for adoption.

I don't want a kid.

He forced me.

Can't I just get this over with?

How could this have happened?

I didn't tell him.

I'm on the pill.

My parents would kill me.

Literally. He beats me.

My girlfriend says she'll leave.

He wore a condom.

Am I a bad person?

Will I go to hell?

It isn't the right time.

Does it hurt?

Yes. Yes, she assured each woman, the procedure would hurt a little, there would be a tug, cramps, like a period, but not much. Or nothing would happen at all. Either choice. Life was about suffering, except when it wasn't. It was filled with hard choices. All gray, not black and white. This hard choice, to end her pregnancy, had broken the last of her heart.

How would she feel if she'd kept it? She would have been a good single mother. But what about the baby? What would the counselor tell this patient? The father was a sex addict, a pothead, a pathological liar, possible sociopath with no sense of remorse, but he was also famous and rich. He had piles of cash to throw at a child with a dark pit in his heart. She did it knowing that all of the love she had to give in the world would never be enough for a kid with an unloving father. She promised herself that she did it knowing that Peter would leave an open wound in a child because he couldn't love. Narcissists only loved their own reflection. She did it knowing that her decision would haunt her for the rest of her life. And there would be a karmic consequence.

When the doctor at the clinic performed the abortion, it had hurt a little, yes, like a tug, but it also felt like nothing for such a big something. It happened quickly; the nurse had offered a maxi pad like it was an answer or a salve to losing the hope of a life. To losing a life. Red stuffed it in her purse and walked away empty.

Sweating and exhausted, Red sat on the ground, finally, spent, all cried out. She gazed up at the dome of stars over the desert, one pinpoint brighter than the rest. Planet or satellite? The moon, a small sliver of white hung on an invisible thread, weightless, magical, and beautiful.

"Fool," she yelled into the darkness. The wind picked up, a quiet growling across the desert floor, sending detritus skipping across the earth, remembering the words, the Buddha turns the wheel of the law: birth, sickness, old age, and death. Jesus wept.

But Red was going to take her fucking power back.

She needed a solid plan, a way to get close enough to Peter's shiny new life so that she could destroy him. Who could be an ally? Who hated Peter as much as or more than Red?

SASHA

"Is our fingertips reach toward heaven with our shoulders relaxed, we take one more deep breath and slowly exhale, lowering our hands in prayer in front of our hearts, opening wide to the Goddess within," Sasha said in a soothing, meditative tone as she exhaled and opened her eyes to see at least two dozen beautiful mothers-to-be, their eyes closed, faces flushed and sweating, blissed out, seated in wide-lotus or open-legged positions on their mats, absorbing one another's energy. They had love, pure love, for the lives growing within their bodies and their own.

Many of the women in her prenatal sessions were six or seven months along, but with the support of Sasha's classes and diet regimen, they'd managed to retain their sexy, sleek figures, energy, and great health. Her hand instinctively went to the growing bump of her own belly. Hey, baby, hey, baby. What's going on? This morning when Sasha had dressed, her swollen feet couldn't fit into her yoga grip socks. Or the ballet flats. She made a mental note to call her homeopath about water retention. So unsightly. What kind of role model's regimen didn't work on herself? Thank God Peter was on the road to miss this ugly part. The thought hit a lonely echo in the center of her chest, and she reached for the bell wand.

Sasha slowly circled the wand around the rim of the large meditation bell. A relaxing circadian rhythm enveloped the room. "Ohm, ohm, ohm," she chanted. The women quietly joined in, humming the higher vibration catching on the twinkling lights swaying from the rafters. *We are one.* The large gold Ganesh on stage emitted abundance. Perfect purple walls soothed. There was an orange energy room next door, yoga and spiritual dancing classes, vibrational energy drinks and snacks, t-shirts, candles, and gemstone healings. In God!ess, Sasha had built a successful healing studio (soon-to-be featured in *Yoga Monthly*'s holiday issue). She had created something from nothing but an idea, a dream. Of course, Peter's name initially inspired Hollywood clients to sign up for packages as well as their first women's yogic dance retreat in Tulum next spring. The success of The Disasters had afforded the down payment on the location so near to the Grove, but Sasha had made God!ess, the brand, what it was, like she was making a baby.

From prayer, hope, intuition, and sheer determination, this was a miracle!

When she was fourteen, Sasha had been in a terrible car accident on the way to compete at the Miss Teen USA pageant; her drunken pageant coach had plowed into a concrete wall and died at the scene. A horrible man, a prick, a narcissist. Every specialist from London to Los Angeles had assured her parents that having a baby would no longer be possible. Even after extensive reconstruction surgery, there'd been too much damage to her pelvic region. The God!ess had kept her alive for a reason. And that reason wasn't to be crowned in a beauty pageant as that was her mother's dream, which she'd never accomplished, or to sing backup in a famous band, which was her former dream. It was to become happy, help other women be happy, and make a baby with Peter.

Peter's first reaction was shock. "But how?" He'd stared at the plastic stick with the red plus sign. "The doctors said you couldn't?"

"The God!ess!" Sasha wiped the tears of gratitude from her cheeks. "She heard our prayers."

How many times while making love had Peter looked deeply into her eyes and said, "I wish I could make a baby with you." Sasha held her breath and waited for Peter's surprise to turn to joy.

"It is good news." He took her in his arms. "It's just, babe, the baby's timing is really bad. What do we do?"

The Disasters were about to embark on their first North American headline tour. The miracle baby's timing was inconvenient, but not bad. How could a miracle ever be bad?

"Don't worry." Sasha had pressed her palms into his stubbled cheeks to calm him, to connect him to her. "I'm still your backup singer. My studio is running smoothly. I have teachers to cover my classes."

But morning sickness had quickly wrecked her touring plans.

Peter had hired Annie, an older woman he knew from the early coffee house band days, as Sasha's replacement. Singing in The Disasters' first headlining tour wasn't a part of the God!ess's great mystery plans for Sasha.

"Annie will do great," Sasha had assured Peter. "And you'll be home for Christmas, in time for your fortieth birthday, and a whole new year with our baby."

She watched the pretty, sleek Westside pregnant moms rolling up their mats, chatting about breastfeeding and doula birth plans and repeated the mantra in her head: Not fat, not fat, I am pregnant, beautiful, and deserve love. Since she'd gotten pregnant, Sasha's normally optimistic interior clock tilted too easily to sad, mean, anxious, or weary.

And jealous.

Why? Two months into the tour, Sasha was getting fat while Peter sang onstage with Annie; toned, thin and hard-edged, Annie was too rough around the edges, too much leather and denim and tattoos, too white, but she was very sexy. Thank God!ess she was too old for Peter; she was at least forty-five. And a heavy smoker. Peter hated the smell of cigarette smoke. And her arms were ropey, veined like a man's. Still, she had a beautiful, smoky, deep voice. Sasha's voice was reed thin.

"Sash?" A yoga mom's voice abruptly brought Sasha's awareness into the class as the lights slowly rose in the room.

Sasha opened her eyes. Her expectant students were staring. "Sorry. I must have dozed off."

A pretty young mother with bright green eyes and a small baby bump laughed. "Rest! Water! Vegetables! No meat! I don't know what I'd do without you."

"Amen," another said.

Sasha felt her cheeks flush. Intimate adoration was the uncomfortable part of owning the studio. "Oh, no, your body knows what you need. Listen to your body. You'll be fine."

The women drank water and chatted as they exited the classroom. She was beautiful in her own way. There was no need to beat herself up about her voice or body in comparison to a woman who wasn't blessed. They were having a baby. Peter was excited about the baby. Of course he was excited. He reassured her with each, "Good night, I love you, and whoever is on its way," from Chattanooga, New Orleans, Little Rock, Biloxi.

Until last night from Oklahoma City, that is, when Peter had sent a text.

PETER: Good night, I love you, and whoever is on its way (baby emoji).
Totally wiped. Call you mañana por la mañana.

It was just Peter, she reassured herself, creativity and nerves swayed his focus. He loved her forever. Exactly as she was. He'd said this repeatedly. He wouldn't leave her because of the change, unexpected event, or the extra weight.

It was a relief that he wasn't home to see her naked bulky body climbing from the bathtub, changing under fluorescent lights in her walk-in closet, her belly slathered in oil to prevent scarring stretch marks. A slight discoloration across her forehead had been expertly covered by her hair stylist in a smart fringe, but the swelling—the unsightly swelling—made her fairly certain that her nose was spreading, so she'd taken out the ring. He wouldn't cheat on the road now. They were married. Yes, they'd cheated on Dani. They'd slept with a lot of people, separately and together. But he'd been living a nightmare, a dead-end marriage with no love to a crazy, desperate woman.

Theirs was true love.

JUST-DESERTS.COM

The bonfire was roaring before we arrived, late as usual. Steve had decided some new girl singer's band rehearsal was more important. My new friends, Iris and Shaun, two Brits I'd met at our local co-op, had extended an overnight beach camping invitation. I was so excited and had been planning and talking about it all week with him.

"This was my thing," I said. My voice was hard, fired up in anger. "Remember when you used to care about the things that mattered to me?"

"I still do, babe." Steve's hands gripped the wheel, knuckles white. "I lost track of time."

Ryan Adams twanged melancholy about loves lost in the background as we drove winding Kanan Dune through the tunnels and back down to PCH, watching the last of the sun set brilliant pink and disappear into the Pacific. I could feel I'd reached the hard edge of his patience, but continued, "If this had been an event with your musician friends, we wouldn't be late. But no, I'm excited for one thing, camping overnight with my new friends. Friends who could be our friends. And we're an hour late."

"I know we're late. You keep reminding me. I can't make it better." His tone sounded exasperated like he was dealing with a small child and not his wife.

"What's going on with us?"

He shrugged. "Nothing. I love you."

This was his answer for everything when he was avoiding a real conversation.

Steve drove in silence while I wiped away tears to keep my face from turning puffy and red in front of Iris and Shaun. I didn't want to look like a basket case. They were hip, lean, did groovy things like the co-op, volunteering at a soup kitchen, hiking the Andes. They had a real marriage. I leaned over and changed the station on the satellite radio. "I'm sick of Ryan Adams." Lucinda Williams, raw and pure edge, came to life, growling, *"I'm learning how to live without you in my life."*

We pulled into the parking lot, watching pit fires flare orange up and down the strand.

Steve parked, turned off the car, and looked to me. "I love you."

Before he could utter another lame fucking excuse, I snapped, "You bring the tent. I'll grab the rest," and climbed out the passenger door. "And try not to hit on my new friends."

Adorable Iris and Shaun were snuggled in a chair in front of the fire, drinking wine, and grilling soy burgers when I stomped to the site.

"Hey," they said in unison, smiling but not bothering to get up from their comfortable seat. They were not people pleasers, like me. They knew what they brought to the friendship table. Their accents, their scrubbed, fresh faces, cheeks rouge from wine and sun and love.

"Hey!" I waved wildly. "Steve is just getting the tent. Sorry we're late. Musicians." I rolled my eyes.

"No worries, mate." Shaun stood. "Beer or wine?"

The Brits were big drinkers. Steve brought the pot. And Woody, of course. Couldn't go one night without being in the spotlight. I drank a lot of wine, more than my usual glass. In my defense, I hadn't realized how beautiful Iris was until I saw Steve see her for the first time. His eyes devoured her lanky legs poking out from her short shorts, her underpants almost visible, with her small round behind, her flat waist to a halter top that revealed an almost flat chest, and her thin, toned arms. All night long he watched Iris playing frisbee, laughing, drinking wine. Iris with her soft blonde bob, big blue eyes, and a wide smile with a slightly crooked eye tooth that only made her sexier somehow. She didn't do anything to encourage it, except maybe flirted a little and maybe sat on his lap at one point after too many beers when they'd started tequila shots. Shaun hadn't seemed to mind. Teasing Steve at one point, "Please, she's a lot. Take her off my hands for the night?"

My heart sank when Steve turned to Iris and strummed the first chord of the song I'd written for him. With his sultry voice, those intense eyes, Steve sang only to her, bewitching Iris with his black magic. I remembered what it felt like to be the only girl in the room and realized that I had been forgotten. Shaun quickly grabbed Iris, taking her into their tent. No one asked where I wanted to sleep, or with whom. I was dressed in old baggy jeans with a big t-shirt, thinking camping, not modeling, my hair frizzy on my head. It was cold. I drank. And drank. I ate a bag of potato chips because I was still hungry, and soy makes me bloated.

Later, inside our tent, as the canvas swayed, and my head spun, feeling slightly nauseated, I forced myself to focus on my husband above me, dry humping, pounding in and out, silently, without looking at my face. My mouth, my eyes, my vagina were dry, but he didn't seem to notice.

"Babe. Oh, God. Yeah," he moaned, his voice deepening. "Fuck me."

"I am." I climbed on top of him swallowing back the vomit. Pretending that I was into it, I circled my hips for emphasis.

"Feel how hard and deep I am. Can you feel it?"

I'd never liked talking during sex. "Oh, baby."

And then, in the most horrible, racist accent Steve could muster, my husband said, "Babe, say, 'Me love you long time.'"

My hips stopped moving, but the tent kept swaying. "What?"

"Say, 'Me love you long time.'"

I pushed his chest away, crawling off of him. "What's wrong with you?"

"Jesus." He didn't sit up. He lay there, his hard cock staring between us. "It's sex talk."

"From some Asian hooker porn site for racists?" I screamed. "You are *disgusting*, disgusting."

He sighed. "Asian women are everyone's ideal."

My stomach lurched as if I'd just been punched. "Why did you even marry me?"

I scrambled on my hands and knees out the tent flap, racing barefoot across the sand toward the public bathrooms. Too late to open the door, I projectile vomited against the concrete wall.

When I crawled back inside the tent with the lit kerosene lantern, Steve was snoring, fast asleep, penis still erect. In the morning, he wouldn't remember what he'd said to me, the woman who worked two jobs to support his fledgling musical career. Even if Steve recalled the unkind words he'd drilled into my heart because he'd been too high, too drunk, and wished he could fuck anyone other than his wife, he wouldn't care. I was tired of feeling like a piece of shit.

The lantern accidentally tipped, lighting a patch of canvas. As the tent went up in flames, onlookers down the beach said the orange glare was like a harvest moon. "The deceased's wife was in the bathroom at the time the fire started," read his obit in the *LA Times*. Camping accidents, warned the paper, happened all the time.

RED

Speechless, she handed back Matt's cell. Peter's ex was writing a revenge blog. She searched for the right words to express the feeling, reading about his death. His murder. She felt

... happy? She wanted to laugh, to cry out, yes! "Wow."

"Fantastic, right?" Matt said, taking a big sip of his Bloody Mary. "So fucking on point. And so fun it should be a TV show or something."

"I knew you of all people could find Danielle."

"Tread lightly." Matt slid over a piece of paper with a scrawled phone number. He looked back down at his phone, scrolling photos of men, probably Carlos.

Red grabbed the paper—818, the San Fernando Valley area code—then tucked it safely into her front pocket.

From her trauma work, she knew that abused women frequently fantasized about killing the perpetrator, or at the very least watching them die a slow and painful death. The victims usually felt guilty about wanting retribution, but she'd encourage her clients that it was natural to feel anger when violated. Patriarchal society taught women to temper rage at abuse. Red encouraged them to work out real feelings through writing, yelling, group therapy, dancing, and even martial arts classes. Red had taken up Tai Kwan Do years before. It was empowering to kick a man, even if he was only the instructor.

Men went to war over the slightest insult or transgression. Kicking someone's ass, using physical force over another, was the king of beasts' job. Aggression was unseemly in the feminine kind. But it wasn't. It was glorious. Teaching a client, who had been punched or kicked, raped, verbally abused, traumatized, to fight back, even emotionally, was rewarding. How satisfying it must be for Dani to kill Peter over and over again. Often, abused women came from dysfunctional homes. On some level, they were taught or encouraged to believe that they deserved it. Rarely did they share with the people in their daily lives their secret desire for an abusive partner to get hit by a car, or the shame or thrill they felt when fantasizing about punching back. Red loved that Dani knew she hadn't deserved his emotional abuse—that she could get away with literary murder.

"I wonder what Peter thinks about it." Matt slurped up the last of his Bloody Mary. "How many of these are acceptable at brunch?" He looked around the pub for their handsome actor-waiter with the sexy Irish accent.

Peter was probably pissed, too, but not enough to file a cease-and-desist order because secretly he loved the attention. That much, Red knew to be true. In his sick heart, Peter knew that his behavior made him a piece of shit. Knowing this didn't make him behave differently, so he let Dani shame him publicly.

Matt was texting away. Red's attention was drawn to the TV screen above the bar.

The cute Irish waiter arrived. They both ordered another Bloody Mary. She turned to Matt after the waiter had left. "I hope the blog gives him an ulcer. Or a heart attack. He's a bad guy."

"Girl, aren't they all?" Matt patted her hand. "Well, not Carlos. He's a darling. Wasn't it sweet of him to let you stay on the property in Joshua Tree? It's gorgeous there! I can't wait for you two to finally meet at Christmas! Did I show you the latest pictures?"

He *had* shown her several times. It was Matt's thing to be passionate for a guy to the point of obsession for about three to eight weeks—his attention span. She nodded again at Carlos' smiling shirtless selfie—a scruffy five o'clock on-purpose shadow, holding a welding tool, shirtless six pack, wearing baggy painter's pants. Matt was her best friend, the one who knew everything about Peter, who loved talking smack with her about him. He had driven her to the clinic for the abortion. He was a good man, generous in his assessment of his friends.

"Did Peter," Matt started, "ever, you know, I mean, did he . . . ?"

"Hit me?" she finished. "No. But he got close enough a couple of times to raise the hair on my arms." She'd been too young and naive to recognize the signs of a potential abuser. "This second go around, we were still in the rosy glow. If I'd shown up in New Orleans, he might have raged. Who knows?"

"Isn't it great that you're not the only one who wants to destroy the son of a bitch?"

"Yes." Red swirled the celery stalk in her drink. "Maybe Dani needs the affirmation, too."

"Oh my God!" Matt laughed. "Are you going to start an anti-Peter movement?"

Her eyes wandered around the dark pub. Why did they choose such a depressing place for brunch? On the corner TV, she saw Peter's beautiful hipster wife, Sasha, exiting God!ess yoga studio.

"Turn it up," Red called out to the bartender.

"Oh, Jesus," Matt said. "Don't."

Two entertainment show hosts, a non-descript, Botoxed brunette sporting angular shoulder pads, and a buff Englishman, were chatting enthusiastically about Hollywood's latest favorite couple—Peter and Sasha—while photographs of the couple's "secret" Bali beach wedding flashed across the screen followed by a splash of pictures of their new Hollywood Hills mansion.

"A charmed life," gushed the male host in his English accent. "Girl, didn't you just love her short wedding gown? Those legs! But, you know, that girl could pull off a burlap sack."

The brunette host smiled, revealing shiny white veneers. "And their lives are just about to get even more charming, Felix." She covered her mouth like a teenager trying to keep a secret.

Sasha was pregnant. Over sixteen weeks. Three and a half months.

"Aw," the hosts cooed in unison.

"Isn't that adorable?" the brunette enthused, like a guest at a baby shower.

"Congratulations to the beautiful couple." Felix raised his water glass. "That will be one gorgeous baby."

The hosts clinked glasses, moving on to a new Hollywood topic about some young actor's drunken brawl at a film premiere.

Red stared in absolute disbelief.

"Turn that off!" Matt barked. Other patrons turned and looked. The bartender obliged, shaking his head. Matt leaned over and gave Red's shoulder a comforting squeeze. "I really didn't want you to know. Jesus, I'm so sorry."

She blinked hard, fighting back the tears. Bile rose in her throat. While they were fucking in Echo Park, Sasha was pregnant. No wonder he'd freaked out. Red had ended their baby, but he got to have one anyway. With the beautiful Sasha. Things always worked out for Peter.

"You have the worst luck in men. Have you considered switching teams? I know a fabulous woman, lawyer, tall, great tits. If you're into that sort of thing."

But Red had already stopped listening. Nausea rose in the back of her throat. She had to get out of the bar. Red jerked her shoulder away from Matt's hand and slid off of the barstool. "I'm sorry, sorry, I need air." She raced for the front door, pushed it open, and burst into the bright Sunday, sunlight glinting off the windshields of cars parked along the street. She threw up in a scraggly bush at the bottom of the bar's concrete steps. Only a small homeless man, sitting on the bus bench with his ratty dog, noticed and nodded his bald head in sympathy.

Walking home, back down Echo Park Avenue, the hot sun burning her forehead, Matt ringing repeatedly from his cell, Red let the salty tears fall without wiping her face, determined they would be the last tears she ever shed for Peter. It was time to stop being a victim, to be brave, and even, yes, reckless. She pulled out the small sheet of paper in her front pocket and dialed the last known number for Danielle Desi Smith.

JUST-DESERTS.COM

Steve's old truck was parked in the garage. My stomach fluttered as I entered the lot and parked beside it, turning off the NPR story about how canning fruits and vegetables was good for the environment. The climate was changing, and the world might have been ending, but I was too chicken to ask my husband if he was cheating.

"Honey?" I juggled groceries as I opened the door into the kitchen. When he didn't answer, I put the eggs and milk in the refrigerator and helped myself to a spoonful, okay three, of Nutella.

I was bored with life as a band widow—sitting alone at a table in a bar until one o'clock in the morning, nursing a drink, listening to the same six songs. I liked writing our songs. And his voice was sexy, beautiful. But how many times was a wife required to listen to her husband's band's set list? Going to see The Calamities play did not count as a date, no matter how many glasses of wine he sent to the table. But if I didn't go, how could I look out for our marriage?

I grabbed the Nutella jar and spoon and moved to Steve's open laptop on the counter.

The Calamities was supposed to be a side gig, but lately, the band had taken over Steve's whole life. Rehearsals had replaced weeknight dinners and often, weekend adventures. Gigs had replaced romantic dates. He was always texting fellow musicians, several women to rehearse, sing backup, and agreeing to play guitar for their bands in exchange. His social media pages quickly filled with new followers, mostly musicians, and pictures of young pretty women wearing low-cut tops or high-cut shorts. Writing comments and posts like, "Hey, S, you looked sexy up there tonight." Or "Hey, S, we should hang sometime." Or "Your hot." *It's "you're," idiot,* I wanted to scream.

"They're fans." Steve shrugged each time I brought up the flirty exchanges or photos. "Part of the gig. If it upsets you, don't look. You're the one who pressed me into this."

I stalked the girls' comments and tags, followed them to their social media accounts, examined their legs in shorts, long and lean, or thin and tan; their flat, bare stomachs, some pierced or tattooed; their breasts full and round, or sexy flat collarbones; eyes, lips, hair.

Was my waist a little too squishy? Were the broken capillaries in my thighs unsightly? Were my plump, round breasts not equally aligned? It was torture, madness, emotionally cutting. It consumed my days while I consumed anything sugary to ease my anxiety.

Yes, okay, I created a fake account with a picture of myself as a striking petite blonde and friended the ones who made me feel the most threatened. I couldn't find evidence of cheating yet, but my gut hurt, jealousy gnawing its edges. I was sick to death of sitting through my six original songs, but I had to show up to gigs or risk losing Steve.

To Vasha. Losing him to the beauty contestant runner-up would have killed me. Vasha, a doe-eyed Persian, always wore a red G-string (it was hard not to miss through her skin-tight translucent outfits) and a t-shirt (with no bra)." Vasha wrapped her arms around my husband on stage while they sang into the same mic. On her page, she claimed to have had past life experiences with Iggy and Elvis. She was batshit crazy, and Steve had a crush.

"Don't be ridiculous," Steve snapped when I pressed. "She's fifteen years younger than me, like a sister. I don't even think she's that pretty."

When his phone dinged, if his face lit up, I knew it was a text from Vasha. I secretly checked his phone. Of course, all wives did. Didn't they? I'd been searching for evidence, building a case. Steve was a naturally private person because of his terrible childhood. He'd always held back words, kept secrets to save my feelings, even over the most mundane things like forgetting to stop for toothpaste or breaking a glass in the kitchen. Why did he lie?

I clicked over to Vasha's social media. Scrolling down her followers list, I didn't exactly know what I was looking for.

"Hey, babe," Steve yawned from the doorway.

I jumped. "Oh, y-you s-startled me." I slammed the laptop shut. Shit.

"Getting in a few winks before the gig." He yawned again. Running a hand through his tousled dark hair, his cheeks flushed from sleep, Steve walked to the counter and straddled the barstool next to me. He opened his laptop to discover the browser still opened to Vasha's page. "Jesus, you're always monitoring me." He shook his head. "I need breathing room, babe."

I wanted to be closer. He wanted distance. I was miserable. He was happy. I'd never seen Steve happier in his life. His eyes were shining.

"I'm not c-crazy." I clenched my fists to stop my insides from shaking. "Show me."

"What?"

"Your pseudonym, alias, fake account. Whatever it is."

"It's not all my fault." Leaning over, he clicked on a profile picture of a cat wearing a sombrero on Vasha's friend's list. A new page opened, revealing a collage of photos:

Vasha and Steve laughing

Vasha and Steve hiking

Vasha and Steve singing together onstage

Vasha feeding Steve a slice of pizza

Vasha straddling Steve's lap in a group photo of a party at some restaurant

Steve was definitely fucking his Persian off-key back-up singer.

"A cat wearing a sombrero?" He stifled a laugh like it was comical.

Reaching for the knife block on the counter, I pulled out the deboning scissors and stabbed him in the eye.

Twice.

SASHA

Anorexic Persian off-key backup singer? Peter's ex was still writing that blog! Sasha was Lebanese, Armenian, Iranian, Italian, German, and Irish—first generation American. And she wasn't about to be skinny-shamed simply because Peter's crazy ex couldn't put down the cookie and pick up a barbell.

Her friend, Renee, told her to stop reading. "It's *very* disturbing," Renee repeated. "Peter needs to file a restraining order." But Sasha couldn't stop herself.

It was disturbing, unbelievable, horrifying. The police said there wasn't anything they could do. It was just words. The names had been changed. Peter didn't want to bother Dani with another lawsuit. "She only has sixty-one followers, babe. Just another sad, dumpy girl. Turn on the alarm if you're afraid." Peter had a bodyguard who traveled with him. She could hire a guard, get a gun, buy a dog. It was a big house, easy to get lost in, easy for a mad woman to lurk behind a corner, hide in a closet with a knife. Oh God!ess, the blog gave Sasha nightmares.

Still, every morning, she read what that crazy woman had written the night before. How will she kill him today, she'd think, opening the blog with dread? Car, gun, poison?

Today, a grotesque eye stabbing. Sasha was trash, evil, subhuman. And Persian? Why point out her ethnicity? "Screw you, fatty!" she whispered. "You're bad in bed."

Stop it, Sasha.

Sasha hated it when she got mean. It was easy for women to fight. She took a deep breath. Why did they have to pit themselves against each other? Especially over a man. When had men appointed themselves the judges? Sasha hadn't faced a panel of men and a few women, who were trained by a man's eye in a swimsuit competition, for years. She'd given away the hours, days, weeks, years of hunger gnawing, ravaging, devouring the calcium in her bones, eating cotton to feel full, smoking, over-exercising. God!ess, how she had hurt her poor body, starved her own beautiful soul. She wasn't that competitive pageant girl anymore. She'd gotten herself healthy through therapy, nutrition, and dance. Yogic dance. Her own creation. God!ess was her brand. The studio helped hundreds of women. Fuck that fat bitch.

Sasha slammed the laptop shut and felt a quick stab of nausea. "I'm sorry, baby." She rubbed the round bump. "I won't read it anymore." Knowing she was lying to her unborn child.

Peter said his ex was crazy. "Dani is a mess, babe," he'd say, stroking her hair. "Screwed-up family is an understatement. Sister's an addict fuck up and has a kid in foster care. Dad's an alcoholic racist. Mom took off, disappeared for a better life somewhere. I think I married Dani because she needed me. I liked being needed. You know I had a problem with saving damaged women after I lost my mom. Until you."

Sasha prayed it was past tense. Damaged women. What did that even mean? Was Peter's ex-wife blaming Sasha for the end of her marriage instead of her own insecurities and lack of support for his career? It wasn't healthy. Peter had said they were over long before Sasha even joined The Disasters and started writing for the band. "In the end, we were only roommates. She's not even that pretty. She was like a sister," he'd promised. "You, babe, are the real deal. You're the only woman in the world for me."

The center of her chest felt like a closed fist. She took a deep inhale and slowly exhaled. Was her singing off-key? People said her voice often reminded them of Iggy Pop. It was a stylistic choice. She closed her eyes and visualized the ocean, the way she instructed her students. *You're beautiful, no matter what they say, words can't bring me down today,* she sang. Fuck that fat bitch. She took another deep breath and held it, rubbing her belly, loving the life growing inside of her.

It wasn't often that Sasha got her feelings hurt. But when another person's opinion burned her quick like a wasp sting, Sasha got down on her knees and prayed to the God!ess for that person's happiness. Danielle and Sasha were a part of the same tribe. Not only had they both loved Peter, they were also women born from the Great Mother. They had to work together, for peace, for the love of God!ess, for the love of humanity. Danielle wasn't fat, but she wasn't starving either. She looked like a perfectly sturdy Midwestern farm woman: soft, with larger breasts.

Sasha pressed her index fingers and thumbs into the circle mudras that the Indian yogi at the Palm Springs retreat had taught her for remembrance—that we are one. She released the image of Dani's breasts. Press harder, Sasha. You'll have to press a lot harder and maybe all day to locate the true essence, which was her love energy. There was no light in her third chakra, the feeling of her heart was lower, which was troubling so near the baby. The thoughts wouldn't stop.

She paced the long expanse of the living room windows that looked out over the city. Think perspective; be bigger. She could be bigger. Sasha had won. It wasn't a competition. But she had won. The windows, tall and wide, covered one side of the house. Most days, she couldn't believe this was their home, not the cramped apartment in Brooklyn where she'd grown up with her parents, not the groovy small studio in Venice where she'd been happily single, writing poetry until Danielle kicked Peter out, and he moved in. The simplicity of those days, a home in one room filled with homemade, colorful art, ceramics, fluffy pillows, a bed, a throw rug, wind chimes, and candles flooded her mind. Some days, Sasha missed simplicity. She should put wind chimes in the baby's room.

Now, they lived in a designer house that resembled a five-star hotel.

It was a clear day, blue sky, faint clouds, easy and cool, not too hot yet. Solar panels and rooftops shone in the LA basin; if she squinted, she could see the blue line of the ocean beyond the faint brown line of pollution. With a baby on the way, Peter and Sasha lived a magical life. "Baby," she whispered. Sasha didn't want to know the sex of their child; she desired the secret thrill of anticipation, waiting, letting the baby, the life inside of her have the power to reveal itself on arrival. Our baby. "Hi, baby," she sang. "I can't wait to meet you."

She moved to the grand piano, placing her fingers on the keys. She played the first few notes of the piece she'd been working on with Enrique, the band's drummer, for Peter's fortieth birthday the day before New Year's Eve. It was a surprise present—a song from her to him.

"Does he make you write all of the music now?" Her mother's voice, the warning again filling her brain. "Be careful. Get everything in writing. What he's done to one, he'll do again."

What did her elderly mother know about Peter? She was a housewife from another country, another religion and time, who'd mastered the art of putting her young daughter in beauty pageants. She didn't know the first thing about being famous in America. Her father owned a dry-cleaning business. Musicians worked nights and weekends. They traveled. They had a different lifestyle, especially now that The Disasters were famous. Fame brought its own troubles. Creativity was fickle. Sasha was more than happy to help.

Her graceful fingers traveled slowly over the ivory. Melancholy, it was a little sweet with an edge, a whole lot of sexy like him; closing her eyes, she waited for the words, knowing that the words would rise like magic from the music. Lyrics were Sasha's strength. "Because you didn't study the piano seriously, jans," her mother often scolded, adding the doting Armenian expression, the only Armenian word she remembered from her grandmother. Sasha's fingers felt the coolness of the keys, the rhythm changing, a little faster maybe, a quickening of light around A-sharp minor? She shook her head, trying it again, the riff, the repeat. Was it better? Yes. She stopped, grabbed the pencil behind her ear and made a note on a liner sheet. "I may be travelin' but I ain't never travelin' away," she sang, "from you." The timbre was high and thin, shrill, and echoed around and down the living room's high-arched ceiling.

Danielle was right. Without reverb, Sasha's voice sounded terrible. She let the shame wash over and sent it away. Get out of this house, and be gone! I am beautiful. I deserve love exactly as I am, Sasha thought. What she lacked in talent and technique, Sasha made up in passion. That's what the pageant judges always said.

On their call last night, Peter had suggested that Annie might be better for backup vocals on the next album.

She slammed down the piano lid. It wasn't that Peter didn't want Sasha's voice on the album. "You'll be busy with the baby," he'd reasoned, "and Annie and I are developing a sound on the road. We've been working it out on the bus.

It's not like ours. She'll never be you. But it might be a natural Disasters progression?"

It was a reasonable choice. "I love you." Why did it feel like the ground shifting beneath her feet? Like she had lost power in her legs. She prayed that it was the natural progression of marriage and family.

Sasha turned toward the window, studying her reflection against the sun and city: bold, strong features, full lips, long, dark hair. She smiled. She was pretty, especially now that she was pregnant. Peter said he liked that her breasts would be fuller—that there would be more to hold. Gentle, she'd said, no, tender but showed them to him on their Sunday call. "I like that your tits are getting huge," he said. He'd ejaculated within minutes. Hers were naturally full, but she'd felt a flash of quick shame. Why shame? They were her breasts, and he'd always nibbled, grabbed, and held them. Danielle had huge breasts. He had left them, for her.

The first time Sasha saw Danielle was from the small stage at Red Bar, a hipster, red-painted room above an Italian restaurant on La Brea. It was The Disasters' regular Thursday night gig. Sasha hadn't slept with Peter yet. When they headed there, she'd known the chemistry, the attraction was too deep. She wanted him desperately, the feeling of his soft, thick hair between her fingers, the musky clean smell of him, his long, muscled legs against her body, inside of her body, pressing on her, taking her over. The river of love coursed through her mind, and she ached whenever their hands touched, setting up equipment, at rehearsals or singing onstage, or while laughing at the bar later. They were both aware of that delicious right before, whispering on the phone late at night and texting sweet emojis during the day from their separate jobs when they'd still had day jobs (hers, yoga instructor; his, graphic designer). It was exciting foreplay without touching before it was real. And she knew what they had was real; that's why whenever a thought traveled through her mind about a wife, it had been easy to let it go. Let her go, the thought floated by. Dance, dance, dance. The world is spinning, turning the revolving wheel of the world. She's not even real to him; she's more like a sister. The God!ess had declared it. Until that night at Red Bar when Danielle had come to hear the band, it was painful to admit how selfish she'd been. Sasha hadn't thought about it much because the marriage was on its way out, according to Peter. Everything happened for a reason. She remembered thinking about bliss and freedom and music together forever.

They'd just finished playing the song, "Sticky Band-Aid," when Peter suddenly changed the set. "Sorry, guys," he'd told the band, turning back to face the small audience, mostly friends or fellow musicians playing after their set. "There's somebody special here tonight. And this is my song for her." Sasha's heart dropped when Peter strummed the first few chords of "Crazy Girl, Crazy Boy, Love." She'd raised a hand to shield the light from her eyes and searched the audience. Danielle, a white girl with light brown hair, a pink denim jacket, and of average size, sat at a table near the window. A very pretty, very real woman.

Peter leaned into the mic and began, *"She spins in circles, she skips across the ocean, sails in on a cloud of moonlight, brings the fury and the rain until it happens again . . . she, she, she drives me crazy, crazy."* Sasha almost missed her cue. Startled, she leaned into the mic, joining Peter, half a note late, *"She, she, she, she."* When she looked back out, Danielle's chair was empty.

After the gig in St. Louis, Peter hadn't called until two a.m. "It's just about the music, babe," he'd promised again. "Me and Annie sat up late writing a new song. You're going to love it."

Sasha took a deep breath and stood up from the piano. Hungry. Baby was hungry, hungry for pears. And chicken. Chicken? God, no, gross. Sorry, baby, no morbid matter for you. She would need to get dressed and go to the store. *Call delivery, jans,* she heard her mother say. *You have the money.*

"No. We need fresh air, baby." She struggled to pull up her jeans. The zipper no longer closed. She peeled them down and found a pair of comfortable yoga pants. There. The widening curve of her hips. "Very sexy." Even though she didn't feel sexy, checking out her puffy reflection in the full-length mirrors of their large master bathroom. Who imagined she would ever have such a house? Double shower heads in a marble shower with a jacuzzi that overlooked the city lights at night. She looked up through the skylight into sky—blue. No need for a jacket. Just get out of the house, see people, maybe call Renee for tea, drop by God!ess to say hi, pick up last night's deposit.

Sasha was a free-spirit, live and let live, live in the moment, dance as if the earth depends on it. The studio was the first expensive gift Peter had given her. A big, beautiful, hardwood floor studio on 3rd near the Grove. With its own parking lot. "Teach yoga, or dance, or just paint the walls with orange mandalas," he'd said and smiled. "Fulfill your dreams."

She loved her studio, of course she did, and she was proud of its success. But sometimes a little thought nagged in the back of her mind. Did he give her the studio so that he could tour alone? It was a silly thought from her monkey mind. When Peter came home at Christmas, she would tell him her crazy thought. They would talk about everything, and everything would be better again.

Waiting for the carved iron front gates to open, Sasha lowered the roof of the BMW. The warmth of the sun on her face felt so good. The scent of blooming jasmine filled her nose, bushes on all sides blooming, blooming in the time of giving thanks. Sasha was having his miracle baby. Peter loved her. It was only hormones making her feel crazy.

Life was beautiful. Thank you, God!ess!

DANI

After circling the small parking lot on the corner of Western and Vermont for twenty minutes, Dani was late. Shit. She didn't want to go inside anyway, but she needed to pee. A silver BMW pulled out of a spot, and reluctantly, she swerved in to park.

"No one can hurt you without your permission," she told her nervous reflection in the visor mirror, double-checking the nude-colored lip gloss. Should she have worn pink? Wait, was that a black whisker on her upper lip? Jesus. She plucked it out with her fingers. Great, now she had a red spot near her upper lip. Why did it matter? It wasn't a contest. She didn't have to be the prettiest woman in the room to keep Peter anymore. Why was she anxious?

The Coffee Bean's air conditioning was on full blast, even though only two people waited in line at the counter. Fruity scones and glazed donuts beckoned inside the pastry case, and Dani quickly looked away, scanning the room for the description the woman, Red, had given over the phone: tall, freckled, long red hair, Peter's ex-girlfriend, about five years older. She waved from a corner table near the window and stood. Shit, Dani thought. Should have used the restroom first.

As Red navigated the tables and chairs to greet her, her flat white belly flashed above her cutoffs. Her long legs and arms were taut, like she came to it naturally, not through starvation or hours at the gym. Dani sucked in her gut. Skinny women always made her feel squishy, short, and fat. Why had she worn the tight white jeans?

"Hi." Red offered a warm, but thin-lipped smile. Her cheeks and nose were sprinkled in freckles. She had big blue eyes for days. Peter's favorite eye color.

They leaned in awkwardly, Red tall and Dani short, for a small hug. Red held on a little too tightly. Dani, pulled back, self-consciously smoothing her frizzy hair.

"Wow, you're pretty." Red sounded surprised. "Can I get you something to drink? I'm having a matcha green tea. It's very good for you."

Good for her, a health nut. Was she suggesting that Dani looked unhealthy? "No, no, thank you. I just drank a bottle of water on the way here." Dani shivered and tugged at the corner of her left eye to stop it from watering. The air conditioning inside the place was on high.

They made their way to the table. A yellow bandana tied to a belt loop on Red's cutoffs made her look like a model for a camping catalogue. Peter loved outdoorsy girls. Red removed a canvas duffel from the other chair, tossed it onto the floor, and motioned for Dani to sit. Dani swallowed a nervous laugh and sat, feeling spongy, the waistband of her jeans squeezing her bladder. Her thighs poured over the sides of the chair, but she didn't dare look down. It was best to appear self-confident, interested, and friendly while internally craving a pastry and an escape.

"Like I said, I love your blog," Red gushed. "I've read a few entries." She stopped, bit her lower lip, like she was trying to figure out the right way to say what came next.

"Yes, that's what you said on the phone." Dani waited for the woman to stop staring. It was unnerving. "I know it must seem weird, or wrong. To write about, you know, killing him. I only have sixty-one followers, seventy-one actually, as of this morning. I'm not really a writer. It was a suggestion from my OA sponsor, Overeaters Anonymous? It's a twelve-step program. Like for alcoholics, but for people who have food issues." She stopped to take a breath. The air conditioning blew in her face. She tugged on the corner of her left eye again. Red stared, waiting. Dani forced a smile. "I have dry eye," she explained, blinking hard a few times. Red nodded. God, she hated silence. "I wasn't an English major, so the writing isn't necessarily grammatically correct. Did it offend you? The content? I know it sounds crazy. I never thought anyone who knew Peter would read it. I mean it's not like I'm promoting it, you know, on social media or . . . I only have sixty-one—seventy-one—followers, and I don't even know how they found—"

"For the record," Red interrupted like a lawyer in court, "I'm not here to bash Peter. We lived together for three years. One of them was the best year of my life." She pointed a pale finger into the air for emphasis, and continued, "Your writing made me feel better. Every bad thing you wrote about him is true. I know he stole your writing credits. Peter can't read or write music." She pointed her index finger at Dani. "I am here to validate you."

"Oh." Dani shook her head, trying to catch up to the woman's words. Red was dramatic, but down to earth and compelling. Luckily, Red hadn't finished. "Peter is a heartless, soulless, spineless, lying sociopathic motherfucker."

For the next twenty minutes, Dani's bladder was held hostage, while she was forced to listen to Red recounting a long-ago tragic college love story.

Recently, Red had briefly returned to the scene of the crime. Why? Who would do that?

"I really believed," Red stopped. She brushed a loose strand of hair back from her face and then continued, "I wanted to believe, that Peter had changed. He's so good at it, isn't he? Figuring out your weak spot. I thought we had come full circle, even dared to use the word 'love.' You know why he fucked me? He wanted me to tour, sing backup. He's terrified that people will realize he's untalented."

Dani nodded. That much was true. Peter was charming but not gifted.

"I'm not a singer," Red said. "I have a job. So, he goes back on tour. Stops returning my calls. I'm a therapist. I counsel abused women, victims of trauma, women in hiding, but I fell for his shit. Again."

What planet did Red inhabit? Dani wondered. Peter's life with Sasha was splashed across magazine covers, entertainment and awards shows. Red's second go around, two weeks of "pure bliss" fucking, had only happened because Sasha was teaching with some famous yogi in Palm Springs. Didn't the woman even casually glance at magazine covers waiting in line at the grocery store? Flip channels and accidentally catch an entertainment show segment? Red may have lived in Echo Park, but her life seemed to be off the twenty-first century grid.

Or she was completely delusional.

When she finally stopped talking to sip her healthy fuck-all tea, Dani seized the opportunity. "I really need to use the ladies' room."

On the toilet, Dani traced the thin, blue spider veins branching along her upper thighs. It was a wonder Barney had wanted to fuck her at all. They rarely had sex anymore. Why didn't that bother her? Did it bother Barney? Had she felt like she needed validation? Wasn't that why she wrote the blog? Wasn't it to be heard? Did it feel satisfying to have Red's validation? A little, yes. But the intensity in her blue eyes? She seemed crazy.

Dani reached for the toilet paper. Great. Empty roll, no extras. Wiggling her hips back and forth to drip dry, she reached around and pulled out a toilet seat cover, feeling the fine paper shred under her hand. Fantastic. She was such a glamorous person. Never. She took a deep breath, pulled up her tight jeans, and buttoned them without tipping forward on the tile. This was surprising, since her insides felt unmoored.

Red was staring out the window, chewing her to-go cup, when Dani stepped out of the restroom. It was a relief to see she *was* nervous. Behind the counter, two bored young male employees stared at their phones, and the butterscotch scone cried out sweet, delicate, flaky, with hardened icing and crystallized sugar. Her stomach rumbled, hunger under duress. She quickly passed the pastry case, making a beeline for the table.

Red set the cup on the table, covering the bite marks along the rim with a freckled palm. "I didn't know that Peter was still married to Anong, a woman from Thailand, when I met him," she continued, as if answering a question Dani hadn't asked. "He told me right before I slept with him. So, karma."

"Well, Anong married Peter for her green card." The surprised expression on the woman's face revealed that this was new information. Dani added, "And she left him, not the other way around, for a rich Beverly Hills lawyer, after her citizenship. They deserved each other."

"Unbelievable." Red shook her head. "He's such an asshole."

Dani nodded, checking the time on her phone. Outside, an ambulance followed by two fire trucks screeched by, sirens blaring.

After the sirens faded, Red stated, "You have very sexy lips."

Dani self-consciously pursed her lips.

"Near the end, Peter started talking about how hard it was to kiss my thin lips. He even suggested injections." Red leaned forward, the muscles in her long neck ropey with tension. "At first, he loves you so much it's like a drug. Right? You're the center of his orbit. The day is brighter. You're floating. You're the smartest, sexiest, most interesting woman in the world. He never even looks at another woman."

"You are the only woman in the world." Dani nodded.

"But then slowly," Red continued, "Peter starts to look at other women. And when, if, he looks at you, it isn't in the same way. Which makes you crave his attention even more. It's a classic buildup, tear down process. You become invisible." The tension in her jaw began to relax. "But you waste the next few years trying to get back the Peter of the first six months. Crying over what happened, what went wrong, what you did, dieting, hair changes, riskier fashion choices, insecurities abound, while he gets colder and meaner and finally leaves you for another woman. Everything is about the natural progression of *his* life."

"A complete narcissist."

They grew quiet. Red picked up her paper cup, realized it was empty, set it back down, and confessed, "I actually considered breast implants after Peter complained during sex one night that mine were too small. And I'm a feminist."

"Unbelievable, but yes. I considered a breast reduction." Dani indicated her ample ones. "Too saggy."

"Really? Jesus, man, your breasts are fucking hot." Red glanced around the coffee house, then quickly lifted her shirt, revealing no bra, just two pink nipples on a flat chest. In a flash, she lowered her top again, the two young male employees still staring at their phones, oblivious.

Dani and Red both laughed. Dani hadn't expected connection. It was refreshing to hear that someone understood, had lived through, been as stupid as you, and couldn't move forward either.

"All these years, I blamed myself," Dani admitted, and she couldn't believe she was sharing this information. She'd never told anybody. "If only I were prettier, skinnier, had longer legs, a flat stomach, or blue eyes. Over time, whenever we went anywhere, even the grocery store, I was obsessed with checking the scene, making certain it was safe. Void of pretty women. It's a terrible way to live." Dani looked directly into Red's pretty eyes. "It's humiliating."

"Emotionally abusive," Red remarked, shaking her head in agreement. "I'm not a jealous person, but after Peter told me that he liked big breasts, I grew really uneasy about this pretty waitress at the coffee house where he played all the time. Hers were huge. I started objectifying, you know? The male gaze, not my own."

"Peter told me that Asian women were his ideal. Note, he didn't say Japanese or Thai or Chinese or . . . ? Is he an equal opportunity player or just a racist?" Dani quickly looked around the room to be certain that no one was listening to her confession. Three tables over a man absorbed on his phone took a sip of coffee. She lowered her voice. "I just freaked out every time any Asian girl appeared on the radar. And not just at gigs. At the grocery store, in line for a movie, even at the dentist. Even when Peter wasn't there, I would compare myself. Every woman became the impossible beauty standard I could never live up to."

Red laughed, slapping the table hard with her hand. Dani jumped. "Oh my God!" she said. "I read that post on your blog." She imitated the horrible racist accent, "Me love you long time," so loudly that Dani glanced around the room again. The guy was still stuck looking at his phone. "It really sucks that he's so good in bed."

Sex with Peter was the best sex of Dani's life. Dani sighed in agreement.

Suddenly, images of Red on top of Peter, riding him, or on all fours, his thick perfect penis in her mouth flashed through Dani's mind. With her short shorts and flat stomach, she looked . . . athletic. Naturally comfortable in her long-limbed, freckled skin.

Dani quickly glanced down at her phone again. She needed to call Karyn and get to a meeting before she bought that scone. "I'm sorry. I have to, well, I have an appointment."

"You need to know, Dani, or Jesus, I'm sorry, did you want me to call you Danielle? I should have asked . . . ." She leaned over and grabbed Dani's wrist. "You're not crazy in the way he said. You're crazy like a fox. You've got his number." She stared, blue eyes intense, into Dani's. "I need to find a way into his life. Do you have any mutual friends?"

Caught off guard, Dani pulled her hand back. "We *never* had mutual friends." Why did Red want *back* inside of Peter's life?

Red's gaze drifted to the coffee house windows. Cars whizzed by on Beverly Boulevard. As if she could read Dani's mind, Red turned back to her and said, "I want to make him suffer."

"Me, too." Dani smiled. "Hey! You should take classes at God!ess! Become best friends with Sasha. He'd hate that!" She laughed.

Red grinned, playing along. "And then, one day, Sasha invites me to their house for a dinner party?" She tapped her skinny fingers on the tabletop. "Peter would flip out."

"Especially when you saunter in, wearing a slinky outfit and drop the bomb on the cheater and the home wrecker."

Red sighed. "But I fucking hate yoga."

"Me, too," Dani commiserated. "Guess you'll never get up to the big house."

"You're smart *and* funny." Red grinned, revealing stained teeth in her pale face.

It was the only unattractive thing about her appearance, but it made Dani feel a little more at ease. She looked at her watch and stood. "Shit, I have to go. Thanks for reaching out to me. It does feel good to know I'm not alone."

Red jumped up from her chair and grabbed Dani in another big awkward hug. "Thank you for being brave enough to come." Her hot tea breath tickled the hair on the top of Dani's head. "I really like you."

"Sure." Dani stepped back. "We should do it again sometime." She regretted the words the moment they escaped her lips.

SASHA

"Don't worry, *I'll* find a nanny," Renee declared over lunch at La Scala. "Alma can ask the others when she picks Liam up from aftercare today."

"God, no," Sasha groaned. She had interviewed enough qualified applicants this past week, young and old women, even a very qualified eager gay man which was ideal, but had come to the realization that she didn't want any stranger raising her baby. She wanted to be the one to change and bathe and clean its spit up, rock him or her back to sleep—the whole thing. "What I really need is a personal assistant, someone to pay the bills, get the dry cleaning. And of course," she added, hoping she hadn't hurt her friend's feelings, "watch the baby while you and I enjoy long Chablis lunches."

"Mommy's little helper." Renee offered a wry smile, held up her Chablis, and took a sip. The new rock on her pale middle finger caught the sun streaming through the window, flashing points of light across the white tablecloth. It was a post-Oscar best-director present from her French husband, Pierre. This wasn't what Sasha wanted, a life filled with ladies who lunched in posh, stuck-up Beverly Hills restaurants, followed by shopping tipsy for designer handbags, the cost of which would feed a small country. That was Renee's reality. Why did Sasha tag along?

She ached for the tiny Venice bungalow, three rooms, the peeling claw-foot tub, loud neighbors, pot smoke, music on all sides, a short walking distance from the beach, Abbott Kinney, places where her friends made art and served coffee. The big, beautiful house on the hill was far away, isolating. Sterilized. She missed it all, her old, single, independent, adventurous life. Teaching free yoga classes on the beach. Listening to jazz late at night, the sound of sirens in the background. Trading up for a new reality wasn't as shiny as it had initially seemed when Peter suggested they buy the mansion featured in *Architecture* magazine. What was wrong with her head lately? Spoiled, she felt rotten, ungrateful.

"If only Alma's English was better," Renee sighed. "I paid for the lessons, but no, she just can't get it." She scraped the sticky white dressing off a grilled Caesar romaine leaf. "Honestly, this salad is so fattening. I should have just ordered steak."

Steak! Sasha's mouth watered. Her stomach rumbled, looking down at her own chopped vegetable salad with balsamic dressing on the side. This sudden craving for flesh, after ten years of veganism, animal activism, was disturbing. God!ess was founded on her personal philosophy of love and climate change in relation to meat and animal cruelty. Instinctively, Sasha put her hand to the growing bump of her belly and massaged an apology to the baby.

"Why don't you hire one of the girls from God!ess to help out?"

"I don't know. Maybe," Sasha started because the reality was too embarrassing. The last thing her strained marriage needed was a trim yoga girl bending over in tight pants in front of her hot-blooded husband home for the holidays. Especially with the way she looked right now—bloated, puffy-eyed. "I guess I want to keep my home and studio life separate," she lied.

Renee attempted to raise a frozen brow. "What's going on?"

"I guess . . . ." Sasha fought back the tears. "I'm not glowing."

"What? Fuck off. You're the most beautiful pregnant woman I've ever seen. Do you remember how many procedures I needed to remove those purple varicose veins? And I was the size of a house. Did Peter say something to you?"

"What? No, no, of course not. Why would you say that?"

Renee paused and thought for a moment. "It's nothing, sweetie. Never mind."

"What?"

"I just . . . ." She paused again. "I'm sorry. Sometimes, I still read his ex's blog." Renee held up her hand to stop Sasha's protest. The ring flashed. "I can't help it. It's thrilling. We all wish we could kill our husbands sometimes, don't we?"

"No." Sasha had never thought about killing her husband, not ever. "Why on earth?"

"Are you okay?"

"He isn't like that." Sasha felt the heat rise in her chest. She grabbed her water glass, pressing the wet cold against her cheek. He was moody, but he wasn't mean on purpose. Peter had demons. He was passionate and alive. "I don't want to talk about that crazy woman's blog anymore. Okay?"

"You're right. Sorry." Renee took a big swig of Chablis. "Sasha, you are so beautiful; honestly, sometimes looking at you, your face, your perfect skin, your figure, even pregnant, I just want to kill myself." She held out her glass of white wine. "Here. One sip will not hurt the baby."

"No. Thank you." Sasha wiped the wet under her eyes with a napkin to keep the mascara from running. She was a wreck. How many people were watching?

Renee finished the glass and changed the subject. "You think you have problems? Look at this ridge between my eyes. It's as deep as the Grand Canyon. I'm thinking of switching to Restylane. Last month's injection left a green stain." She shuddered. "What do you think?"

Grateful, Sasha smiled and looked closely. The skin between Renee's small brown eyes was as smooth as marble. "You look perfect."

Quick as a flash, Renee pulled a compact out of her purse and closely examined her forehead. "Thirty-three is not looking good on me." She sighed. "You'll see."

A slender male waiter set a basket loaded with warm rolls and a ramekin of soft butter down on the table. Sasha eyed it longingly.

Renee turned, pretending to look for someone, and nonchalantly scoped out the crowd. "All clear," she whispered, sliding the bread basket closer to Sasha.

Sasha quickly grabbed a warm roll and tore it in half. The aroma of fresh bread filled her nostrils, and her mouth watered again. She wanted to spread the butter across its flaky surface and watch it melt into the dough. Never in her life had food felt this necessary and sensuous.

"Enough, hurry up, eat the fucking thing," Renee said. "Sorry. You know, I've been hungry since I was fourteen."

Sasha shoved half the biscuit in her mouth, shielding her face with a linen napkin.

Her friend watched closely, licking her lips. "God, I miss bread. Maybe I should get pregnant again."

Giving in to the bread heightened Sasha's craving for meat. It could no longer be deferred with vegan cheese substitutes. If Peter found out, he'd laugh. "I told you so, babe. People need meat." But if her clients knew, God!ess would be out of business forever. The baby needed to eat meat. Sasha had to comply in secret.

She tucked her hair under a Dodgers cap, donned wide-framed sunglasses, and put on Peter's big black hoodie. Then she found the keys to his old truck and backed it out of the garage, lowering behind the steering wheel as she drove through the gates and down the hill, taking an out-of-the-way route to avoid the most populated area where she might be recognized. She turned right again on Sunset in Little Armenia and parked on the street in front of Haykazuni Meats, a market that got amazing reviews on Yelp. Inside, the only customer, *thank God!ess!* Sasha purchased a thick, bloody cut of organic New York strip steak from a smiling elderly Japanese man, who only nodded his head.

Minutes later, back in the truck, Sasha ripped open the package and tore at the rich flesh with her teeth, the baby finally satisfied. It was delicious.

JUST-DESERTS.COM

Steve and I were married on a sunny spring day at the Van Nuys County Courthouse, a non-descript concrete block ten stories high. I wore a sundress and carried pink flowers. He wore black jeans and a starched white shirt with a bolo tie. The inside of the courthouse was chopped up into small rooms with bright white walls and shiny formica floors. We passed opened doorways featuring rows of black plastic chairs where people waited, chatting happily or reading books and magazines. At the bank of elevators, I pressed the UP button. When the doors slowly opened, Steve quickly grabbed my hand. A group of people rushed out, an elderly couple, also holding hands, a tiny smiling woman, several police officers, a judge in his robes, and two men holding coffees. They swam around us like a school of fish oblivious of the bride and groom, focused only on their destination. We stepped into the empty elevator. Steve pressed the button for Level Three. The steel doors slowly closed to reveal the radiance reflected on our smiling faces. It was the most beautiful place on earth.

After we'd submitted the marriage certificate to the clerk, we stepped back outside into the sun, and Steve swooped me into a movie-star kiss. It was May, the month when the jacarandas with their sticky, purple blossoms burst to life across the desert floor. We were young and broke with big dreams for a future together.

We crossed Erwin street and walked to Sizzler for the all-you-can-eat salad bar and steak, ice cream cones for dessert. It was the best meal of my life.

Five years later, we stood side by side at a counter on the crowded third floor of the same concrete courthouse and filed for divorce. The bright white of the walls were yellow and the formica floors dulled by years of scuff marks that no amount of hard wax could remove. A baby's wail echoed down the hallway. The air was humid and stuffy, as if the air conditioning was kept on low to save on electricity.

"Grounds?" The large middle-aged clerk inquired, his swivel chair squeaking as he turned to us.

"Irreconcilable differences," Steve replied.

I shook my head. "Adultery."

The clerk blinked twice, nonplussed. His watery eyes scanned Steve, a quick up and down, and then lingered on my breasts.

"And emotional abuse," I added.

The clerk scratched his stubby cheek with a dirty index finger, imagining *what*, I wasn't too sure, but maybe something sultry instead of Steve's basic body shaming: "You're getting fat," or "Wow, your breasts are droopy," or "You're okay in bed. I mean, I like your enthusiasm."

"Very much emotional abuse." I re-emphasized because it seemed that he didn't get how bad it was.

Steve sighed. "Just get the paperwork." He walked away.

The clerk lost interest in our story and pulled forms from a plastic tray. "Take these. You can finish and pay online."

"How much?"

"Three hundred dollars."

Steve was leaning against the wall, arms folded, watching a pretty Latina girl with a fan of long straight hair and a short skirt walking toward him. I'd always wondered why he never dated Latina women. It would have made his Guatemalan mother happy, even from heaven. As the young woman passed, Steve's eyes devoured her like the predator he was. I pulled my ratty sweater around my body.

"Not the marrying kind," the clerk said.

"Thanks for stating the obvious." I grabbed the forms from the counter. It *was* obvious, wasn't it? Steve was only interested in games of conquest. I was yesterday's news, last week's trash, not the thrill of fresh and new.

Steve joined me, Vans sneakers scuffing across the floor, long arms swinging at his side. "It's three hundred dollars," I informed him.

"I'll cover it." Like he was doing me a favor.

"Yeah, you will."

The clerk snickered. Steve looked at him, and I took advantage of the edge, clenched my fist, and punched him in the face. My hand hurt.

"You broke my nose." He screamed in pain, his hands rushing to stop the blood pouring onto his vintage Van Halen t-shirt. Good riddance, I thought.

The clerk quickly rolled his squeaky chair away from the counter as an elderly security guard raced toward us.

"Arms up. Both of you. Arms up where I can see them."

Steve bent over, small red dabs hitting the white linoleum floor. "Bitch," he yelled. "Bitch!"

People stared, frozen at the scene. I raised my arms high over my head, but Steve didn't. "She punched me," he cried. "That bitch punched me." Steve lunged, an angry bull, eyes red with rage, at me. Before I could step back, his hands were around my throat. He squeezed me tightly, and I couldn't breathe. I clawed my fingernails at his strong hands. I heard screams. I heard the security guard yelling. Then, a pop, pop, pop, and suddenly, Steve released his grip on my neck and fell to the ground.

DANI

The phone rang. Dani's hand shot out, searching the surface of the dresser. Two a.m. It could only be one person. Monica's words tumbled out in a rush, and Dani wondered if Monica was anxious or high. God, Dani hoped not the latter.

"Who is it?" Barney mumbled from the far side of the bed.

"My sister," Dani replied. "Monica, slow down, slow down. Where are you?"

"I just told you. I'm at the hospital," Monica snapped. "I found Jack. Passed out. In his driveway. He was naked. Dehydrated, maybe? And . . . shit, all messed up."

"Is he still . . . ?" Dani couldn't finish.

"Alive? Jesus. Dani, I would have told you straight up if Dad was dead," Monica said. "Yes, of course, he's alive."

Dani turned on the lamp. "Jack's in the hospital," she told Barney.

"Again?" He pulled the pillow over his head.

Dani glared at Barney's wide acne-scarred back, the crack of his hairy ass exposed above the boxers' waistband. "Don't be a dick," she hissed.

"Sorry, babe. Sorry. I've got that five a.m. call in Sylmar."

Dani crawled out from under the covers. She'd felt a little dizzy lately. Her doctor said it could be stress, or hormones, maybe inner ear, any number of things, but probably, it was nothing.

"I'm fucking freaking out here," Monica said, as the panic rose in her voice. "I can't do this. You know that I can't do this. I don't know where I am."

"Breathe," Dani replied. "Take a deep breath." Sisters were always slightly annoyed with each other, weren't they? But Dani's annoyance with Monica fell into an entirely new category: shut the fuck up or please go away. "Okay. Tell me what's in the room?"

Monica exhaled. "Um. There are a few chairs and an ugly brown couch. Some Christmas lights around the window. Really sad, you know? There's a TV. It's playing some old, black-and-white movie. One with that beautiful actress, when she was little, the one who fell off the yacht and died?"

"Natalie Wood. *Miracle on 34th Street*? Seems a little early." Dani grabbed a glass from the kitchen cupboard and filled it with tap water, her hand shaking a little under the weight. "You're in the waiting room."

"Jesus, I'm not an idiot," Monica said. "I can't remember the name of the hospital."

"Ask someone."

"And seem like a fucking idiot? No, thanks. When can you get here?"

"I have to work today."

"Aren't you a temp?"

Outside the kitchen window, a half-moon hung in the dark. The yard was still and quiet. Shadows of the barren fig tree branches fell across the lawn like something from a scary movie. Dani wondered where Buddy and Stan, the two feral cats she'd been feeding, wandered to at night, probably down the street to the park with the possums, raccoons, skunks, and homeless people. She sent a silent prayer for their safety in the open spaces.

"Dani?" Monica interrupted her thoughts. "I kept saying, 'Jack, it's me, Monica. Monica.' But he just . . . ." She started to whimper. "He didn't even know me."

A drop of water fell from the faucet into the aluminum sink. Why hadn't Barney changed the washer yet? Dani didn't want to call maintenance. Every time she called with an issue, Armen went from irritated to mad and then completely enraged, as if she were bothering him on purpose to ruin his day. She was sick of asking Barney to fix things. What good was letting Barney move in if he couldn't replace a goddamned washer in the sink? Another drop fell, spreading like a small flower in the basin.

"I want to drink," Monica confessed.

Dani pressed an index finger into the spigot, feeling around for what was loose. "You need to call your sponsor," she told her sister. "Is Violet with you?"

"She's at home. Thirteen is old enough to be left alone."

Was it? Dani had no idea. She hoped Violet's social worker thought it was.

"Everything's shit right now, Dani. I thought a person was supposed to like her own kid."

Violet wasn't anybody's favorite. Dani was happy that Eddie, the surfer drug dealer deadbeat boyfriend, was out of the picture, but certain, like herpes, he would return.

"I found a brochure! Southern Culver City Hospital," Monica announced.

According to Google maps, the current drive from Pasadena to Culver City was only fifty minutes. In a few hours, rush hour would more than double the drive time. She left a voice message with the temp agency, claiming a cold. After quickly brushing her teeth, Dani pulled her frizzy hair into a ponytail. God, her hairline was receding on the left side, a half a widow's peak before forty. She wave kissed Barney from the kitchen doorway.

"Good luck, babe." He kissed her cheek. His dark curly hair was still wet from the shower. "Don't let the turkeys get you down." What was wrong with her? He was chubby handsome in a big lug regular guy way. Why did he get on her nerves?

"Take the rest of the vegetable frittata to work if you want." She smiled.

"Great, thanks. It's delicious," he said, as he watched her grab the laptop from the counter. "Hey, babe, maybe you don't need to kill him today. Seems like you have enough on your plate?"

Backing the car out of the garage, it occurred to Dani that she'd never asked Barney if the blog bothered him. He'd never said anything. Was he stuffing his feelings? They went to the same home OA meeting but didn't share their programs with each other, which had been recommended by his sponsor. Instead, they kept their lanes separate. They met at an OA meeting. Barney was an overweight boom operator filling a childhood trauma with apple pie, curly fries, and porn. Not always at the same time. Dani was a fat and broken woman, fresh from what the judicial system called a divorce but what she called a psychic cut to the bone.

Having Barney by her side had dulled some of the heartache. He was steady-eddy. A good egg. Barney liked coming home at night, eating a sensible dinner and watching TV together. He wasn't into art or music, or even talking, but what she needed at that moment was simple, and until recently, he'd been kind. They weren't madly in love, but they were doing all right. Who was she kidding? She wouldn't have given him the time of day in her old life. She knew they were marking time and counting calories, keeping each other distracted from eating their feelings. For today, wasn't that enough? Even though he never said it, she knew that Barney felt the same. They'd had enough toxic relationships to last a lifetime. Settling could be a good thing.

Merging onto the 210, Dani wished that she didn't always have to be the best daughter. She didn't want to help her father. She hated being a thirty-five-year-old woman who held onto twenty-year resentments, stamping her feet over events that each family member remembered differently, or not at all.

That was the crazy thing about memories; the brain naturally filled in the gaps, missing or forgotten components, to make sense. Everyone's stories were rewritten over time, until they were made anew. Dani had recently learned about neuroplasticity, as well as the unreliability of memory, from Jack's neurologist. "The brain doesn't retain a fixed moment but grows and changes like the Universe," the neurologist had stated several times. Jack had no memory whatsoever of his daughters crying when he threw the Thanksgiving turkey at the wall. But every day he drank too much Schlitz and waited for his wife's return. The neurologist had posited a theory: the truth was too complicated and painful, so it was easier to believe his wife was coming home.

Dani's brain had tried a different healing tactic. It had worked until Peter's abandonment ripped the scar from the primary wound. Her memories of what "Peter had said" and what "Peter had done" and "when" may have been completely unreliable, but she still clung to them. She reshaped them every time she murdered him on the blog.

Jesus, she was sick of reflecting, therapizing, and reprogramming all over. She was over it. She had no business making promises to addicts like Monica and Jack without thinking things through. At least that's what Karyn said. She said that Dani was a person who rushed toward impending disaster, instead of safely stepping out of the way. Was that the reason for her current unsteady, undiagnosable, vertigo?

The wide-open freeway curved around the dark hillside with the shadow of the eagle in the rock, wings spread, that had inspired the name of the newest gentrified town. A smattering of raindrops hit the windshield, wipers blurring her favorite southeast view of downtown LA. Its high-rises flickered against that velvet gray backdrop of early morning, an electric desert hum before humans awoke, stamping, honking, and spewing, across the city's rolling back.

Dani was burned out on narcissists, people who shined because they'd stolen the light (and lyrics) from those around them. It made her feel cold and alone, helpless while dangling, wriggling on the hook, trapped and ashamed. Wriggling? she thought. Fish hook? Fish line? Wire? Death by hanging!

Peter could accidentally hang himself. She would provide the rope.

Leaning across the passenger seat, Dani opened the glove box and pushed aside registration and insurance papers, fumbling around, eyes glued to the road, until she felt the cellophane package and exhaled. Inside the crinkling material awaited three small, perfectly round, powder-sugar donut holes. The emergency stash she'd been told not to keep. Like a recovered smoker hiding one cigarette in a drawer, she caressed the package. Her mouth watered with anticipation merging from the 134 onto the 2, seeing a snake of red taillights in the distance.

Dani imagined placing one sweet mound in her mouth, feeling the flour melt on her tongue, dough and sugar thickening on the roof of her mouth, filling herself like yeast dough rising.

Merging from the 5 onto the 10 West, traffic growing heavier, a chemical reaction in her brain cried, *you can have just one bite*. Who would know? She wanted to devour them desperately. The sweet sugary plastic smell of chemicals, the dryness of the powdered sugar rough and sticking to the roof of her mouth—

she knew the trip. It would be sweet going down, but too quickly dissolved and not enough to stop it, this pain, this ever-present hovering anxiety, anger, fear, and out-of-control-ness. The truth was: "You can't have just one." One rolled into the next and the next until it all slipped downhill. "I am powerless," she told the car. "Take it from me."

She jerked her hand out of the glove compartment and opened the driver's window, letting the wet fall on her arm, hoping the cool would take away the yearning. What an idiot, playing with fire.

At the hospital parking lot entrance, Dani pulled a ticket from the kiosk and watched the black and yellow arm lift. Driving into the lot, she found a space and parked, looking up at the windows of the white stucco building where her dad, Jack, teetering on the precipice of dementia, fed on the fuel of life-longisms: alcoholism, racism, narcissism, you-name-it-isms, and her sister, the (hopefully still) recovered drug addict, awaited her rescue.

At the hospital's door, Dani tossed the package of donuts into the trash. Her sobriety was worth more than that.

An hour later, watching Jack's exposed, sagging, hairless, patsy rear limp toward the bathroom in the hospital gown, she wondered if she could retrieve them. He'd refused to use the bed pan. "I don't take welfare from illegal sissy boys," he said to the young male nurse.

"My parents are from Malaysia, but I was born in Iowa," The nurse replied, forcing a smile. "My father teaches math, and my mother cooks in a restaurant. Where are your people originally from, Mr. Smith?"

"Hell," Dani whispered, offering an apologetic, automatic shrug, *sorry, my dad's an asshole*, to the nurse.

The bathroom door closed. Jack's foul mood wasn't unusual. He needed a beer. She suspected the nursing staff had put him alone in the small single room because his unpleasant personality had distressed other patients. She rubbed her sore neck. She needed a hot shower. Where the hell was Monica with the coffee?

Outside the hospital window, a fine layer of mist glistened in the morning light. She wrapped her arms around her body for warmth.

"Here you go." Monica entered the room. "I had to put a lot of Sweet'N Low in for taste." She held out a cup, and Dani suddenly noticed how thin her sister's arms looked, even inside the sleeves of a thick turtleneck. Plus, she reeked of cigarette smoke.

"Thanks." Dani blew on the steaming brown liquid.

"Where is . . . ?"

Dani nodded toward the bathroom door.

Monica took a sip of coffee. "The guy in the next room is dying."

"Oh, no!"

"Can't you hear the crowd keening around his bed?"

Dani shook her head.

"You can't hear it? There must be like twenty people."

Monica's sensitivity to pitch was remarkable. When they were little, Monica and Toby, the terrier, were the only ones who could hear a fire truck's high-pitched wail long before it passed the house. When he grew old and deaf, Toby was hit by a car. "Hey, remember our dog, Toby?"

Monica sadly nodded. "You're so lucky you can't hear things."

"Yeah. I have no superhuman talents."

Monica's pale face broke into a wide grin. "You're great at killing your ex-husband." Her yellow teeth made Dani shudder. She remembered the stains on Red's teeth.

"Glad that makes you happy."

"You have no idea." She grinned. After a beat, Monica added, "Hey, you've lost more weight."

"Yoga," Dani lied. She wasn't ready yet to tell her sister that she'd been right about OA. Monica loved to gloat.

"I'd rather keep smoking," Monica said, groaning. Her brown hair lay flat against her cheekbones. If she'd wanted to, Monica could have been a model. She definitely had the looks in the family, but she preferred to keep her beauty hidden under dirty hair and baggy clothing. Monica glanced up at the muted TV bolted in the corner. "Dad loves that food competition show," she said. "Have you ever watched it? What's it called?"

"I don't watch food shows."

The toilet flushed, and the door reopened.

"It stinks in there." Jack's voice was raspy, probably from yelling at nurses. "This place is a dump. Let's go."

"You can't go until they say you can, Jack," Dani said. "How's your wrist?"

"My wrist is right as rain." He held up his left arm to display the white cast. "Where's your mother?" His eyes scanned the room.

Monica looked at her phone. Dani instinctively looked out the window as if Diane had momentarily stepped out. Dani knew if they waited five minutes, he would forget that he'd asked.

"You, Dani," he barked at Monica. "Where are my pants?"

Dani's cell phone rang. Thank God. "It's Barney," she told them.

"I don't know anybody named Barney," Jack growled. "I won't talk to him."

"Uh, Dani's boyfriend?" Monica rolled her eyes. "Jesus, Jack, you met him at Thanksgiving."

Jack shrugged, shuffling over to the bed. Dani averted her eyes again from his sagging backside. "I don't want another Mexican. Get an American."

"Asshole," Monica said.

"What? Now, they don't want to be called Mexicans? Jesus, people are such crybabies these days."

Monica sighed. "Peter was born here. His parents were from Guatemala."

"Why is it my job to keep track of everybody?" Jack threw his hands up in the air.

Dani answered the phone, "Hey," grateful to be interrupted.

"How's it going?" Barney's voice was raised over the sound of traffic in the background.

"Oh, the usual. Where are you?"

"Shooting right off the 210. Brilliant, just brilliant. The actors can't even hear each other talk over the traffic."

Jack threw a small blanket off the bed onto the floor. "Where are my shoes?" He lifted the bedsheets.

Dani suddenly remembered Monica saying that the paramedics had brought him in naked. "That sucks," she told Barney, turning to Monica. "Can you go to his house to get him some clothes?"

Monica looked up from texting, her brown eyes filled with alarm.

Jack opened the built-in cabinet in the wall, discovered it was empty, and slammed it shut. "Jack, you don't have clothes here," Dani said. "Let's wait for the doctor."

"Did that chink take my clothes?" he bellowed.

"Jesus," Barney said. "Even I heard that."

"Jack, be quiet," Dani snapped. Then back to Barney, "We're waiting for the doctor to release him."

"We're not waiting for anybody," Jack yelled. He pulled the curtain away from the window to inspect the area. "I'll call the cops."

"Sit!" Monica scolded like he was a misbehaving dog.

Dani put the cell closer to her mouth and whispered, "I don't think I can do this. I almost had a donut."

"Babe, do you want me to see if I can find someone to cover me?" Barney asked.

Yes, please come rescue me even though I think we're breaking up very soon, she wanted to cry out watching her father rummaging through her purse. "No, it's okay. I'll try Karyn," she heard her voice falter. "Plus, I'm not by myself. I've got Monica."

Barney stifled a laugh.

Monica texted, watching Jack get down on his hands and knees near the bed. "Where the fuck are my goddamn shoes?" He crawled under the bed.

"Monica!" Dani barked.

"Where is my Jew doctor?" Jack crawled out from the other side of the bed.

"Jack," Monica sighed from her chair. "You can't say that."

Jack turned his head and stuck out his tongue, giving her the raspberries. "I'm allowed to say Jew." He gripped the side of the mattress and slowly got back to his feet. "It's the one that starts with H you can't say anymore. Like calling black folks colored or negro. You can't do that anymore. One day it's African American, then it's black. What the hell is this Latinx crap?"

"Dani?" Barney's voice called out.

"Barney, I need to call you later," Dani said, sighing and hanging up.

Jack looked at them, confused. "My ass is cold," he commented, turning around and opening his gown for emphasis.

Why was everything always rotten? Had it always been like this? No, of course not.

For instance, when Dani was ten, her poem, "The Butterfly," was published in the local paper. "Wrapped tightly, I work my wings. Build muscles. Becoming strong. To break free. I make the whole world sing." Jack was so proud that he'd taken her alone to JCPenney's and purchased the beautiful white faux rabbit fur coat she'd been dropping hints about for weeks; it was soft and luxurious with a slender silver buckle at the waist. Dani had wept with gratitude, clinging to the box the whole drive home, terrified in the fragility of closeness, afraid the fatherly pride was temporary and that as soon as they reached home the light would fade into a can of Coors or Schlitz, followed by another into the night. Which it had.

Later, Diane, furious with the extravagant purchase, allowed her to wear the coat only on special occasions: Halloween, Thanksgiving, church at Christmas. In between, Dani had modeled alone in her room until the shoulders grew too tight. Eventually, Monica mailed the faux fur coat COD to PETA. By then, Jack couldn't have cared less about poetry, coats, or his daughters because his wife had left them all behind.

For some people, a great loss sparks the awakening of deeper compassion and empathy toward others. Jack's disappointments turned into a dark, persistent rot.

Years ago, in a session at one of those twenty-five-dollar therapist training places in the San Fernando Valley, a young therapist surmised that the single event of the butterfly poem and faux fur coat was the reason that Dani had quit writing all together. It hurt too much to know what was missing. In writing the blog, was she also trying to recapture the girl who'd once had Jack's love?

Pointing up at the TV, she called out, "Sriracha sauce in a dessert? C'est impossible!"

Jack stopped and looked to the screen. Hopefully, that would shut down his racist anti-Semitic diatribe until Dani could find a pair of men's pants.

RED

A small group of fit, shiny younger women exited the God!ess studio. They chatted in pairs or alone, walking to their BMWs, Mercedes, and Audis. It was ten o'clock on a Wednesday morning.

Red watched, crouched low behind the steering wheel of her old Toyota, her heart beating fast, scanning the group for Sasha. Which car did she drive? Mercedes? Maybe the hybrid BMW? That would be in keeping with her brand. Her name wasn't on the teaching schedule for the day, but a young woman who'd answered Red's call earlier had said that Sasha would be at the studio, "From eleven thirty to three mostly. I think, maybe?"

Meeting Dani had sparked a flame. The woman was charming, chubby yet pretty, and slightly neurotic, but who wasn't these days? The lot quickly emptied, leaving only a white Escalade, white Range Rover, and the white BMW convertible, hybrid model. It was the BMW.

Red sat up, rolling her stiff shoulders around a few times to loosen the muscles.

Fuck it, she couldn't hold it any longer—she had to pee. She opened the creaky car door and stepped outside. Her pace quickened as she made her way across the parking lot. She pulled open the silver double doors painted with the God!ess purple and white logo and felt a blast of cold air conditioning hit her face as she stepped inside the studio. White walls, white paintings, white roses in white ceramic vases, white blocks to hold shoes, a gleaming light wood floor—it was simplistic, stylish, and clean. Perfect. The sound of the ocean played subtly from hidden speakers.

A young woman with a thick, blue ponytail and several face piercings looked up from behind the white reception counter. She raised a pierced brow.

"Bathroom?" Red asked.

The girl smiled at Red and pointed down a long white hallway of closed studio doors. "Please remove your shoes," she whispered, holding a finger to her shiny lip stud.

Red flipped off her sandals and put them in an empty, white wooden box. Then she tiptoed hurriedly across the slippery floor, hearing a soothing voice instructing behind one closed door. From behind another, the gong of a large bell rang out. She sped past the door marked "Office" and to the bathroom.

It reeked of sandalwood and vanilla, her two least favorite scents. She locked the door and sat on the toilet, wiping the sweat from her brow.

It took a moment for her eyes to adjust to the subtle light. The bathroom was painted lavender and featured a round, purple porcelain sink and toilet. The sconces on either side of the large ornate mirror were small chandeliers. God!ess hand soap and lotions were lined along the white marble countertop. The plush white hand towels must have cost a small fortune. Red hated purple, preferring greens or blues, but the bathroom was exquisite.

When she was done, Red slowly reopened the bathroom door. Her exit line was clear, thank God. Just as she was about to step out, the office door opened.

A very tall, beautiful woman wearing a white turban stepped into the hallway, followed by Sasha. Red quietly closed the bathroom door again. Shit. She held her breath, straining to hear the conversation.

"Thank you for coming, Abebi," she heard Sasha say. "And again, I'm so sorry that we can't offer you the position at this time."

Position? What position? Another class ended, and the hallway filled with life. Red stepped out safely into the stream of yoga students, making her way back to the front desk where the ponytailed receptionist sat, furiously texting away on her phone.

"Is Sasha still here?"

"No, no she went out to run a quick errand."

Women in yoga pants with perfect rear ends passed the receptionist, guzzling water from their glass bottles. Red waited for the room to clear, moving slowly through the spacious white reception area, pretending to be interested in the displays of crystals, yoga wear, nutritional supplements, and other God!ess vegan lifestyle products for sale. Sasha knew how to milk her brand. Maybe that was another reason Peter had married and impregnated her? Steady money?

When the room finally emptied, Red sauntered back to the receptionist. "I'm really sorry to bother you, but do you happen to know if there are any open positions at God!ess?"

"Probably mine. Just kidding." The girl looked around and then whispered, "I did sneak a look at the resumes. They're like for mother's helpers or maybe a nanny?"

Red nodded. Perfect. A mother's helper. "Oh, wow. I used to be a personal assistant," she lied. "Is Sasha hiring right away?"

"Yeah, I think so. She's pretty uptight with Peter on the road. Needs help. She has a bunch of interviews scheduled again tomorrow."

"Cool, thanks. I'll bring my resume by later." Red offered a warm smile.

Mother's helper. Red may have just found a way into Peter's life.

DANI

Jack's darkened house looked small and forlorn in the midday light. Its gutters sagged with leaves from the withered walnut tree. A single shutter was missing from the front window. A wave of sadness filled Dani's chest.

Monica pulled her beat-up Mazda into the driveway, its nearly-bald tires skidding on wet concrete. Dani parked beside her, turning to Jack, sleeping, in the backseat. She said, "We're home," adopting an authoritative tone.

Jack, wearing sweats with hospital socks stuffed into the large boots of a dead man, grumbled. He uncurled a middle finger.

"Real pretty." Dani stepped out of the car.

"We can't carry him like that big paramedic did," Monica said, her voice low enough for only Dani to hear. Monica's whisper was filled with fear.

"We can try."

Monica nodded but looked doubtful. Dani hoped they could manage without getting shoved or hit. She leaned in and grabbed Jack's bony arm. "Be careful of the cast."

"I won't touch it." Monica shuddered.

Jack peered around them, outside the opened car door, looking confused like he didn't recognize his own untended front lawn. Finally, he acquiesced and slowly stood; his body swayed, then found its strength. Dani moved in closer. A wave of dizziness washed over her. Oh God, no tipping over now, please.

"Move it, sisters," he growled. "It's cold."

Slowly, the three shuffled toward the front door. Dani knew they couldn't expect help from the neighbors. Jack had alienated every do-gooder within a ten-mile radius. Why hadn't she taken Barney up on his offer?

Monica jiggled her key in the door. They helped Jack step through. "Oh, God!" Monica commented as she covered her nose with her hand.

The house reeked of cat urine, rotten food, and—Dani was certain—sewage. She flipped on the light. How was it possible that it looked worse than it smelled? Monica started to dry heave.

"Breathe into your turtleneck," Dani commanded. She wasn't about to spring for a motel or bring them to Pasadena. "Jack, we're going into the living room."

"I heard you fine the first time, Danielle."

She took a deep breath and held it. Monica ducked her mouth and nose into her turtleneck. They hobbled across the living room. Each held Jack in place with one hand while swiping away old newspapers, empty beer cans, a rotting banana off the sofa onto the carpet. Dani knew that Diane would kill herself if she saw the carnage; her once prized blue damask sofa was soiled with a large brown stain on one cushion. Please, let it be mustard or ketchup or coffee, Dani thought.

"Let's lie you down, Jack." She turned him around, helping his buttocks slowly lower to the cushions. Jack fell back with a sigh, sinking in. The white stubble on his sagging chin caught her by surprise.

Monica stared at the wreckage, frozen in place.

Dani wanted to grab her sister's small hand and lead them out of this mess, back through the chasm of broken childhood promises to a better place where they could start fresh, get new parents, better attitudes, and mental health. She wanted them to be women who still stood a chance. She also wanted a dozen Winchell's chocolate sprinkled donuts with a gallon of whole milk and her mom or some other grown-up to pull up in a big car and drive them someplace clean and warm. She wanted Jack to change. But somehow, the girls were the grown-ups now.

"I'm gonna turn up the thermostat and make some coffee," Dani said, forcing cheer into her voice. "Mon, wanna help me? Maybe you could get Jack a fresh pillow and blanket from upstairs?"

Monica looked at her phone's screen, then furiously texted back.

"Maybe you could find a clean blanket upstairs while I make coffee?" Dani didn't bother to hide the annoyance in her voice.

Monica gazed up the darkened stairway but didn't move.

"Jack, we'll be right back." He was already snoring.

She eased her sister into the hallway and flipped on the stairway light. "It won't be as bad up there as it's going to be in the kitchen. He probably doesn't go up there much anymore."

"It smells like vomit. Right here. Where I'm standing. Vomit," her sister observed. She crossed her thin arms in defiance.

"When you said you visited him, I thought you meant inside of the house."

"Mostly, I drop off stuff. Groceries. Pick up mail." Her cell beeped again.

Anger bubbled in Dani's throat. "Why did you tell me you'd been taking care of him when you clearly haven't?"

"What have you done lately, sis? For our father?" Monica sent a quick text and put the phone away.

Dani waited, tapping her foot. "Was that your sponsor?" She was sick of adulting her sister.

"It's none of your business. Jesus!" Monica snapped, starting up the stairs. "That's why it's called anonymous," adding, "Should I monitor your diet, Lady Good and Plenty?" She disappeared down the upstairs hall.

Bitch. What a bitch.

Hoping some drug dealer wasn't on his way over, Dani stepped into the kitchen, turned on the light, and cried out. The sink was filled with dirty pots, bits of dried food on the stove and the counter; the freezer door was open, which accounted for the horrible stench of rotting meat. Plastic grocery store bags bulged with crumpled beer cans. She dragged the over-flowing trashcan out the back door—let the skunks and raccoons enjoy it—and left the door open to get the flies out of the house. Where was Dick, the cat?

"Danielle?" Jack interrupted from the kitchen door.

Dani turned and tipped forward, knocking an empty whiskey bottle off the counter; it shattered across the floor. "Shit. Don't move, Jack. Don't move." She dropped to all fours, picking up big shards of glass.

"Are you drunk?" Suddenly, he was interested in her.

"No," Dani replied. "I just, I tripped."

"Well, I just took a piss in these pants. Good thing they aren't mine." He looked down at a wet patch on the front of the dead stranger's gray sweatpants.

The bad dream was turning into a full-fledged nightmare. "Okay. Hang on. We'll just put them in the washer. I'm gonna draw you a nice, warm bath."

"I can't climb the stairs." He shuffled back out of the room. "Monica!"

Dani swallowed back the bile rising in her throat. One thing at a time. Draw a bath. You can handle it. Bath first, clean the kitchen tomorrow, Dani thought. God, she needed a warm Cinnabon with extra frosting.

"Monica?" Dani called out with a note of false cheer. "Can you help Jack up the stairs to the bathroom?"

"I already am!" her sister yelled back.

She grabbed a broom and dustpan and started sweeping the tiny fragments of glass into a pile. Where was the fucking cat? God, she hoped Monica wouldn't find it dead upstairs under a pile of mildewed clothes.

"We can do this," Dani encouraged herself. "We've done it before." She searched for a safe place to dump the broken glass. Was that black mold on the ceiling?

She opened the back door and set the dustpan down on the concrete step. Jack needed a bath. She needed to cover that cast. She grabbed an old plastic grocery sack from the counter.

Climbing upstairs, Dani gripped the banister and felt a stab of pain. She pulled a shard of glass from the soft flesh of her palm, and little drops of blood dribbled onto the beige carpet. The whole place screamed demolition.

Dani knocked on the bathroom door, her heart pounding, trying not to remember that memory, that one time, from long ago. "Jack? Are you decent?" When he didn't respond, she took a deep breath and slowly entered.

Jack stood alive and naked, staring at his cast in the full-length mirror. He turned to her, surprised, but did nothing to cover himself. She squeezed her eyes shut and quickly turned away. God, she was sick to death of being a good person. Why did she feel compelled to do this? Filial piety for a horrible man. Other people dumped their horrible parents, refused phone calls, took jobs in Alaska or Japan to escape. But no, not Dani. She carried too much shame, was a glutton for punishment. Was a glutton, plain and simple.

Fuck it. She steeled herself and turned back to face him. "We need to cover that cast before you take a bath." She held out the bag.

Jack held out his casted arm.

None of it was going to be easy. Dani quickly tore a hole in the bottom of the plastic grocery sack and then fitted it over Jack's cast. "There we go," her voice singsong light as she tucked it tightly on both ends.

For an old, out-of-shape alcoholic, Jack still had serious muscle tone in his arms and legs. He stared at his image in the mirror. He had small, dark eyes taking in the sunken chest covered in white fur, a protruding small round hard belly, a flaccid penis, and scrotum.

Her father was an old man.

"Now, I'm going to start your bath," Dani announced. Her loud voice was irritating with false cheer.

She pretended not to notice his sour odor. Dani grabbed the box of Epsom salts from the shelf and knelt down at the edge of the tub. She pretended as if it were the most ordinary thing, to be alone with her naked elderly father in the bathroom where the Smith family nightmare had taken place. She turned on the faucet, praying the hot water heater still worked, praying he'd paid the bills. "Do you want bubbles or oil or anything fancy like that? This old tub always heated up so fast. They made them better in the old days. Mine just leaks out the heat." Jack didn't respond. The tub was sparkling clean. She hoped at least that he'd showered this month. She grabbed the bottle of shampoo and squeezed it under the running water. It was best to fill the tub with soap in case he forgot to wash himself. A drop of blood dripped onto the suds. "Do you want help getting in?" Dani tested the water.

Jack watched the water rise in fascination. Her stomach felt queasy at the nearness of his sour smelling flesh.

"Jack? It's time to get in the bath." She prayed he wasn't remembering that night—the one she didn't want to recall—with Diane in this same bath. She waited for him to say something. No one had mentioned that night since Diane had left them. She held out her hand.

As if reading her thoughts, Jack said, "I'm glad my wife hired a pretty white girl," he took her hand and gripped the shower rail with his free one, "instead of a colored."

"Put your left foot in first," she instructed. He did as he was told, legs shaking. "Is it too hot?" He shook his head no, swaying a little. She let go and grabbed his sides. "Now put in the right foot. It's okay. I've got you," she said. Dani prayed that her hands wouldn't slip. His pale hindquarters lowered into the tub, his sagging gray-haired balls hitting the water first. "There, great. Perfect. Now you relax for a minute. I'm going to find a clean towel."

She headed back into the hall but heard a small splash and turned to see Jack completely submerged underwater.

"Jack!" She raced back to the tub.

He bobbed up coughing and sputtering.

"Are you okay?"

He spat a mouthful of water in her face. The act was so unexpected that Dani laughed. Jack grinned.

"All right then, playtime is over. Be sure to soap under your arms," she commanded.

"You should have laughed more, Dani. Maybe then your husband wouldn't have dumped you for that towel-head."

SASHA

"**B**abe." Peter's handsome face cut in and out on the iPhone screen. "It's going to be okay."

"You don't know that." Lately, he'd really been getting on her nerves. She had a pounding headache. And fat fingers, fat feet and fat ankles, thick cankles. Jesus, sometimes Peter was dense. She hated feeling this way. Especially when they were far apart. "Los Angeles to Kentucky is too far."

"Babe." His tender voice enveloping her in his arms. "You're right here. In my heart."

By the time Peter returned for his birthday, she would be a squishy, veined, baby delivery system with stretch marks and flabby breasts. Ugly. Plain stupid ugly. And uncomfortable. Her sides were hurting. The baby was spreading quickly, as quickly as her nose had started to spread. What did her clients at God!ess think when they saw her swollen, cranky frame? She was only twenty-five. Why was her body betraying her? Craving things that weren't good for her, but tasted amazing? She hadn't lived this way her whole adult life so that she could look like a fat, lazy housewife. Stop! She thought. Breathe. Be kind. You're such a shallow bitch sometimes. Imagine. Flood the room with light. Feel your husband's love.

"I love you, too, my husband, my heart."

The door opened. Sasha's sturdy English OB/GYN entered smiling, holding the test results.

"Is it preeclampsia? Is the baby going to be okay?"

"Sasha, all seems on track. Your blood pressure is slightly elevated," Dr. Simone reported. Her accent made her sound like Mary Poppins delivering bad news. "But the protein level in your urine is normal. Does high blood pressure run in your family?"

"No." Sasha heard the tremor in her voice. "And mine is usually a little low. Is the baby all right?"

"We're going to check in on your baby's growth and heartbeat in a minute. All is good, Sasha. Are you still practicing veganism? How about trying some fish?"

Sasha paused. Would her doctor leak her meat lapses to the press? No, patient doctor confidentiality, but assistants read charts. And were notoriously underpaid. That's how her carnivorous turn would be leaked and destroy her brand, by a curious, bored, or angry underpaid assistant. Also, she didn't want Peter to know about her flesh cravings. Not yet. "No, meat," she lied. "Or fish. I'm worried about the mercury." But what if it was the meat spiking her blood pressure or hurting the baby? She'd look at WebMD online later tonight.

"Hey, doc." Peter's voice interrupted her anxiety.

"Dad, thanks for joining us." Dr. Simone chuckled. "How's the tour?"

"Great. In Louisville for the next few days. Gorgeous weather here."

"Sunny here, also. As I was telling Sasha, Peter, I don't think it's anything to be worried about. Over halfway through. Let's see what the baby wants to reveal to us today."

Oh, God!ess. Sasha took a full breath in, expanding her chest—baby, my baby, please be okay—and released the air back out through her nostrils. Her heart was pounding. What if there wasn't a heartbeat?

"Let's do this," Peter called out.

Dr. Simone reached for the bottle of gel in the warmer. Sasha leaned back and raised her shirt. The gel felt warm. She stared at the static image on the monitor, waiting, holding her breath, praying, *please, God!ess, please*, as the ultrasound wand glided over the smooth surface of her belly, the small sounds and whooshing of the placenta revealing ghostly shadows but not a form.

"Well, hello, little one. Hello. Don't be shy," Dr. Simone started.

"Is it . . . ?" Sasha stopped herself before she finished the sentence. Alive?

"Baby just has its back to us now. Come on there, turn around, baby," the OB/GYN cooed. "There it is. The heartbeat." She pointed the cursor at the small, white, pulsating dot.

"Oh!" Sasha exhaled with relief, watching the rise and fall of the white line on the grid at the bottom of the monitor. Thank you, God!ess!

She nodded yes, squinting small tears at the strong pulse beating on the screen, feeling the wet pooling into her ears.

"Babe, I can't see anything," Peter said.

Sasha held the phone closer to the monitor.

"Oh," Dr. Simone exclaimed. "Well. Oh, my. This could explain a few things."

"What?" Peter and Sasha asked in unison.

Dr. Simone grinned at Sasha. "You've popped out, Sasha, because you're having twins!"

"Oh my God!" Two? She was carrying two babies, two to love! "Oh my God!ess! Peter!"

"What?"

"You're having twins, Daddy," Dr. Simone repeated. "I know it's a bit of a shock."

"Twins? Two kids?"

"Honey, it's amazing." Stay positive with me; don't be afraid of change, Peter. It doesn't hurt the tour. It doesn't hurt anything, Sasha thought. "It's going to be so wonderful." She sent him a silent plea.

Dr. Simone pointed the cursor. "See? The spine?"

Sasha squinted hard, trying to visualize the form her OB/GYN was pointing to. Was that the head? "Oh, I see it!"

Dr. Simone moved the cursor to the other curled bean. "This one, the one closer to the cervix, we call Baby A. With twins, it's Baby A and Baby B, at least until we learn the sex."

"I don't want to know the sex," Sasha interrupted. "Hi baby, Baby A."

"Babe," Peter said. "Hold the phone the other way." His voice sounded irritated, not elated.

Sasha wanted to yell at him but adjusted the phone in silence. She would not let him ruin her experience. "Better?"

"Peter," Dr. Simone said. "We'll have printouts to show you, too. Don't worry. Now, let's see if I can get a better picture. There! Head, arm, heart, oh!"

"Is that baby, Baby A, lying on its back?" Sasha was mesmerized.

"And the outline of the head. The chin." Dr. Simone adjusted the wand, and Baby B's heartbeat, strong and steady, scratched up and down on the graph at the bottom of the monitor screen. "Recording." The staccato sound of printing, the readout being ripped from the machine. "163. Good! That's two cycles. Baby B's heart rate is 163 beats a minute. Very strong and healthy."

"Peter, oh, my love. Baby B has a strong heart. Just like us! God!ess is good. Dr. Simone, where's Baby A?"

"Baby A is kind of curled away now, so it's going to be more difficult to get a measurement. Ah, there! That's right, little one. Let us see you. Can you see baby, Sasha?"

Yes. Two. Such joy. "Peter?" Sasha looked at her phone. Peter had disconnected.

He rang back. "Sorry, babe. Sorry, doc. Radio interview's about to start. Big local station."

"I can see the sex of Baby A," Dr. Simone interrupted. "Are you sure you don't want to know?"

"I want to know," Peter said at the same time that Sasha repeated, "I don't want to know."

The doctor's expression remained static.

"We've already discussed this." Sasha tried to keep her voice even but heard the sharpness.

"Men don't get a lot of choices. Why even fucking ask?"

Dr. Simone rolled her eyes and quickly turned her gaze back to the machine.

Sasha hung up on Peter. "He's on tour," she vented to her doctor. "While I'm home, getting fat, lonely and scared. I mean, I know he had to go. I'm just, it's hard, you know. I'm sorry."

Dr. Simone placed a strong hand on Sasha's shaking shoulder. "There, now, Mommy, there now. Daddies often take a while to come around. Don't worry. He will in time. Do you have a support system?"

Her mom always made excuses about visiting. She hated Los Angeles and was afraid of the traffic, but she was excited to have them visit New York after the baby was born. Sasha missed her old friends, the starving artists and true yoga granolas from Venice. Her life was now filled with new slightly famous or famous-adjacent friends. Peter had been hounding her to hire a personal assistant. Sasha pulled back and hiccupped. Twice. She nodded. "I'm going to hire an assistant."

"Excellent."

That night, home alone with the security system on, especially the sensors outside of the master bedroom, Sasha lit candles on her dresser and sat cross-legged in meditation, feeling her belly heavy against her thighs. She was determined to draw into her life a larger support system. She imagined rings of peace emitting out from her heart chakra, blue-green and soft, reaching out across the city, connecting with beautiful women, a tribe. Maybe even a few mothers from her class would be interested in getting closer? I deserve love and support, she chanted mentally. I am worthy of good friends and relationships. "I am having twins," she said aloud, though it didn't seem real. Miracles often felt unreal, but for others, they were ordinary every day.

Her thoughts wandered to lists of things that needed to be done. Tomorrow, she would hire an assistant. Someone from the stack of resumes waiting on her desk.

Sasha couldn't push away the sound of Peter's cold response, "Twins?" It was more than fear; it resonated like a slap, a push, a loss. It wasn't her Peter. "I wish you could have my baby," he'd always said. They were having miracle babies! Not just one baby, oh baby, but two. "A and B. You and me." No man in his right mind would have scheduled a radio interview during his wife's ultrasound. Shouldn't flowers have been delivered to her with Peter's apology and expression of enthusiasm? Maybe the band's publicist couldn't change the time?

What was she thinking? Meredith, the publicist, hated her.

Whenever they had a band meeting at her office, Meredith had treated Sasha like a groupie, a minor blight in the light of Peter's rising star. Even if Peter had told Meredith—cold, sneering, menopausal Meredith—about the appointment, she wouldn't have cared less. She was all business, and frankly, mostly inhuman.

Sasha would not look at the band's socials' tonight. She didn't need to see the evidence of his distance. Sasha wasn't controlling and didn't demand one hundred percent desire from anyone, but things had changed and expectations needed to be expressed and met. This is what their therapist said. Conscious coupling, being a real partner for another imperfect, real human. They were married now. Counseling had started teaching them a new way of creating a sacred union, but then the tour had begun, and she'd gotten pregnant. What was the state of their marriage? The quiet still night of meditation offered no comfort. Sasha held onto her belly. The bed was a raft, floating with the babies, headed toward a strange, exciting, terrifying, new land.

RED

The morning of the interview, Red pulled her thick red hair into a ponytail, leaving her face free of makeup. She chose loose-fitting khakis and an oversized, light green, button-down shirt—something subdued to hide her long, toned legs and flat stomach—and slipped into sexless flats. She smiled at her reflection in the full-length mirror on her bedroom door, and then took a deep breath, grabbed her car keys, and headed out.

Creating alter ego Lynn Pickerton—Midwesterner, gardener, ending a bitter divorce and starting over—had been fun. Sasha would subconsciously size her up for competition within the first few seconds, so Lynn had to be warm and matronly, sexless, slightly boring, and smart. A friend. Never a threat.

When she entered God!ess, the same young, pierced receptionist greeted Red, leading her down the quiet hallway. She knocked on Sasha's office door, quietly calling out, "Your next appointment, Lynn, is here."

There wasn't any way that Sasha knew about Red, but still, her stomach rumbled with nerves.

The décor in Sasha's office was tasteful but overly ornate, in stark contrast to the simplicity of the rest of the God!ess studio. The walls were a light lavender, with pastel-painted mandalas in various shapes and sizes. A large glittering chandelier hung over a sitting area furnished with a fluffy white chair and large purple sofa. Marble planters featured tall, green palms in every corner. A gold and glass antique side table displayed a neatly placed stack of fashion photography books beside a tall, delicate, white, and pink orchid. Three long skylights poured natural light across Moroccan Boucherouite rugs.

Sasha, seated behind a large, ornate desk, stood up from her faux-sheepskin chair. She was dressed in white leggings and a crop top. Pregnancy suited her. Her curves were only more pronounced. In person, the woman simply glowed.

Red forced herself to stare at Sasha's face and not the pregnant belly. She needed to remember why she was here. Hating her wouldn't accomplish anything.

"Lynn, hi, please shut the door, and join me." Sasha stood revealing her round baby bump, the navel protruding slightly, skin stretched tightly over her naked belly. She moved like a graceful bowlegged cat around the desk.

Red closed the door, amazed at how easy it had been to get inside the inner sanctum. The ease made her anxious. She crossed the room and sat on the velvet cushion near Sasha, crossing her shaky legs at the ankles, remembering to keep her body language open and warm. "Your office is gorgeous."

"Thank you." Sasha smiled, revealing overly whitened teeth. "Feng Shui says that the center of a business establishment should be bursting with vitality. It spreads to the rest of the company." She offered a nervous, friendly laugh. "I know, my husband thinks it's silly." She reached for Lynn's resume on the round, gold coffee table, scanning the paper in her hand.

Had something in Red's expression betrayed her? "I don't think it's silly," Red assured, even though she did. "Ancient Chinese wisdom. Older than everything."

"It is!" Sasha exclaimed. "I just hate it when people think New Age beliefs are shallow. *The Secret* changed my life."

Red had no idea what secret Sasha was talking about but played along. "I'd love to hear more about it."

"It's like the Laws of Attraction. I think I have an extra copy in my desk," Sasha offered with another genuine, warm smile. She was slightly irresistible. "Hailey says you're the best."

Hailey? The receptionist. Remain calm, Red told herself. Stay the course. "Running a business is tricky." She took a breath and launched into Lynn's fictional backstory. "When I was married, I quit my job as a family therapist to help my husband start his small business—home insurance. We had three employees. This was in Iowa. I handled the hiring, the books, most of the day-to-day business tasks, while he focused on building his clientele. The business grew into six figures. A good six."

Sasha listened, nodding. "Marriage is a compromise, especially for women." She stopped herself and quickly added, "But true love means everything."

Eager to get off the true love subject, Red reiterated, "I am qualified to help, Sasha and reliable."

Suddenly, Sasha leaned over and hugged Red tightly. She reeked of essential oils and patchouli. She pulled back, her eyes bright. "Lynn, would you be my personal assistant?"

Caught off guard by the burst of affection, Red laughed. "I would love it!"

"Then it's settled." Sasha smiled. "Fifteen dollars an hour." She used a hand to push herself slowly up from the couch.

Her naked belly met Red's eye-level gaze like a splash of ice water. Whatever inkling of fondness had begun for Peter's wife vanished. Red stood, remembering her mission. "Did you want to call any of my references first?"

"Oh, no." Sasha placed a well-manicured hand to her heart. "I'm very intuitive. I knew the moment you walked into the room that you were the person I've been praying for. Thank you, God!ess! Your chakras are clear. Monday morning, my house, ten a.m.?"

And like that, the door of Peter's life opened widely, and Red stepped inside.

DANI

After making Jack a grilled cheese with tomato soup and getting no thank you, Dani left him to yell at the Food Network (chocolate cake recipes threatened her sobriety) to finish cleaning his kitchen, hoping Monica would return soon from whatever "errands" she'd needed to run. Hopefully, they involved Violet.

Months of grime disappeared—dried eggs in cast iron skillets, ice cream containers, take-out pizza boxes, half-filled beer cans, not to mention what lurked in the microwave, gone. Still no sign of Dick, the cat.

Following Karyn's guidance, she created a plan: go grocery shopping, cook several casseroles to freeze for Jack to reheat for suppers, and then get the hell back home to OA meetings and Barney. She had been of service and taken care of herself.

She felt okay.

When her cell rang, she thought it was Monica, but it wasn't.

"Aunt Dani?" a sharp young female voice asked.

"Violet?" Her niece sounded almost adult-like. She'd always been old for her age and not in a good way.

"I need you to pick me up from Young Librarians."

"Libertarians?"

"Librarians." Violet exhaled exasperatedly. "We're not affiliated with any political party."

Such a difficult kid. "Where's your mom?"

"Your guess is as good as mine. I've been waiting for an hour."

Shit. "Where are you?"

"John Adams Middle School. 16ᵗʰ Street in Santa Monica."

Dani couldn't believe it. Since her last round of rehab, Monica had been fighting to keep custody of Violet. Now this? "I'll be there in twenty minutes. I just have to get Grandpa dressed."

"I'll be sitting on the front steps. I'm wearing a red cap and a denim jacket."

"Violet, don't worry; I know what you look like."

"I'm not worried. I just don't have money for the bus."

Violet was acting in a way that didn't seem possible for a twelve year old.

Thirteen. A thirteen year old.

Jack was asleep, slack-jawed, on the sofa. Little bits of spittle and bread crumbs gathered in his white chin stubble. She was afraid to leave him alone so soon after the incident. Dani sat down on the edge of the sofa, gently touching his shoulder. He growled and pulled away, covering his eyes with his arm. "We need to go pick up Violet."

"Nope," he said into his sleeve. "I don't like Violet."

Dani sighed. "We have to."

"And it's not because she's a Mexican, or God knows whatever mix she is." He started, crawling out from under the covers. "It's because I don't like her."

"Well, she's your granddaughter. You have to."

"Who do you think I am? Nelson Mandela?"

They headed north from Mar Vista on winding Walgrove Avenue, passing neighborhoods of overpriced homes through Venice and into Santa Monica. The sea breeze was soft, the afternoon light—that never-changing blue hint of golden happiness, while Jack stared out the passenger window, silent and brooding.

As promised, Violet, wearing a red cap and denim jacket, sat hunched over her phone on the front steps of the middle school. Dani gave a beep, pulling to the curb. Her niece looked up at them through large, round, black-framed glasses, too big for her face. Maybe that was in style now? Violet stood without a smile. The denim jacket was too tight on her chubby frame, the sleeves too short. Dani stepped out of the car because it seemed like someone should do more than wait for her to open the back door and climb in.

"Hi, Violet," she cried out cheerfully, coming around the front of the car with her arms outstretched. Violet's eyes filled with terror, and she pulled slightly back as Dani pitched forward, banging her head on the front fender.

"Dani?" Jack opened his car door.

"I'll call 911." Violet pulled her phone out of her back pocket.

Jack made his way to Dani's side. "She looks fine."

"She fell hard."

"It's okay. I'm okay." Dani tasted blood. Had she lost a tooth? "I just slipped." She struggled to her feet, a little woozy. "Did I lose a tooth?" She'd let her dental insurance lapse.

"You bit your lip." Violet put her phone away.

Jack held out a dirty handkerchief. Dani pressed it to her lip. "Show's over. I'm tired. Monica, give me the keys."

"You can't drive, Grandpa," Violet said. "And that's Dani."

Jack's eyes widened.

"They took away your license."

Boy, Dani thought, the kid was rough.

"What's this kid talking about?" Jack jerked a thumb in Violet's direction.

"You failed your driver's test last year." Violet crossed her arms. "I won't get in the car. It's illegal."

Dani glared at her niece. "I'm driving."

A look of confusion passed through his eyes, and then Jack laughed. "It's my car, girl. You can climb in the back and shut your pie hole or walk your brown ass home for all I care."

"Jack!"

Violet's chin jutted out in defiance.

Jack held a hard, blue-eyed stare.

Dani opened the driver's door and waited for Jack and Violet's standoff to end. The wind picked up, scattering middle school debris, waded-up exam papers, candy wrappers, crumbled McDonald's bags, across the sidewalk. A horn honked. A traffic light changed. Above, palm trees swayed. Finally, Violet pushed her big glasses back up her button nose.

"Hello?" Dani interrupted. "I'm bleeding?"

Jack shuffled around to the passenger seat. Violet reluctantly climbed into the back and slammed the door. She put in ear buds and closed her eyes. Her small arms crossed tightly over her chest. She looked nothing like her mother, but that posture was full-on Monica. Full lips set hard, soft and wide dark eyes, were her mystery father's contribution. Once her preteen phase passed, Violet would transform from awkward duckling into natural beauty. It was obvious. As long as she didn't inherit the Smith's list of isms, everything would be okay.

Dani looked back at the road, making a right on Lincoln, entering the bumper-to-bumper traffic headed toward Venice, and then Mar Vista. The story of Violet's father was as shifty as Monica. Sometimes, he was an American Indian lawyer who Monica had met at a bar in Tarzana. Other times, he was a Brazilian singer playing at Desert Daze in Joshua Tree. Once, he was a Canadian hockey player staying at the Bel Aire Hotel. Did Violet know who her father was? Why hadn't Dani ever asked?

Back at Jack's, Violet headed upstairs to do homework in Monica's old bedroom. "Aunt Dani?" she called out. "If you talk to Monica, tell her I won't say anything to the social worker, okay?" The door shut without waiting for a reply.

"This family needs an intervention," Jack remarked as he opened a can of Coors and took a big swig.

Dani headed into the kitchen to make a simple dinner—Greek lemon garlic chicken.

"Intervention," Dani scoffed. She wished she could say to him, "We've come together today to tell you how your behavior has adversely affected us and to beg you to seek treatment. Your life is going down the tubes, get professional help, get us back on the right path." Could anything or anyone have altered their sad downhill trajectory? Maybe Diane had sought intervention. Maybe that's why she left. Who knew? They were kids, busy with their own problems. Dani hardly noticed her mother's unhappiness. Unfinished, abandoned, they were girls left alone to survive a war zone. Jack versus the people of the world. But they'd done it. They'd survived.

"We're survivor bunnies," Monica always said.

Monica was bold, high-strung, and sensitive, which probably fueled her teenaged drug experimentation into full-blown addiction. Dani was a worrier, in a constant state of panic, a good girl, the saver, and a realist, which probably led to her choosing fucked up men. To Jack, neither of them showed exceptional talent in any area except the ability to truly not succeed at anything. When he was drunk and angry with his lot in life, Jack had often pointed accusingly. "You two are the reason," he'd yell. "For my bitter unhappiness." Or the feminists, hippies, the IRS, or the President of the moment, regardless of the party.

Where was Monica? She was on probation; the court would take Violet permanently. Was she using again? After dicing the oregano and garlic, Dani added it to the marinade for the chicken. She rinsed off her hands and texted her sister again.

DANI: I picked up Violet. We're at Jack's. Dinner at six thirty.

When Monica was eleven, she tried vodka for the first time. Monica didn't take to alcohol as much as to the combination of marijuana and alcohol introduced later by a high school boyfriend. Through eleventh grade, Monica had managed to stick to a strict rule of getting high only on the weekends with football players, until one of them introduced her to cocaine. The fleeting bliss even while shaking in her own bed, plus the weight loss, made it her absolute drug of choice. She told Dani it was the only cure she'd found for bulimia. Until crystal meth. But the meth came after Violet.

Dani was in the middle of the lawsuit with Peter when Monica announced her pregnancy. Dani assumed the father was Monica's Scandinavian-looking boyfriend, Rolf. Imagine blond, blue-eyed Rolf's surprise when beautiful brown Violet cried out in the delivery room. After Rolf kicked them out, Monica and Violet lasted six months at Jack's. Then she met Juan, and crystal meth came along. It was the beginning of the end for them. Dani, too consumed with destroying Peter, hadn't noticed. Violet entered the foster system around five, living with a kind elderly couple for several years until Monica succeeded in kicking the habit. Violet returned home at nine, left again for six months, and finally had been stable with Monica for over a year.

Why hadn't Dani taken Violet when the social worker asked? She was a wreck from Peter, trying to rebuild. It wouldn't have been a stable home. Those were the reasons she still told herself.

Earlier at the hospital, Dani had wanted to believe, to hope, that her sister was only playing around with anorexia again. Monica hadn't seemed high, but the texting, the forgetting to pick up Violet, the lying about checking in on Jack—it didn't look good.

When her sister hadn't called by sunset, Dani sautéed some green beans to go with the lemon chicken and rice. She set the table for three and called the others in to eat. At least the kitchen was now clean. Jack didn't say a thing.

"Green beans?" She passed the bowl to Violet.

Violet shook her head no.

"You've hardly touched a thing. Aren't you hungry?"

Violet shrugged.

"Eat." Jack stabbed a piece of chicken with his fork. "Kids are starving."

"Clearly, *I'm* not starving." Violet looked down at the phone in her lap.

"Do you want something else?" Dani asked. "Do you not eat meat?"

Violet texted away on her phone.

"Put that goddamn thing down at the dinner table, girl." Jack chewed the chicken with his mouth open. "Or I'll break it."

Violet put the phone on the table.

"She." He pointed in Dani's direction. "She went to all this trouble to cook dinner. You'll eat it or go to your room."

Violet scooted her chair back from the table.

"Permission to leave?" Jack asked.

"May I please be excused?" Violet inquired between clenched teeth.

"After you thank Dani for the lovely meal."

Violet stood. "Thank you for the lovely meal, Aunt Dani. I do love a good dead fowl eaten under duress."

In a flash, Jack grabbed Violet's wrist with his good hand and twisted. She let out a yelp. Dani jumped up. "Hey, hey!" She grabbed Jack's good arm, her heart racing, heat rushing to her chest. Violet was breathing like a trapped wild animal. "Let go." Dani tightened her grip on Jack, watching his skin turn white.

Jack released Violet. "You two don't know your place." He rubbed his arm. "Freeloaders in my house."

"You're a terrible person!" Violet cried out, running from the room.

Jack laughed. "High strung." He tore a piece of bread from the baguette near his plate and sopped up the last of the lemony-garlic sauce. "Just like her mother." He shoved the bite into his mouth.

Dani stood from the table. "We don't hurt kids in this house." Her voice shook with rage. "Not anymore. You hear me, old man?"

He rolled his eyes and squished the bread out between his teeth.

"I will put you in a home," Dani said. She curled her fingernails sharp into her palms.

Jack closed his mouth.

Dani picked up their dirty plates and carried them into the kitchen. Desperately wanting to get in the car and find the nearest Dunkin' Donuts, she carried the dirty dishes out the back door, down the steps, and into the side yard where she threw each plate with gusto against the side of the house, watching the cheap china shatter to bits.

As her anger subsided, she climbed the stairs up to Monica's old room. Without knocking, she opened the door.

Violet sat on the edge of the twin bed, her head in her hands. Her small shoulders shook.

"I'm sorry. Jack's a mean, old asshole."

The mattress springs gave a small sigh as Dani sat beside her niece. Was she fatter or was it the bed? Violet didn't move. Her arms ached to hold the girl, even though Dani knew it wouldn't make up for bad love, for hurt, for things that shouldn't happen to children.

"Let's get out of here," Dani said. "We've been cooped up. I've got cabin fever."

Violet mumbled something inside her sweater.

"In-N-Out?"

"It's late." Violet sniffed, rubbing her nose with her hand. "Besides you're a terrible driver."

"Oh. Okay. Thank you for that."

Violet shrugged, wiping the tears from her round cheeks.

"Help me out here. Toss me a line? Give me a break."

"From what?"

Dani folded her hands, begging but smiling. "Please. What do you like to eat? Really? I love to cook. And I'm trying not to eat it all myself anymore. I'm good at it. I'll make whatever you want, Violet. Give me something to do here, or I'll go crazy. I cannot sit in the living room and watch TV with Jack. You get that, right?"

Violet took her time chewing on the question. "I'd like steak. But it's too expensive."

Dani smiled. "Girl, I know where Grandpa keeps his wallet."

"That's called stealing." Violet kicked her shoes off. "Can you take me to school in the morning?"

"Of course."

"Then we have to leave by seven fifteen."

It would take more than a trip to Target to build a relationship with her niece. Where in the hell was Monica?

RED

The cat waited patiently on her haunches in front of the screen door, peering out into the late-night dark air, ready to be set free into the shadows. Yes, there were coyotes in Echo Park, cars, mischievous kids, and unseen danger around every corner, but Red had never been able to bring herself to keep a wild thing captive. She opened the front door and watched its silver, brown fur sprint for adventure, certain each morning that she'd be tacking posters to street signs offering a reward.

Monday, she would drive to Peter's house above Sunset Plaza. The fact made her stomach flutter again. Sasha had made it easy. Red's earlier elation had faded into a bitter melancholy after one too many glasses of Chianti. Now, her thoughts were woozy. It was almost midnight, and she'd been crying.

To soothe the anxiety, Red googled how to get away with murder, but only found information on some hit television show. She hadn't owned a television in ten years. She poured another glass of Chianti, which she shouldn't have. It was

Peter's favorite, and drinking too much wine made her sad, made her make late-night phone calls she shouldn't. Too much wine made her anxious the next morning. She tried googling, "how to kill a person," but the images were shocking, horrible. How did Dani think up so many creative ways without falling down the rabbit hole? Did she research famous serial killers or kings murdered throughout history? The local news? How was Dani able to be creative and keep Red reading each sentence carefully, instead of skipping to the satisfying end? Red would ask her the next time they had coffee. It was thrilling to know they could become friends. She didn't make friends easily, especially not with other women. What would Dani think of her new position? Her stomach fluttered again. It was too late to call her now. Red took a sip of wine and clicked on the bookmarked page hoping that Dani had written a new entry on her blog.

That would calm her nerves.

JUST-DESERTS.COM

For Steve's thirtieth birthday, I made spaghetti with homemade tomato basil sauce and veal meatballs. Dessert was a chocolate cream pie. When I first met Steve, his culinary tastes were what you'd imagine a latchkey kid's would be: hot dogs, hamburgers, and mac and cheese. Slowly but surely, as I learned to cook for the man I loved, his tastes developed. With the table set, I opened a bottle of Chianti, lit candles, and waited for him to walk in the door from work. Since his temp job at Disney had turned permanent, we could afford good food. Soon, we could move out of the dump on Van Nuys and into a sweet place in Toluca Lake or Burbank.

I checked my phone again. Seven. Maybe there was traffic. I texted him. "Hey, birthday boy. Can't wait to see you." Heart emoji, eggplant emoji, taco emoji, flames. I freshened my red lipstick and readjusted my tight skirt. I reached underneath and pulled my panties down, peeling them over my high heels, tossing them into the corner. He'd often begged for "commando." Tonight, I wanted to make him the happiest man in the world.

The truth was, we'd entered a rough patch. All of the marriage books told me not to worry, but to engage, try new things, take up a new interest to make myself more attractive, interesting, and spice up our sex life.

At my encouragement, Steve had not only picked up his guitar, Woody, but started playing new pieces at The Rex X, a coffee house bar around the corner from our apartment. I had gone and watched a few times, but decided it was better to give him space. Sometimes, we wrote songs together. Or at least, he tried. I liked to write, and he always said I was talented at writing lyrics. Steve was happy, happier than I'd ever seen him, and I'd continued to encourage him, even though the last two weeks butterflies had started flitting around in my stomach. New names: Annie, Samantha, Vasha, Ty, casually crossed his sweet lips. Friendships formed via text, social media, an occasional rehearsal after work. They were new friends, fellow musicians, I'd told myself—even though the tone of some texts seemed flirty. I had encouraged this. I wanted him to be happy. Steve had married me. He had encouraged my learning to cook. Paid for the classes. I encouraged his creative life. He hadn't needed to marry me. Steve loved me. "The Rex is a very supportive environment," he would reassure me. "There's nothing going on but that." This morning, when I'd asked if he wanted to go together to The Rex and catch a set and grab a beer for his birthday, he had replied, "No, babe, I'm good with just you." So, happily, I'd cooked veal meatballs and spaghetti, shaved my bikini line, and made certain that I was clean as he had slight difficulty with any sort of musky scent.

At eight fifteen, I pulled my underwear back on, blew out the candles, locked the front door, and walked to The Rex.

Steve was seated with his back to the door at a table in the middle of the room, with two pretty girls, a blonde and a brunette, and some guy with a beard and ear stretchers I think I'd met before, who looked like he was trying too hard. I knew it wasn't right; it didn't feel right. The four huddled like old chums, drinking beer out of bottles, people I'd seen but never really met because they were no longer interested in me once they'd learned that I wasn't a backup singer and didn't have a stage where they could play. It was his birthday, and he hadn't called or answered my texts. He was *my* husband. The pretty brunette spotted me first, leaned into my husband, and said something into his ear. Close. Steve laughed and then turned, but he didn't get up. My feet were slippery and swollen in my heels. I unclenched my fists, pasted on a smile, and walked to the table, aware of my heart pounding in my chest.

"Hey." I was trying to be the best, cool, casual wife.

Steve nodded, no surprise registered, no worry, nothing. It was almost as if my discovery didn't matter—like it wasn't a big deal. A look of indifference crossed his face, and I thought I might be sick. Who was this stranger? The other guy, maybe his name was Brett, jumped up and offered his chair. "Hey, hey." His voice sounded uptight and nervous. "Steve was just saying if he didn't go home soon, you'd come and find him. Dude, you were right."

I didn't sit down. The girls pretended to suddenly be interested in their drinks. Steve stared at me daringly, his eyes dark, almost empty.

"Hey, your birthday dinner is getting cold." I wagged my finger, as if this were our routine, him the negligent husband, me, the old ball and chain.

Steve reluctantly stood and pushed his chair back. There was tension in his clenched jaw, as if I had done something wrong, as if he were the one who should be mad.

"No," the brunette whined. "I thought you were going to do that song with me. I'm up next." She was beautiful, exotic looking with large brown eyes and pouty red lips.

I felt myself shrink in my jeans and t-shirt but pasted on a smile. "I'm Steve's wife. I don't think we've met."

She stood revealing her taut stomach with a belly ring. She held out a limp hand and offered a wide, warm smile, "Vasha."

Jack always said that a limp handshake was a sign of an untrustworthy person. I grabbed Steve and led him outside, forcing myself not to think about her flat stomach.

Walking back to the apartment, Steve offered the silent treatment, while I limped in high heels, listening to the gravel under our feet.

"I'll just reheat it," I heard my voice sounding natural, my hands steady as I turned a burner to medium heat. Steve went into the bedroom and shut the door. I tiptoed after, listening for a moment to his soft whispers on the other side, and then I went into the kitchen, pulled the Drano out from under the sink, and stirred it slowly into the bubbling red sauce in the pot on the stove.

We sat at the table while my husband enjoyed the birthday meal that I'd spent all day cooking to make him happy. I watched him chew and swallow, his prominent Adam's apple bobbing, while I sipped another glass of Chianti. Finally, my synapses started firing again. "Vasha is fucking my husband."

Steve twirled pasta on his fork, saying, "Grow up." He slurped in the last big bite. "I can't do this anymore."

He was right. The Drano took his life, painfully, by six the next morning.

RED

She exhaled, the final words spreading like heat searing open the center of her body. It was nearly perfect. Every entry, poetic justice. She chugged the last of the Chianti and threw the empty glass at the wall, screaming out a lion's roar. The bad guy did not get to keep winning. He was *such* a bad guy. This would not be another year of suffering. It was her year of revenge. Their year.

It was midnight, but she dialed Dani's number anyway and left a message.

"I'm Sasha's personal assistant!" she cried out with glee.

DANI

She sat on the edge of her squeaky childhood bed, swinging her legs and listening to the TV blare downstairs. The walls were covered with music posters for Duran Duran, Tears for Fears, Madonna, and Dani's 80s pop music favorite—The GoGo's, *Beauty & The Beat* album.

Smiling, she still remembered the lyrics. "*Hush, my darling. Don't you cry. Quiet, angel. Forget their lies. Pay no mind to what they say. It doesn't matter anyway. Hey, hey, hey. Our lips are sealed.*"

A band of only girls, she'd once considered punk, fresh new voices. Dani had danced to that song repeatedly in her room.

She suddenly cringed with embarrassment, remembering Peter's reaction the first time he'd seen her "white girl tribute wall." Like she hadn't known that people of color also made great music.

After that, Dani had made a point of discovering new music and realized a deep love for Nigerian jazz—anything played on steel drums, Latin salsa, and the buttery voice of Bill Withers.

How could she find Monica? She needed a cruller. Oh—a crème-filled donut. Something, anything, to take the edge off. She dialed Karyn, who answered on the first ring. Really, it showed true progress on her part that she'd chosen such a reliable sponsor.

"I imagine it's rough. Maybe you could find a meeting in Mar Vista. How's it going with your eighth step?" Karyn asked. "Any progress?"

She was stuck on the 8th step. Making a list of people she'd harmed by overeating and using food to stuff her feelings didn't make sense. Her addiction only affected her happiness, her blood sugar, and her own waistline.

Dani ignored the question. "Jack grabbed Violet tonight. I should have called the police. Who does he think he is? Who does Monica think she is? Disappearing on us like that? I should call social services." She felt the heavy grip inside of her chest, heard the anxiety in her breathing, the raised pitch of her voice and took a breath.

"Then, call the police," Karyn stated over the line.

That stopped her. "Wait. What?"

"Call social services."

Call the police? "On Jack? He's an old man."

"So?" Karyn's voice was suddenly hard. "Why are you doing this, Dani? Stay in your own lane."

"Stay in my own lane?" They were all in *her* lane. Where was the sweet, soft understanding sponsor? "I can't send Violet back to a foster home."

"Why not?"

"A foster home?"

Karyn snorted. "You write a blog about killing your ex-husband."

Dani leaned back against the creaky headboard and stared down at her bare feet, peasant feet, square and solid. A sliver of a hangnail protruded from the side of her big toe. Juggling the phone with her right shoulder, she lifted up her left foot and picked the hanging skin off with her front teeth, feeling the rip and burn, spitting the piece of skin on the carpet, seeing the droplet of blood. What she wouldn't give for a cupcake. Or a Hostess cherry pie. "You're the one who encouraged me to write."

"Revenge is not the message of sobriety."

Dani hung up. Karyn rang right back. Dani didn't answer. Karyn sent a text.

KARYN: You need to get to a meeting and keep working program.
DANI: You come over here and deal with this crazy bullshit.

That's when she noticed she had a voicemail. From Red? Oh, God. It was three minutes long? Oh, God. Delete or play?

"Dani, hey," Red's voice sounded different. Relaxed, warm, and slurred. "I took your advice. Guess what? I'm in! Sasha hired me as her personal assistant. Can you believe it? I start Monday. My name is Lynn. It was much easier than I thought . . . ."

Dani felt like she might be sick. Her arms shivered in goose bumps as she quickly hit delete. Oh my God. Had Red thought she meant it? They were playing around, having fun. What sort of person pretended to be a personal assistant to get back at an ex? A crazy person. A stalker.

Had Dani set the wheels in motion for something that would spin out of control? What if she got caught? Would Red say that it had been Dani's idea?

As if Dani didn't have enough on her fucking plate.

She texted Red's number:

DANI: Got your voicemail. We were joking around. I didn't mean do it for real.

She watched the text box quickly appear below as if Red had been waiting, phone in hand, for Dani's response.

> RED: It's going to be great!
> DANI: What if you get caught?
> RED: Why are you freaking out?

Dani stared at the texts.

> RED: I'm not going to murder him. (smile emoji)

Fuck, Dani thought, shit, shit, shit. What have I done?

> RED: Hey? It's funny. I thought you'd get a kick out of it.
> DANI: I didn't. What about your job?

So lame. She quickly typed.

> DANI: He's not worth getting into trouble.
> RED: Good night, Dani. (kiss emoji). Talk soon.

Jesus, why did Dani bother with people at all?

She climbed off of the bed and grabbed her laptop from the dresser, before this anxiety turned into a fucking trip to 7-Eleven and several packets of Hostess Cupcakes, or whatever version they sold there.

Damn, cupcakes. She licked her lips, opened a browser window, and started typing.

JUST-DESERTS.COM

A heat wave was suffocating the San Fernando Valley. The window A/C unit rattled, spewing out only a weak stream of cool air. It was so hot and still that even the beige carpeting felt oppressive. We lay beside each other, drenched in sweat, naked on top of the sheets of his futon. Our hands rested on each other's damp thighs, too hot to get close again. Steve smelled sweet like sandalwood and rain forest shampoo. I loved him, of course I'd loved him from the first date, tall and muscular brown with long, wavy dark hair pulled back into a ponytail. The Webster's definition of the word, *man*. He was quiet, calm, reassuring. Back then, I thought that quiet meant deep, interesting, a vast well of soul to share a little at a time. Later, I would realize that quiet meant secrets and lies. Quiet meant that Steve was thinking of someone else.

But in the beginning, it was love brought on by chemistry, endorphins, early-stage addiction, and my need to be loved, his need to be free, pushing and pulling, the drama of conflict.

"What's your secret dream?" I stared up at the wobbly ceiling fan as it squeaked from a loose bolt.

"To have a famous band," Steve confessed. "I know, it's embarrassing."

"Really?" I was surprised he'd never mentioned music to me. "You play music?"

"Yeah, I used to noodle around on the guitar." He pointed to the reddish-brown guitar waiting on a stand in the bedroom corner. "That's Woody."

"I used to write poetry in high school. I don't know why I quit. Why did you?" I softly caressed his muscled arm.

He shrugged, pulling away from my touch. "I had a bad experience onstage."

I crawled over his naked torso, retrieving Woody from the stand in the corner. I strummed the three chords that I knew: A minor, D, and C. It was in tune. "Play for me?"

Steve took the guitar. "You're pretty cool, babe."

An ambulance siren screamed past, lights flashing against the side of the building, reflecting off the bedroom window. Then it disappeared, receding into the night while Steve strummed a little Joni Mitchell, Chelsea Morning, and "I could drink a case of you." His playing was all right, but his voice caught me off guard. The deep resonance, slight rasp at the end of the phrase, interesting and unique, raw and real.

"You have to do it!" In my desire to repair broken things, I asked, "Isn't it just like falling off a bike?"

"My mom used to say the same thing." And then Steve told me the tragic story of his life.

"My mother, Valeria, brought us here from Guatemala after my father died. She cleaned houses, working like a dog, for rich people who treated her like shit." Steve wiped tears from his eyes. "It was just the two of us. We always had the radio on in our apartment. Music made my mother happy. Old-time country was her favorite. Boy, could she sing and dance." He sniffled and smiled. "One of her clients had a baby grand piano, and when they were out, she'd sneak me into their house, and I'd noodle around on the keys, and we'd sing. *Here you come again, just when I'm about to make it work without you.*"

"I wish I'd met your mom."

"She would have loved you even though you were a white girl."

I smoothed his worried brow, imagining him as a young anxious boy.

"She'd say, 'You have real charisma. One day, you'll be famous. And I'll be so proud! Look at my son, the famous rich musician!' And I promised her that I would make her proud. But she smoked too much, and the stress killed her. I went into the foster system at fourteen."

It was a horrible story, and it bound me closer to him. "I will support your dream however I can," I promised. "Maybe we could write a song together?"

Steve smiled. "That's an idea." He laid the guitar on the floor.

I snuggled up into his side, smelling the musk of him. "I have a secret dream—" I started.

"I think I know what it might be." He slid a sexy hand between my legs.

"No. Seriously."

"Okay, babe. What is it? What's the dream?"

"To be happy."

"You're not happy?"

"No, no, no, I'm very happy right now, with you," I said, grabbing his hand in mine. "I mean, you know, the kind of happy that just is. To feel happy."

"Like abiding," he replied.

"Exactly. Abiding happiness."

That was the impossible dream: to just be happy. With the moment, with life the way it was, with myself, my thoughts, my body, my job, whatever. Another fire engine blared past, almost midnight. What kind of tragedy? A dog barked, dishes clanged in a sink, a TV murmured, the air conditioner was too old and tired to filter anything out, even hot air.

"Babe. Nobody feels happy all of the time. It's really unrealistic."

"And being famous is realistic?" I climbed out of bed feeling the sting of rejection. "It's hot. I have to go to the bathroom."

He didn't stop me. Why not? Or why hadn't I walked out? Why had I supported him to pick up Woody again, when he hadn't encouraged one moment of abiding happiness? Why did I start writing songs with him when he'd discounted my dream?

That night, and several nights after, there were many lies, discoveries, and tears and screaming, fights, and apologies. For what? That toxic dance, that unreal love, the things that people did to each other in the name of broken, in the name of horrible childhoods and alcohol and drugs, and an inability to believe in the best things, in happiness without conditions.

For years after, every time we'd argue, Steve pulled out my secret, my "impossible" dream, like a small, sharp dagger. It was an accusation and a shame. "Are you *happy* now?" During the divorce, he'd used it as a character assassination. "So, you're still not *happy*, huh?" Or a surgeon's scalpel. "I thought you didn't care about my money. I thought you only cared about being *happy*." He was always sarcastic, leaning in on the word, stabbing, mean. So, *not* happy. He'd gotten everything. There was no way to prove that I'd written, mostly, the hit, "Crazy Girl, Crazy Boy, Love," one night after a bottle of wine in the candlelight of his shithole apartment.

Crazy girl, to love a crazy boy like me. Crazy boy, to love a crazy girl like you. This love, what is abiding. Abiding. Crazy girl, I will never break. You will never break me. We will live forever together. Love is not crazy, not crazy. Her, her, her, her, me me me, happily. See, see, here, here, here happily. It's wonderful. Good luck, crazy girl. Crazy boy dreams come true.

"Are you *happy* now?" What was wrong with wanting to feel loved, to be loved, to have a sense of real security? To belong, to be tethered on the earth. We tether each other to keep from spinning out of orbit.

Seated on the toilet in Steve's shithole apartment that night, many years ago, I should have stood up and walked back into his room. I should have watched his peaceful face slumbering deeply in the way that only the wicked could and then gently picked up my pillow and smothered him dead.

That might have made me *happy*.

DANI

She was finally drifting off to sleep when the scratching sound started. She bolted up, her heart pounding. Were there rats in the ceiling? No, the noise was below in the yard. Was a raccoon in the trash? She climbed out of bed and went to the window, looking out into the pitch dark of the backyard. There it was again. Was someone breaking in?

As Jack's neighborhood had slipped into dead lawns, peeling house paint, and broken-down cars, the way neighborhoods sometimes went, the crime had increased. Dani had suggested that Jack vamp up his security since he hadn't wanted to downsize into a townhouse or condo; he thought Diane might come back. One old man in a two-story house with a Buick out front was an easy target. "At least get some motion sensor lights, or a security system," Dani had said.

"Smith & Wesson are all the protection I need." He'd grinned. "Second Amendment until I die."

In order for Jack's safety plan to work, he would first need to remember where he'd put the gun and find the bullets, then load it, aim, and shoot straight. She should have made Barney come stay with them. He hadn't texted his usual good night.

Cell in hand, Dani tiptoed in the dark down the creaky stairs, listening through the sound of the blood beating a rhythm in her eardrums. The scratching was at the kitchen door. Then, a howl. Jesus. It was Dick, the prodigal cat.

"So, you're not dead?" she asked the hard-bodied, old black cat with the missing tail and left eye. He meowed, more demand than hello. He brushed against her leg, sauntering into the kitchen, and stopped in the middle of the room to lick his balls. He had the biggest balls she'd ever seen on a cat. The oozing red scab above his good eye proved he'd recently succeeded in a battle to breed another generation of feral kittens that would get shot or hit by a car. Jack didn't believe in neutering animals. "It's inhuman is what it is," he'd repeat. A man who didn't believe in "mixed" marriages, gay rights, or even equal pay for women, took a humanistic stand when it came to tomcats. Everybody could access some of their humanity. Dani found the Meow Mix in the pantry and grabbed a bowl from the dish rack.

The cat dove in.

"You're welcome." She bent down to scratch him. He acquiesced, raising his butt, and kept eating.

Love is food; food is love, Dani agreed. Maybe she would make chocolate pancakes for Violet for breakfast. Did she even like chocolate? Probably not. No sweets, no greens. A cheese frittata with green onions, no greens, maybe tomatoes? Her stomach rumbled. The blueberry coffeecake with its cinnamon crumble beckoned from the counter, like an open bar for an alcoholic at a wedding. Late night snacks were her slippery slope. Tomorrow night, she would make Violet that promised steak dinner.

"Hurry up." She nudged Dick with a toe. He offered a low growl and kept shoveling it in. What would food entitlement feel like? To eat and eat without self-shaming? Dani missed the brownie days. Devouring a whole pan. She grabbed her belly fat in both hands and squeezed to remind herself how far she still had to go to not be disgusted. Honestly, children were starving around the world.

She was going to have to sell Jack's house. They needed the money for assisted living and Violet's care. Temp work barely paid for groceries and gas. Now she wasn't even temping. Barney covered most of their bills. What little money Peter had been forced to begrudgingly give her in the divorce was gone. He lived in a mansion above the Sunset Strip. Wouldn't he discover Red working there when he came back from tour? She'd just rid her mind of today's encounter. Get the image of Peter touching Red's nipples out of her mind.

What if she fostered Violet until Monica returned? Fostering paid a stipend, plus Violet's medical and therapy, which she probably needed more now than ever. The last time Violet had needed her, Dani had been too preoccupied suing Peter. Maybe fostering now would make up for the past. Would Violet even want Dani to be her foster parent? What if Dani were horrible at it? What a mess.

The cat went to the backdoor and mewled. "Wham bam thank you, ma'am." She opened the door, watching his scraggly butt disappear into the dark adventures of the beyond. Freedom. There wouldn't be much freedom taking care of Violet full-time. Freedom? People associated free-spiritedness with getting in a car and driving the 10 freeway across the Mojave at a hundred miles an hour, hair flying in the wind, dancing and singing under the stars—a picture of freedom but not its reality. Freedom meant too much time on her hands to think.

If she *had* been born a free-spirit, Dani'd never had the time to develop it. There weren't any summers as a kid laying in the grass, looking up at the clouds, and daydreaming. She had to get Jack sober and out the door for work, go to school, make dinner, and help Monica with homework. Hooky from class? She had to get straight As. Get drunk at a kegger? Sex behind the bleachers? How could she have skinny dipped or auditioned for a school play or even learned to horseback ride? There wasn't any time for college. Get Monica into a good state school. What a waste of student debt.

Well, if nature had wanted Dani to be the kind of person who took off on a whim, leapt and let the net find her, moved to another country, studied a new language, taken up skydiving or kayaked, it was too late to find out now. Her environment had shaped her steady, boring personality and poor life choices.

Try as she may, her thoughts kept returning to Red. *You write about killing him, but you don't really do anything.* Six months without sugar had seemed like a big accomplishment, until today.

Dani turned the bolt on the back door and listened for a moment. Far off in the distance, a dog barked, and another chimed in. She hoped Dick wasn't getting into a battle that he was too small to take on. What would happen to the cat? What if she fucked it up? It wasn't just her life anymore that she couldn't get together. Violet was a pain in the ass, but she deserved better. Was Dani the best that her niece could get? Monica hadn't turned out that great under her supervision. She knew what it was like to live without a mother, or mothering influence. Hopefully, her sister would return home and take Violet back.

Back upstairs, snuggling under the covers, Dani texted Barney. They'd barely spoken since Jack's hospital visit. Barney had yet to come to Mar Vista and hadn't even asked Dani out to dinner. He'd been busy with work, catching up on hours. Did she miss him? She felt relieved, knowing that he was still in her apartment. It was comforting to have a man in the house. Although he hadn't changed the washer in the kitchen sink, he was feeding the two feral cats. How would he feel about the new living arrangements? Did she even care?

The answer was obvious.

SASHA

Sasha walked into the kitchen and found Lynn standing at the far center island arranging colorful vegetables, cut julienne style, in a bowl with homemade vegan pesto dressing. Her thick red hair, tucked behind her ears, cascaded straight down her long, thin back. Sasha hadn't noticed her height during the mostly seated interview. A moment of serenity, almost comfort, entered her heart at the sight of such an efficient older woman in her home. "Thank you," Sasha acknowledged. How old was Lynn? Late-thirties? Of course, she wouldn't ask, but redheads always looked older. Maybe forty?

Lynn looked up, the blue of her eyes intense. "I hate to see fresh food go to waste," she replied. She smiled, a tight smile from thin lips and then indicated a single table setting at the end of the other island: a fine china plate, a linen napkin, and a glass of water with a slice of lemon. Was Sasha paying her enough?

Sasha pulled out a stool and sat. "It's beautiful."

Lynn tossed the salad and then poured some into a smaller bowl, sprinkling pine nuts over the top, and setting it in front of Sasha. Should she ask Lynn to eat with her? What was the protocol for personal assistants? "Are you going to join me?"

A startled look crossed Lynn's face. "Sure, okay," she replied, as she opened a drawer and pulled out a fork, diving right into the big bowl of salad. Was that a little too comfortable already? "I haven't eaten vegan in years." Lynn offered an awkward laugh. "But I love raw vegetables." Lynn was stiff, attractive but a little off, eager to please, with a crooked slope to her mouth.

Was there anything worse for a woman than being almost pretty? Ugly wasn't the worst. Ugly got to take math and science, excel in corporations, conduct symphonies or open-heart surgeries. But almost pretty? Boys walked across bars for girls like that only to get closer and swerve. "Pretty from a distance," her mother called those girls. Girls who hovered between not ugly but not quite good-looking enough suffered the most. If anyone knew the harm of the beauty ideal, it was Sasha. She'd been competing in pageants since the age of four. The truth she'd discovered was that the world hated pretty women, which is why she worked hard to be a kind and good person to balance out the equation.

Sasha speared a chilled stem of bright asparagus. "God!ess be great; these vegetables are gorgeous. Farmer's Market?"

"They're from my garden."

"You have a garden? That is so cool. I always wanted to be a person who had a garden. It must feel wonderful to be so close to the Mother. Peter says it's hilarious that I didn't know beets grew in the ground until I became vegan. I grew up in Brooklyn."

"I thought you grew up on Long Island." Her assistant quickly covered her mouth with a freckled hand, continuing to chew as she added, "I must have read that somewhere."

For a moment, Sasha had forgotten the fact that fame bred familiarity, made relationships uneven. "I was born on Long Island," Sasha continued. "This salad is delicious. How do you get the asparagus so crisp?" She held up a green stem and took a crunchy bite.

"Shock them."

"Oh, right." Sasha hated to admit that she didn't know her way around a kitchen except to microwave ramen or ask the chef to make Peter steak again. "What's that again?"

"Blanching. You toss the vegetables in boiling water to briefly cook, and then immediately immerse them in an ice bath. It halts the cooking process. That's how they stay crunchy, but also it really brings out the color."

"I love the bright orange of carrots." Sasha felt her spirits rise with the healthy conversation. "It's so cheerful."

"Vegetables are beautiful, aren't they? I have to get my hands in the soil every day," Lynn said and looked out the kitchen window at the sloping uphill of the backyard. "Feeds the soul. You could container garden up on that deck at the top of the hill. Tomatoes, zucchini, squash, even strawberries. It's easy. I'd be happy to show you."

"Oh, thank you! I would love to feed the babies food from my own garden," Sasha replied, rubbing her protruding belly, grinning. "We're having twins! Twins. By the blessings of the God!ess! I can't even believe it. I'm eating for three!"

Her assistant quickly turned away, carrying the salad bowl to the sink. Were Lynn's shoulders shaking? Had Sasha somehow hurt her feelings? It was too soon for that. She crawled off the barstool, knowing a boundary had been crossed and needed to be reset.

"Congratulations." Lynn turned on the garbage disposal.

Since high school, girls like Lynn, those almost pretty girls, tried but found it impossible to be Sasha's friend. The proximity to her beauty had always turned them mean and vicious with jealousy. The last thing that Sasha needed was another difficult female relationship. She had to stop being such a people pleaser. She was pregnant now, with twins! And married, a grown woman with a house.

"I'll clean up here and then maybe you could show me your online bill pay?" Her assistant's voice sounded far away, almost angry.

Sasha leaned back in her chair, taken aback by Lynn's sudden change in behavior. What had she triggered? Something about children? Poor woman. Maybe she couldn't have any, wasn't blessed. Stop using that word, Sasha, she thought. It sounds like you think you're better than her. "Perfect. Feel free to grab a beverage from the refrigerator under the bar. I think there's a few Le Croix left. Or would you rather I buy flat water?" Sasha asked. She wanted Lynn to stay. Needed her to stay. "Maybe we could plant strawberries next week?"

RED

R ed's old Corolla barely made it up the steep concrete, palm tree-lined drive to the house. My God, it wasn't a house. It was a mansion, a small hotel, opulent white with contemporary angles. It had windows that reflected the morning sun, a lush green lawn, flowering bushes, and fruit trees. God, this is what the word fecund looks like, Red thought with a rush of jealousy.

"Lynn," Sasha greeted her, opening the wide, beveled glass front door. Light spilled across the contoured angles of Sasha's face, a little swollen from pregnancy, but wrinkle-free, smooth and beautiful in the prime of her life. Her new boss was dressed in all white again, tight white leggings and a billowy sheer blouse over a white crop top.

"You're right on time," Sasha said. Her smile revealed those perfect white teeth. She turned, waddling slightly, and Red followed her into the house, checking out her shapely frame, as they crossed the light hardwood floor of the giant foyer, taking several steps up into an all-white living room: sofas, rugs, and art.

"It's breathtaking," Red observed. It made her feel smaller than six feet.

"I didn't know that I was good at interior design until Peter's album went platinum and we could afford more than a futon." She giggled and turned down a wide hallway. "You should have seen his studio apartment in the Valley."

An image of Peter's dingy hellhole from their college days flashed through Red's mind: a black futon, that stained gray carpet, the broken plastic blind, sash half down, stopped by an air conditioning unit that spewed dirty warm air. Woody, the acoustic guitar, on a stand in the corner. A small desk with an old PC and folding chair. The kitchenette with gold appliances against the opposite wall. Posters of rock bands and Uma Thurman in *Kill Bill*.

They wandered down a long hallway between framed photographs of Sasha and Peter laughing, kissing, and smiling, artfully hung between windows revealing an outside of ivy and jasmine. They passed an arched entrance to the giant kitchen. Red peeked inside; it was all white again. There were two center islands, one with a sink and stainless-steel appliances, an eight-burner Viking stove, and a three-door refrigerator, with a pretty breakfast alcove almost the size of her messy bedroom in Echo Park.

Red felt rumpled inside Lynn's sexless apparel, following Sasha's perfectly heart-shaped ass. Of course, Peter had married her. Sasha was exquisite, a delight to watch entering and leaving a room. Sex on a stick. And that friendly, bright smile, teeth probably purchased at the highest price. Big, warm, liquid, trusting eyes. Today, she seemed genuinely happy, enthusiastically holding up a small Venetian bust from their Italian honeymoon, sharing a photo of Peter swimming with a sea turtle from a last-minute adventure to Galapagos, and even her first nude pregnancy photo shoot for the cover of a pregnancy magazine.

At the end of the last hallway, Sasha stopped in front of a closed door. "Peter doesn't like to call it an office," she explained. She turned the knob. "He calls it a testament to single-minded determination." She opened the door to reveal a white room with all black furniture, his Grammy on a bookshelf, two framed LP covers on the wall, as well as artistic, black-and-white backstage pictures taken with various other famous people.

The house was easy to move through, with its graceful arches and wide steps. "Architectural unflawed beauty," proclaimed the framed cover of *Architectural Digest*, with the photo of Sasha seated on a white couch, unflawed beauty revealed in white, beautiful red lips and voluminous, shiny hair. "That shoot. It was like a dream." Her voice was filled with genuine humility. "You should see the walk-up I grew up in!"

From all appearances, they seemed genuinely happily married. The idea horrified Red. It had to be a delusion; Peter was good at smoke and mirrors in a love relationship.

The home tour took forty minutes, the lap pool with waterfall and cabana included, but did not include the master bedroom suite, for which Red was grateful. During the tour, her thoughts had often turned to Peter's ex. What would Dani think about the mansion her lyrics had helped build? Would it make her angry enough to finally take real action?

Later, over lunch in the bright, beautiful kitchen, Sasha had gushed over Lynn's simple salad, even asking Lynn to join her. There had been a few polite questions about Lynn's past, but no real interest, just good manners. It was a positive sign that Sasha didn't have her guard up. Why would she? She was prettier, younger, richer and married to the man.

It had all been going well, until Sasha revealed she was carrying twins.

Sasha had rubbed her growing belly, grinning, and declared more good fortune, "We're having twins by the blessings of the God!ess! Twins. I can't even believe it. I'm eating for three!"

Red felt like someone had punched her in the stomach. She'd quickly grabbed the almost empty salad bowl and turned away, carrying it to the sink. Her heart was on the floor, but she'd managed not to cry, squeaking out a forced, "Congratulations" and then turned on the garbage disposal so that she didn't have to hear another word about how wonderful Sasha's life was with Peter.

She needed to get right to his money and get the fuck out. "I'll clean up here, and then maybe you could show me your online bill pay?" She'd felt uncomfortable with Sasha's concerned eyes boring holes in her back.

After only three hours of employment, Sasha had granted Lynn full access to her God!ess bank account, and their joint home checking account. It was a good start. Email address, user names, and passcodes. But not Peter's Morgan Stanley account, which Sasha said held their steady six million. It was in his name alone.

"Everything, stocks and house, are in Peter's trust. Should something happen to him, I'll be taken care of." Was she naïve or an idiot? Was Sasha's name even on the deed of the house? Probably not.

If Sasha had bothered to check one, just one, of Lynn Pickerton's job or personal references on her resume, the girl would have hit a dead end. Maybe that's the way it was with beauty contestants and swimsuit models turned wannabe singer or actresses; they grew up with people telling them what to do. How did the girl run a business? A successful business, according to *Self* magazine. When Lynn had asked who ran the day-to-day business of God!ess, Sasha waved a hand as if it were nothing. "Oh, I do. I loved math in high school. It's fun," Sasha had said.

Peter and Sasha's joint checking account had twenty-five thousand dollars in "spare change." Twenty-five thousand, six hundred thirty-five dollars and seventy-two cents to be exact. Over half of Red's yearly salary.

"We call it spare change." Sasha had laughed, blushing. "I mean, really, we don't need anything. It's to buy things that well, you know, are too expensive like Lululemon pants and hiring a private chef, I don't know. There are nights when you just feel like ordering a masseuse, or you want to fly to Mexico for the weekend. Or San Francisco. I just love San Francisco! It's pretty. I'm so blessed," Sasha had continued, placing her hands on her belly. Again. "*We* are."

Blessed. God, Red hated that word. She wanted to slap people who used it. Isn't that nice, to feel favored? Red wanted to ask her.

Sasha had prattled on to Lynn, her fifteen-dollar an hour part-time personal assistant, as if they were friends, equals, as if everyone had that kind of "spare change" lying around. Red had to bite her tongue. Truth was, Red hadn't worked full-time since the abortion. The shelter and clinic work with abuse survivors had become too personal and painful. She'd felt impotent, unable, and that wasn't good for anyone. Her meager earnings from Sasha plus savings would keep her in wine and cat food for two months. Destroying the man who'd broken her heart hopefully would pay off in the end.

The first thing was to start taking small bites from the personal checking account. Siphon off donations from the accounts to which Red had access, to see how long, how much she could get away with. Women's shelters and charities. After that, she could start siphoning small amounts into the Banxico account that Carlos had helped her create in Oaxaca, Mexico where his parents still lived.

But she needed to get into Peter's Morgan Stanley account with the big bucks; she wanted to drain his fortune, ruin his property, invest poorly, make certain it couldn't come back. Somewhere in Peter's office, he'd written down a password that opened the door to his financial ruin.

The trick, she thought, might start with forging a letter from Sasha to the stock broker saying that Peter granted her full access. Could it be done in an email? Perhaps there was a way to plant a seed of doubt in Sasha's mind about the vulnerability of a wife blocked out of her husband's wealth. Tomorrow, she would find articles to print and plant around the house, maybe even tell a tale of an imaginary friend whose husband recently left her for another woman, sending their money overseas where the poor wife had no access.

That evening, back home in Echo Park, exhausted but amped, Red put the key in the front door lock and turned the knob, opening the small blue door of her little mortgaged-up-the-ass house. Inside, it looked dusty and dark. There was the shabby, red antique sofa picked up for fifty bucks at a yard sale, the bamboo chair with the bright orange throw, the nickel-plated coffee table, gifted from a moving neighbor, the travel photography books from Vietnam and Croatia, two places she'd always wanted to visit, the single, half-full wine glass, and above all was her prized, Moroccan purple gold-fringed rug, which probably cost a quarter of the one in God!ess's office. Her indoor plants in various stages of rebirth hung in macramé, the succulents gleamed in ceramic stands, boho chic with her favorite shades of living green.

She loved her small home. But now, it felt claustrophobic, cramped, a college student's apartment decorated with yard sale furniture.

She kicked off the ugly loafers, unzipped, and stepped out of the khakis, pushing the front door closed with her toe. Calling out, "Cat?" she carried the empty wine glass into the kitchen, retrieved a new one from the dish drainer, emptied last night's bottle of Chianti, and grabbed the last wedge of cheese without mold from the refrigerator and sat on the back stoop.

Since Sasha was pregnant with twins, she ate far too little, in Red's estimation. Sasha had nibbled at an asparagus, carefully dipping a piece of cauliflower in the pesto dressing. Tiny bites, chewing for a long time, too much water. Did she have body dysmorphic disorder? Was Sasha nervous to be liked by her new assistant? She was a people pleaser with body issues. Did she experience sexual abuse as a child, or was she just a product of all the years of scrutiny under the parent's gaze? Being beautiful wasn't all it was cracked up to be. Red wasn't there to diagnose or treat the young woman but knowing the cracks in Sasha's foundation would definitely help her plan.

Why had the discovery of twins upset her? What was the difference between one or two babies?

Fecund. That word kept repeating in Red's head. It seemed that everything Sasha touched, by hand or mouth, or vagina, bloomed into a giant, beautiful fucking flower, like the God!ess actually had blessed her.

Later, slightly tipsy, feeling less of a shadow and more like herself, Red sang out with Lou Reed: *Just a perfect day. You made me forget myself. I thought I was someone else, someone good*, as she fingered herself, imagining Sasha's breasts full and round in Peter's mouth until the sweet release, and she would sleep.

DANI

Exhausted and on edge, Dani drove north through the smoky haze in bumper-to-bumper traffic up Sepulveda, Jack and Violet quarreling, while orange flames shot up, licking the darkening sky on the other side of the 405-freeway, closed due to another seasonal fire. Dick yowled inside his carrier. She turned up the air conditioner and swallowed a scream. What a life. They were making a wide detour first to Panorama City to pick up the rest of Violet's clothes, toothbrush, and personal things from Monica's before moving on to Dani's place in Pasadena. Jack's suitcase and twelve-pack, plus Dick's cat food and litter box bumped in the trunk. Violet would have to transfer mid-semester, because her mother was still MIA, and Jack's house had termites, rats in the attic, and black mold. The house would need to be tented for a week; the mold cut out. Jack had agreed to pay for repairs from his meager savings, but he would not agree to sell the house. A realtor had told Dani that houses in the neighborhood were going for over a million.

A million dollars, she'd told Jack. Imagine. His response? "You can get your hands on the cash when my dead body is cold in the hard ground."

Dani didn't even have enough money for them to stay in a motel in Mar Vista through Christmas break. Jack would sleep on the sofa bed. Violet had the guest room, which meant Barney had to move his clothes into Dani's closet. He wasn't thrilled via text.

BARNEY: You know how I feel about your dad.
DANI: I know. Sorry. Family. (heart emoji, crazy emoji, smile emoji)

She hadn't yet told him about the cat because he was allergic. Four people and one cat in a two-bedroom, one bath apartment was far from ideal, but it was the only solution for right now.

As they crested Mulholland, the heavy smoke dissipated into mist, and the Valley spread out below, the most beautiful stretch of the longest street in Los Angeles. Sepulveda. What was the song? And then she remembered; it was "Pico and Sepulveda!"

Rolling down the window, Dani turned off the air and felt the warmth on her cheek, a pleasant high-seventies. *"Pico and Sepulveda, Pico and Sepulveda,"* she hummed, that cheerful 40's tune with the Latin beat that Diane sung washing dishes.

"Pico and Sepulveda," Jack piped in singing off-key, horribly off-key, then growing silent again.

A collective memory. There wasn't a reason to be this angry. She was excited to sleep in her own bed. *"Pico And Sepulveda, Doheny . . . Cahuenga . . . La Brea . . . Tar Pits! La Jolla . . . Sequoia . . . La Brea . . . Tar Pits!"*

At the red light at Ventura, Jack turned around to Violet. "Listen, girl, beer is good for your health. Ask that TV doctor. What's his name?"

"One beer, maybe two," Violet responded, as if they were in the middle of an ongoing conversation. "Not a case a day."

"Ha!" he snorted, turning back to face the front. "Think you're so smart. Wine comes in cases. Beer in packs."

"The red veins all over your nose are from too much alcohol."

"I'm fucking old, girl." Jack laughed. "One day, you'll get uglier than you are now."

"Guys!" Dani interjected, white-knuckling the wheel. "Enough. All right?"

"You're ugly inside!" Violet yelled.

Dani looked into the rearview mirror. Her niece was on the verge of tears. "Jack," she slowly drew out his name for emphasis. "Apologize."

"Jack, apologize," he mimicked.

"Right now, or so help me God," Dani lowered her voice, making it hard, like steel, like anger, like a fist, "I will pull this fucking car over and put you out in front of that shitty motel." She put her blinker on and moved into the right lane, pointing to a dilapidated white stucco one-story with a flashing vacancy sign.

"Christ on a cracker, relax." Jack raised his hands in defeat. "You aren't ugly, Violet. Nobody in this family is. I'm not bullshitting. You're a good-looking kid, but you're a real pain in the ass."

"Takes one to know one," Dani muttered under her breath. Violet heard and snorted.

The temperature rose, and the air quality diminished as they passed car dealerships, strip clubs, apartment buildings, strip malls with liquor stores, homeless people lying on sidewalks or pushing grocery carts, and young girls with too much makeup and too little clothing acting bored, waiting for business on street corners and motel parking lots. *"Pico and Sepulveda, Pico and Sepulveda,"* she hummed again, trying to distract herself from what they might find in the apartment: Monica, high and alive? Or dead?

A Winchell's Donuts sign called out ahead. The sensation of small, hard chocolate sprinkles melting in her cheeks increased. Dani fought the urge. She cried out, singing, "Vine may be fine, but for mine I want to feel alive and settle down in my Pico and Sepulveda."

"Pico and Sepulveda . . ." Jack chimed in.

"Turn right," Violet interrupted.

Dani braked and made a sharp turn, jerking their bodies right back to reality. "Sorry, sorry," she said. Following Violet's terse instructions, she went left at that street, another left, then right, parking in front of a six-story chipped stucco apartment building with iron railings, a brown lawn, sandwiched between an auto parts store and a Lavanderia.

"Mom," Violet called out, in a singsong voice. "I'm home."

Jack laughed. "You're funny, kid."

Her voice was all bravado, but Dani knew her niece's stomach was churning. Oblivious, Jack was having difficulty unbuckling his seatbelt with his arm in a cast. "Goddamn piece of shit," he growled under his breath. "Fuckin' Jap car." Dani leaned over to help, but he swatted her hand away. "Get your hands off of me."

"Suit yourself. Come on, Violet," Dani replied. She climbed out of the car, turning back to Jack. "Lock the doors. Oh, and crack a window for the cat." She slammed the driver's door shut before he could speak again.

With the elevator broken and after four flights of concrete slatted stairs in deep-valley eighty-five-degree heat later, they reached Unit 419A. Violet pulled a set of keys from her backpack and unlocked the front door. She hesitated and then let go of the doorknob, turning to Dani, her bushy eyebrows knitted in worry.

"Why don't you wait out here?" Dani took a deep breath and stepped inside the apartment. It reeked of old cigarette smoke and beer. She felt along the wall for a light switch. Please don't be dead. Please don't be dead. "Monica?" Dani called out. The light revealed a small living room with a black vinyl couch that also served as an unmade bed, pillow and blanket, gold table lamp with a stained shade, a plywood coffee table covered in mostly empty beer bottles. A bong filled with dirty water. An over-flowing ashtray with cigarette butts. The place was the drugged look of doom and impermanence.

A queen-sized mattress with a cheap, blue comforter and a chipped blue dresser were crammed into the one small bedroom at the end of the hall. On the corner of the dresser was a framed picture of a smiling black couple, maybe in their mid-sixties, conservative and well-dressed. Violet's foster parents?

Three teen girl shirts and two pairs of pressed khaki pants hung in the small closet. Violet was neat and practical. Dani laid them on the bed. She opened a dresser drawer, where three pairs of balled socks, two training bras, and several white cotton underpants were neatly stacked. She placed them on the bed. The other drawers were packed with cheap, brightly colored lingerie, stained boxers, men's white V-neck t-shirts, and athletic socks. Dani shuddered.

The bathroom was relatively clean, except for a heap of dirty towels in the middle of the floor. Thank God Monica wasn't dead in the bathtub.

Outside, Violet leaned on the railing, staring down into the concrete courtyard with the small umbrella table, minus the umbrella, and scattered plastic chairs in various states of disrepair. Nearby, a neighbor's TV blared some daytime show, and Dani could hear distant laughter and applause. "She's not here," Violet stated matter-of-fact, turning and walking into the apartment. Dani followed.

While Violet stuffed her meager belongings into a green trash bag, Dani stepped out of the room and tried calling Monica's cell again. It went straight to voicemail. Dani would have to call children's services and destroy what little progress Monica had made toward keeping her daughter. She desperately needed to wash down a cherry pop-tart with a Coke slushie. Maybe she should try to make a night meeting?

"I'm ready." Violet dragged the trash bag behind her across the brown-stained carpet. In her hand, she held the framed photograph of the elderly couple from her dresser.

The sight was enough to break the coldest of hearts. "Hey, it's so hot. Let's get ice cream," Dani said.

Violet sighed, rolling her eyes. "I'm not seven, Aunt Danielle. I know she's using again."

Dani had a lot to learn about children and preteens, and she didn't know Violet. They were strangers. "I don't have kids." A lame excuse, yes. But it was better than what she really wanted to say which was, give me a fucking break. "I use food as a coping mechanism," Dani confessed. "I'm in OA."

"Okay," Violet replied, closing the plastic bag with a knot. "But I don't like ice cream."

"That's insane. You're a weirdo. You know that?"

"Yeah, sure. *I'm* the weirdo."

"Did you get everything?"

"Of course. It's not like I haven't done this before."

"I'm sorry, Violet." It wasn't enough of a consolation for a shitty childhood.

"I have to shit," Jack announced when they climbed back into the car. "And I want ice cream!"

"Then you can shit in Baskin-Robbins."

And there it was, her life.

"What'll it be?" the perky, fresh-faced girl in the pink-striped uniform behind the counter asked Jack.

"Two scoops of chocolate chip on a cone," Jack responded, as he smacked his hand down on the glass countertop. "Not a fancy bullshit cone. The regular kind."

"You hate chocolate chip." Dani turned back to the sincere teen. "He'll have a scoop of peppermint in a cup."

"Anything else?" the girl asked, opening the glass case and pulling a steel scoop out of the water bucket.

Dani's eyes scanned the colorful tubs of butter-brickle, strawberry cheesecake, cookies and crème, salted caramel, coffee chocolate bits, peppermint, vanilla with swirls of chocolate. "Just a lid and spoon," she replied.

When they climbed back into the car, Violet, wearing earbuds, was texting away on her cell. Could the girl actually have a friend? She was probably harassing a politician on social media or setting up a small country coup. Wasn't she too young to be on those sites? Who was monitoring Violet's online presence? She would be the perfect victim for some sex trafficker or pedophile, an unwanted child. She wasn't unwanted . . . she wasn't. Was it Monica?

"Who are you texting?" Dani asked.

Violet didn't look up.

Jack scooched down in the passenger seat and slowly spooned a bite of pink ice cream into his small, hard mouth, happily humming, *"Pico and Sepulveda."*

Dani repeated, "Violet, who are you texting?"

Her niece turned up the volume on her phone. Ah, male voices, a podcast? The banter was loud. Something about librarians, she hoped, PG-13, not anarchy.

"Turn that down." Dani raised her voice. "You're going to blow out your eardrums."

Jack sang, *"La Brea Tarpits?"* and slurped his ice cream, staring out the window without a care in the world. Did he remember where he was? Violet turned the volume up even higher and then went back to texting. What a brat.

Dani put the car in reverse and started backing out of the parking space when it occurred to her just how frustrated she felt, overwhelmed, under-appreciated. She wasn't a servant. Or their assistant. How rude and ungrateful—Violet and Jack. They weren't her responsibility. She wasn't Violet's mother, or father wherever he was and whomever he was, and Jack was an ass, and Monica was using again. And now, they were moving in with Barney, who had one foot out the door. She slammed on the brake.

Jack lurched forward, catching the dash with a casted arm. The ice cream cup fell to the floor. "My ice cream!"

"Damn it. Sorry, sorry."

Foamy, pink-white cream and bits of red candy spread between his feet on the dirty car floor. He leaned over and started scraping it up with the small plastic spoon. "Oh no, oh no, oh no," he said.

"No, Jack, don't eat that. I'll get you another one. Hang on." She turned around and stared at Violet. Violet looked back, widening her eyes, like a dare. Dani held her stare. "Are you texting your mom?"

Violet turned up the podcast volume. She waited for her niece's ears to bleed. Violet was just like her mother, impossible, defiant, unyielding. But Dani knew a thing or two about setting boundaries. She wasn't about to let some twelve-year-old girl—Thirteen?—end her sobriety. Violet had no idea what a bitch her aunt could be when she needed to feed. Dani revved the engine for effect, put the car in reverse, stretched an arm across Jack, and backed out of the space. Then she slammed on the brakes. Violet lurched, and her glasses slid down her nose. The cat carrier slid across the seat, causing Dick to yowl.

"Hey!" Jack cried.

Her niece pushed her glasses up, and with a stare of defiance, she braced both hands on the backseat. Dani revved the engine and waited, fuming, daring back. "Who are you texting? Answer me," she demanded.

Finally, Violet pulled out her earbuds. She turned her phone to face Dani. "I was texting my social worker. To save you the hassle."

Grabbing the pink plastic spoon from Jack's hand, Dani commanded, "Stop it!" She scooped the sweet crunchy bits off the floor and back into the paper cup. Then she climbed out of the car and threw the cup in a trash can. She was a real asshole. *"Pico and Sepulveda. Pico and Sepulveda. La Brea . . . Tar Pits . . . where nobody's dreams come true."*

RED

Sasha was snoring, out like a light, on the chaise in her office, snuggled, without a care in the world, safely cocooned inside an Egyptian cotton blanket with a thread count Red hadn't known existed. Red rarely fantasized about wealth, but if Sasha's riches could buy that kind of sleep, that kind of deep slumber, riding on the waves of a lullaby, the kissed sleep of well-loved, well-fed children, then maybe she was ready to inherit her parents' money. Had she ever slept like that? Not without the help of at least two glasses of wine.

She spent the morning sitting at Sasha's desk working on the iPad while the computer was being repaired, and her boss slept. She tallied and entered receipts into Sasha's checking account ledger from her expenses for the last two weeks. Over one hundred dollars in cashew smoothies? A camisole for five hundred dollars? Laser facial treatment for five thousand? Ten thousand dollars spent on personal care, clothing, massages, facials, superfoods, and her shiny hair. Almost a third of Red's yearly salary at the clinic.

She stared at the sleeping beauty, feeling older and unkempt, awkward, and ashamed. Her gaze lingered on Sasha's exposed, silky-smooth thigh, and just like that, Red clicked a key, sending a two-hundred dollar donation to a women's shelter in Riverside; five-hundred to a rape crisis hotline in Redlands; one-thousand to Planned Parenthood.

It felt amazing.

Red wanted to meet Dani for a glass of wine and share, laughing and shaking their heads at her escapade. Think of how much money they could get away with before Peter was even home for his birthday.

Maybe that's why Peter lied and cheated on women. It was fun to get away with it.

A text from TrueLoveP flashed across the iPad screen.

TRUELOVEP: Hey, Baby?

Red's breath caught. She slammed the iPad shut. Fuck.

Sasha moaned and stretched her toned arms over her head. "How long did I sleep?" She offered Red a sweet smile. Red never woke up pretty and fresh-faced. These days, it was puffy eyes, red-faced, hungover.

"About an hour," Red answered, making her voice light. "How are you feeling?"

"The usual. Nauseated and starving." Sasha sighed.

"I brought kale from my garden. I could make a smoothie."

Sasha rubbed her eyes and yawned. "No. The babies hate kale."

"What about a strawberry cashew smoothie?" Red nervously picked at a cuticle on her thumb.

Sasha gave a half-hearted hum and sat up. "I think I might run out and grab something. I need to swing by the studio anyway."

"I could do that," Red offered. "Tell me what you want." She was dying to escape the rarified air, get out, drive down the hill, see real people living in the real world.

"No, it's okay. Just finish here." Sasha picked up her phone from the table with a "thanks" and grinned when she saw Peter's text. Red felt queasy as Sasha walked out the door and down the hallway, texting.

Red re-opened the iPad and read the conversation between TrueLoveP and God!essS:

TRUELOVEP: Hey, honey! How's my baby? (heart emoji)

GOD!ESSS: Your babies. (three baby emojis)

TRUELOVEP: Three, yes! Love you.

GOD!ESSS: We're good. We miss you. (heart emoji, heart emoji)

TRUELOVEP: (heart emoji, heart emoji) Video? (eggplant emoji, taco emoji)

GOD!ESSS: Ugh, no. Too fat. (sad face emoji)

TRUELOVEP: (Picture of Peter's half-hard cock.) Come on, baby. I need it.

Red barely made it into the office bathroom before throwing up last night's wine and cheese and this morning's coffee in the porcelain sink.

SASHA

She started making up reasons to leave the house—a lunch, a hair appointment, drop by the studio—any excuse to get out and secretly eat barbacoa tacos from a truck near a construction site. The babies were raving mad for dead flesh. Like Mia Farrow's character, innocent and unsuspecting, in the movie, *Rosemary's Baby,* Sasha couldn't stop dreaming about it.

Each morning, when the sun warmed her face, she promised herself, "Today, I will stop this behavior. I won't feel angry, ugly, or edgy. I will not partake in animal torture for food. I will go to the studio, teach prenatal class, say hello to the girls, get a fresh juice and not stop on the way home for steak or burgers. I can up my protein intake in shakes. If I ask Lynn along, I won't be able to make any detours." But after her Yerba Matte, she was out the door calling to Lynn that she would be late; she said she needed a pedicure after teaching, but this was only an excuse to drive to another new meat market in another part of town wearing her disguise.

It was getting hard to think up new excuses. Lies, Sasha, she reminded herself. Stop it; stop the lying it can't be good for the babies.

Sasha dreamt again about Rosemary and that demon baby, even though she'd never been able to make it through the whole movie. Mia Farrow's emaciated boy body with a swollen belly, gaunt cheekbones, those beautiful contours, the horror, the screams, the drinking blood from a glass—yes, cow's blood—meat sizzling on a skillet, sort of alive. Were *her* babies possessed? Her hormones were all over the place, making her feel crazy. But she wasn't horny. Had craving meat replaced her sex drive?

She had faked sex on FaceTime with Peter because if she'd said no, he'd go out and find a groupie, Sasha knew.

"I'm grabbing your big juicy tits!" he'd said, ejaculating on the dark hairy stripe of his muscled belly. It disgusted her to watch the way he behaved in front of the babies. It made her feel sick.

But Sasha had played her part, pretending to climax. "Oh, Peter, oh, Peter!" she moaned.

God!ess, Sasha loved Peter. That wasn't a question. Would her desire return? Once, her yearning hadn't known any limits. She'd fantasized about touching his skin, tracing her fingers along his taut arms, the sinewy muscles, his round buttocks. She'd daydreamed about fucking him while driving to gigs, after gigs him fucking her, imagined while teaching yoga class, even during lectures to women's groups preaching the God!ess. Her mind had wandered to her desire. Sasha hadn't cared that he was married, and when she made her move, neither had he. Peter believed in openness, the fluidity of sexual preferences, that fantasies were meant to be lived.

In the beginning, Sasha had also pretended Peter's sex life was natural for her. Free love. Open love. But sharing Peter sexually had required shutting down the most natural parts of herself. Watching his eyes fill with desire over a naked beautiful woman or a pretty girl they would bring home had initially turned her on, but later there would be a moment, during the act, when Sasha caught herself, hovering above outside of her body, lying alone and untouched on the other side of the bed. Peter's mouth, hands, his gorgeous cock inside a groaning stranger. Sasha would feel the familiar sensation of becoming invisible, numbing, curling into the pain in the way she'd felt winning second place, always second. Not good enough, never good enough, a kind of panic as if being turned into mist over the sea, above a rough current, unable to grasp the sandy shore. Measuring herself against another woman in bed, comparing another woman's smooth or muscled legs to her own curvy thighs, smaller, perkier breasts in his hands compared to her heavy full ones, pink nipples against brown, white teeth, whiter than hers, a fuller mouth, a longer torso, tall or short, shorter or longer hair, a different skin tone. Was she as good in bed? Peter made all the women speak to him like prostitutes or porn stars. Peter's moans were different with them. Panic forced Sasha back into the action, mimicking sexual moves of a stranger to get his attention. Sliding deeper into the hazy sex dream, losing boundaries until the morning's hangover, shame and bright light spread across their naked bodies. She rose to make them coffee. The sheets had to be washed. They didn't speak of such things during the day.

Sasha had told herself that it wasn't cheating if she was included. But they were married now, about to become parents, and their life had been blessed by the God!ess with so much good fortune. They'd agreed to continue therapy, after the tour, to marriage counseling. Peter loved her enough to quit the women. This was his promise during their wedding vows.

Danielle had lost him because she was bad in bed, insecure and neurotic, unadventurous. Peter's exact words. His fantasies weren't the secrets that lovers whispered behind closed doors. He liked acting them out. Sasha participated, not as willing as she'd appeared, but engaged in the action. Sasha loved being the object of his and his friends' desires. When they were married, she thought it would end. Was it foolish?

What if their out-of-control sex life had given birth to the babies' cravings, turning them into rabid beasts? "A mother rises like the great earth," she'd read once in a Buddhist text. One is the mother of ten thousand. The God!ess had blessed her. Blessed be the God!ess!

A woman with babies, a mother is a world, a safe place of love, kindness and dignity and abundance. And there was nothing left in her for the sad exploits of a beauty contestant runner-up, always fighting for first place performing debased sex acts.

"What will we do after the babies are born?" Sasha had asked her sleepy husband after fake phone sex.

But Peter was already snoring.

The next morning, a beautiful voice awakened Sasha with a familiar song. *"What do you say we'll put on a day, and we'll talk in present tenses?"* She smelled cinnamon sweet and opened her eyes to the bright sun. Who was playing Joni Mitchell? Peter? She threw back the fluffy duvet and awkwardly tumbled out of bed. Joni was their shared favorite.

"Peter?" Sasha cried over the banister down into the foyer. "Peter!"

"Hi, no, just me," Lynn replied, suddenly appearing below. "Sorry, didn't mean to wake you." Plain Lynn, dressed in baggy jeans and another white button-down shirt.

Sasha's heart sank. "You're early." She felt crabby with disappointment.

"It's ten-thirty. I made vegan cinnamon rolls. There's fresh juice from the orange tree in my garden. Come eat while they're still warm."

Sasha's stomach rumbled. The babies wanted bacon, ham, or pork chops for breakfast. Shit, Sasha was tired, but she had boxes of merchandise to drop off at the studio and then the meeting with that new interior designer, whose name she couldn't remember, for lunch at some hip new vegan restaurant in Highland Park to talk about the babies' rooms. Shouldn't the babies stay together? She yawned and lied. "I'm so tired, but I have errands."

"Hello?" Lynn offered a big smile. She was such a down-to-earth person. "Isn't that part of my job description?"

Had they ever discussed her job description? Could she ask Lynn to buy pork chops when she'd lied to her about Peter's Morgan Stanley account? Of course, Sasha knew the password and had full access. She wasn't an idiot.

"What errands do you need to run?"

She was being difficult and felt too emotional. "Okay," she answered. Now she had to create a fake list of errands. "Let me just make out a list." She turned from the banister, slipping on the shiny hardwood floor. She grabbed for the railing but fell hard on her knees. "Ow," she cried out.

Lynn was suddenly at Sasha's side. "Are you okay? Don't move." Intense eyes stared level with Sasha's. "Why are you wearing Peter's socks? You need to be more conscious."

Sasha looked down at Peter's thick blue socks on her feet. "He doesn't miss me." She burst into tears.

After her hiccups quieted, Lynn helped her to her feet.

Sasha felt ungrounded, shaky. Why had she slipped? What was happening to her body?

"You're taking the day off," Lynn directed in a strong, warm voice. "I'll bring you whatever you want in bed." One is the mother of ten thousand.

Juicy chicken. The babies want Zankou chicken and rice with loads of extra garlic sauce, Sasha thought, letting her assistant lead her like a small child back into the master bedroom. But Sasha couldn't reveal her secret, so she said, "You have a really pretty singing voice." She touched Lynn's arm, and it felt cool and smooth. "I thought it was Joni singing through the house speakers."

Lynn gave a dry laugh. "That's not what my ex-boyfriend said."

"Well, then, he was just jealous. I am. My voice is hideous."

"You write beautiful lyrics," Lynn told her. "Sometimes when you're at the piano, and I'm in the office, your words take me to another place." Lynn offered a big, warm stained-toothed smile.

Later, after Lynn had supplied Sasha with sugary treats and tangy juice delivered on a tray, Sasha snuggled back under the soft duvet, feeling the comfort of a woman's care. What good was money if she didn't enjoy the comfort? Still, she felt a heavy pit, an anxiety, quaking in her heart. Wasn't this supposed to be the happiest time in her life?

Why couldn't she convince her younger self, the scared girl, that nothing wrong was happening? She wasn't ten years old standing in only underpants and a bra, arms folded across her chest, acutely aware of the size of her breasts in relation to the other preteens in the pageant. There wasn't a leering old coach with dentures or manicured shaky hands, offering to brush her hair in private or unzip her pink dress. Peter wouldn't let anything terrible happen to her or the babies. He'd promised to create a safe space together. A man wouldn't make that promise, say those words aloud, claiming them to the entire Universe, unless he'd meant them in his heart. No one had forced Peter to marry her.

Peter's fortieth birthday was only a few weeks away, and she was close to finishing the song. It made her feel better knowing that Lynn appreciated the lyrics. Normally, Sasha loved to plan parties—Christmas, Thanksgiving, birthdays, baby showers, anything. People always commented that she had a knack, a certain style, for capturing exactly what people wanted, what they loved.

But what if he wanted another woman for his birthday and not his pregnant wife? God!ess, how could she tell him? She wouldn't do that, or *watch*, that anymore. Would he understand? Or would he go ahead, without her?

Images flooded her mind: the short white girl with the nose ring that played the zither, a Malaysian singer who Peter said had "the most beautiful ass I've ever seen," the Norwegian foreign exchange student, or the voluptuous redheaded actress starring in that new movie. Remembering the captivated look on Peter's face, his raw desire, was like cutting herself with a razor repeatedly. "God!ess," she cried out. "Please make it stop."

The only answer was not to have a party.

She threw off the covers and climbed out of bed. She was a successful business woman, wife, and mother. She needed a shower and to make plans. It was time for their marriage to grow up. When Lynn returned from the fake studio errands, Sasha would ask her to help plan something small, intimate, but not at home where there was a danger with alcohol and flirtations and too many bedrooms. Maybe she would make a reservation at a restaurant in a private room, somewhere they'd never eaten, except there wouldn't be any belly dancers or waitresses in skimpy outfits.

The showerheads pulsed cold water on the kinks in her neck. She let out a long sigh, forcing her muscles to relax. She slathered coconut body gel on the growing mound which had once been a flat stomach, her fingers swollen, no longer able to wear her sapphire ring. "All is well in my world," Sasha exhaled. Visualize the white light on the path, creating sparkling, glittering happiness for all who attended, especially her talented and loving husband, she thought.

Of course, they would have the party here at the house. Any up-and-coming or on-their-way-down great band would be thrilled to play. She would invite the Disasters and their current wives and girlfriends, some studio friends, a few clients, key players from the label. Meredith would invite the best press. Lynn could call that bitch.

Lynn, capable, sturdy, sensible Lynn, like a big sister, would help. *Hello? That's what I'm here for.* Capable, athletic, fresh-faced, strong, and intense Lynn was Sasha's watchdog and protector. Lynn had offered to help coordinate with Delilah, the new decorator, for the babies' rooms. It was such a relief. Delilah was overpowering and intimidating. Lynn would not be easily intimidated.

Lynn could be in charge of the party. That's why rich housewives had personal assistants, wasn't it? To do the things that their rich husbands were too busy or too bored to help with. What had Sasha thought? That it would be just she and Peter excitedly making plans? Painting the babies' room, or rooms, together, laughing and singing, flinging paint at each other like a happy couple in some romantic comedy? They would hire someone to stencil the walls. Visualizing the babies' room, Sasha felt lighter, imagining her aura glowing bright green and blue. Health and wealth, wealth is health; babies are my fortune, she thought.

Lynn. Peter didn't know about Lynn. Sasha wanted one person she could have to herself. Would she tell Lynn to take two weeks off over the holidays? Would Sasha not invite her to the birthday party she'd helped plan? That seemed mean and wrong. Sasha wasn't jealous of Lynn. She looked like everyone's eighth grade PE teacher—slightly familiar, yet a stranger. In fact, this afternoon, the drummer's longtime girlfriend, Emiko, had mistaken Lynn for someone else.

The doorbell had rung around two, waking Sasha from her cat nap. She'd listened to the female voices, Lynn's and Emiko's, faint, but still audible, rising and circulating in the arching foyer. She heard enough to ask Lynn: "Emiko thought she knew you?"

Her assistant had laughed. "Apparently, I could be a twin for one of Peter's old girlfriends. I guess the girl was a redhead, too. People say I just have one of those faces. But I'm not pretty enough for Peter," she replied. She shrugged like a person who never worried that being pretty wasn't enough. Like a woman who rarely thought about her physical attributes.

Alone in bed that night, staring up at the ceiling, light filtering through the windows of the clerestory above, Sasha entertained how it would feel to be free from Peter's scrutiny, which was a kind of tyranny, wasn't it? She imagined herself floating high in the stars above arms outstretched. "You are braver than you believe, stronger than you seem, and smarter than you think." But she didn't feel like it.

She couldn't locate the purple light in her third eye.

Her thoughts returned to the conversation she'd heard in the foyer. Emiko mistaking Lynn for someone else. Lynn assuring the woman that she wasn't. Why did Sasha care? What was needling in her brain?

It was the simple fact that one of Peter's ex-girlfriends resembled Sasha's assistant. Plain, pale, and freckled, an outdoorsy, ordinary, no-nonsense sort, tall, no breasts. A white girl with stained teeth. Seriously?

Not pretty enough, and yet, pretty enough. For Peter. It never stopped.

RED

The plot had almost been ruined.

After running a bunch of errands for Sasha that felt more like an excuse to get Red out of the house—CVS for nail clippers, Whole Foods for bottled water, Sephora for hair crème, Red had returned with Sasha's lunch order: a cashew smoothie and vegan burger, no bun.

Sasha was asleep, so Red snuck downstairs into Peter's office to hunt for the passcode to his private bank information. She was rifling through opened Morgan Stanley statements in Peter's desk when the doorbell sounded its long, cheerful tone, like theatre bells. Red stuffed the statements back inside the folder, slammed the filing cabinet shut, and raced down the hallway.

When she opened the front door, Emiko stood in front of her.

Red couldn't find any words.

"Red?" Emiko's startled expression melted into a smile across her wide, pretty face.

Shit, Emiko, shit. They had once been friends, during those first Peter days.

Emiko stood holding a cardboard box in her arms. "Red?" she repeated, incredulous.

She stepped into the entryway uninvited and set the box down. "Girl, man. What in the hell are you doing *here*?"

"Sasha's upstairs taking a nap," Red finally offered because she couldn't think of anything else. Thank God Sasha wasn't there.

"Enrique wanted me to drop off this unused old merch. I guess Sash wants it for some volunteer thing. Wow, Red. What a trip." Emiko shook her head. "Rebecca, sorry, Red. Man. What's it been, like twenty years?"

It had been fifteen, and Red was scrambling on her feet. Think, think, don't think. Just play stupid. "Do I know you?" Red prayed that playing confused would work.

Emiko laughed. "It's me, Emiko. Enrique's girl? Come on. Red, you taught me to drive when I first moved here from Kyoto. You *remember*." She offered a sly, sexy smile. They'd drunkenly kissed at a party one night.

"I'm so sorry." Red shook her head with confusion. Stick to Lynn, the story of Lynn. "But you must have me confused with someone else. My name is Lynn. I'm Sasha's personal assistant."

"No. No way." Emiko leaned in closer, peering at Red's face, slowly, nodding up and down, as if trying to find a way to make it fit. "Seriously? What's your name again?"

"Lynn." Please make it fit, Red thought, holding her breath. "Lynn Pickerton."

"Lynn Pickerton. Wow, man. This is trippy. Like, do you have a sister, or a cousin named Rebecca? Red for short. The red hair, freckles, even your long, skinny arms. Are you from LA?"

"No. The Midwest," Red replied, trying to sound calm, relaxing the tensed muscles in her jaw. She forced a laugh. "Guess I just have one of those familiar-looking faces."

"Trippy, man." Emiko shook her head and set the box in the entryway. "K, then. Peace out." And she left Red, feet sweating in her shoes, shaking.

Had Emiko walked away convinced? Red wasn't certain.

Red rolled out of bed, knocking the sleeping cat onto the floor and almost tripped over an empty wine bottle on her way into the bathroom. She ran her tongue over her teeth. Her mouth was as dry as the desert. Drinking the tepid water from the sink faucet, Red wondered how much longer she could keep it up. She didn't need a Ph.D. to know that drinking a bottle of Chianti a night was a symptom of a problem.

Her mind wide awake with anxiety, Red wandered into the living room. She pulled the front curtain aside and looked out across her shadowy garden into the dead night silence, taking in cars bathed in rose from the street light. The cat appeared and rubbed figure eights around her ankles, but she wouldn't open the door.

If she'd purchased the big house her parents had loved in the sterile, safe suburban neighborhood, she and the cat could have sat on the front porch. But these Echo Park hours were reserved for the unstable, the homeless, and the truly dangerous to pace up and down in the alleys, seeking God-knew-what kind of food, shelter, or trouble.

Red loved Echo Park.

"Rebecca, you know that we are not comfortable in that *atmosphere*," her mother always said.

The exact reason that Red loved it.

Echo Park represented different parts of all things and people Los Angeles. Every kind of food, art, religion, and socioeconomic status.

The old and the new mingled together. Shiny BMWs, pick-up trucks, and her beat-up old Toyota parallel parked curbside. Cracked sidewalks were littered with newspapers, dog shit, and colorful kids' stick figure chalk drawings. Tiny houses with browning lawns visible behind chained-link fences, feral cats lounging on cement porches, bird cages swaying from opened windows. Unimaginative square nineteen-seventies apartment buildings with carports exited alongside elegant nineteen-twenties Spanish homes with bougainvillea-covered walls and palm trees. Bars and coffee shops and upscale restaurants were beside taquerias and lavanderias, in mini-malls featuring used-auto parts and discount clothing stores, where colorful piñatas swayed from pollution-worn awnings. Fresh fruit stands that sprinkled spicy red Tajin over pineapple competed for business with trucks that offered street tacos for a buck.

The hipsters had encroached with their wine and cheese stores, small art galleries, and even a new French designer wedding gown retail shop, but hopefully, they were only another layer of Echo Park's rich history, another footprint.

She would take her vibrant Echo Park neighborhood over Peter and Sasha's sterile shiny life above Sunset Plaza any day of the week.

What if Emiko told Enrique, and he told Peter? She was running out of time.

She had to get into the Morgan Stanley account. She was starting to suspect Sasha knew more than she let on and was playing the part of the trusting wife more than she actually trusted Peter with her money.

How could Red bring up the stock market over lunch?

DANI

"Listen, Dani." Barney stood in the dark of the backyard, a packed suitcase waiting at his feet. "I've rented a furnished apartment at The Oakwood until this situation with the racist, the cat, and the kid sorts itself out."

"Ssh." She glanced back at the apartment. They were huddled a far distance from the back windows, but still close enough to hear if Jack fell or Violet tried to run away; she hadn't yet, but why wouldn't she? "I'm sorry. I'm sorry. Barney, what am I supposed to do?" she hissed.

"Put him in a nursing home. Let them deal with his crazy 1950s white male shit. I still can't believe you didn't tell me about the cat, Dani. Not cool."

"Sorry, I know, sorry, but I didn't know how to tell you."

"So, you just let me have an asthma attack? Put your dad in a home."

"I don't have the money for that right now. You know that. They're very expensive, even with Medicare. There are waiting lists. I have to get him to agree to sell the house. Violet has to get registered for a new middle school tomorrow.

Do you know how stressful that must be for her? I don't even know how it works. She's smart and deserves a real shot at a good life."

Barney put a big hand on her shoulder and squeezed. "Take a breath, Dani. You'll do great with Violet. I'll pay the rent and utilities for a couple of months, but I'm sorry . . . I can't stay," he replied.

Dani clutched his hand. Why had she considered a breakup earlier? "Thank you, but that doesn't seem right. Jack said we'll use his social security check. I'll get back to temping once Violet is settled in school." She took a deep breath, but it did nothing to dislodge the cement brick in her chest. "Please," she whispered, feeling desperate. "Just stay."

Barney pulled his hand away. "Dani," he said in a firm tone. "Yesterday, I ate a sheet cake from Vons in the car and jerked off. Then, I attended meetings back-to-back." He looked directly into her eyes. "I lost eight months of sobriety. I don't want to be that guy anymore." He lightly kissed her forehead and then stepped back. "I finally like myself."

"I'm sorry."

Barney picked up his suitcase. "Me, too." He walked to the back gate and turned around. "I think we moved on a long time ago," he acknowledged.

Dani forced a smile. "See you at the meeting tomorrow night?"

He shook his head. "I think I might find a new home meeting. Fresh start."

"No, no, I will. I'll find a new meeting. You love that meeting."

He nodded. "All right."

"Keep coming back!" She cheered the twelve-step motto, but her voice didn't sound convincing. "It works if you work it."

"And you're worth it." He offered a soft smile. "You are, Dani. I think what you're doing for your family is amazing."

Dani locked the back gate and stood in the dark, listening to the late-night talk show audience's laughter blaring from elderly Mrs. McAuley's apartment next door, waiting for a feeling of sadness, sorrow, or emptiness. Anything to wash over her as Barney's old pickup sputtered down the alley.

Had she used him to cross the bridge of loneliness after the divorce? Or had they helped each other on a part of the journey? She hoped it was the latter.

Inside, Jack was passed out, snoring, sprawled on the couch. Dani pulled the blanket over his hairless legs, and Dick hissed, jumping up to curl up on the back of the sofa. She collected several empty crumpled Schlitz cans, put them in the recycling bin, and turned out the lights. A yellow glow seeped from under Violet's bedroom door. Dani knocked, entering slowly when there was no reply.

Dwarfed in Dani's large pink flannel pajamas, Violet had fallen asleep leaning against the headboard, her thick glasses resting on the bridge of her nose. The book she'd been reading for school had fallen from her hands onto the faded bedspread. Violet's meager wardrobe was still crammed in the green trash bag on the floor.

On the dresser, Violet had stacked her schoolbooks and the silver-framed, black-and-white photograph of the couple just as it had been in her room at Monica's. Upon closer inspection, the gentleman in the photograph looked to be in his late sixties: tall, reed thin, with the demeanor of a professor. His wife wore a halo of short white hair and a housedress with an apron. Posing for the photographer on the porch of some old house, maybe their home, they'd fallen into each other, his arm around her shoulders, hers gripping his waist, as she leaned in. This was love, she felt.

"Clifford and Irene," Violet mumbled, and her groggy voice surprised Dani. "They once lived in Mexico where he preached before they got a church in Los Angeles. They moved to North Carolina to be closer to their grandchildren."

"Oh, he's a pastor." Dani put the photograph back on the dresser. "They look like kind people."

Violet nodded with a yawn. "They are," she replied. She closed the book and took off her glasses, placing both on the nightstand. "They were my favorites."

Dani sat on the edge of the bed, feeling the give of the springs, wondering if she could afford a new mattress. She thought about what she was supposed to say next and held her breath.

"People thought I was their granddaughter."

"Really?"

"I look more like I could belong to them," Violet said, "than Monica or you."

Of course, she was such an idiot. "Right, right. Of course." The stark contrast between Monica and Violet's skin. What would it feel like to look different from your parent? Dani was different from Jack internally, but people had never doubted that she was his, much to her childhood dismay. Why hadn't Dani ever thought of that?

Violet continued, "I want to write them, but I don't want to make them sad, especially Irene."

"I'm sure they'd love to hear from you," Dani encouraged.

"They don't want to foster kids anymore if that's what you're thinking. We could try to find my grandma. Diane. Maybe she has room for me?"

"I don't know where Diane is," Dani said. "I want you here. If you want to be here."

Violet bit her lower lip, obviously considering the options. "Would I have to share the bathroom with Grandpa Jack?"

Reasonable consideration. "Unfortunately, we both will have to, unless we make him poop in the backyard."

"Gross," Her niece said, raising one bushy eyebrow. "How would that work? Sharing. Because I'd obviously need it first thing in the morning to get ready for school."

"Could you shower at night?"

"I don't like to do that."

"Well, then, Grandpa Jack would have to wait. Lots of families, bigger than ours, have to share one bathroom."

Once again, Violet took a minute. "How far is the school from here? Can I walk?"

"It's about a fifteen-minute walk. I'd rather drive you. Okay?"

She rolled her eyes.

"For safety. It's a new neighborhood."

"Hello? I lived in a crack dealer's apartment."

"But now, you live with me," Dani replied, a parental tone becoming apparent in her voice. "My rules. Safety first."

"If you say so." Violet scooted down under the covers.

So that was how it worked, Dani noted. State the rules clearly with authority. "Do you think you'll need another blanket? Sometimes this apartment gets drafty."

Violet shook her head. "I'm fine. I don't get cold at night."

"Okay," Dani said and stood. "Tomorrow, after registration at school, let's go shopping. I want you to pick out a new bedspread, and maybe we can get some things you'd like for your room. Target has some cool stuff. Right?"

"No, thank you." Violet's voice was quiet. "I'm good."

"It'll be fun. What's your favorite color?"

"It's okay, Aunt Dani. I don't need anything."

"If you change your mind, remember, I've got access to Grandpa's credit card. I've been wanting to fix up this guest room forever. Now, it's yours."

Violet reached over and turned off the lamp on the nightstand. "Thank you, but I really don't like shopping," she responded.

What did Violet like? Dani closed the guest room door, pausing outside, listening. She heard sniffling, quiet crying. Should she go back in or let Violet cry it out? What was the right thing to do? After the ice cream debacle, how could she win Violet's trust? How could she get control of her anger shit?

Maybe Pasadena City College extension offered a crash course in parenting? What did a thirteen-year-old girl need? Did Violet have her period yet? How should Dani ask that question? Why hadn't she? She should tell Violet the boxes for feminine products were in the cabinet under the bathroom sink. And birth control! Had Violet and Monica had that conversation? Probably.

Tomorrow morning, she would call Jackie, Violet's social worker, and take real action. And get to an OA meeting before she wrecked this new, fragile beginning. Dani needed to call the social worker and start the foster process. How did they find her other relatives? Her father? Her sister wasn't coming home anytime soon. Was she ready? It didn't matter. No one was ready for motherhood.

The steaks! That's what she could do for Violet to make her feel welcome.

RED

She pressed on the brakes, feeling the BMW glide to a perfect stop at the red light on Fairfax and Beverly. It did feel great driving a car more powerful than her old Toyota, but she would never admit that to anyone.

Tired and overwhelmed, Sasha had begged Red to drive her to the meeting with the intimidating interior designer, Delilah. Just *Delilah*, like Cher or Madonna.

"I know that Delilah feels that the energy of Arun, the Warrior Prince, would give the babies courage to fight their lesser inner selves," Sasha prattled on nervously from the passenger seat. "But I don't know, doesn't that seem a little . . . ." She searched for the right word.

"Ridiculous?" Red suggested. Just like the hot new LA designer. "They're babies."

"Right?" Sasha nodded her head.

"And excessive," Red added. "Like her retainer."

When Sasha's regular designer, Marc Macrone, indefinitely suspended new projects in favor of seeking sobriety at Promises Malibu, Renee had swooped in with the gift of Delilah, the "impossible-to-hire" designer. It was all such bullshit. Why did Sasha feel she needed to try this hard to fit in? Maybe that was Red's value judgment. Maybe Sasha actually enjoyed her lifestyle.

The light turned green, and she inched the car forward into the intersection, waiting with three other cars, determined to turn left on the yellow and red without getting hit. What did Los Angeles have against turn arrows?

Red steered the silent white BMW east on Beverly entering Koreatown, the sun beating down into the heat of the day. It was almost the holidays; yet temps were in the eighties. Her fair skin hated this heat. Maybe when she was done ruining Peter, she'd take the money and move to Alaska while there were still a few icebergs. She wouldn't run into anyone who recognized her. As she'd learned from Emiko's visit, leaving the house could be dangerous.

"Hello?" Sasha sang out. "Earth to Lynn. What should we do about the babies' room?"

"Sorry. What do *you* want to do about *your* babies' room?"

"I thought *Finding Nemo* would be cute," Sasha chatted on. "Nemo is so hopeful and colorful, every color on the chakra spectrum, but then Delilah reminded me that Nemo is orphaned throughout most of the movie, and Disney is a marketing racket. So, I don't know. What do you think?"

"Keep swimming," Red quoted. "It's nice." Insecurity was Sasha's most unattractive quality. "I'm confused. Why can't you do what you want?"

Sasha flashed her warm smile. "You're funny," and continued, "I also suggested Winnie the Pooh and Christopher Robin, but Delilah feels a more spiritual theme—"

"What's more spiritual than the Tao of Pooh? Fuck Delilah and her pretentious name. You're paying. What does she know?"

As if on-cue, Sasha's cell dinged. "Delilah." She read the text. "Puppy emergency. Must reschedule." She exhaled a sigh of relief. "Thank God, the babies are starving."

Red found a small Korean barbecue restaurant that opened early just off Western.

At the front door, an older dumpy woman handed them menus, indicated they should seat themselves, and walked back into the kitchen without a word. The interior was utilitarian, all black with aluminum tables and chairs. There were only two other occupied tables: a young couple, heads bent into their individual phones, and an older man, staring out the window. Still shaky from the Emiko encounter, Red was relieved this wasn't a part of town she frequented. Sasha chose a table in the dark back corner away from the sunlight shining through the large front window.

"Paparazzi," she explained.

A dumpy young girl, clearly related to the older woman, with a shiny forehead of red acne approached. Red ordered a Bulgogi Plate, minus kimchee, and a beer. Sasha chose Bibimbap and tea, then glanced down at her phone.

Odds were Sasha was scrolling through pictures of the band's after-party last night. Red never glanced at her phone, unless it dinged. She had impulse-control problems, but social media wasn't one of them. Did Dani's blog count as social media? Christ. Dani hadn't posted in ages.

The waitress set down the beer bottle with a glass and the tea. Was it unprofessional to drink at eleven thirty with her pretend boss? Sasha sipped at her tea and didn't seem to notice. Day drinking was probably a typical activity with her upscale Beverly Hills lunch pals. "It smells good in here. Now I'm starving, too."

Sasha looked up from her phone. "I've been starving my whole life," she stated as a matter of fact. "You wouldn't understand because"—she made a quick, up-and-down gesture to indicate Red's slender physique—"your slim body type and high metabolism."

Red nodded. "Women have hated my metabolism my whole life. I get it from my mother."

"Women are the worst, aren't we?"

"We can be." Red reminded herself to tread lightly. "Society pits us against each other for a man, the ultimate trophy."

"Women in my family competed for a crown."

This piqued Red's interest. "As in monarchy?"

"No. Just beauty contests between my mom and her sister. Whose daughter was the fairest? Me, or my cousin, Scarlet. Scarlet was a beast. I'm sorry. God!ess, but it's true. She was very mean, just like my aunt. She used to put glue in my shoes, and Ex-Lax in my Diet Cokes. In fairness to her though, it's exhausting to starve yourself for the love of your mother."

The waitress put down their plates. Sasha's reeked of sour kimchee. "God, I really hate that stuff."

"Me, too." Sasha spread the kimchee over her food. "This way, I don't overeat."

How deep was her eating disorder? "I read the craziest thing once," Red said, adopting a casual tone. "Some models eat cotton balls soaked in milk to stave off hunger? Is that possible?" She dipped a piece of steak into the sauce.

Sasha's dark eyes followed the bite into Red's mouth. She licked her lips. Was she salivating? "I didn't do that. But I tried herbal remedies, protein shake meals, exercising three times a day, eating a grapefruit before every meal, colonics, juicing, intermittent fasting, and of course, the best, starvation. Or smoking, but it made my hair smell terrible. I was addicted to the hunger high for a while. Plus, it's the perfect method for a controlling person like me. Nobody can *make* you eat . . . ." Her voice trailed off, staring at the food on Red's plate. "Is that juicy?"

"It's delicious." Red chewed. "Would you like a bite?"

"Sarah Jessica Parker eats an apple and a bag of unbuttered popcorn a day," Sasha replied as she leaned over and pinched a tiny piece of meat from Red's plate between her fingers. "At least, that's what I read she did when she was young." She put the miniscule piece on her tongue and sucked. After a moment, she wiped her tongue with a paper napkin and then took a sip of water.

Red watched in utter fascination, dumbfounded by the ritual.

Suddenly, a look of panic crossed Sasha's face. "Lynn," Sasha begged in a whisper. "Please, can I trust you to keep a secret?"

Intrigued, Red didn't promise anything. She nodded her head and waited for the confession.

"You must think I'm crazy."

"You should see me eat a block of cheese," Red said. She held a skewer out to Sasha. "Chrissakes, Sasha, eat, you're pregnant. You're hungry. Eat." This wasn't what she would have said to a client at all because she knew it could backfire. It was too soon; she had to easy-does-it.

Sasha blanched and pulled back, shaking her head furiously. The older customer stood from his table. Sasha waited for him to step outside and then leaned over. "God!ess, please help me."

Was she having an affair? Were things rotten in Denmark? Red nodded, silent. She offered a small smile.

"The babies want meat," Sasha confessed. She took in a deep breath and then continued, "I dress up in disguises and go to markets to purchase meat for them. Then I eat it sitting in my car." She looked as if she might burst into tears.

"Raw meat? That's it? Jesus, I thought you were going to tell me you'd murdered somebody."

"I have."

"Sasha, of course you're craving meat. Your body wants and needs the minerals. Not everyone was born to live vegan. Wisdom is learning to listen to your body. But perhaps raw meat might make you sick? Take it home and cook it."

"What if I was in an accident on the way home, and they found meat?" Sasha's voice was desperate. "If this got out, my whole brand could be ruined. Would be. My life, God!ess, would be ruined."

Meat. This was all for the need of nutrition; Sasha was acting like a fugitive, an addict, lurking and slinking in the shadows because women weren't allowed to be hungry, to indulge, to gorge, or to gnaw or tear away at flesh. She had set herself up to fail. Rigid rules led to chaos. It explained the odd behavior, the secretive meetings, the furtive looks, the unexplained purchases, the disappearances. "You could update your brand. It's much healthier to live your truth," Red said. She heard the hypocrisy as it escaped her lips.

"Just cut me a piece of meat, all right?" Sasha hissed. "The babies are desperate."

"Hang on, hang on." Red was delighted by the intimacy. Why? It was sad, and desperate. It was human. They were more alike than different. This was the healing connection in comedy, dark comedy. She slipped a cube of rare steak from the skewer. It was a fantastic revelation of Sasha's humanity. She wasn't perfect; she kept secrets.

This was the key to the storehouse, Red thought, her breath quickening. The real secret.

"Wrap it up in the napkin," Sasha instructed. "And hand it to me under the table." Only the young couple remained in the restaurant, heads leaning in together as they watched a video on one phone.

"You have to admit. This is a little fun crazy." Red wrapped the piece of meat in a paper napkin. "And weird. Like we're getting away with something illegal."

The young waitress interrupted. "Okay?"

They both jumped.

"I really need to pee," Sasha announced as she scooted her chair back fast and wobbled off to the restroom. She was torturing herself.

"I'll have another." Red signaled the waitress with an empty beer bottle.

The waitress nodded and left.

Red shook her head. Crazy pants. Sasha, the creator of God!ess, the all-vegan lifestyle brand, was a carnivore. The secret was meat. Should Red call Dani? No, Dani would use it to hurt Sasha. But Sasha was not her friend. Peter had hurt them both. Sasha was collateral damage. But she truly was a sweet person.

Shit, a moral predicament. What in the hell? She needed to stay mission-focused.

"Sorry." Sasha sat back down. "One of them stuck my bladder with his elbow. I mean, its elbow. I keep thinking they might be boys." Her big eyes looked vulnerable and afraid.

"From now on, I will buy you organic veal, venison, beef, and buffalo and stock the garage freezer. No one will know," Red told her. Reaching under the table, she offered her new friend a small, wadded meat napkin. "Bon appétit."

Sasha looked like she might burst into tears. "Thank you. Thank you." Had the woman never had a confidant?

Sasha slowly moved the napkin to her mouth, popped in the meat and sucked, moaning and humming, as if in a sexual trance. God!ess, people deserved their own secret weirdness, but now Red had real information. "Swallow," she encouraged. "It's good for the babies."

Sasha swallowed, and Red handed her another piece under the table, talking to help ease Sasha's anxiety. "So, who was the best contestant? You or mean Scarlet?"

Sasha vigorously chewed and swallowed. "Yum yum. Scarlet. She had the perfect skinny with curves figure. Just born with it. Ate whatever she wanted. And had incredibly thick red hair. Like yours."

"I get my ginger from my grandmother."

"I still can't get over Emiko thinking you were one of Peter's exes." Sasha ran her tongue over her lips, licking up the last of the meat juice. "What are the odds?"

Red offered a casual shrug and speared another piece of meat. Sasha watched in anticipation. "What were your talents?"

"Well, Scarlet could sing. Judges said she had the voice of an angel."

"You can sing." Red wrapped more meat in a napkin.

Sasha pursed her red lips. "Peter's ex-wife, Dani, says the sound of my singing is like fingernails on a chalkboard."

"Not very nice."

"She has every right to hate me. I understand." She took the napkin from Red's outstretched hand. "I pray for her happiness every day. Hate leads to cancer." She popped the meat into her mouth.

Who prayed for anyone else's happiness every day? Red didn't know anyone who prayed at all anymore. Only Sasha, gullible, bright, open-hearted, Sasha. "Every day? Come on."

"Why not? She's a person."

In getting closer to destroying Peter, Red would have to hurt Sasha. Goddamn. Her kindness wasn't an act.

DANI

After a hectic week of cohabitating, Violet was attending classes at Wilson Middle School—*Every Child, Every Chance, Every Day*—and said that the kids were "all right," and the teachers were "boring," except for the political science teacher, who was a "badass with dreads and a nose ring." It was a reason to celebrate with grass-fed, free-range, filet mignon from the Armenian market on Altadena.

Strolling down the aisles, salivating over jars of brown sauce, stuffed grape leaves, Middle Eastern spices, and mixed beans, Dani mentally tallied future recipes; food was the love she had to offer her niece.

Rounding a corner, headed to the meat counter, smiling and hungry, the dizziness hit. And then, she was on the floor, surrounded by cans of stewed tomatoes from a display pyramid.

A young woman knelt down beside her. "I called 911," she said. Her voice was irritatingly high-pitched.

Dani looked up at the round face leaning over her, partially hidden by large sunglasses with a Dodgers cap pulled low, the natural full red lips, perfectly sculpted nose, and cheekbones appearing familiar. The scent of amber and patchouli on the stranger's skin was overwhelming, nauseating. Amber and patchouli? Oh my God. Sasha.

Sasha pulled back and clutched a white paper packet to her ample chest. A stain of red spread from the corner of the paper. She was holding meat?

A young guy wearing a Jane Doe band t-shirt held up his phone to take a photograph. Dani grabbed Sasha, pulling her face-to-face in a close whisper. "You're about to go viral." Her eyes gestured to the meat package against Sasha's breasts.

Sasha's eyes widened. Shoppers started to gather around them. Dani grabbed the package of meat. What in the hell was going on?

"Nothing to see here. Give them room!" An older female employee wearing a dark wig and blue eye shadow parted the onlookers for the paramedics.

"She fell into the canned tomatoes pyramid," Sasha explained to the younger paramedic, gesturing to the fallen cans. "I don't know if she slipped on something, but she hit her head. Look, there's blood." She pointed down at the bloodstain on her own overalls.

Angry, Dani shoved the meat package back into Sasha's hands. "Hold this," she said.

"Oh." Sasha's cheeks turned crimson. "Sure, sure. No problem."

"We need you to step back, ma'am." The paramedic gently moved Sasha's pregnant frame aside.

"Ma'am?" Sasha asked, startled. "Me?"

Dani pursed her lips to keep from laughing. Jesus, she thought, that's insecure.

"You fell pretty hard," the EMT said. "Are you dizzy?"

She shook her head no.

"Can you tell me what day it is?" He shined a bright light in Dani's eyes.

"What day?" Between Jack's midnight snoring, driving Violet to and from school, and tossing and turning without Barney, her brain felt mushy. "Um, Wednesday?"

It was Friday. They brought in a gurney and wheeled Dani past Sasha, who still clutched the white packet to her breasts like a precious object, through the smattering of onlookers and out of the Armenian market into the waiting ambulance, speeding south down Fair Oaks while Dani dreamed that her mother was standing on a hill, overlooking cattle grazing below. Diane turned, raised a hand to shade her eyes, and Dani waved. "Diane," she cried. "Mom, up here."

An hour later, Dani woke up in the busy hallway of an ER, sad that her mother wasn't a ranch hand with a wide lasso and a big brown horse. Instead, she was only a woman who'd left her family for a better life. Emptiness reopened in her chest. A warm hand touched her foot, causing her to jump. Red stood beside the gurney.

"Sasha phoned after the ambulance took you away. She said that you were very nice to her," she said. Red's turquoise eyes shone like a bright, warm sea of compassion. "That must have been uncomfortable."

What was *she* doing here? Dani searched for an escape route down the brightly lit corridor. "I need to get home and make dinner for my niece," Dani replied. Why was she on a gurney in the middle of the afternoon? She felt along the cold metal of a lowered siderail and gripped it tightly riding out the wave of anxiety.

A young doctor with a heavy dark beard headed down the hallway towards her, just as an elderly female voice cried out, "Someone, help, please help me." The doctor turned in her direction.

"I couldn't remember what day it was."

"Did you know before you fell?"

Had she known? What day was it? Dani's thoughts were mush. She shrugged.

"Maybe you have a lot on your mind, or maybe the fall hurt you. I'll stay here with you while we wait for the doctor to check."

Dani didn't feel sick, just tired. "I have a lot going on," she responded.

Red nodded. "Stress can make us forgetful."

"I am stressed." Dani was surprised how easily the confession tumbled out. She felt her tense shoulders relax. "I just moved my dad, his cat, and my niece into my two-bedroom apartment because my sister is off the wagon again. And my boyfriend broke up with me."

"That's a lot," Red sat down on the edge of the gurney. "Those are big life changes." She loosely crossed her arms. Her voice softened, "I'm sorry about your boyfriend."

"It's okay. He's allergic to cats."

"Oh," Red replied. "And I'm really sorry about your sister. Are you thirsty?"

Why was she treating Dani like a mental patient? "What are you doing here?" Dani finally asked.

Red laughed. "I know. It's crazy. Don't think I don't know it looks unstable."

"Then what are you doing here?"

The redhead shrugged. "You're the only one who'd understand my experience."

Suddenly, the image of Sasha clutching the meat wrapped in white paper appeared in Dani's mind. Did Red know that her vegan "employer" secretly ate meat? Was she keeping the fact a secret from Dani, or was she still in the dark?

Red leaned in. "It's surreal working at Peter's house. And Sasha's different, not that bad. She's insecure."

"The woman is a fucking cunt."

"Wow, okay," Red replied, lowering her voice. "You have a lot going on."

"I don't give two shits about the home wrecker and her shiny life," Dani grumbled. But it felt amazing actually—to say what she was thinking about the shitty new hand she'd been dealt.

Living with Violet and Jack had not been easy. Their constant bickering and the absolute lack of personal space had left Dani in a state of constant panic so animal in nature that she knew it was only a matter of time before she started eating sweets. Dani spilled the whole shit, the big life stuff: Monica missing, Jack losing his mind, Barney living at the Oakwood attending different OA meetings, her sponsor Karyn's constant texting and badgering about her absence; it was the little things that threatened her sobriety. Jack and Violet were not house-trained. Divulging, purging, all of it.

"You're a good daughter. A good aunt. It's all going to work out," Red assured her. "Just growing pains."

There wasn't a kind way to say it. And Dani wasn't about to tell a total stranger when she could hardly admit it to herself—that she wanted Jack gone. She wanted him to be tucked safely away with three hot meals and a solid roof, preferably without elder abuse, where Dani and Violet would never have to hear his hard words or see that mean face. It sounded cruel, but Monica would have chosen the same. It wasn't healthy for Violet to be around his racist diatribes. "This is temporary until Jack's house sells," Dani said. Then it was adios. Dani had found a real estate agent, an uptight no-nonsense white dude, who was rough around the edges but skilled at his job and who had informed Jack what houses were going for in Mar Vista. It was the same speech Dani had given, but when

Jack heard it from a man, a white man, he listened and agreed to put the family home on the market. There weren't any offers yet, but the realtor said not to worry. It was a matter of time. After that, Dani and Violet could get on with learning how to live with each other until Monica returned. Monica was probably alive but unable to parent. Dani hated missing her sister. "It's the missing her, the worrying, and the wondering," she confessed to Red. "That keeps me up at night. Not the cat, or Jack's TV. It's Monica. Where in the hell is she? Doesn't Violet feel the same?"

"Why don't you ask her?" Red gently suggested.

Why hadn't she? "We don't talk that way in my family." Which was a hard fact. "I don't want to pry or make her sad. We stuff our feelings with drugs or food and cling to inappropriate people as shields."

Red nodded, looking down the corridor again for a nurse or young resident to finish gunshot wound victims and heart attacks. And probably to escape from Dani's verbal diarrhea.

"Well, at least you know your brand."

Why couldn't Dani shut up? And why couldn't she remember what day it was? Did she have a brain tumor? No, the MRI six months ago had revealed nothing. It was Friday!

"It's Friday!" Dani exclaimed, as she swung her legs around, planting her tennis shoes on the floor. There wasn't any dizziness, only a vague sense of fatigue. "I was going to make Violet a steak." She stopped as the image of Sasha's white paper package with the blood-stained corner filled her mind. "I'm sorry for rambling on like that."

"I'm a counselor, remember?" Red offered a genuine smile. Her teeth were slightly stained. From bad hygiene, coffee, or wine. Had Peter liked those teeth?

"I can't afford to pay you." Dani grinned. Red could be kind. Maybe she wasn't a terrible person. She was a therapist. "Can you drive me back to my car at the market?"

Moments later, Huntington Hospital's wide glass doors slid open, and they stepped out, the bright sun hitting their faces as they crossed to the parking structure's elevator.

Dani shielded her eyes from the light. "How much is an ambulance ride without health insurance do you think?"

"Yikes," Red said, as she pushed the down button for the elevator. "Hopefully, you gave fake information?"

"I would never lie about my name—" She caught herself and didn't look over at the woman who was currently lying about her name. "Why don't you come to dinner, since I can't pay you for our therapy session?" It seemed an unwise choice to bring Red home only to escape an awkward conversation. When in fear, Dani always moved closer to the danger. "Do you eat meat?"

The elevator doors opened, and they stepped inside the humid box.

Red pushed the Level 3 button, and the doors slowly closed again. "Sasha hasn't converted me to veganism." She snorted. "I love meat."

Clearly, Red wasn't aware of Sasha's hypocrisy yet.

"God!ess!" Red proclaimed. "No meat, no dairy, no animal products of any kind. Only love."

"I always said, 'Does God!ess know you're fucking my husband?' Such high moral standards."

In the apartment an hour later, Dani stirred more dried oregano into the homemade sauce while Red, chopping the romaine, enjoyed a large glass of red wine. Violet was at the sink, filling the pasta pot with water.

"Maybe just a little less," Dani advised.

"Like this?" Violet dumped out a little bit of the water.

"Oh," Red said. "Next time, use that on your plants. California is a desert in a drought."

Dani rolled her eyes in Violet's direction, and her niece stifled a grin. "I managed to kill the roses in the backyard, Red, so there's nothing to water."

"I could help you with that." Red turned to Violet. "Do you like to garden?"

"I don't know." Violet lugged the heavy pot to the stove.

"There's nothing like getting your hands in the soil and learning to grow things yourself. It's my therapy."

"Maybe." Violet sounded utterly unconvinced. "How high do I turn it up on the stove, Aunt Dani?"

"Cover it and turn it on high until it boils," Dani replied, feeling a bit of wonder at this new kitchen dance. It was the kitchen, of course it had to be the kitchen, where she and Violet were free from Jack, able to connect. Teaching, learning, nurturing. "When it boils, we'll put in some salt, then pour in the pasta, and turn the heat down a little."

"Okay," Violet said. "I want bacon with cheese again. Can we have that?"

"Carbonara. I have pancetta. It's ham-like bacon. We'll chop it thin, adding crème and eggs at the end. Oh, please get out the frozen peas."

"Not with peas," Violet said. "We didn't have it with peas before."

"Peas are delicious."

"And they're so pretty, Violet," Red added. "You'll impress your friends."

The girl shook her head. "I don't have any friends."

"Yet," Dani said. "You don't have any new friends, yet."

"Can I go read?" Violet's cheeks suddenly looked hot red and her eyes watery. "It's for class." She left the kitchen without an answer and Dani turned to Red.

"Oh, God, I'm failing. I know. I fail every day. It's not like she came with a guidebook," Dani said.

"How old is she? Thirteen?"

Dani nodded. "I'm trying to catch up on thirteen years. It's a lot of homework."

"How long have you had her?"

"Ten days."

"Oh, well." Red gulped down the last of the wine in her glass. "You should be perfect at mothering by now." She grinned, revealing those purplish teeth.

Maybe Red wasn't a horrible woman, Dani thought. "Next time, I won't bring up peas. I'll just put them on the side."

"Perfect. Don't argue over peas, but don't give up on them either," Red picked up the wine bottle and refilled her glass. "Do you want me to shave some carrots into the salad?"

"Please." Don't argue. Don't give up. This kind of practical advice made Dani think of Monica again. Had she done the best she could?

When Diane abandoned mothering, Dani became the defacto woman of the household. Jack never took up cleaning and cooking, nor did he hire anyone to do it for them. Dani was in charge. Being the eldest sibling and afraid that her little sister might hurt herself in the kitchen, Dani practiced small things first: cereal and sandwiches, moving up to boiling water for spaghetti, anything stove top, before the oven challenges like roast and chicken. That first year, they ate a lot of spaghetti, especially pasta carbonara, which became her specialty. And Monica's favorite. She would tell Violet that story and that her mother loved peas.

Dani was never seriously hurt in the kitchen. There were a couple of close calls, a few burns, a slice or two, but no ER. Shouldn't she hate food? Resent having to cook for them? No, it was the opposite. It had made her feel like a pioneer, of sorts, trying new recipes from Diane's cookbooks, or women's magazines, until Jack had cancelled the subscriptions, and she went to the library, checking out more adventurous recipes, cooking Mediterranean foods like spanakopita, chopping up spinach leaves with feta and spices and rolling in filo dough to bake, or creating Indian staples from online recipes like creamy spicy chicken tikka masala, which Jack had devoured until discovering that it wasn't "American food." Cooking, feeding her family, had given Dani a sense of purpose, a steady head-held-high esteem.

Dani had learned resilience.

Children were resilient. The only adults she'd known to use this phrase were parents of divorce who harbored guilt over their own parental shortcomings. Not all children were resilient. Some broke into a thousand pieces and could never put themselves correctly back together again. There was a huge difference between surviving and thriving.

"This is too hot!" Jack spit the pasta back onto his plate. "Nearly burnt my damn tongue off."

Violet looked over at Red and rolled her eyes. "Grandpa, blow on it," Violet groaned and spiraled a forkful of pasta, blowing on it. Red stifled a laugh.

"I know how to eat spaghetti pasta, girl," Jack growled. Picking up his knife and fork, he sliced the spaghetti into tiny pieces.

"Hey, Jack," Dani started. "How come you never paid me to cook and clean the house?"

"What?" He slurped a cheesy wad off his spoon, biting down on the metal and pulling it through his teeth.

Dani winced at the sound. "Monica and I did everything, remember?"

"I paid the bills. Put a roof over your head. What did you do for me?"

"We grocery shopped. I cooked. I was ten."

"Yeah, you were the females."

"Oh my God, really?" Red started. "Sorry." She quickly refilled her wine.

"Do I know you?" Jack growled and turned to her.

Red looked at Dani, a thin red brow raised in concern. "I'm Red. We met earlier?"

"I meant, do I *know* you?"

Red shook her head no and took another sip of wine.

In an effort to save her dinner guest, Dani continued, "So, why didn't you pay us?"

"It's called an allowance," Violet chimed in. "Parents pay for grades, chores, all kinds of things. The Graysons didn't pay us, but we got points. And the points added up to things, like a trip to Baskin-Robbins or choosing the TV program. It was a good idea, I think. Better than money."

Had Violet lied about not liking ice cream? Dani filed the idea for later, as Jack continued, his voice raising, "Points? Ice cream? For contributing to your own family?" He shook his head. "No wonder America is going down the drain. Entitlement."

Red guffawed, slapping her hand on the table.

Jack turned to her. "You think we're funny, ginger?"

"You're like a character in a 50s television show."

He grinned. "*Father Knows Best.*"

"I think she meant Jackie Gleeson," Dani said.

Jack continued pontificating. "They don't make shows like that anymore, which is why I watch food television." He leaned closer toward Red, whispering conspiratorially, "Always did love myself a redhead. True American color."

"Grandpa, gross. She's young enough to be your daughter," Violet said.

"Ha! You think you're so smart, smartass." Jack laughed. "I don't have any daughters."

"Salad?" Dani held the salad bowl out to Violet.

Violet passed the salad without taking any. "I like pasta carbonara. Thank you."

"You're welcome." Dani smiled. She was making progress. She needed to develop patience. "I'll show you how to make it."

"Cool. I think I might like to learn to cook."

Red gave Dani a small eyebrow raise. "I'd love to teach you to grow what you cook."

"Well, I like the idea of being capable. But I have the thumb of death. Hence, the dead roses."

"No such thing, Dani. We could put some tomatoes in pots out back." Red turned to Violet. "Gardening is a healing meditation."

"My mom meditates. It doesn't work."

Jack farted, loud and long.

"Grandpa!" Violet jumped up from the table. "Gross."

He looked around. "What?"

"We have company."

"I think you need to use the bathroom, Jack." Dani plugged her nose, mouthing the words, "I'm sorry," to Red.

Red pulled her t-shirt collar up over her nose.

"I don't know who the fuck you think you are," Jack said to Dani, crimson anger flushing up in his neck. "But we're ready for the check."

Dementia would have been hard even with the kindest, funniest of fathers, but it was much worse when the father was a class-A asshole because it was hard to bring compassion to the surface. His doctor had assured her that much of the confusion would clear up when Jack was used to his new home and to keep steady the course.

Dani cleared Jack's plate. "That will be twenty-five dollars."

"For bacon and egg pasta? Go fuck yourself. Where's the manager?"

Red stood and helped to clear the plates. "Can I get you another beer, Jack?"

After the dinner dishes were cleaned, and Violet had gone into her room to do homework, Dani and Red left Jack with his beer staring at the Food Network and went out to the backyard. Red pulled a joint out of the pocket of her flannel shirt and lit up. After taking a big drag, she held it out. Dani had never been into drugs, but she took a small puff. It felt hot. "He really should have given us an allowance." Dani coughed out hot smoke.

"Uh huh." Red sucked on the joint like a straw and held it in her lungs.

"One day, Monica opened the refrigerator door, and the smell was so bad she threw up."

Together, they'd wheeled the big green plastic trash can up the driveway through the garage and into the kitchen, placing it in front of the open refrigerator door. Holding their noses inside their small t-shirts, they emptied its bowels of everything from rotted lettuce to lumpy milk. How hadn't they gotten food poisoning?

"We're doing spring cleaning this weekend," Monica had announced with great enthusiasm.

After the refrigerator, they got the idea to do the whole house, bottom to top. They tied bandanas on their heads, donned rubber gloves, and filled a bucket with dish soap and bleach. It was spring. Diane had been gone since before Christmas. Months of neglect.

Jack left them most nights and weekends to drink with buddies. He still had a few friends then, vets, like him, screwed up from some tour somewhere and unable to assimilate back into their families and daily life.

Dani had rolled the trash can through each room on the first floor. Upstairs, the girls scrubbed the bathroom together, making their own beds, putting away shoes, folding sheets as best as they could in the linen closet until there was only one room. The master bedroom. Monica, the braver sister, opened that last door, the one not even Jack had opened since Diane's departure.

Unable to take another step, Dani peered from the opened doorway into the dark room, musty with a faint scent of her mother's rose lotion.

"What's wrong?" Monica passed her, lifting the window blinds, a ray of sunshine illuminating the fine layer of dust. On their parents' dresser were two framed prints, Monica in a yellow shirt, ponytail, and a wide grin and in the other, Dani, short hair with bangs and big glasses. Their mother had left them behind.

Dani looked out into the darkness. Dick's feral body raced in front of them, chasing something crawling in the grass. "That was the last time we opened the door to our parents' master bedroom. Jack slept on the couch, which is why he's fine sleeping on mine now. Nobody went in there. For all I know, the pictures are still there."

"Jesus." Red exhaled a long bluish plume. "That is sad."

"Yup." Dani took the roach from Red's outstretched hand. She glanced back at the apartment windows. The last thing Violet needed to see was her aunt sitting in a chair in the backyard, smoking pot with Peter's ex-girlfriend. Not exactly a great role model. She inhaled and coughed—too hot, harsh, too strong—handing the joint back. "I'll stick to Entenmanns."

"Hmm, I liked those as a kid."

"I love the way you can pull the chocolate wax frosting off and eat it first, then dip the cake in coffee or save it for later."

Red let out a hearty laugh. "Sasha does not eat donuts . . . ." She paused, hesitating. Was she going to disclose the meat? "Or if she eats them, she throws them right back up."

"God!ess can go fuck herself," Dani said and leaned her head back against the old Adirondack. The stars were buried in a dark marine layer and smog.

They listened to a car pass by on the street out front. The sounds of Mrs. McAuley's television wafted through the night.

Red extinguished the joint between her fingers. "Some children get mothers who make picnics, drive them to swim lessons or piano, teach them to fold towels, make pasta. Can you imagine?"

Dani's brain felt a little fuzzy and thick. How could she not have asked Red anything about her family? "Here I go on and on venting about mine, and I never asked you anything. Do your parents live here?" she asked.

"My parents are *activists*," Red replied. She rolled her eyes. "They like to travel to exotic places, stay in fancy hotels with five-star restaurants, visit an orphanage or two, and call it saving the planet. Eco-tourism. It's like a thing for rich people."

Red's parents were rich. Why was she driving such an old car? "I'm afraid of flying," Dani confessed. "And strange insects. Any kind of bugs or spiders, actually. And I don't wear a swimsuit, not even shorts, in public. And usually exotic places mean humidity, which would make my hair five times frizzier."

"So, you're good. No rich people activism for you. Just daily life. Sasha is really big into talking about activism. And I guess she thinks her company helps people. Maybe it does."

"Only people who can afford her *lifestyle*," Dani said, groaning. The wind picked up, and the dried leaves of the fig tree rattled. "You can tell me what the house is like but not too much."

"It's a beautiful fucking house. All white. Shiny. Clean. Huge. I know you didn't want to hear it, Dani, but unfortunately, Sasha is a kind person."

"Yes, she's a super, lovely home wrecker. Really lives her truth," Dani said bitterly. She turned her anger to picking at a piece of splintered blue paint on the arm of her Adirondack chair. The pair was a great yard sale find one lazy Sunday afternoon. For Peter and Dani's old age on the front porch, they'd laughed. Sundays then were for sleeping in, and sex followed by a late breakfast and yard sales. Peter had promised to paint the chairs bright green. Dani had liked bright colors back then. But instead he'd chosen a deep navy blue, dark like his soul, his favorite. Years of disregard had left them a cracked mess, ready for the dumpster. Like everything he left behind. Why did she hold onto them? She couldn't afford another pair.

"I can't figure out Peter and Sasha," Red continued. "Their marriage. They seem happy, genuinely happy together, Dani. At least in the photos and by her account. But of course he's cheating on her—"

"He is."

"Sasha's hard to figure out." Red leaned forward, resting her bony elbows on her bony knees, and peered at her long bare feet. "She follows all these women's lifestyle influencers on social media; trendy diets and exercise routines, shoes, and home design. They're more damaging than women's magazines. And I hated women's magazines."

Dani thought of all the times she'd stood in line avoiding eye contact with a pretty model on the cover of one of those hideous rags. "They made us all crazy. Like, I'm supposed to make the greatest chocolate cake of all time but have a flat stomach. And be politically active. I should also write a memoir before forty. And stay single. Or get married."

"And you must be good at blow jobs!" Red made a loose fist and imitated giving a hand job. "Monitor Violet's shit online."

Of course, she was an idiot. Dani needed to start monitoring Violet's phone.

Suddenly, Red turned to Dani. "Don't freak, but when I look at you, sometimes I think of Peter and you having sex. Is that weird?"

Dani's stomach was churning. Was it the pot or too much oversharing? "It's the first thing I thought when I saw you. That he loved your flat stomach," Dani replied.

"Not enough to marry it."

"You dodged a bullet."

"And a lawsuit," Red added. "You're very sexy."

Uncomfortable, Dani switched topics. "Do you write music?"

"No. I like to sing, but Peter said my voice wasn't that great. Sasha writes though."

"Really? Is she any good? You know, she can't sing."

"She knows she can't sing. I've heard her at the piano composing, but she stops when I enter the room. From what I hear, she sounds talented. The music is beautiful. There are stacks of colorful journals filled with lyrics in the corner of her office."

"What do they say?" Dani was intrigued and hoped Sasha's true thoughts were filled with unhappiness and regret.

A strange look crossed Red's face. "I wouldn't read her journals. That's personal."

"You're in her house under false pretenses," Dani pointed out.

"I am. But I'm not inside her head."

So, that was the line Peter's ex-girlfriend wouldn't cross? Dani closed her eyes and took a deep breath. Sea, so far from the sea, she could still smell it. "It smells like the ocean."

Red stood up from the chair stretching her long arms over her head. "I wish he had cancer. Is that rotten?"

"Prostate cancer. Super slow and very public."

"Asshole."

"Rectal cancer, then." Dani yawned. She was exhausted. High. "When I have time again, I'll write that one on the blog."

Red grabbed Dani's hand tightly and squeezed. She looked deeply into Dani's eyes, hers shining. Dani smelled the woman's garlicky breath and sweat. She felt her finger bones crunching.

"Let's kill him," Red whispered.

RED

Back home in bed, Red tossed and turned, watching the pale moonlight pass across the ceiling until dawn.

Dani was neurotic, but very likeable, genuine, and down to earth. She was in a constant state of overwhelm. It was hard to ascertain whether it was her usual approach to life, or a more recent condition with the two she'd taken into her small apartment.

Getting to know Dani and her family had felt like reconnecting with old friends, or maybe distant, long-lost relatives. Red hadn't realized how lonely she'd been for company, real company, not just Matt at Sunday brunch, or pretending with Sasha. Connecting with Dani felt honest and real. It wasn't only because they'd slept with, loved, and been hurt by the same man. They mirrored similarities, easy to laugh and easy to cry, vulnerable and tender-hearted. Sasha was the same.

Good women.

Had Peter thought their proximity would make him a better person? He hadn't accounted for their darker natures. Awakening a beast of anger. It hadn't happened yet for Sasha, but it was only a matter of time. She was bright. The babies would multiply her rage.

Taking advantage of their vulnerabilities would be his downfall. It had to be.

Like Dani, Red had revealed her true self with Peter. She had shared her struggles with self-esteem after being molested at age ten by an older male babysitter when her parents were traveling first class to save chimpanzees. Peter had held her in his arms while she'd cried, releasing years of loneliness and shame. What had she hoped to gain by sharing this center, her vulnerable core? Wholeness.

Red finally crawled out of bed and walked into the predawn living room, to the bookshelf where she kept her vinyl stacked and protected, choosing the Pretenders' latest album with Chrissie on the cover, fist bump, tattoo. Alone.

"We weren't meant to be alone," Red told Chrissie's image. Women were meant to congregate. There was power in numbers. Was she discovering the piece missing from her life in the company of Peter's exes? Wouldn't that just be the shit.

Red wasn't alone anymore. And it felt good. She was playing this role to its end.

SASHA

"Hey, what about a mariachi band?" Lynn asked, furiously scribbling notes on the small pad she'd pulled from a worn leather purse. She yawned, covering her mouth. "Sorry, couldn't sleep last night."

"Me neither," Sasha replied. The accidental run-in with Peter's ex-wife at the market had left Sasha shaken.

The late morning light drifting through the office windows revealed hints of beautiful golden natural highlights in the dark red of Lynn's hair. Peter also liked redheads, she thought. Stop it, Sasha! Maybe she'd like to have it professionally done for Christmas. That was a good idea for a gift. What else could Sasha give? Something Lynn couldn't afford. That was the wonderful thing about having money; she could support all of her friends. How did Lynn make ends meet?

"Do you have another job?" Sasha inquired. Startled, Lynn looked up from her notes. There were dark circles under her eyes. "I never even thought to ask that." Sasha felt earnest to connect. Lynn's brows knit into a thin orange line.

Was it an unreasonable question? Was it too personal? Sasha scrambled, "I mean, do you need to work more hours?"

"Do you need me to work more hours?" Lynn was as direct as ever.

God!ess, forgive my weakness. The equilibrium of their relationship was off. Sasha needed to get back the upper hand as boss, or if not, at least even the playing dynamic. Pull it together, Sasha. "I don't know that much about you. And after the other day—"

"I made a promise, Sasha," Lynn interrupted in a brusque tone. Was she mad? "I won't break it."

Sasha nodded.

Lynn put the pen and pad down on the glass table top and leaned back in the desk chair. "It's true you don't know that much about me except that I love gardening. So, ask away."

"I just, I'm sorry. "It's weird to have someone working in your home and then realize you don't know anything about their personal life," Sasha explained. "Where do your parents live? I mean, I'm sorry. Are they still alive?"

"Yes, they're alive. They like to travel." Lynn offered a wry smile. "All over the world. They call themselves *activists*, but it's very bourgeoisie. You know, they fly to Delhi, stay in a five-star hotel, dine on twenty-dollar hamburgers, and then go to an orphanage and hand out Nikes for a day."

Sasha thought it sounded lovely, but then realized that her assistant found it shallow. No matter how hard she tried not to, Sasha did like what money could buy. A person didn't have to live in another's hovel to help their pain, did they?

God!ess! It was okay to like buying expensive health food and outfits made of good fabric and staying in luxury five-star hotels. "First world problems," Sasha said and hoped her sarcastic tone implied that she also thought Lynn's parents were ridiculous. "What else?"

"I'm a counselor." Lynn's face softened, the tight muscles around her mouth relaxed. "For women who've experienced trauma. Abuse. But after my breakup, I mean divorce, I just didn't . . . I don't have the energy to help."

"Oh. Wow." Sasha felt her face redden in embarrassment. In her mind, she'd formed a different picture of Lynn, a broken woman without a college education, poor, dumped by her husband searching for a better life. The image was completely wrong! Lynn was helping Sasha reach the edge of her limitation—thank you, God!ess—by opening a door.

As if reading her mind, Lynn said, "Never judge a book, right? It's okay. I needed a break. I wanted to be engaged in something more light-hearted."

"Like decorating the babies' room." Sasha nodded, also wanting to feel light. Everything was dark these days. Where was this light? she wanted to ask Lynn. Why am I unhappy when I have everything I've ever wanted? Sasha needed this conversation with a strong woman, a real person, who told the truth, as much as air and sun. She kept the dialogue flowing. "I feel that way about the studio. How light and happy it makes me to help others. I mean, women come in with all kinds of problems. They may look rich and pretty, but I feel their sorrow and angry energy. It's a gaping hole. When they leave, they seem refreshed, reenergized, filled with the light. That is the God!ess! This is my prayer," Sasha continued. She heard the naive hope in her voice and saw a tremble in Lynn's lower lip. Was she holding back a laugh? Did she think Sasha was an idiot? "I mean, I don't have a degree. The God!ess taught me to bring out my intuition, which I think is better—no, not better, but wiser or deeper than only intellectual education. Maybe that sounds silly."

Lynn shook her head. "It sounds beautiful, Sasha. Most people don't think like you. You are a special woman."

Surprised, Sasha took a moment to feel the compliment. Breathe it in and out, don't push it away, she prayed. Let it envelope your body in a glow. It's okay to feel good about yourself. Feel and share it back. Why had she thought Lynn was judging her? "You should come take a class at my studio!" Sasha said, clapping her hands. This is how she could help Lynn. "Maybe even spiritual dance. It feels good. You would love it. Feet on the ground. You like working with the Mother, the earth."

"I'm not really into yoga," Lynn quickly replied. "I mean, thank you. I know it's good for your body, but I prefer hiking on terra firma. Or gardening in it."

Sasha felt the air let out of her excitement. Maybe Lynn thought Sasha was special in a way that wasn't a compliment. Moving close to another person is a fragile dance. Expansion, contraction. She felt Lynn's energy pulling back. What secret had broken her heart? Love, or the lack of it, was always the reason. "I like to hike Runyan sometimes. Maybe we could hike together. I mean, the babies are making me so fat. I could use a walking partner. There is a lot of dog poop though."

Lynn laughed, a true genuine laugh which made Sasha feel better again. "You're my only job, Sasha. And I like working for you."

"Gosh, I hope so. I'd hate to be one of those female bosses who's uptight and bitchy, unreasonable. Working for me should be fun!" Sasha said. Why couldn't she say what she wanted to Lynn? Here's my secret: Peter is breaking my heart. Can you help me understand how to get him back again?

"Working for you is a lot less stressful than my last job. And the working environment is beautiful."

"I know this isn't all it's cracked up to be. Doesn't mean real happiness." Sasha gestured around the exquisitely decorated room. She was being ridiculous, embarrassing herself. Her life was light. She had everything she'd ever dreamed of. "I'm sorry. I don't know why I just said that. I guess I felt embarrassed, you know? It's all new to me. You should have seen my studio in Venice. I was so broke, but when I look back, it felt like good times—laughing and being around friends. It's quiet up here. I get a little lonely. That's all. It's embarrassing."

"People in mansions suffer, too." Lynn's voice was quiet and soft. "I'm here, Sasha, if you ever need to talk."

Sasha's felt the pressure of a headache begin in the center of her forehead, her third eye, from trying to gain clarity. She hadn't slept well all week. It was awful enough that Peter had forgotten to video chat her at her last OB/GYN appointment, but then she'd seen an after-party photo on The Disasters' socials' and run into his ex-wife at the market where Sasha was holding a slab of meat. "I haven't been able to sleep. I can't believe Dani saw me holding a hamburger. She will ruin me. She has this blog about killing Peter."

Her assistant picked up her pen and pad again. "How didn't you recognize Dani at first?"

"Remember, she was on the floor." She paused. "It wasn't what I expected."

"In what way?" Lynn replied.

Sasha still couldn't believe the encounter, the way the woman had come to her rescue, only to have Sasha lie about the stain on her overalls. She had forced herself not to think about it and hadn't mentioned it to Peter. "She was kind. She looks different."

"She's lost weight." Lynn's head was bent, scribbling on the pad.

Sasha shook her head, wanting to change the subject. "They never do that with men."

"As long as they're rich or famous, men can be as fat, ugly, and bald as they want and women will still want them."

"Especially, if they have a band. Peter's drummer is fat," Sasha said. She liked sharing a little gossip with her new friend. "You met his girlfriend, Emiko. Groupies love him."

"It's probably the reason some guys become musicians."

The photos from the Disasters' after-party, the whole gamut of temptation floated through Sasha's mind again: half-dressed girls and women, exposed breasts, thighs, short and tall, black, brown, white, mixed, shaved heads or long hair. "My mind is creating problems that may not exist, crazy monkey mind, and meditation isn't helping. I miss Peter. And the babies are always hungry. And Danielle writing about my carnivorous activity could destroy my brand." She felt her lower lip quiver and bit down hard. "Or worse."

Lynn looked directly at Sasha. "Why don't you reach out to her, if you're worried? It might help you sleep better," Lynn suggested.

Sasha stood, picking up their empty teacups and saucers from the table. The hard truth, no filter, was that Danielle deserved her apology, a coming-together, for them to move forward. "You are a good therapist," Sasha replied, nodding. She needed to practice what she preached, reach out, and apologize. Be in the moment. Appreciate the journey. "Peter will be home in two weeks, and everything will be great!" She shrugged off the unhappiness, adopting an upbeat tone. "I need to go focus on finishing his birthday song. I think a mariachi band is a great idea! Can you find one?"

As Sasha was leaving the room, it occurred to her—how did Lynn know that Dani had lost weight?

DANI

Dani spread the coarse sea salt over the filet mignon and massaged the granules with her fingertips, Violet watching at her side. What was it about the feel of flesh, the smell of blood? Earthy iron and minerals. Her mouth watered at the trickle of pink juice gathering on the wax paper under the meat. At the end of the day, they were all animals, weren't they? And animals must be fed. She thought again of Sasha's weakness. Appetite was labeled as unattractive in a woman, wasn't it? "Here." Dani handed the ceramic ramekin of salt to Violet.

Studious, ever serious Violet carefully pinched some crystals between her fingers, then sprinkled them over her steak.

"You can add a little more," Dani suggested, to which Violet complied, hesitating to touch the flesh. "You can't hurt it."

"Anymore," Violet stated. "Is this hormone-free, grass fed?"

Oh God, no, but Dani lied. "Yes. These three steaks cost more than I make in a day."

Violet's eyes grew wide with alarm. "But I thought you said you used Grandpa's money. I'm sorry . . . ."

What the hell had Dani done, shaming her niece over a desire to try steak? Think. Think before you speak, she admonished herself. "I did, I did. Grandpa is excited to not have pasta or stinking fish stew tonight. But I'm sorry, they aren't grass fed. We simply can't afford that kind of meat."

"Okay." Violet's dark brows knitted together with concern. "Then why would you lie about it?"

Right, right because Dani was weak. Violet liked the truth, needed it. "Because I wanted you to enjoy them."

"I will, Aunt Dani. I promise. But don't lie again, okay?"

"You're right. We have to trust each other, right? I promise."

Violet shrugged the way she did, shoulders quickly up and then slumped straight down like an old woman, as if to say, *Why bother? Life is what it is.* She was too young to be old.

"They're going to be delicious." Dani smiled. "Now, let's massage the salt in."

Violet did as she was told, fingers kneading into the flesh on the wax paper, as if the exchange hadn't happened, or she was over it. It was a good trait she had, not holding grudges. Dani wished she had it, too. "This feels really weird. Like, I like the feeling of it. It's cold. Poor baby cow. I shouldn't like it." Violet looked at Dani for reassurance.

"This cow wasn't a baby." Dani replied. "He had a full happy life with friends on a farm. His death was swift and painless."

Violet shook her head, a few strands falling from her ponytail and addressed the steak, "Aunt Dani is a little delusional about the meat industry and its contributions to global warming. Poor cow. Thank you for letting us eat you tonight. I do wish you'd felt the grass under your hooves."

What a kid, talking to a steak. Monica once had that kind of delight, telling stories, talking to animals. Dani forced herself back into the present. "How was school today?"

Violet shrugged. "Fine."

"What's your favorite class? Mine was always choir because we didn't have homework."

"I like homework."

Potholes, hills, and sharp turns were everywhere Dani steered. She needed a break, gesturing to the washed leaves waiting on the cutting board. "How about you make the salad? But wash your hands first."

"How?"

"With soap and water."

"Aunt Dani," Violet said, and her voice quickly rose with frustration. "I know that. I mean, how do I do the lettuce? With a knife? How tiny should the pieces be? God."

One minute she was enchanting, the next so exacting that Dani yearned to escape. Hadn't it been easier living alone with Barney? Wasn't loneliness better than this? "Just tear bite-sized pieces with your clean hands," Dani instructed. She was exhausted just making her niece dinner once. Poor kid. "It doesn't have to be perfect."

"I don't want olives on my pizza," Jack hollered from the living room.

"We're having steak," Dani yelled.

"No vegetables either!" Jack yelled back.

"I don't eat lettuce," Violet informed Dani, ripping away at the leaves. "Remember?"

"Butter lettuce is very mild. Red dropped these off, so we know they're organic from her garden. Look how they grew just for you."

"Yeah, I still don't want it. Did your mom teach you to cook?"

"No. I taught myself." Dani finished massaging the last filet.

"What happened to your mother, my grandmother?" Violet carefully tore the lettuce in her chubby hands and tossed it into the salad bowl. "Monica won't talk about it."

It was innocent, a normal question. Where was Violet's grandma? Where was she? How could Dani begin to answer a question that had no explanation, no happy ending?

The history of mothers and daughters is a fabric woven from intricate stories of joy and pain, birth, sickness and aging, secrets, wisdom, competition, jealousy, misunderstandings, hurt and anger, love and death, and sometimes, abandonment. The waves of repeated mistakes—family karma. When she was little, Dani hadn't understood, or cared about, the reasons Diane left them, her small daughters, and never returned. As she grew older, living with Jack, she understood a part of it, the escape, but never leaving *them*. "We don't know where our mother is," Dani finally said. She kept her tone even. "We don't even know why she left."

Violet placed her warm palm on the center of Dani's back. "It sucks."

Dani turned to her niece, looking into her warm brown eyes. "It really does, doesn't it?"

Violet nodded. "I don't think mine's coming back either. Sometimes, I don't want her to. Is that bad?"

The timer on the stove dinged.

"No." Dani put an arm around her niece's shoulder. "That seems like a perfectly reasonable feeling."

Violet swayed into Dani's embrace, leaning her head against Dani's chest. Dani bent and kissed the top of Violet's head. She smelled like coconut shampoo, fresh and new. I like having you, she wanted to say. I want you to stay, but I'm afraid. Will you help me be the person you need? Forgive my mistakes. Hold my hand along this way?

On cue, the timer dinged again.

"Turn off that goddamn noise," Jack cried from the kitchen doorway. "I can't hear my program." He stopped and stared at the two. "Who died?"

"Nobody, Grandpa." Violet quickly moved away from Dani. "It's called a hug. You should try it sometime."

Jack grumbled.

"Time to grill!" Dani turned off the stove's timer feeling the connection pass. "Grab your plate, Violet. I'll get mine and Grandpa's. Let's get some fresh air."

Jack stepped down the back stairs, into the yard, just as Mrs. McAuley stepped inside the gate, arms loaded with grocery bags. Her spindly frame was well-dressed in a smart, black-and-white pantsuit, her hair neatly pulled into a tight bun. She was even wearing makeup, which Dani had never seen.

"Hey there, hey now!" Jack sprinted toward the elderly neighbor. "Let me give you a hand, Doris."

The meat sizzled as Dani placed each steak carefully on the grill.

"Grandpa's got a thing for the neighbor," Violet whisper-informed her aunt. "They met over some mail mix-up."

"Ssh," Dani replied.

"Why, thank you, Jack," Mrs. McAuley gushed in her sweet English accent. "There are so few gentlemen around anymore."

"One hand is better than none." Jack grinned. "And America is going to the devil." He took her bags, following the woman to her back door.

"Infidels and immigrants," she cheerfully agreed. "It is. It is."

"And the Mexicans."

"Grandpa," Violet cried. "Stop that."

"Oh, hello, Violet." Doris waved from her stoop. "Goodness, I didn't see you standing there."

"Good evening, Mrs. McAuley." Violet offered a big, obviously fake, smile.

"Let's go check on the baked potatoes." Dani waved and guided her niece back inside.

How could she surround Violet with kind people? Wise and strong women? Protect her? Defy the odds? Should they look for her father?

"Maybe we should take Red up on her hiking offer?" Dani suggested later, putting the salad dressing on the table.

"I'm not going," Jack said.

"*You* aren't invited." Dani plopped a hot baked potato down on his plate.

Violet sliced her baked potato open with a steak knife. The steam covered her thick lenses. "Are we in good enough shape?"

Jack laughed and sliced into his medium rare steak, blood pooling around the edge of the plate. "This is good. Meat is good for you," he told no one in particular.

"I think we could handle it," Dani replied. "Butter sour cream and chives."

Violet looked doubtful.

"How about just butter and chives?"

Violet cut a thick pat of butter and wedged it into the potato, sealing it tightly, watching yellow pool around its base. "I've never had those green things though." She indicated the chives in the ramekin. "What are they?"

"Chives. They're a mild herb. Tasty. They'll bring out the flavor in the potato. How about you try a small bite and see what you think?"

Violet shrugged.

"Be brave."

"Brave?" Jack scoffed. "World War Two was brave. It's a fucking potato. Eat it."

"Jack," Dani warned.

Violet opened the side of her baked potato with a fork and sprinkled a few slices of green in one place. "Gross."

"They aren't slugs." Jack ladled a spoonful of chopped chives into his palm, popped them in his mouth, and chewed. "Hmmm, delicious!"

Violet scooped out a small portion with a spoon and slowly put it in her mouth, swirling it around and swallowing. After a moment, she decided, "I could have a few."

"Help yourself." Dani slid over the ramekin of fresh herbs. "Now eat, before your meat gets cold."

Violet held the fork and steak knife poised above the meat. "Do I just cut it anywhere to start?"

Oh my God. She hadn't eaten steak before. Was Dani such a clueless idiot? "Just dive in anywhere."

"Knock yourself out, girl." Jack cut off a big hunk of meat and stuck it in his mouth.

Dani turned her attention to her own plate so as not to embarrass the girl.

Violet picked up the steak knife and sawed through the tender meat, juices spreading on her plate. "Oh! Um. There's blood."

"That's what medium rare means."

Violet looked like she might pass out.

"I can cook it more. Okay? Let's put your potato on another plate to keep it separate from the juice."

"You mean, the blood," Violet corrected as she shuddered.

Jack opened his mouth, revealing the masticated meat. "Jesus H. Christ. Are you my granddaughter or not? Try it first."

Challenged by Jack, Violet stabbed a small piece with a fork and stuck it in her mouth, chewed it repeatedly, and finally, swallowed. "Huh, buttery." She pushed her dark glasses back up her nose. She needed better frames. "Why do only rich people get the good food?"

Dani's eyes watered, and she quickly stood. "We forgot the salad."

"No greens." Violet sawed away at her steak. "How could you already forget that?"

This kid. This kid would drive her to the brink. "I'm sorry, Violet, please have some patience with me. I'm new to this."

"I don't like greens either," Jack agreed. "The apple doesn't fall far from the tree."

"Well, I like salad, so maybe it's an acquired taste. You should try it, Jack, like you made Violet try the steak."

Jack laughed, big and hearty, setting down his knife and fork. "Nice try, Danielle Desi Smith, nice try." He wiped his whiskered chin with a paper towel so hard it sounded like sand paper, then bunched it up and threw it on the table. "Get to these dishes, quick." He pushed his chair back and stood. "My food murder mystery show starts in ten minutes, and I think you two will like it. Tonight, some baker kills a groom with a poisoned cake because he was having an affair with the bride."

Cake and murder? Dani thought. Perfect.

"Okay," she and Violet piped up in unison.

RED

She pulled up to Dani's blue four-unit apartment building and honked the horn. It was already seven thirty. They needed to get on the trail before the marine layer evaporated. Her skin had suffered enough sun damage, and Dani was so out of shape that the heat would make climbing worse.

Holding a to-go coffee mug, Dani stepped out wearing a baseball cap, jeans, and a t-shirt, even though Red had stressed shorts for Malibu, or she'd be too hot. Dani hated her legs, which Red thought were perfectly fine. So what if there were a few veins? They were all getting older. Hiking wasn't a beauty contest. It was about seeing beauty. Dani waved and held up a finger as if to say, one minute, then yelled something inside. A second later, Violet emerged, dressed appropriately in shorts and a t-shirt and of course, wearing her earbuds. She reluctantly scuffed her sneakers behind Dani to the car. There was something familiar and likeable about the kid.

"Violet, it's so cool you want to hike." Red turned around as the teen climbed into the backseat. "Who's watching Grandpa?"

"Mrs. McAuley, our neighbor," Violet said. "I need to finish listening to this podcast." She turned up the volume on her earbuds, and Red faintly detected the sound of arguing men's voices.

"Politics," Dani explained. "She's addicted. The parenting blog I follow affirms it's the new trend. How are you?"

"Good, fine. I planned Peter's party, hired the mariachi band, and decorated his unborns' room with poufs, lavender, and wind chimes. Now it feels like a new age bookstore. Sasha beat me twice at Rummikub."

Dani laughed. "Wait? She can play games?"

"Sasha always wins. She's really bright."

"Right," Dani replied, her voice dripping with sarcasm.

Red shook her head, disappointed at Dani's refusal to see things differently. No wonder the woman was so miserable. "People will surprise you," she replied, wondering if Sasha had left Dani a voicemail yet, seeking forgiveness. If so, Dani would spill the beans today. They rode west on the 101 across the San Fernando Valley, traffic moving at a good pace, early weekend sun glinting off of the windows of houses and office buildings. "Dani, I can't believe you've never been hiking," Red commented and looked up into the rearview mirror at the preteen completely unaware of the conversation from the backseat. "Malibu Creek State Park is where they shot the TV show *MASH*."

"That's cool."

"Have you ever heard of *MASH*?" Red called out.

Violet stared out the window, listening intently to her podcast.

A semi's red lights flashed ahead, and Red changed lanes and slowed around a minor fender bender while she filled Dani in on Sasha's latest behavior, sans the carnivorous: the melancholy piano playing while weeping, staring at her pretty reflection in the living room windows, afternoons of pointless appointments for pedicures and color stylists and shopping or lunch in Beverly Hills with her stretched-too-tight, pumped too full, girlfriend. "Emptiness to fill the void between prenatal yoga class and spiritual round-up," Red said.

"Do they dance around with their eyes closed or sit in a circle and share fucking uptight new agey Westside problems?" Dani asked.

"I'll tell you after I go this week. Maybe it helps? It's strange, being so close to his life," Red admitted. "It hurt at first, but now, I guess it's just so strange. Their life seems too big but is a post-pubescent teenager playing a grown woman.

It's sad, really. Twice last week, she asked me to spend the night because she was afraid."

"Oh God. That is sad."

"Right?" Red took the Kanan Dune exit off the freeway. "I'm her friend, but she isn't mine. Working in someone's home, that's the way it goes, I guess. A personal assistant is an extension of her, like the cleaning lady, gardener, or floral delivery person. It's assumed familiarity due to proximity. Sasha makes few attempts to get to know Lynn."

"But you don't want her to know the real you," Dani pointed out. They passed a public school whose grounds looked more like a private college, Spanish-style stucco buildings surrounded by lush green grass, the drive lined with palm trees. "I wish Violet could go to school here," Dani sighed.

Red lowered her voice. "Peter comes home soon, and I haven't gotten access. Here's what I've uncovered so far that doesn't help us at all." The light ahead turned red, and she slowed the car. "Sasha hasn't had a bowel movement in two days, and she's booked a colonic. She hides Mallomars cookies in the bottom of the guest bathroom cabinet but doesn't eat them   and surfs handbags online, like some addicts do porn. I know her mother had a dental appointment this morning for a new cap and that her younger brother just got his third DUI. Her family never visits. I know she stopped getting her pussy waxed while Peter's on the road because I've cancelled the appointments. I also know that she has a mole on her lower back that she finds repulsive but is afraid to have it removed in case it scars. She created a very successful brand and keeps it successful like some kind of magic. You wrote the song that launched The Disasters, and now she's the writer who has expanded their success. He sleeps with women to use their talents and then discards them. I sense she also knows this. She's very edgy and insecure when he doesn't call. We have to do something. It's illegal. He's a phony."

"Stepping on the backs of women to rise to the top isn't new," Dani said, cutting her off. "From Rodin to Fitzgerald. Don't ask me to feel sorry for the home wrecker. God!ess is a snake-oil saleswoman." She turned from the window to face Red. "When I fell at the market, Sasha was holding a bloody steak and tried to pass it off as mine."

"You *do* know!"

"*You* knew, but didn't tell me?" Dani was clearly upset. "So much for being partners in crime."

"I'm sorry." Red lowered her voice again. "What are you going to do?"

Dani sighed. "He won't care if I hurt her."

They grew silent, staring at the road. Around a lush, green hill, the land opened widely, offering a view of the Santa Monica Mountains. Ancient red boulders dotted their outline like the curved spines of prehistoric creatures.

"Don't worry. Things aren't so great in happy town." Red hoped to change the trajectory of the day. Get Dani back on the same page. Feeling terrible that she hadn't trusted Dani with Sasha's secret, Red confessed another. "Peter forgot to video chat during the last OB/GYN appointment. Said he was in sound-check. Sasha acted like she believed him, but I heard her crying in the bathroom after the phone call."

"He's fucking Annie!" Dani proclaimed.

"The older guitarist who replaced Sasha on tour?"

Dani nodded. "That's her first AA chip on his guitar strap. They go way back."

"He's not in AA."

"They met in SLA, Sex and Love Addicts Anon. Annie's a total slut. No moral compass."

"I know what SLA is." Red rolled down her window for air. She hated that word—slut. Female musicians slept around; they were sluts. Male musicians fucked everything in sight, and they were just musicians. Was Dani aware that she sounded like Jack?

"Would she leave him if we told her?" Dani asked. "She'd get some of his money. That would hurt him."

Red shook her head. "She sees his social media posts and looks the other way."

Suddenly, Violet sprang to life from the backseat. "Aunt Dani stalks Peter online."

Red laughed.

"To look for blog ideas," Dani replied defensively.

"Nice of you to join us, Violet." Red smiled in the rearview mirror.

"Aunt Dani, you haven't written your blog in weeks," Violet continued to torture her aunt.

"Hello?" Dani turned around to her niece. "I've been a little *busy?*"

Red laughed again, looking over at Dani. "How can you view his behavior online without it bringing up feelings?"

"Don't you work in his house?" Violet asked.

Touché. Red turned her eyes back to the curvy road ahead. "Violet, you haven't been in love yet, have you? It's hard to explain."

"If you're helping plan Peter's birthday party," Violet stated, "you should poison the cake." She giggled, and Dani shot Red a look of alarm.

"Jack turned us onto this food murder show. It's really good," Dani explained in an apologetic tone. "I know, bad aunting."

Violet leaned forward. "My aunt likes to take a true event and then add a fictional murder. She does a lot of research. Her writing is not that bad. But is it bad that she's doing it?"'"

Dani looked like she might physically be sick. Red tried not to laugh. "We can't poison the cake, ladies. Real, innocent people would die. Violet, I think it's great that your aunt is able to work out painful personal stuff, fictionally, not in reality. It's very healthy," Red said. But of course Red had already considered poisoning the cake. It wouldn't work. She was currently ruminating, just as a therapy exercise, on making it look like an overdose. Which form of murder would be the hardest for police to trace back? She'd considered shoving the drunken birthday boy off the balcony, making it look like an accident, or maybe strangulation from an intruder, but she wasn't certain she had the physical strength. Or inebriation followed by drowning like in *Sunset Boulevard*, the man in a suit face down in a pool. Peter couldn't swim. But drowning seemed too kind a reckoning. What would be so slow and painful that in his final moments Peter would scream for absolution? How about a sincere apology? "Is an apology too much to ask for?" Red once asked him. Dani said he'd never apologized to her either.

"Look at that blue sky," Dani observed, rolling down her window. A gust of wind blew the hair from her pretty face. "It's nice of you to take us hiking." The woman was clearly ready to steer the uncomfortable conversation in a different direction.

"My pleasure." Red glanced up again in the rearview mirror. Violet had put her earbuds back in and was staring out the window at the red rock formations in the distance. "Any word from missing in action?"

Dani shook her head no.

Ten minutes later, perched on the open trunk of the Toyota in the dirt parking lot, Violet removed her earbuds and stuffed them in her back pocket. At nine a.m., the sky was already a warm autumn blue, the air smelling of burnt grass and Manzanita from a brush fire weeks ago. Red took a deep breath and felt the peace of her favorite hiking spot, thinking about how much Sasha would love this open space.

Dani and Violet stared nervously ahead at the dirt trail, which wound through a large meadow of brown grass and snaked up a sparsely forested hillside, disappearing around a bend deeper into the Santa Monica Mountains. Red smiled to ease their worries. "We'll go easy the first time," she promised. "Got your water?"

Red loved introducing friends to the California beauty of Malibu State Creek Park; its rocky trails covered eight thousand acres once owned by SONY Studios to shoot Westerns and TV shows. There were succulents, Manzanita, the occasional oak or walnut tree and a host of living things, such as red foxes, coyotes, mountain lions, rabbits, rattlesnakes, and lizards. The park also offered the prize of wide ocean vistas and a dip in the water if you didn't quit too soon.

"Isn't it breathtaking?" Red slowed her pace, measuring their steps behind her, listening to their labored breath. The idea of living mostly indoors, or only in the city, without any connection to the earth was beyond her imagination. Hiking and gardening were how Red worked out her stress. As they neared the first bend with a view, Red stopped and waited for the two to catch up. In the golden-hued blue sky above, a pair of red-tailed hawks circled, seeking breakfast. "Look at that." Red pointed up to the sky. "They mate for life." She would tell Sasha about the animal sighting. The woman believed in the magical thinking of animal medicine and totems.

The two arrived in silence, heaving. Violet's t-shirt was sweat stained around her chubby middle. Dani's cheeks were bright red from the heat. She looked miserable in her jeans. "Everybody okay?" Red asked. Violet wiped her brow with the back of her hand. They both nodded, drinking copious amounts of water. Red gestured to the outlook, past red rock pyramids formed by volcanic eruption millions of years before, the ocean flat and blue, smooth before them. She turned back to them. "Isn't it amazing?"

Violet asked, "What do we do when we have to go to the bathroom?" Since Violet made it clear she was "absolutely disgusted" with the idea of peeing in the wind of the great outdoors alongside beetles, possible snakes, and humans, they turned back toward the port-a-potty, which was much worse than a hole in the sand.

Red suggested they adventure the rest of the way over Kanan Dune, so they climbed back into the car and drove north up PCH to Leo Carrillo State Beach, another favorite, with tide pools of anemones and a strip of sand less inhabited by other humans.

They scrambled down the hillside and crawled over the black rocks, wading through the ankle-deep cold water through a small cave into a secret cove. Red and Dani sat in the sand, watching Violet test her toes in the cold water, looking back at them, nervous about sharks and jellyfish.

"I haven't even asked what the doctor said," Red said and felt like an ass. Dani gave her a blank stare. "About falling over in the market?"

"Oh, I'm sure it was nothing. Nerves. Anxiety. I haven't had an episode since." Dani quickly brushed off the question, raking her fingers through the wet sand.

"Are you afraid of doctors?" Red remembered something that Peter had once said about his ex-wife's hypochondria.

"Not doctors," Dani clarified. "Diagnosis." She punctuated her clarification with air quotes. "I'm sure it's all tied up somehow with my unstable childhood. Completely emotional. Nothing to worry about." She looked back out at the ocean. Violet splashed and kicked at the edge of foam.

The girl wasn't tentative like her aunt, but maybe the bravado was a front. She looked so small and alone that it tugged at Red's heart. What kind of mother leaves? It left a sinking in the pit of her stomach. Red scrambled to her feet, calling out, "Last one in is a rotten egg!" Rushing into the sea, she grabbed Violet's hand. Together, they turned and braced the cold, holding their breath as a wave broke over them. They dove under, popping up on the other side. Violet's dark hair was matted to her cheeks, and she coughed, choking out water and wiping sand from her eyes. "You're okay," Red encouraged. "You're all right."

"Duck!" Violet cried, as another large wave circled overhead.

This time, when Violet popped up, she shrieked with joy. Red laughed, too, wiping sand from her eyes and saw Dani walking in the water toward them, unable to cross the wave lines. Suddenly, Dani disappeared, caught in an undertow. When she popped back up, her shirt was over her head, one large breast free from her bra. Violet pointed and howled. The three of them laughed so hard that Red's sides hurt. Violet dove back under for another ride to rescue her aunt, and Red followed, wondering who'd taught the girl to swim.

Later, at Malibu Fish Company on PCH at an outdoor table, they ate grilled mahi-mahi tacos, the women drank beer, and they all watched the sun's rosy glow toward its nightly end at the edge of the ocean. "I think I saw another dolphin," Violet spoke with quiet reverence.

Red gazed at the teenager's profile. One day, she'd be a stunner. A real beauty. That mass of dark hair and distinct features waiting to be chiseled after the loss of the baby fat. Those long curvy lashes much have come from her father, Dani's and Jack's were sparse. What would it be like to grow up without a mother *or* father?

Dani reached over and touched the back of Red's hand, interrupting her morose thoughts. "Thank you," she said.

"No problem." It was hard not to like Dani, Red thought, despite her neuroses and victimhood, the way she shoved food into her mouth without tasting, never stopping for a breath. There was also the way she watched Violet, eyes searching and motherly, the way, earlier, she'd noticed a seagull with a broken wing and fought back tears, her gestures all kindness. Still, it was hard not to compare herself, seated next to the woman Peter had chosen to marry after their relationship. Why her? Red wondered. When Dani laughed, it was infectious, not a loud guffaw like Red, or an empty trill like Sasha, shiny Sasha. As Dani sat beside her with a pretty hand on Red's capable, muscled one, trimmed nails not gelled and painted like Sasha's, but well-tended, clipped short, probably for cooking in her kitchen and that laugh, Red realized Peter must have been smitten to conquest. Women were trained at an early age by advertising, Red knew and also by their parents, boyfriends, each other. They competed and loved. For what?

Red smiled. "I can see why he loved you."

"Oh," Dani said. "I was thinking the same thing about you today."

A black dolphin crested the glassy sea, followed by a few others. Violet stood and watched the small pod roll south with hands on her heart. "This was the best day ever," she said.

Red shivered wrapping her arms around her body feeling a warmth expand like a flower inside of her chest.

SASHA

"He's a Dutch Shepherd, Border Collie brindle mix," the young guy with the braids standing at her front door said. A brown and black striped puppy whimpered inside the large crate by the courier's feet. "I can carry him in if you'd like. He's a little on the heavy side. Sixteen weeks old. He's going to be a big boy."

"I didn't order a puppy," Sasha replied and was wary that the stranger might be a fan, or worse. It was Lynn's day off. Why had she answered the door? "I think there's been a mistake. Just let me check with my husband." She started to close the door.

"It's a gift." The guy flashed a friendly smile. "From your husband."

Who gives a pregnant woman a puppy? "I'm sorry." Sasha offered a wide smile back, even though inside she was still seething, crabby with heat, uncomfortable, and nauseated. It wasn't the delivery guy's fault. She took the small blue card from his outstretched hand and opened it.

"Dear Sash," it read, in Peter's handwriting. "Something warm to keep you company until me. Love, P."

She was warm already, too warm, all the time, throwing off the covers at night, standing in the pool under the stars to cool off. A puppy wasn't a fix for Peter's lack of attention. Did he think . . . God!ess, stop, Sasha!

"He's a rescue, if that helps your decision?" The stranger held up the crate, and the puppy whimpered. "From a puppy mill in Northern California."

The puppy scratched on the carrier to be let out. She poked a finger into the crate. "Hi, little guy," she greeted. He pressed his brown nose against the metal door and whined. He had big brown eyes, and his red tongue tickled her hand. "He's wearing a purple bow," she said, surprised.

"Your favorite color, right?"

Sasha felt her heart soften. Hadn't she told Peter they needed a dog to guard the house, but also for the babies? He'd remembered. Children needed dogs. She just hadn't wanted such a young dog right now. She'd been thinking of rescuing an older one, more well-trained, one that required less work. A retired military or police dog. She'd never had a dog before. She looked up at the guy. There were beads of sweat on his upper lip. It was hot outside. The puppy whimpered again. "I'm sorry. Thank you. I'll bring him in. Thanks." She pulled a twenty out of her pocket for a tip.

Hours later, the puppy had soiled the floor, chewed the corner of her white living room sofa, eaten the leaves of a possibly toxic palm, and fallen fast asleep under the piano, refusing to reenter its crate. Exhausted, Sasha texted Lynn a photo of the pup.

SASHA: Please find it a good home. I cannot do this.

She loved Peter, but he was messing up. She felt an anger surging from her solar plexus, a feeling she'd never had with Peter. When he came home, after his birthday party, she would set him straight. This wasn't her idea of a happy marriage. Whatever he was afraid of wasn't her priority anymore. The babies were their priority. If Peter loved her and the babies, it was time for him to participate in the pregnancy. Or else.

Oh, God!ess, or else what?

Or else he could sleep somewhere else.

DANI

"Aunt Dani, get in here," Violet demanded from the living room. "The small town chef chopped off his wife's head and hid it in the restaurant freezer. For two years!"

Dani pulled the steaming popcorn bag out of the microwave. "Oh, my God. I'll be right there."

Murder had bonded them. Second only to cooking. True crime was a family thing. Jack liked yelling at the non-union actors during the serial killer simulations. "Fuckin' cracker, don't bury the next-door neighbor in your own backyard." He didn't always remember that it was reenacted.

Was it bad that she loved sharing murder with Violet? That she'd grown accustomed to those big, warm eyes hidden behind giant frames, the sharp tone and edgy retorts? Violet was smart. At night, Dani stood in Violet's doorway, watching her chest rise and fall, terrified that the phone would ring. Did it make her a terrible person for praying during OA, not for sobriety, but for Monica to stay happily far away? Violet had said the same, hadn't she?

"They found her right hand," Jack declared when Dani entered with the popcorn.

"Was he serving her to the customers?" Dani squeezed between them on the couch.

"They think he was eating her all by himself," Violet said. "She slept with his sous chef—what's a sous chef?"

"He makes soup." Jack shoved his hand into the bucket of popcorn, pulling out a fistful, kernels dropping on his flannel shirt.

"Aren't you supposed to take out your teeth first?" Violet asked.

Jack opened his mouth, showed the chewed kernels, and chomped again.

"You'll be sorry, Grandpa." She reached for the bowl and took a small handful. "Popcorn is very bad for your teeth."

This new camaraderie made Dani want to get up and dance in front of the television. "A sous chef, Violet, is second-in-command to the head chef."

"Like what I do for you in the kitchen?"

"Exactly." Dani nodded.

On TV, a sonorous male voice-over explained that the chef's wife, a much younger blonde and former pro-wrestler, had gotten tired of her husband's early morning at the docks and late night hanging with bartenders and flirty waitresses and had gotten back at him by having an affair with the handsome South African sous chef. "She did it with the sous chef in the dessert pantry." The simulated, shadowy sex scenes, thank God, weren't too steamy. The chef had walked in on them, during fellatio, chased off the chiseled South African with a knife, and then tied his wife to the chopping block, grabbed a meat saw, and quartered her like a hog while she screamed, bled out, and died.

"What's fellatio?" Violet asked.

"Ice cream." Jack shrugged. "In Italian." Emphasis on the *I*. This time, Dani didn't correct.

They feigned being squeamish, squinting their eyes, yelling words of disgust, but secretly, Dani knew they loved sharing this experience together, watching the idiot trophy wife's comeuppance. Even Jack applauded the bad actress's fake screams as, "Very convincing."

"Emmy award?" Violet asked him.

"Maybe, maybe," he said. "You're pretty enough to be an actress."

"Never! I don't want to get into drugs, or dieting."

"Good choice, Violet," he said. "Hollywood is for nut cases and alcoholics." He drained his beer, crumpled the can, and belched.

"Grandpa, gross." And then she belched, and they laughed.

It had been a while since Dani had thought about killing Steve, but the meat saw on the show inspired her. She stored away the idea in the back of her mind for blogging later when she had time again. Maybe she would once Jack's house sold, or Violet went away to summer politics camp. If there were such a thing for thirteen-year-old girls. She made a mental note to find one.

Violet wriggled, pulling a piece of clothing out between the cushions. "Gross." She held up a pair of boxers. "Laundry hamper in the hallway, hello?"

"Are you Dani?" he asked her.

"I'm Violet, your granddaughter."

He stared at her for a long moment. "Am I black?"

She shook her head, no.

"Am I a goddamn Mexican?"

Violet shook her head again.

"What are you?"

Violet shrugged. "For the hundredth millionth time, Grandpa, I'm your granddaughter."

He thought about it for a minute. "Well, nobody really knows who they are anymore. It's very mixed up."

Dani nodded. "We're all a great melting pot of homosapiens."

"Race is a construct," Violet said. "We are all part of the same race. Human.

Jack listened thoughtfully, and then he ruined it. "America is a diversity shit show. Whatever happened to assimilation? Learning fucking English. Press one for Spanish?" And he was gone. "When is my wife coming to get me?"

"In about twenty minutes." Violet gently patted the sagging, bluish-bruised elderly skin of his forearm. This kindness must have been inherited from her father's side of the family.

Jack patted her hand. "You're a good girl." Then turned his eyes back to the television. "My bets are on the Puerto Rican busboy for accomplice."

Dani and Violet agreed; the busboy seemed shady, but maybe it was the way the actor played him. The inside of Violet was all warm mush. The hard exterior was only an outer casing of protection. It was love; Dani was falling in love with Violet. She was a self-centered idiot to have spent so much time being sad about Peter and missing the first twelve years of Violet's life, leaving her to live with foster parents in-between living situations with Monica. Violet hadn't offered information, still wasn't interested in talking about her mother, and Dani hadn't brought it up.

They had finally gone to Target—mission accomplished! Violet's new friend, Charity, had come along as fashion support. Charity wore skirts that were too short, but Violet assured that it was all the rage and not a call for help.

At one point, Violet had even begrudgingly modeled a pair of jeans. The fit was a little tight across her bottom, revealing too much of her niece's budding preteen curves, so Dani had gently suggested, "I think you'd look better with the next size up."

Violet had turned around, assessing her reflection in the mirror. "Why?" she'd asked. "Am I fat?"

"Oh, God, no! You're beautiful," Dani had quickly replied, anxious to stop body issues from forming. "It's just—"

"Girl," Charity had interrupted, looking up from her phone. "You look like a badass."

The kid was a straight shooter. Dani held up her hands, busted. "I'm not ready, Violet. Those jeans show everything."

Violet had beamed and wiggled her fanny.

"I wish my butt wasn't so flat," Charity had commented, scrunching up her cute nose. "They make butt implants. But they're probably too expense."

Dani had felt her face grow warm. "Girls! Flat or squishy or hard. You have to love yourself for who you are." She'd heard the passion rising in her voice. "Trust me, people will try to tear you down. Because they don't like you. Or to get you to buy stuff. You're perfect as you are. Understood?"

Dani's impassioned speech had left the girls wide-eyed and silent. Finally, Charity had turned to Violet and said, "Your *aunt's* a badass."

The stretch jeans were left behind in the dressing room. Walking to the cosmetic's section for acne creme, Violet had moved closer into Dani and whispered, "Aunt Dani, don't worry. I'm not ready for any kind of action yet."

Violet was interested in learning math, science, and of course, politics, but wanted nothing to do with popular culture like Charity who loved pop music, hip clothing, or trending teen social media topics. Dani wondered at the trajectory of their teen girl mutual attraction. Violet would either be bullied or become the most popular eclectic genius with friends from all the cliques.

At home, they had fallen into a rhythm with mornings up early, breakfast, and driving Violet to school with Jack in tow, days spent watching Jack, cleaning, shopping, dropping him next door at Doris's when she needed to be alone, evenings of Violet's arrival home, cooking and sharing dinner followed by TV, sometimes playing Scrabble or cards.

On the weekends, they made lists of dishes to cook. Violet wanted to start with desserts, but Dani was keeping that at bay, uncertain it was the wisest choice. They watched Jack so that he didn't escape out the front door. He'd tried several times. Dani was on hiatus from temping. Jack signed over his monthly social security check for rent and groceries. They picnicked in the park down the street, went to movies, swam in the local pool. It was almost Christmas, warm, every day closer. And there wasn't any sign of Monica.

All of the parenting blogs and the book Dani had read said that modern parents were letting kids make their own life decisions, and this was causing long-term harm. The prefrontal cortex of the human brain, the area of logic and reasoning, didn't fully develop until the mid-twenties. Thus, kids, whose area of logic and reasoning wasn't yet completely developed, were being asked to make larger decisions, making emotional, instead of practical, choices, which often led to disastrous ends. A wrong choice could also lead to poor self-esteem. A vicious cycle. A mom blog Dani read, MDKE, Mom's Don't Know Everything, preached the opposite approach to parenting: give the child the freedom to make one's own decision and watch one fly. Free-range parenting was the new hip thing. It was a balancing act, Dani decided, working between two extremes. But everyone agreed the problems for kids today were social media and poor parenting.

Dani and Violet struck a deal: Violet was given free access to her phone as long as her aunt was given free access to check it at any time. After a few checks, all Dani discovered were political podcasts, NY Times recipes, and Instagram photos of puppies and Charity pouting. Thirteen was the age, MDKE said, to stay alert. Be a bear, or a police chief. The opposite of free range.

This was the hardest time for teenage girls, and Violet had enough strikes against her in the fucked up genetic categories: alcohol, drugs, sex, food. "The talk" was coming, but it wasn't yet time. Violet hadn't discussed boys specifically, but she had mentioned that the "not-guilty" Puerto Rican busboy from the show was cute. Did Charity have a boyfriend? Charity was probably trying to get a boyfriend. Those legs. Teenage girls saw a gynecologist at the onset of menses. Violet hadn't yet had her first period. Had she? They would talk about everything. Smart Violet deserved all the good Dani could give her and more.

Jack's house hadn't sold yet. It needed too much work: new toilets, windows, paint, pipes, and a roof. Basically, it was a tear down. He hadn't saved enough money to do repairs. Dan, the House Sell Man, had lowered the price, again.

Inexplicably, none of this mattered. Dani was feeling optimistic, certain it would somehow all work out.

RED

I n a race to open Sasha's iPad before she returned with more tea, Red tripped over the puppy. It cried, and she picked it up. "Sorry, sorry, buddy," she said. It still didn't have a name. Peter was an idiot. A goddamn dog apology? Why not diamonds, or a nanny? Or a spa retreat? And why did they have to drink hot tea all day long? Sasha swore black tea would keep them young forever. Red didn't want to be young again; she just didn't want to feel old. She clicked open the iMessages app and searched the last stream of text messages between the happy couple.

GOD!ESSS: Where were you?

An hour later.

GOD!ESSS: You missed the babies' checkup. They're fine. I'm fine. In
case you still care.

Two hours later.

GOD!ESSS: We have to talk.
TRUELOVEP: At sound check. Call you later.

There it was. Trouble in paradise. Of course, Peter had missed another appointment. Hence, the puppy. The puppy which Lynn now had to find a home for. Peter clearly did not want those babies. He'd only told Sasha that lie because he'd thought she couldn't get pregnant. They hadn't expected a miracle. Her prayers were so sincere that the God!ess, or whatever, had responded. He was discarding his wife and children. At sound check? More than likely, Peter was having a beer with the band, getting high on the bus, or receiving a blowjob from a groupie behind the venue. Or all of the above.

Red quickly pulled up Sasha's browser history. There was a long list of home designer sites with décor ideas for the twins' rooms, maternity wear, nontoxic candles, local butchers, dog breeders, and The Disasters' page.

There was a photograph of Peter and Annie singing on stage, sharing the mic. Their heads were lightly touching, as they looked out at the audience. Dani had nailed it. What kind of person got so wrapped up on stage that he willingly wrecked his real life? Destroyed all who loved and supported him in search of that first high? The next "score?" Peter was addicted to the highs of new love, which usually lasted about three months, or in Red's latest case, only two weeks. But he was good at it, at new love.

It was a simple shot, probably taken by a fan or paparazzi hoping to get a backstage interview. Like a punch, a wave of nausea, a sickness passed through her mouth. Red knew that Sasha had felt that too when she'd first seen it.

Peter and Annie were sleeping together. That pig. She pulled out her cell and sent Dani a quick text. "Check out the band page."

She was scrolling down to read the latest venue review when Sasha entered carrying a tray with tea cups and saucers. "I forgot if you take raw sugar or Stevia. We should do some research on fun tequila recipes," Sasha said.

Here was an opening; Sasha was ripe for an intervention. It might not make her leave him. She was pregnant, and it was her first break. There would have to be many more. But it might get her access to his finances. Red needed to rip off the band-aid. Make it real. She started to read a music writer's review of the show aloud.

"Darkened hot room, twilight on the stage, stale smell of beer and old cigarettes, sweaty bodies packed shoulder-to-shoulder, heads moving in syncopated rhythm to the raw energy, electric sexual stylings of The Disasters with the new lead guitarist and backup singer, Annie D (short for Deville). With her talent and androgynous, taut body in black leather, reminiscent of old-school Jeff Beck, Keith Richards, and Chrissie Hynde rolled into one, Annie D ruled the stage at Clancy's on Friday night. The addition of D to the band was a flash of brilliant insight. Peter Palmieri pursued Deville for months before she agreed to tour. We are all grateful that she did. One day, music enthusiasts will regale their children with 'I saw them when' stories. Like The Stones and The Beatles, The Disasters are the new world-class band. Run. Get tickets. Before it's too late."

Red looked up. Sasha placed the teacups gently on the coffee table and then walked to her desk. In one swift motion, she cleared the desktop with the swipe of her arm.

The iPad crashed to the floor, leaving a small spider web crack in the glass.

SASHA

Lynn picked the iPad up off of the floor. "The screen is cracked. But I think it's okay."

Sasha clasped her fingers and squeezed them tightly to stop the shaking. She wanted to strangle her assistant. "Why did you read that?" Sasha asked. She tried to take a deep breath, but it caught in her throat. The heavy sinking weight of blackness—her old friend—was quickly invading the room. No, no, she would not sink down! The God!ess is light. I am filled with light. I am beautiful and loved, Sasha thought.

Lynn just stared, waiting. What did the woman want? "I'm sorry," her assistant finally said.

Sasha sat down on the edge of the couch, letting Lynn's fake apology fade into the plush white carpet. The turquoise polish on her big toe was chipped from where she'd stubbed it stepping out of the shower. She was a clumsy, fat, insecure pregnant woman who needed to schedule a pedicure.

"I know he's sleeping with Annie. I didn't need you to point out the obvious," Sasha admitted. She dropped her face into her hands, feeling the crushing, the falling, all of it tumbling down.

"You have to tell him that you know." Lynn sat down beside her on the couch. She put a warm hand on Sasha's back. Slowly, she rubbed a small circle between Sasha's tight shoulder blades. It felt irritating.

Sasha was hyper-aware of Lynn's proximity, the scent of lavender shampoo, the tingling sensation of fingers in her hair. "Can you please *not* do that?" Sasha asked. She moved away to the edge of the sofa.

Lynn squared her shoulders back. "Sasha, I'm on your side."

She felt sick. He needed her, but she was too far away to help. "You don't know him. He has problems. Real struggles. But he loves me," she said, trying to calm her shaky voice. "We all have problems."

"We all do have problems. It's just that . . . ." Lynn paused, like she was considering how to say something. Sasha didn't like people who calculated their words.

"What?"

"I have been working here for a few weeks. And all I see is a wife who loves her husband, who takes care of him, who supports his dreams. And I just don't think you get the respect that you deserve. There." Lynn stood. "I've said it. You can fire me if you like."

The voice of reason. "I'm not going to fire you. But I'm not going to confront my husband over the phone. I have to wait until he's home."

"Well, until then," Lynn said, "you have to take care of yourself."

"I am." Sasha felt her defensiveness rise again. "I'm doing the best I can."

"I mean real life care. For you and the babies' future." Lynn started pacing in front of the coffee table. "For starters, as his wife, you should have access to the money. All of the financial accounts. Is your name even on the deed of this house? Why isn't it on the stock portfolio? You're married. Sasha, you're really good with money."

Sasha sat back, startled by the confrontation. It wasn't the answer she'd expected. Was her name on the deed of the house? Oh my God. Could Annie move in?

Lynn continued, "Demand access." Her voice was heated now. Her pale fists clenched so tightly that the edges were blood red. "Sasha, wake up! You have no idea how many women I've seen financially ruined because they trusted their husbands to handle the money."

She was right. Lynn had her back. "I don't know why I never bothered. I guess I was busy with the studio, the house. He kept telling me he'd handle it. I'll call our accountant and rectify that." Her mind was spinning.

"You're good with money, Sasha!" Lynn was suddenly excited. "There's no reason you shouldn't have access to the stock accounts. The whole portfolio. You helped make that money."

She had helped make that money. "You're right. My mother told me to do it months ago," Sasha said and remembered with embarrassment her mother's pleas. "I don't have any excuse, except that I felt like I couldn't push. I mean, I have the money from the studio. I'm not touring." She was a Pollyanna, gullible maybe, but she wasn't an idiot. She knew the truth of Peter. He couldn't write music. She hadn't minded helping, guiding, and supporting. "Peter helped me create God!ess studio. He wouldn't hurt me like that. But you're right. I'll take care of the accounts."

"Good. Show him that you won't be made less."

Peter didn't think Sasha was less. He just didn't think. Lynn didn't know the depth of their relationship.

"You need to call the broker now. Don't even tell Peter. He didn't bother to tell you. Do you know where we can find a copy of the deed to the house? I'll bet it isn't in your name. After everything you did to make this home beautiful. Unbelievable." Lynn's voice was raw with anger. "The man is unbelievable."

Sasha couldn't allow her assistant to continue. It wasn't the truth of their marriage. Instead, it was of love, created by the God!ess. Their union had made a miracle. "Lynn, stop!" she said sternly. She held up a hand. "I know my husband better than you. Unless you're also having an affair with him." Lynn's face flushed scarlet under her freckles. "He has demons," Sasha continued. Peter's weakness wasn't any of Lynn's business. "I will take care of it." Why didn't she feel certain? "I know him in my heart. Annie means nothing to Peter." She wiped her wet cheeks with a sleeve. She should have had phone sex with him after his gig in Cleveland, but she'd been too tired lately; the babies were wearing her out. Plus, he hadn't wanted to talk to the babies, which had made her angry.

On the road, Peter was lonely, filled with anxiety before he played; onstage, the adulation of screaming fans created a sexual electric high that he needed to release and not just with alcohol and drugs.

Tonight, he was in Indianapolis, and then the Disasters had two travel days until they performed in Raleigh. He needed her now. Sasha would unwind him back to normal, back to her Peter. She turned to Lynn, assuming a voice of authority, "Please book me a first-class flight to Raleigh, North Carolina this Tuesday." She knew she'd have to hide the late-stage pregnancy or she might not be allowed on the plane.

No small town, anorexic, chain-smoking electric guitar player on the backside of menopause could tear apart what the God!ess had brought together.

DANI

Tonight's meal was a secret for Dani's birthday. Violet led her through the apartment blindfolded, Jack and Doris tailing behind. When they reached the kitchen door, Violet removed the bandana.

A few colorful balloons, tied with string, floated in the air from the back of the dining chairs. The kitchen table was covered in a plastic cloth and prepped for cooking with staples like flour and sugar, utensils, and mixing bowls. A dark wicker picnic basket with a red ribbon waited in the center.

"Doris, Jack, and I created you a basket!" Violet's voice was high-pitched with excitement. "Like on *Chopped*!"

She handed Dani a white apron that featured shiny red apples. Dani laughed, tying it on. "I thought you guys were taking me out for pizza."

"Don't blame me." Jack smiled and patted Dani's shoulder unsuccessfully hiding his enthusiasm.

It made Dani feel almost excited about another birthday.

"Honey," Doris spoke softly to Jack. "You chose the marshmallows. Remember?"

Jack nodded. "I do love marshmallows. The pink ones."

"Yes." Doris took his hand.

"Guys, can I *please* finish?" Violet rolled her eyes. She grabbed an empty paper towel roll and held it up to her mouth like a microphone. She assumed a TV show host's authoritative tone. "Danielle Desi Smith, using only the ingredients in this basket and staples available in the kitchen, you have twenty minutes to create your birthday-themed appetizer. The ingredients are: bacon, barbecue sauce, beer, smoked pork chops, and pink marshmallows."

Doris and Violet giggled, elbowing each other. Was this her life now? Dani could barely contain the bliss swelling in her heart. A family in her kitchen on her birthday. OA be damned. Tonight, she would eat sugar-laden marshmallows. Violet didn't know about the program's ridiculous food restrictions. It was only one night.

"We're the judges," Violet said. "Your dish will be judged on a scale of one to ten. Since you're the only one playing."

"What do I get if I win?" Dani beamed.

"A fucking Gold Medal," Jack replied.

"Grandpa," Violet started.

"Sorry, sorry, kidding." Jack waved his hands in apology. "We got you something nice. I think."

Doris held up the kitchen timer, turning it to the twenty-minute mark. "All right, then," she said. "Ready? Set?"

"Go!" Violet yelled at the top of her lungs.

"Let's eat," Dani cried out, opening the wicker basket.

Dani grabbed an iron skillet, put it on the burner, and turned the heat on medium. Quickly, she chopped up some yellow onion and sauteed it in the pan with olive oil, placing the chops on to sear while she diced the garlic and parsley. After turning over the chops, and adding the garlic, Dani lowered the heat and covered the pan.

"Sixteen minutes," Violet bellowed.

Huffing, she grabbed another skillet, turned on the flame and laid the bacon strips side by side.

"I'm hungry," Jack grumbled. He grabbed the can of Schlitz from the basket.

"Grandpa," Violet shrieked, taking the can away. "That's a basket ingredient."

"Goddamn it, kid. I'm lost here."

Doris called out, "I'm getting you a beer, Jack."

Violet put the can back in the basket. Dani pulled out a sauce pan, set it on the stove, and turned the burner on to medium. She opened the barbecue sauce and poured it into the pan. Dani then pulled the pink marshmallows package out of the basket, ripped it open, and poured them into the sauce. She popped open the tab on the beer and slowly poured it in, stirring, waiting for the heat to boil like a dance, a happy dance.

"What are you making?" Violet asked and held up the cardboard microphone.

Dani leaned in, whispering, "A little appetizer I like to call 'Pigs in a Blanket Birthday Surprise.'"

That's when she smelled the bacon burning. "It's burning, it's burning," Violet cried out, as the smoke detector went ballistic. The kitchen quickly filled with smoke. Jack opened the back door, and Dick raced out with the smoke. Doris chased after the cat, but Dani focused on rescuing the blackened raw meat. "What will she do now?" Violet asked the imaginary audience. "Twelve minutes left! Will she make it in time?"

Dani threw out the burned meat, took the last of the uncooked bacon, laid it onto the skillet, and lowered the heat. Then she raced to the cupboard and found a can of pineapples. After opening the can, she poured some pineapple juice into the barbecue beer sauce and stirred. "This is unnerving," Dani remarked. She wiped the sweat from her brow. "Completely insane."

Dick raced back into the house, as Doris followed with a broom hot on his tail. "Everything smells delicious."

"I'm hungry." Jack chugged down the last of his beer.

"Two minutes," Violet yelled.

Dani turned the bacon strips over, grabbed several green onions, and sliced them thinly.

"Time to plate. Time to plate!" Violet cried.

"Plate, plate, plate," Jack and Doris piped in.

Dani set four small plates on the table.

"Will the pork chops be too dry?" Violet asked the imaginary camera.

Dani placed the chops on a platter and quickly carved the hot meat into thin slices. Stomach rumbling, she grabbed a piece of bacon and slowly rolled the pork slices inside, praying the overcooked bacon wouldn't crumble. After plating the sliced meat, she sprinkled green onions over the top.

"One minute! We're running out of time," Violet hollered. "Get all of the plates done. Get them done!"

"Oh, my!" Doris clutched her hands to her heart. "It's very exciting."

"Go faster, Dani, hurry, hurry," Jack yelled. "You can do it!"

Dani's heart was pounding. She wiped the sweat from her brow with the back of her sleeve. Her fingers couldn't work fast enough.

She grabbed four ramekins from the cupboard and filled each with the pink sauce, practically flinging a ramekin onto each plate.

"And five, four, three—"

Ding!

"Done!" Dani raised her hands in the air.

The three applauded, cheering.

Violet stuck the cardboard microphone in her aunt's face. "You barely made it."

Dani nodded, trying to catch her breath.

"Judges, this is going to be a tough one."

They carried their plates into the dining room and sat at the table. Dani followed, watching as Violet dipped a piece of meat into the sauce and then popped it into her mouth.

Jack stabbed a piece of pork with his fork and stuck it into his mouth.

Doris carefully sliced a small bite, daintily dipped the ends in the pink sauce, and politely nibbled it off of her fork.

Jack spit the meat out of his mouth into his palm. "Disgusting!"

This encouraged Violet to follow. Doris, ever the lady, gently raised a napkin to her mouth and spit out the food.

"Well," Doris said. "My goodness."

Dani grabbed a piece from Violet's plate, first dipping it into the gooey pink sauce before she ate it. The consistency of the sauce felt like melted bubble gum but tasted more like glue or paste. As it melted, she could feel the bits of burnt bacon flake onto her tongue. The bacon was burnt, and the pink sauce was gooey and sticky, a terrible contrast.

The three watched in fascination as Dani chewed the tough piece of pork, cooked beyond recognition. She spit it out into her napkin, laughing, "It's like eating yesterday's trash. I'm so sorry, you guys."

Violet jumped up and grabbed a rectangular-shaped wrapped present from the coffee table. "Here." She placed it in front of Dani. "We forgot to get a card."

Dani ripped the blue tissue paper away to reveal a *Chopped* recipes cookbook.

"Ah, you guys are the best," Dani said and hugged her niece. "I love this!"

"It was my idea." Violet beamed with pride. "I knew you'd like it!"

Jack added, "And Violet also made a gold medal in case the dish was any good . . . ."

"I, for one, think Dani deserves it," Doris finished. "For being such a good sport!"

The medal was a piece of cardboard painted in gold and glitter. *Chopped Champion!*

"It's perfect." Dani bit her lip to keep herself from tearing up.

They celebrated Dani's birthday dinner at an affordable favorite, Abbey's Burgers, on Colorado. Jack brought Doris, her presence always putting him at ease. Violet even laughed at one of his slightly misogynistic jokes about a priest, a rabbi, and a nun in a bar. Dani wasn't certain that the joke was age-appropriate, but any time Violet laughed, the mood was elevated; it was pure magic. They shared two slices of chocolate cake. Dani had only taken three delicious bites, letting the sweetness and flour melt on her tongue. Fuck Karyn and OA; a piece of cake wouldn't affect her sobriety. Dani deserved every sensation. It was her birthday.

After dinner, Jack went home with Doris, where he stayed some nights when he remembered her name, and Violet brushed her teeth without a fight. "Thank you for the best birthday I've ever had." Dani hugged her niece, inhaling the sweet scent of the girl's shampoo.

"I knew you'd appreciate the *Chopped* theme." Violet gently extricated herself from the tight embrace. "Happy birthday, Aunt Dani." Her big eyes were shining.

Dani wiped happy tears from her cheeks, patted Dick good night, and went into her room to read, listening to the wind pick up outside, wondering if she should get Violet a puppy for Christmas. Warmth blossomed in the center of her chest.

At three a.m., the phone rang. Dani rolled over and picked it up. Monica? Unbelievable. She turned the phone to mute and let it go to voicemail. Fuck her. Three months and she picked three a.m. the day after Dani's birthday to make contact again? Happy birthday. The phone dinged. Message left. What a bitch.

She stared at the ceiling for several minutes, knowing that she wouldn't sleep until she listened to whatever Monica had to sell.

"Dani." Monica's voice sounded nervous. "I hope you had a happy birthday." She took an audible breath and then continued, quickly stumbling over her words. "Can I? Can we, I mean, I'm sorry, can you meet me? I need to tell you something. It's important. This time, I'm ready to tell the truth." Her sister's voice broke, and the message ended.

The truth?

How could Dani have forgotten that like a cold or flu, a car careening around the corner, out of control, a tornado, a tsunami, or an earthquake, that Monica's secret sixth sense would alert her to the fact that they were almost... Yes, they were happy.

DANI: Tomorrow, 9 a.m. Vroman's Bookstore on Colorado. Don't be late. I won't wait.

SASHA

Sasha settled into her first-class seat. The attendant who'd scanned her ticket had not commented on her belly. Thank God her behind wasn't too fat yet that she couldn't. Was it safe to fly? God!ess, she prayed, it had to be. She put in earbuds and pressed play on the new link Peter had uploaded to the band page.

Was he writing his own material now? Or was someone else helping him? Her nerves gave way to rage as soon as the melody started.

My love, Peter sang, his voice slow, deep, and sexy, that far away melancholy careening joined in by piano.

Ask the sky, ask the trees, ask the dust that kicks up under the wheels of this bus, Moving down the way, ask anybody no matter where we roll. I ain't travelin' away from you.

A single violin keened.

Ask Johnny, ask Don, Elvis, and Janis, anybody on this lonesome road, girl, Traveling away but not from you.

Ask the birds singing from passing trees, the baby wailing in a car at the station,

The waitress pouring coffee, she's worked here a hundred years,

Ask any stranger you meet today out on those lonely old streets,

I'm driftin' for a time, but coming back home to you.

He'd stolen her birthday gift!

She had sent him the link to his birthday song early as a reminder of their love, of hers, and the babies with the message that she was headed out to see his show.

And that narcissist had recorded the song and released it without even so much as a thank you.

"Ladies and Gents," a hipster flight attendant with a man bun interrupted over the intercom. "The pilot has just cleared us for takeoff. Please turn off all electronic devices and make certain your seatbelts are tightly fastened as we three super sexy attendants also buckle up. Bon Voyage."

The plane slowly backed away from the gate, turning in the direction of the runway.

The panic spread in her chest. He didn't love her. He'd used her. Lynn's intuition had been dead on. Sasha tried to unbuckle her seatbelt. "Stop," she yelled, fumbling with the clasp.

Outside her window, the plane's speed increased passing loading jets and parked baggage vehicles down the runway. Sasha felt the front wheels lift off and the nose point toward the sky. They were only feet above the ground, Los Angeles not yet in the distance, as its velocity increased.

"Stop the plane," she yelled. "Stop! I need to get off!"

A male passenger dressed in a tan business suit seated across the aisle turned to the elderly woman beside him. The elderly woman leaned forward; her wrinkled face full of concern. "Honey, is everything all right?"

Sasha finally got the seatbelt unfastened. She looked out the window. They were ascending to circle over the wide blue Pacific. "I can't go to Raleigh," Sasha said, listening to the hysteria rising in her voice. "I can't go."

Suddenly, an older flight attendant was at her side. "Ma'am?" Sasha bit her lower lip to stop from quivering. "I need him to turn around and take me back to the gate. Please."

The flight attendant offered a small, impatient smile, revealing a red lipstick stain across her front teeth. "This isn't possible, ma'am. We are in flight." The scent combination of the musky perfume and floral hair gel made Sasha suddenly nauseated.

"Are you having a medical emergency?" the attendant asked.

"Yes," Sasha declared. "Yes. I am having a medical emergency!" Yes, her heart was breaking. She might be having a nervous breakdown. "Oh, God!ess." This couldn't be happening. Peter couldn't be doing this to *her*. Releasing his birthday song, having an affair, not returning phone calls. It wasn't real. Lynn was right. Lynn had been right.

Was the house in her name? Would he move Annie in?

"Is there a doctor on board?" the hipster male flight attendant requested over the plane's speaker, while the flight attendant, wearing pantyhose, of all things helped Sasha out of her seat, lying her gently onto her back in the aisle. Interested coach passengers leaned out of their seats, necks craning to get a better view of the woman in first class, clearly having a mental breakdown.

"What seems to be the problem?" an older, taut woman with beautiful salt and pepper hair asked in a commanding tone. She leaned over Sasha. "I'm a doctor. You can talk to me. What's happening?"

"My husband stole my song," Sasha sobbed. "He stole my song. And he's singing it with Annie!"

"Excuse me? What is your medical emergency?"

"He doesn't even want our babies," Sasha bawled, wiping away the tears on her cheeks. "I am alone."

"Ssh," the doctor comforted. "There now, Mommy. Let's not forget about the baby."

Sasha hiccupped. "Babies." She put her hands on her belly and started rubbing up and down. God!ess, why was this happening? I'm so sorry, my little ones, Sasha thought.

"Twins?" the elderly woman passenger across the aisle exclaimed. "How lovely." The woman stood up from her seat, her head bent slightly forward from the overhead bins, and twisted around, calling out to the interested passengers. "She's having twins everyone. Twins!"

Several people wildly applauded, shouting, "Congratulations" and "Woo-hoo!"

The hipster flight attendant barked into the plane's speakers. "Not now! She's not giving birth this minute. Everyone, relax. Back to your seats."

"You're having an anxiety attack," the doctor told Sasha in a calm tone. "Just lie here for a minute longer. Try to take deep breaths."

Sasha felt the tears leak from the corners of her eyes and slide into her hair. "God!ess, I'm a mess."

"Trust me, you're fine." The doctor squeezed Sasha's arm for comfort. "I left my husband three times when I was pregnant with our first. And once, after the birth. Those hormones can make us feel crazy."

The doctor didn't understand. Sasha slowly sat. She was alone. No. She had Lynn. And Lynn understood, she knew, somehow, exactly who Peter was.

The flight attendant and the doctor helped Sasha back on her feet while passengers lost interest, returning to their electronic devices.

Sasha wasn't going to be fine, but she wasn't going to cry again. Not on this flight. She reached into the pocket in front of her seat and pulled out the iPad. Logging onto the plane's Wi-Fi, she bought herself a return flight from Raleigh, getting her back to LAX less than twenty-four hours since she'd departed. She thought about texting Lynn to pick her up but decided against it.

She needed one night in their home, if her name was on the deed, one night before she made any decisions that would change their lives forever.

DANI

After breakfast, Dani told Violet and Jack that she had to get to a meeting, then drove to Vroman's Bookstore. She'd chosen the bookstore café as a meeting place because it had free parking. Even though she was pretty sure Monica would arrive by bus—or new boyfriend—Dani wasn't about to pay for parking on Monica's behalf. Or let her sister come to the apartment.

Violet deserved a window of time before the tornado that was Monica sailed back in to flatten them, that is if Dani ever decided to let her see Monica. She'd also left an urgent voicemail for Violet's new social worker, Anita. They needed a plan. What were Dani's rights? Monica couldn't take Violet back; she couldn't. The idea of it, the loss, stuck in Dani's throat like a scream, a pain she couldn't name.

It was cold and gray. The bookstore café's outdoor aluminum tables and chairs were empty, with the exception of one. Monica hunched, wearing a torn jean jacket and red ball cap. She jumped up when Dani approached. Dani stepped back. Reeking of cigarettes, the logo on Monica's cap read "Texas Hold 'Em," and Dani wondered if it belonged to a new boyfriend or if that was where she'd been. Her hair was dirty and stringy. There were deep circles under her eyes, but they appeared clear.

"Hey." Monica's voice was breathy with nerves. "You wanna sit here or inside?"

Dani shrugged. "I need something warm." Without offering to get her sister one, Dani went inside and ordered a large mocha with extra whipped crème and shaved chocolate. And a double chocolate chip cookie.

When Dani returned, her sister was rocking back and forth on the edge of her chair, tapping an unlit cigarette on the table top. Dani took a seat across from her sister. "Okay, shoot," she said.

Monica started nodding her head, as if convincing herself to ask for money. Or maybe she was coming down from a bad trip? "Okay, okay," Monica replied. She was fighting tears. She pulled a note out of her jacket pocket. "It's not easy. So, I wrote it out." She slid the folded paper across the table.

Dani removed the plastic lid from her drink. She stuck her tongue deep into the sweet airy cream and lapped it up. "I don't feel like reading right now." She was going to suck it down, and there wasn't anyone like Karyn to stop her. She could have one fucking hot chocolate and not destroy her life. OA was a cult, a goddamn cult. People were afraid of sugar . . . which was such a slippery slope of bullshit. Oh, my God, why had she ever gotten caught up with them? Home, home, the whipped crème felt like coming home. Sweet Jesus, what a fucking relief.

Monica could wait, Dani thought because whatever long tale she had to tell could wait. After years spent with addicts, Dani knew, the taller the story, the bigger the lie. Dani gently bent the cookie in half, then dipped a corner in the whipped crème. It wasn't too crunchy, or too soft; it had hardened slightly on the outside but still had gooey dark chocolate in the middle. Delicious.

Monica stared hard.

"What?" Dani asked, mouth full, faking a casual tone. What a bitch. Like Monica could judge anybody. Fuck her.

"You can read the note later, I guess." Monica stared at the letter.

Dani picked it up and stuffed it in the pocket of her jean jacket. "Don't you want to ask about Violet?" Dani inquired. Hearing the hard tone in her voice, she loved the feeling of sticking in the knife. For Violet, stick in the knife.

"Of course, I want to know about Violet." Monica's voice trembled.

"She got an A on her last science essay, loves murder shows, can cook pasta now. Oh, and she made me an amazing birthday gift—thanks for the card by the way—and she wants a dog for Christmas. What do you think? Am I up for another responsibility right now?" The words hit as bitterly and meanly as intended. Dani watched a tear slide down the side of her sister's pretty nose. She wanted to hurt Monica as much as Monica had hurt Violet. Yes, she wanted Monica to feel as much suffering as she'd caused interesting, weird, smart, and difficult Violet to feel. The way Violet was hard like Monica. The way she was sharp-tongued like Jack. The way she loved murder and justice and food like Dani. She took a swig of the hot, sweet liquid. My God, she'd forgotten the amazing earthy bitter taste of chocolate. "We just painted her bedroom walls purple because she said it helps with relaxation. She didn't want to at first, just in case, you know, you came back. But then we were like, 'Why wait?' Oh, we also hung fairy lights from the ceiling. I mean, she won't let me call them fairy lights, of course, because she doesn't believe in magic. She calls them sleep-enhancers," Dani continued. Her jaw felt hard, her heart just. "And she's a size five shoe now. Can you believe it?" A fist of love-filled anger stuck in the base of Dani's throat.

At any moment, she would start crying. "Can you guess the name of her best friend? No? It's Charity."

Monica leaned back in her chair and looked out at the light traffic on Colorado Boulevard. Her lip trembled, but she didn't break down. What an actress, Dani thought; with years of training, addicts were the best. She gulped down the last of her mocha, savoring the thick sweet syrup at the bottom, immediately wanting another. The corners of an abandoned newspaper on the next table fluttered in the cold breeze. It smelled like rain.

"What else? The first night, she cried herself to sleep. But not anymore. Is that what you wanted to hear?"

"Don't," Monica whispered. She clasped her pale hands, pulling them into her abdomen.

"Why did you leave her this time? Booze or meth? Oh, I got it. Let me guess, glorious new boyfriend out of prison? You don't even know which guy you were fucking is her father, do you?"

Suddenly, Monica lunged across the table and grabbed Dani's arm tightly with her small bony fingers. "Dani!" Her grip was hard, her voice as sharp as a razor. "Peter is Violet's father."

Dani ripped her arm away. "What?"

"Peter is Violet's father," Monica repeated and scooted to the edge of her chair. "I'm sorry, but it's true."

"Bullshit." Of all the low blows, this was the worst. Hurting Violet to get to Dani. "How much fucking money do I need to give you to make you go away forever?"

Monica's shoulders shook. She wrapped her arms around her body and started rocking back and forth.

"Peter hated you."

Monica's eyes turned hard. "Yes. He did."

Dani stood. The force knocked over her chair. In a flash, her hand shot out and slapped her sister across the face. Monica's palm rushed to the red spot on her cheek. "I hate you. Stay away from us."

She walked back through the bookstore and out the door to the parking lot. Her legs were wobbly climbing into the car.

Driving back home on Walnut Avenue, that ugly commercial street running parallel to the beautiful San Gabriel's, she pulled over in front of an auto body shop, put the car in park, and shoved her index finger into the back of her throat, gagging, until she puked up the mocha and cookie onto the asphalt.

Later, in the canned goods aisle of the 7-Eleven across the street from her apartment, Dani ate a box of cinnamon donuts, six, downed with a pint of whole milk. When both containers were empty, she paid her friendly cashier, Adebowale. He shook his head sadly as if in agreement that yes, he'd known that it was true.

Peter was Violet's father.

She climbed back into her car but couldn't go home and sit with Jack, yelling at the TV. Hopefully, he was still inside with Doris. It was twelve thirty. Violet wouldn't be home until after five. Charity's mom was dropping her off.

Was Peter Violet's father?

Dani sat in her car in the 7-Eleven parking lot, staring through the spotty windshield at her building. It looked miles away. The jacaranda branches practically covered the yard now. Doris hated their purple flowers' sweet scent. She'd asked the landlord to chop the beautiful tree down before it bloomed again next May. So far, he'd ignored her requests, but it wouldn't be long before she had Jack onboard complaining to the city that their landlord, Mateo Morales, wasn't a citizen, even though he'd been born in Boyle Heights and was third generation.

A few raindrops hit the windshield, but Dani didn't turn on the wipers. Of course. Violet had his eyes, the deep brown with full lashes. The beautiful skin, though hers was lighter. Thick dark hair. How had Dani missed the obvious? He had that crooked eye-tooth that made his smile inviting. Violet had that eye-tooth, that wide smile.

Her sister had slept with her husband. While Dani and Peter were separated but still married.

How would she tell Violet? Should she tell Violet?

Peter wouldn't want Violet any more than he wanted Sasha's unborn babies. Oh my God. For the past year, Dani had kept a blog about murdering Violet's father. She would delete the blog. That was the right thing to do. She should read Monica's letter.

She pulled the folded note out of the pocket of her jean jacket, sliding her thumb and index finger along the crease. What sort of amends had Monica written? Why would her sister have betrayed her in this way?

Dani turned on the radio. A slow, melancholy crescendo filled the car, and suddenly, Peter's voice sprung to life, singing a beautiful new song and making everything hurt a hundred times worse.

Ask the sky, ask the trees, ask the dust that kicks up under the wheels of this bus,

Moving down the way, ask anybody no matter where we roll. I ain't travelin' away from you.

She turned off the radio, feeling the rage take over her body. "I'm not forgiving you this time," Dani whispered. She stuffed Monica's letter back inside of her pocket, pulled out her cell, and left a voicemail for Red.

RED

With Sasha safely in the air, Red wandered freely from room to room in the house above Sunset Plaza, acutely aware of the sound of her bare feet padding across the marbled alcove, the puppy's nails clicking at her side, such a sweet, cute unwanted thing.

Should she have convinced the woman not to fly?

It was thrilling. She was close to having her hands on Peter's money. It had all happened effortlessly. How easily she'd been able to manipulate Sasha into the realization of her own worth. Because Red believed it. Sasha was the reason for the growth of Peter's fortune.

She almost skipped with excitement into the sunroom, blinds at half-mast to preserve the orchids delivered and tended monthly by a quiet young man with a ponytail. It was a beautiful room, thoughtfully created by Sasha with her former designer. For whom? Sasha wasn't on the deed to the house. Red had found it filed away in Peter's office—in his name only. Had he purchased it before marriage? She would tell Sasha when she returned from North Carolina. Just in case Peter had managed, which he probably would, to convince her out of what she knew to be true.

Red remembered the color and depth of Sasha's studio office. There wasn't anything of Sasha in this opulent mausoleum. She'd made the house beautiful for visitors. Like her body.

Poor Sasha.

Red followed the curious puppy into the giant library with its plush red sofa. "No puppy, no chew," she commanded. The tall shelves were lined with acclaimed and important literary works whose spines would never be broken.

They moved into the kitchen. She grabbed a bright red apple from the large ceramic bowl on the second island, took a big tart bite, and chased off after the puppy again. To her delight, she discovered him at the door of a wine cellar near the service entrance. She opened the door.

Wall-to-wall shelves were filled with wine bottles, waiting, resting in the cool room. Red shook her head again in disbelief. Sasha didn't even drink. She had done all of this as if instructed by a women's magazine. As if to prove Red's theory, a framed article, "How to Impress Your Guests with a High-End Wine Collection," hung hidden just inside the wine cellar. The article featured an actual graph of high to middle to low-end wines for even the snobbiest of connoisseurs.

Red pulled out bottles, examining the labels. Some wines were from California vineyards, others French (Rhone) or Italian (Tuscan), a few Australian, arranged and ordered exactly as instructed. Not a single divergence from the list. She grabbed a bottle of Screaming Eagle 2010 cabernet because the label was cool, and it cost thirty-five hundred dollars. Peter owed her at least one good bottle of wine considering how much cheap Chianti he'd brought to her house the last go around. She found a wine opener and popped the cork. She'd never spent more than twenty-nine dollars on a bottle of wine. It was time.

Red filled a giant wine glass, taking a big sip without letting it breathe. She strolled into the miraculous white living room, glass and bottle in hand, the puppy at her heels. The horizon was turning winter's pink early; its reflection in the city windows was breathtaking. Without smog, she could imagine a hint of blue sea. If Red could play the piano and write songs, looking out over that view, she'd never leave. Setting the bottle on a magazine on the glass table, she wandered over to the Steinway. Its lid was closed and covered in charts featuring a trail of half-started songs with lyrics about betrayals, breakups, and true love. Half-starts, over-written, some perfect words.

Her cell rang, and she pulled it out of her jean pocket. Dani, again? Third time in two hours. She wasn't in the mood. She needed a minute to not be needed.

She hadn't touched a keyboard since high school. Red placed her fingers on the keys and pecked out a few notes of a chart resting on the stand. It was pretty, mostly fits and starts, not yet a song. Her mother had forced Red to take piano lessons once, believing that music was part of a well-rounded education. Red was proficient but didn't have any passion or natural talent for playing, only singing, which her mother had deemed "too showy."

She reached for another chart, "Traveling Away from You." A note scrawled at the bottom, in Sasha's handwriting, read, "Happy 40th Birthday, Peter. We may travel distances apart, but never in my heart."

Red had been listening to Sasha write for a few weeks now. The song was haunting, slow and easy, desolation, open-road woeful. So much feeling created by Sasha. But would Peter ever acknowledge it, or would he release it and collect the accolades again?

Red chugged down the glass and poured another. Sasha was the band's only songwriter, the breadwinner, the woman behind the curtain of Peter's bigger fame and fortune. It all added up. That's why Peter left Dani. Sasha could write better, and she was younger and therefore willing to take a lot more abuse and make a lot more excuses for Peter's poor behavior. Dani had known that she deserved credit, whereas it appeared that Sasha never asked for it. Dani's voicemails waited, but first, more wine. And food. Red was starving.

The refrigerator was loaded with spinach, chard, kale, carrots, raspberries and tempeh, cashew butter, and chia almond treats that tasted more like dirt, every healthy option and absolutely nothing that Red could stomach on so much wine. She ordered a large sausage and mushroom pizza with garlic breadsticks from Joe's and grabbed another four thousand-dollar cab from the cellar. The puppy whined, and she carried him outside, watching the red smoggy sunset from the terrace on the second floor while he scarfed down his kibble.

After over-tipping the flirty delivery guy on Sasha's credit card, Red ate the pizza straight from the open box in the theater-like, six-rowed entertainment room with padded gold walls and too much gold engraving on the ceiling, while the puppy licked her greasy fingers. Red's favorite guilty pleasure, *The Holiday*, was in Sasha's cue.

During her favorite scene, the dinner scene in the Beverly Hills Italian restaurant between Eli Wallach (the widowed, elderly famous screenwriter) and Kate Winslet (the lovelorn, English wedding column writer) Red spoke along with the actors.: "Iris," Eli Wallach's character leaned over the two-top. "In the movies, we have leading ladies, and we have the best friend. You, I can tell, are a leading lady, but for some reason, you're behaving like the best friend."

"You're so right," Kate (and Red) said in unison. "You're supposed to be the leading lady of your own life for God's sake!"

Red finished the last cheesy slice and took the bottle upstairs, tipsy, laughing, almost slipping on the dog. It followed her, nipping at her heels into the large master bathroom with the windows opened to enjoy the night view. What if the neighbors saw her naked in the tub? She crated the whimpering pup—"Be good, I'll be back"—and slid into the bubbles that smelled like a symphony of roses. Leaning back against the cool porcelain, the room spinning a little, water too hot, thinking what strange kismet it would be if she died in Peter's elegant tub. Her hands were rough with calluses, but when was the last time she'd touched her garden? Last week, lettuce for Violet? She climbed out of the bath, wrapping a big white towel around her body. She hadn't felt the luxury of such a soft towel since leaving her parents' home. But her parents weren't rich *rich*. What would it be like to have so much money that your towels were plush, your refrigerator always stocked, and *how many* bottles of expensive lotion were lined along a marble counter? Ten. Red had never bought more than one bottle of body lotion from the grocery store or CVS if she had a coupon at a time. She cut open the end of her toothpaste tube and scraped out the last. Waste not, want not. So much waste in this house, Red thought, disgusted and yearning at the same time.

Red pulled on one of Sasha's silk white robes with the God!ess logo and weaved into the master bedroom, calmed by the muted purple and crème theme, the painting of sensual lotus flowers, and the scented candles. A giant California king waited with a million small, decorative pillows. A designer's dream. Was it Sasha's? Peter hated the look; Red was sure of it. Probably made his wife have sex in the bathroom or the closet. She put the wine glass and bottle on the nightstand and settled into the pillows against the fabric headboard, surprised by the giant flat screen hanging on the wall. Had Sasha hired a designer with no knowledge of Feng Shui? A TV in the bedroom was the end of good sex. He'd knocked her up somewhere else in the house. Red remembered the last time, the sex, against the back of her sofa, him turning her face away, and her feeling like she might be sick.

The puppy whimpered, and she dragged the crate beside the bed.

An urgent need to pee woke her several hours later. She stumbled naked, giggling, grabbing furniture toward the bathroom, a heat suddenly rising up inside of her body. And then it was too late: thousands of dollars of red wine and pepperoni splashed across Sasha's white cowhide rug. "Shit," Red cursed.

Minutes, or hours, later, the bell at the gate woke up the puppy, who started yipping until Red came to, cold and naked, lying on the floor. She looked around, disoriented. Something smelled horrible. Where the fuck was she? Crawling on her hands and knees—Christ, her mouth was dry—she came face to face with a giant lithograph of Peter and Sasha, holding hands, faced forward, grinning for the camera. "Oh, shit." The bell rang, and the puppy yipped louder. "Coming," she said, feeling the wall for a switch and flipping it on. Crimson vomit everywhere. She grabbed the robe hanging over a chair, freed the barking pup from its crate. The bell rang again. "Jesus," Red yelled into the intercom. "Come on up." She pushed the button to open the iron gates, praying for Advil and a hot cup of coffee, hoping it wasn't a crazed fan, or who? Who else would be coming today?

Following the barking puppy down the stairway to the front door, Red scooped it up in her arms and opened it wide.

Dani's face was swollen and red.

"Peter is Violet's father," Dani blurted. She crumbled into Red's arms, squishing the yapping puppy.

"Jesus Christ," Red said. "Jesus fucking Christ."

SASHA

When the Lyft arrived outside of LAX, the middle-aged driver with the kind eyes felt he had to explain first that he'd fled Iraq and loved America. "I'm going to get my citizenship. America is the greatest place in the world," he repeated. "Praise Allah for letting me come to this country."

"I'm Lebanese Armenian with some Iranian, on my mother's side," Sasha replied. She hoped to quiet him more than silence his fear. "Can we take La Cienega home instead of the 405?" She needed to keep moving, keep the car going. Her courage on the plane ride home had dissipated into dread. Think, Sasha. Remember what Peter's done to your marriage.

A year, she reminded herself, it was a year she'd spent working on the lyrics for "Traveling Away from You," perfecting the melody, making certain that each word captured her exact feeling, the emotion when they were separated, of pensive sadness, a melancholy as holy and pure as their love.

She placed both hands on her heart and pressed against her ribs to calm the rapid beating. Sasha was to Annie, as Dani was to Sasha, and so many before and after them. She laughed bitterly, and the driver looked up in the rearview mirror.

"You are lucky," he said.

She shook her head.

"It will be all right. Praise Allah." In the rearview mirror, his eyes were kind, with a sunburst of crinkles at their edges.

Sasha had a lot of things to make right. And God!ess help her, she would right the wrongs she had done to others. Make a better karma for her children. Still, she dreaded returning to the house, she was fuming over Peter's big, empty gesture, and the babies were hungry.

"Can we please stop by In-N-Out?"

DANI

"Animal Style with large fries?" The perky cashier held out a large bag. Dani passed it to Red.

"Thanks." Red pulled out a fistful of fries and shoved them into her mouth. She reeked of alcohol.

"Large coffee and chocolate shake?" Dani passed over the hot cup and put the shake in her drink holder.

Construction had stopped traffic on Sunset. She took Fountain west to Plummer Park and pulled into a spot, leaving the car on with the air running. Temperatures were supposed to rise into the mid-eighties, which was how winter happened now in California. It was a week until Christmas. Dani wanted a do-over for the last fifteen years, but there wasn't such luck. She sucked sweet, cold cream up through the straw, feeling the freeze in the back of her throat, the ache in her head, sensing Red's eyes on her. She waited desperately for the dopamine rush. "I fell off the wagon," she finally said. Red only shrugged, making her feel a little less ashamed.

"Have you ever been on Echo Park Lake?" Red asked and squeezed the last of a ketchup packet onto her burger. Her dirty red hair tucked behind her ears revealed a slender tattoo of a blue dandelion on the side of her neck. Dani hadn't noticed it before. "They have pedal boats for rent. Peter took me there once, after a big fight. I'd caught him flirting with my younger neighbor. He bought wine and cheese, a really big splurge, you know?" She closed the lettuce leaves and took a big bite, chewing with her mouth open. "We rented a boat, and he rowed us into the middle of the lake. It was late afternoon. Magic hour, Peter called it. We just sat there, silent. Watching the light fade, listening to the water lapping against the plastic boat. It was the first time he hadn't brought a guitar to make me listen to him play. It was nice and easy. We just drank wine, ate cheese, and watched the evening pink fade over Echo Park. It felt like love. I'm not excusing your sister's behavior, Dani. But he is very good at what he does." Sasha's puppy whimpered in the back seat. Red wiped ketchup from the corner of her mouth. "Know anybody who wants a dog?"

Dani thought about how much Violet wanted a dog; it was number one on her Christmas list. She'd told Dani that a wish list was stupid, but Violet had made one and posted it on the refrigerator along with Jack's yellow post-it requesting a Smith & Wesson. Dani's voice caught. "I don't know what to do," Dani said flatly.

"What did your sister want? Did she want you to tell Peter?"

"I don't think so." Dani had tried to imagine every Monica angle, from money to guilt or shame, running the gamut in her sister's crazy addict head. She realized the simplest answer was the truth. "The eighth step." Monica, with her sunken cheeks dotted in red acne, rail thin, parentless, sisterless, shaking and alone at a table in the rain, wanted to make amends. "She's sober."

"She's sober?"

"Seemed to be," Dani said. "She wanted to come clean. Pretty ironic considering my OA sponsor dumped me for refusal to do the same." She slurped the last of the shake. It wasn't as sweet as she'd hoped, but she still craved more of that sensation in the back of her mouth and ears. "She gave me a note. I'm sure it's an amends. But I'm not interested in reading her excuses or stories."

"You don't always have to be the best person in the room, Dani." Red looked out the car window. "Forgiveness is overrated."

"I once had a therapist who practiced Buddhism. She told me that families are karmically connected. Jack, Diane, Monica, and I are together throughout eternity. Working our stuff out. To get better, more enlightened or something. I don't know. I didn't go back."

"Happiness is about taking responsibility. For our pain, our shit, our goodness. I preach it but . . . ." Red sighed. "You could get a paternity test?"

She hadn't considered it. "What would that do to Violet?"

Red pulled out her cell phone. "Maybe we can do it without anyone knowing," Red replied. Dani watched her type, pushing away the desire to go back through the drive thru. "Voila!" Red turned her phone screen to face Dani. "Online paternity testing company with ninety-four percent accuracy. You really can find everything online." She scrolled, reading the information. "We'll need to get hair follicle samples from Peter and Violet. Probably the hair brush, right? Then we just mail it in and wait three to five days." Red paid for the expensive DNA service using Sasha's credit card. "She never looks at her account."

The car inched west in traffic again on Sunset Boulevard, headed for Peter's hair brush, sunlight shining on the billboards of Amazonian half-naked models cuddling in jeans, advertisements for rock tours, comedy specials, and films, while Dani's thoughts hurtled lightning speed between the what ifs and how-tos, life and death urgency. Peter couldn't take Violet away from her, could he?

Would he? What if he did? He had a lot of money. Or it might not be him. She had to learn to think more positively. Isn't that what experts encouraged? Believe in possibility. Maybe Peter wasn't Violet's father. If he was, Dani didn't have to tell anybody. They wound their way up the sharp curves lined with houses perched against the shifting sandy hillsides.

"That's it. The iron gate up on the left," Red said and tapped the entrance code into the app on her phone.

The giant gate slowly slid open. Dani held her breath to slow down her anxiety and drove up the curved asphalt between waxy, green shrubbery and palm trees, parking near a fountain in front of the California modern, steel and glass mansion she'd seen featured in the architecture magazine.

"Come on, dog." Red pulled the puppy crate out of the back seat. "The cleaning lady and gardener come tomorrow. We're on our own." She opened the crate and put the puppy on the grass to pee. It was adorable, black and brown with white spots on its big paws. Violet deserved a dog. After it was finished with its business, Red picked the puppy up in her arms, unlocked the massive front door, and stepped inside.

Dani followed and immediately froze. "It's so . . . ." Big, clean, shiny. Huge.

"White," Red finished. Her voice echoed across the tiled floor, curving up the iron railing stairway, catching in the high, domed ceiling of the vast entryway. "You get used to it."

If Violet was Peter's daughter, she could live in this house. Would she walk around in amazement, up and down the curved staircase? Would she play the grand piano, while gazing through the big living room windows at the city below, her eyes reaching the thin, blue horizon of the coastline? Would she luxuriate in an overstuffed chair in the sunroom while reading each book in the mahogany library, marveling at the contemporary furniture so well-made and beautiful?

Would she wonder at her good fortune, afraid it might change at any time, feeling like an imposter, a pauper in the play? Or would she adapt and turn into another bratty private school celebrity's kid? No. That wasn't Violet. She didn't care about shiny things, but she did want her own bathroom. Would Peter even want her?

Dani rubbed the center of her rib cage trying to ease the sharp pain in her heart.

Leaving Red inside, Dani stepped onto the back veranda, shading her eyes from the sun. The tiles of the infinity pool were so blue that the water shaded indigo. She walked over and dipped her fingertips, warm but not too warm. Perfect. "Violet would go crazy for this spa jacuzzi," Dani observed. And then there was the miniature golf course with a steaming, warm stream that meandered down the hill. She gazed at the cement path up the back hill enveloped by fragrant lavender bushes. Near the top, a wide wooden deck offered lounge chairs under an umbrella, like the sundeck of a European hotel.

Dani turned and followed Red and the scampering puppy through another wide door and was stopped cold by the sunlit kitchen. Light gray hardwood floors spread out... hardwood floors spread out toward white walls and wide windows; the room revealed a slanted, open, high-beamed ceiling, with three sparkling crystal chandeliers hanging and two center islands with marble countertops. One had a deep tub sink for cleaning large pots; the other counter was surrounded by high-backed acrylic stools where Violet's friends could drink sparkling juice or diet soda while the chef cooked on the six-burner Viking stove, with supplies from a Subzero side-by-size freezer and a wall rack of stylishly-arranged copper pots. The kitchen was efficient, beautiful, and perfectly white with hints of color in the green apples in a clear bowl, like watercolor sketches of food. The placement of a single crystal vase with a white rose on a small white table was perfection. Violet could lose hours in this kitchen baking and concocting.

"And Sasha uses this room to make smoothies." Red slid open a frosted glass door. An overhead light illuminated a well-organized pantry, shelves neatly packed with canned goods, clear canisters arranged by height and labeled with ingredients like flour and sugar, nuts and crackers.

"How much food could two people need?" Dani questioned.

"There's another huge freezer in the garage. Filled with the meat."

During the past few weeks, she'd cooked on the wobbly, old gas stove in her apartment's cramped galley kitchen, bumping into Violet or yelling back at Jack, unable to open the dishwasher and refrigerator at the same time, overwhelmed maybe, busy or tired, but cooking there with Violet had made it feel like living in a home for the first time. The butcher block on wheels had to be rolled in from the dining area, the freezer had to be defrosted the old-fashioned way—with a knife and steaming water. Feral cats cried at the back door in the morning and evening to be fed, while Dick hissed and tried to get out. The smell of Dick's stinky canned food, combined with Jack's burned toast and Dani's coffee—even all that—had been pleasant. Violet's haphazard stacks of sugary cereal boxes on top of the refrigerator were comforting. Dani's apartment had become a home with a calendar that featured puppy photographs hanging on the side cabinet. It was a reminder from Violet so that Dani wouldn't forget important school dates or birthdays.

"At first, this house made me envious. Even though I know the truth about ridiculous wealth," Red said, "it's beautiful, but it doesn't pass for life's richer experiences. Who cares what your house looks like when you're unhappy living in it?"

Standing in Sasha's kitchen, the strange mix of feelings weren't what Dani had imagined on the drive there. All she wanted was to be home. To be with Violet.

Dani followed Red up a wide back staircase. "Let's just get the sample and get out of here." What if someone discovered the woman who wrote the blog about killing her ex-husband in his house, uninvited? There would be a restraining order. Dani might get arrested. "Where's the master bathroom?" Her eyes darted back and forth in escape, anxious to get the fuck out of his house and back to her own, coming to her senses. She followed Red down a long corridor and into Peter and Sasha's bedroom.

The huge master suite included a sitting area, a fireplace, and a large bed of white linen and pillows. The walls displayed several still life drawings and one floor-to-ceiling, black-and-white photograph of Sasha, naked, artfully lit. No wonder he married her, Dani groaned. She was a masterpiece.

Red strode across the hardwood floor. "Step around the rug there. Sorry." She pointed to a beautiful crème and brown cowhide splashed in pink and, oh God, vomit? Not from the dog.

Dani carefully made her way around the mess, covering her nose from the putrid smell. "You might want to take that to a dry cleaner."

Red disappeared through a frosted glass door, then returned, a large hair brush in her hand.

Dani's stomach flipped a little. She took the brush. "Thank you." Forcing herself not to look at the mass of dark hair meshed in the boar bristles, she stuffed it in her purse hoping it held the answer.

Red walked out of the room. "Where in the hell is the puppy? Dog!"

Dani lingered for a moment, staring at the California king bed, its mound of soft, white pillows. It was surreal, standing in his life again, feeling nothing for him, no loss, only anger and worry, worried for Violet.

"Jesus," she heard Red cry.

Dani raced out of the master bedroom and into the laundry room.

There sat Sasha, pregnant, wearing only a bra and underwear, semi-cross-legged on the floor. Her pretty face was covered in tears. And ketchup.

"Holy shit." Red dropped to her knees.

Dani stood, frozen, in the doorway.

Sasha looked up, registering Dani's presence. "How did *she* get into my house?" She pointed at Dani. "That's Peter's crazy ex . . . ."

Red cut her off. "It's Dani. It's okay." She helped Sasha to her feet, the puppy nipping at their ankles.

Sasha looked from Red to Dani and back to Red again. "Lynn?" she asked, shaking her head in confusion.

Red glanced to Dani and then back to Sasha.

"I'm not here to hurt you," Dani said.

"What is she *doing* here?" Sasha demanded. Her face and neck turned bright red.

"We're friends," Red finally said.

"You're *what*? What's going on? I don't understand."

This was the last thing that Dani needed right now.

"Let's go downstairs to the kitchen, Sasha," Red said, in a soothing tone. "And we'll tell you the whole story."

Sasha growled, lunging toward Dani like a cornered bull. She placed her hands flat on Dani's chest and shoved. Dani fell to the floor.

"Sasha, no!" Red chased her toward the master bedroom.

Dani scrambled to her feet. The puppy was barking its crazy head off. She ran for the stairs, to get the fuck out of the house, and was halfway down when she realized it was too late. She couldn't run away.

Dani found Red, foot wedged between the master bedroom doors.

"I'm calling the police," Sasha screamed. She stomped on Red's foot. "Get out!"

Red yelped, pulling her foot back. Sasha was tougher than she looked.

Sasha slammed the sliding doors closed. Dani heard the lock click into place. "We need to leave," she yelled at Red. "Now!" But her legs were frozen.

Red knocked on the door. Her voice was calm. "Sash, think about the babies." How she managed to keep her cool, Dani had no idea.

"The police will be here in five minutes." Sasha's threat didn't sound convincing. "Don't you talk about my babies." Was she crying?

"I know you're confused. Give me a chance to explain," Red said and used her finest talk-the-patient-off-the-ledge voice. "Peter hurt me, too."

Silence. Dani shrugged, but Red put a finger to her lips. Dani took a breath. Her hands were balled into tight fists. She released them, shaking her fingers, and started to pace.

Red held up her hand. Dani heard the click of the lock, and then the doors slowly slid open.

"Who *are* you?" Sasha asked Red.

SASHA

"What are you saying?" Sasha heard the hysteria in her voice. Lynn helped her squeeze her belly into the kitchen nook, whispering, "Ssh, Ssh, it's going to be okay," like *Sasha* was the mental patient. Lynn wasn't Lynn. She wasn't her friend. Her name was Red. The redhead Peter had fucked a long time ago, and apparently, had recently fucked over again. Emiko had recognized her correctly.

Lynn was sorry. No, Red said she was sorry, *very sorry*, with a troubled look in her eye. Sasha needed to call the police. What type of person would pose as a personal assistant just to get back at an ex-boyfriend? The woman was decorating the babies' room. Oh God, had she taken a Jacuzzi in the master bathroom? Thank God, she hadn't tried to hurt the babies. Thank God, she hadn't hurt the puppy. She was mentally ill and had brought Dani into their house. Dani: the woman who wrote about killing Peter.

"I want you out of my house," Sasha said. Her thoughts were trampling like wild elephants all over the place. What did they want? How could she get them to leave? Why had she come home? Did they really want to *help* her?

Sasha shut her eyes to block out their faces. She felt the racing blood in her ears. Breathe, breathe. She took small sips of air as if through a straw, exhaling hard in a burst. Anxiety, fear, panic. Deep inhale, Sasha, push it out. Almost like giving birth. Don't give birth. Not now.

The puppy cried out from its crate in the living room.

Wasn't Lynn supposed to have found it a home? Red. Her name was Red.

God!ess, help me, she prayed, trying to remember where she'd left her cell phone. 911. She opened her eyes and looked across the kitchen to the yellow panic button on the alarm pad. She would run out the back door, down the hill, to the neighbor's house.

Peter's ex-wife's gaze followed Sasha's to the panic button, then returned to Sasha.

Sasha forced herself to glare back at her and to look straight into her hazel eyes. Dani responded with a furrowed brow, her sad eyes puffy as if from crying.

"We're not here to hurt you," Dani said. "I promise, Sasha."

"*You* promise me?" Sasha snarled. "I've read your blog."

Dani averted her eyes.

"Sash," Red said. "How about some tea?"

"You are trespassing. There are security cameras." She didn't even sound convincing to herself. She was alone. They knew it.

Lynn/Red, quickly pulled her phone out of her pocket, unlocked it, and dialed 911. She handed the phone to Sasha, who stared first at Red and then at Dani while it rang. And rang. Dani's face was the perfect shape of a heart. Feminine. Sasha felt like she might be sick. *What you have done to one, will be done to you one day.* God!ess!

"911, what is the nature of your emergency?" a sturdy female voice asked.

Sasha hung up. "I want you both to leave." She slid awkwardly, belly-first, out of the nook. The puppy barked and yipped. "Be quiet," Sasha snapped. She handed Red her phone back, turned, and left the kitchen.

Dani followed at her side through the house, talking still talking, toward the front door. "I'm very sorry that I came into your home uninvited, Sasha." Her voice sounded sincere, warm. "I'm sorry that we scared you. We thought you'd be gone. I had some really disturbing news that might involve Peter . . . ."

"Is Peter all right?" Sasha stopped in the front hallway, feeling her heart quicken again.

Dani bit her lower lip. She was about to answer when Red interrupted, touching Sasha's arm. "He's fine."

"What disturbing news?" Sasha asked, the pitch of her voice rising too high again.

"That he may have cheated on me with someone besides you." Dani stared directly into Sasha's eyes. "Someone I loved."

Sasha bowed her head, feeling the tip of the fiery arrow through the center of her chest. A clean, clear hit. Because Sasha had procrastinated, hadn't known how to apologize to Dani, hadn't reached out, even though she'd written several unsent apology emails, unsent texts, hadn't wanted to admit that she had ruined another person's happiness, the God!ess had brought the mountain to Muhammad. "I am deeply ashamed for everything that we did. That I did," Sasha finally replied.

"Good," Dani said. "I don't forgive you. Forgiveness is overrated."

Was it overrated? Is that where the unhappiness in her heart was bred, from her behavior toward another woman? "I should have apologized a long time ago. You didn't deserve it. And I don't expect your forgiveness. I am sorry. I wish you only happiness."

"I don't need your prayers, Sasha," Dani replied. "Just be a better human."

Lynn/Red, looked from Dani to Sasha, shaking her head, as she said, "I can't believe this is happening."

"Fuck you." Sasha turned away toward the foyer. The two women followed in obedient silence. When they reached the front doors, Sasha opened one and turned back to Red. "I am blocking you on my phone and changing all the passwords on my accounts. Now. Give me your key."

Sasha knew that people thought she was just another new age LA hipster in yoga pants working an image. Deep inside, she'd known they were right. God!ess had been an attempt to change that, use their money to do something good, ground herself and help others. What did sending light to her third eye matter if she didn't stop to consider her actions?

The iron gate slowly closed as the old Corolla's taillights turned the corner, leaving the midday street empty and quiet. A small breeze rustled the palm fronds. Sasha shivered, looking up at the branches. With hands on her belly, she took a breath, inhaling the ocean's salty and clean scent, feeling the babies curled into each other, sending them waves of pulsing love, and exhaled, awakened to the truth. Peter was coming home next week for his birthday, but he would never belong to her again.

She went inside to find her phone and to call a locksmith. And to shut up that crying dog.

RED

Exhausted and spent, Red drove back home, up Hyperion, passing five-story stucco apartment buildings, their windows lit with colorful trees and holiday salutations. Old cars were wedged bumper-to-bumper, along with strewn bicycles, even an old Big Wheel. A homeless teenager sat on the corner with a handmade sign that read *#FuckSanta*.

At the red light, Red grabbed her cell from the passenger seat.

RED: Let's talk.

The weight of what she'd done was sinking in, and it didn't feel great. She hadn't gotten the justice she'd felt she deserved. She deserved? What about Sasha?

"Well, it's over," she reasoned with herself. "Sasha needed to know the truth."

What a mess. And a relief? Yes. Pretending had been exhausting.

Red squeezed into a parking space across the street from her darkened little house. She looked at her cell again. No replies.

RED: Are you okay? Call me when you get the paternity results. I am here for you.

With Lynn fired, would Sasha see the credit card bill now? Would Sasha connect the DNA text dots? She was bright. Poor Sasha. What had Red done?

The cat raced down the walk, beating her to the front door. "Cold, buddy?" It slid in figure eights around her legs, nearly tripping her. She flipped on the lights. The cat mewed again. "Sorry, I know, sorry, buddy." The house was chilly. She shivered, picking up the mail dropped through the slot in the door and made her way into the kitchen.

Car payment overdue, phone and credit card pink notices, KCRW radio renewal subscriptions, *Gardening Monthly*. She needed to call the clinic. Get back into rotation. See patients. Clear her head.

Tossing the bills on the kitchen counter, she hunted for a clean glass, but the cupboard was empty. After rinsing one in the sink, she poured the last red wine from a bottle of Cab.

She carried the wine glass into the dark bedroom, flipped on the light, and saw her unmade bed, dirty clothes strewn across the floor, dry-crusted, half-eaten toast on dirty plates, empty to-go containers, two half-filled wine glasses.

"Enough." She set her wine glass down on the dresser. "It's time you pulled yourself together." She started picking the dirty clothes up from the floor.

DANI

It was the last day of school before holiday break. Dani waited in her car, idling in the pick-up line.

She had barely slept since seeing Monica. She was running on fear and anxiety fumes. She kept waiting for the phone to ring with more bad news. Please, she prayed, don't let anything else happen before Christmas.

They deserved one good Christmas.

The school doors opened, spilling half-grown, awkward, and loud kids from the building, racing across the lawn in every direction.

Dani spotted Violet wearing that silly, oversized purple shirt she loved, running down the front steps, holding hands with her friend, Charity. Wasn't that girl chilly in her short skirt and midriff top? Thank God Violet didn't want to dress like that.

"Hey." Violet climbed into the backseat out of breath. "Can Charity come over to help us make the Christmas cookies? Her mom said it's okay."

Charity climbed into the backseat. "Hey, D," she said, like they were on a first-vowel basis. It was a bit much.

Dani turned around to face them. "C," she replied. Wait, was Violet wearing makeup? The dark smudges around her eyes made her look like a raccoon. Charity's blonde head was bent over texting.

"What did your mom really say?" Dani asked Charity, eyes boring into Violet's. Why would Violet lie?

Charity shrugged. "She hasn't texted me back yet, but I'm sure it's fine."

"Buckle up, ladies. Hey, Violet, who did your eye makeup?" Dani tried to sound casual as the car inched slowly forward in the long line.

"Moi," Charity bragged. "Smokey eyes. It's the thing. Sexy. Do you like it?"

Sexy? Not today with this shit. "It's very, um, smokey."

"*Sexy*," Violet repeated in twang. "Oh, my God, oh my God, Aunt Dani," Violet interjected, words rushing out. "Mr. Wilson, our science teacher, was sent home today. He wore a t-shirt . . . ."

"That had a polar bear giving us the middle finger," Charity finished, sticking up her middle finger for emphasis.

The girls burst out giggling, then quieted. "Because you know, even the coral reef will be gone by twenty-fifty," Violet said.

Charity's phone dinged. "My mom says *yes*," she announced. "Told ya."

"Yes!" The girls high-fived.

They were pre-teen girls, Dani reminded herself. Nothing bad was happening with Violet. It was smokey eye makeup. Nothing else.

Witnessing Sasha on the floor of her laundry room, covered in hamburger shame and sorrow, had made one decision crystal clear: Peter ruined every woman who came into his life.

How could Violet be saved? The thing about love, truly loving another human, Dani realized, without need or agenda, is that it sneaks up on a person. Dani had been getting by, trying to make it all work, keeping everyone alive, crossing her t's and dotting her i's, figuring out algebra for Chrissakes, but then Monica's revelation had revealed something deeper.

How could Violet be saved?

Finally, cleared by the elderly school crossing guard, Dani exited the school driveway and merged with the other parents, caretakers, and nannies driving chatty or sullen teenagers.

She would teach Violet and Charity how to make sugar cookie dough the old-fashioned way, rolling it out on wax paper, using the holiday cookie cutters to cut trees, Santas, and hearts.

After the baked cookies had cooled, they would decorate them with buttercream frosting dyed green and red, sprinkles and red hearts, licking the delicious remains from the bowls. She would let them eat cookies until they fell into sugar comas, and Dani returned the probably troubled Charity to her own parents.

Maybe she needed to encourage Violet to make more friends? Whatever had happened to the Libertarians? Librarians?

"Last day of school! Woo-hoo. How does it feel?" she asked the girls, feigning excitement.

Her niece shrugged, "Good."

"*Sexy,*" Charity replied, drawing out the word.

Dani was startled. Oh my God, didn't the girl know any other words? She longed for one big fucking doughy soft, buttery cookie covered in sugar shoved in her mouth whole. Like a sugar plum fairy, Karyn's voice appeared in her head. "We can't have just one," and "Why can't you finish your eighth step?"

The girls giggled, watching something with a laugh track on Charity's iPhone. Since when did Violet like anything but political podcasts? Monica had started drinking at their age. Charity looked like the type of girl to get Violet into trouble. The MDKE (Mother's Don't Know Everything) blog said that this was the age when friends became more influential than parents.

It had to be a good Christmas. OA be damned.

Monica and Peter and Sasha and Red could all be damned, too.

Dani wouldn't reach out, and she wasn't responding to Red's texts. Enough! There would be no decision about running the paternity test before Christmas. No reading of the amends letter from Monica. Whatever it said, Monica had waited this long to tell her story. It could wait a few more fucking days.

There were presents to be bought and wrapped, lights to be strung, old movies to be watched, and time together to be loved. *"Haul out the holly. Put up the tree before my spirit falls again,"* Dani sang with forced cheer, parking the car in the garage.

The girls jumped out of the car, racing for the back gate.

"For I've grown a little leaner. Grown a little colder. Grown a little sadder. Grown a little older. And I need a little angel sitting on my shoulder," she continued alone in the car.

"Aunt Dani," Violet yelled out. "Last one in is a rotten egg."

"Need a little Christmas now." By God, Violet was going to have the Christmas she deserved, if it was the last thing Dani did before the whole world came crashing down.

SASHA

Renee had begged Sasha to meet at the Beverly Hills Parisian Café for their annual Christmas Eve lunch. The bright red awning, cheerful string lights, and bistro tables and chairs with black-and-white, nineteen-twenties gay Paris were an affront to Sasha's sad mood. Renee was mostly in it for the notoriously handsome waitstaff. The place was packed.

Why had Sasha come? The pretense of holiday cheer made her feel like clawing someone's eyes out.

Renee lowered her sunglasses as an attractive waiter passed carrying a tower-high burger on a plate. Sasha speared a piece of frisee salad, craving something warm. "I don't *want* to plan a C-section. It's completely unnatural," Sasha said. She was more than irritated at Renee's suggestion, imagining an unsightly, thick scar, a ridge of purple above her pubic bone.

Renee's eyes widened. "My. Someone woke up on the wrong side this morning."

Sasha gritted her teeth. "Sorry."

"I'm just saying," Renee continued. "Sweetie, everyone wants a natural home birth at first. Listen to Dr. Simone. She's the best OB/GYN in Beverly Hills. Liam came out perfect and pink, and more importantly, I didn't feel a thing." She took a sip of low-calorie Chardonnay, the newest craze in LA. "Unless you'd prefer vaginal rejuvenation laser surgery to keep your husband?"

The thought of Peter inside of her vagina made Sasha want to vomit. "We want a loving, quiet home birth," Sasha replied. She desperately needed to maintain the appearance of a happy marriage, a "we" through the holidays, even though she was facing Christmas alone. Renee probably knew that Peter was having an affair. It was Hollywood. Gossip traveled faster than chlamydia.

Another handsome waiter passed their table carrying a plate with steak and fries. Sasha called out, "Excuse me! Is it too late to order fries?"

Renee stifled a gasp.

"No problem." He offered a warm, friendly smile. "You're aware they're cooked in lardon, right?"

"Delicious," Sasha said and grinned back. "Lardon away!"

Renee leaned forward and whispered, "Seriously, what in the hell is going on with you?"

Sasha glanced around the crowded room: two tables with Beverly Hills' agent types, a lone, pretty girl wearing bright orange lipstick, two elderly women, their faces taut and stretched above small salads. Where was the paparazzi? She and Peter hadn't spoken since he'd released her birthday song without a conversation, or permission, or even a thank you. He hadn't called her when she didn't show up in Raleigh as promised. Every day that passed, the chasm of grief in her chest was filled a bit more by outrage. He had used her, like the others. She would not beg. When he came home for his birthday, they would have it out.

"I'm hungry," she replied with a shrug.

"I remember pregnancy cravings," Renee laughed. "Salt and vinegar potato chips were my downfall. It took six months to get my body back. Don't give in."

Why were they friends? They didn't have anything in common. They had never discussed anything deeper than the benefits of Paleo versus blood type diets. Renee spent more time in and out of stores and plastic surgeons' offices than she spent with her only son. How could Sasha explain her feelings and fears to a person like Renee? She'd managed to construct a life in which her only trusted ally was her lying husband. She missed quick-witted, big-hearted Lynn. She missed a fake connection. "I'm lonely," Sasha finally confessed.

Renee held her gaze, as if settling an inner debate and then decided to speak. "Evan and I have been married for fifteen years." She took another sip of Chardonnay. "What I'm sharing with you is very private. Not a word of it to anyone."

Sasha nodded. "Of course." Renee's husband was a famous film director with two Oscars.

"We follow a strict marriage code. When Evan is in town, we are devoted and enjoy one another's company and our son. When Evan's away on location, we speak once a week, unless there's an emergency about Liam. There are no questions asked. We are each free to seek other sexual company, but not relationships. This is why I'm not lonely." She raised her wine glass, nodding at the older suited agent at the far table. He held up his soda and raised an eyebrow. "That handsome devil is meeting me later at the Beverly Wilshire, and I am happily married."

Renee's matter-of-fact marital advice deepened Sasha's anger. She didn't want to have an open relationship again. That had been the point of getting married. She had never enjoyed watching Peter receive oral sex from another girl, no matter how turned on she'd acted. She hated the feeling of too many bodies entwined. She'd realized the truth was that her only talent had been faking it to make Peter happy. The babies helped her to see the truth. She loved being married, the monogamy, the story of growing old and boring with another person. She let the revelation flood her body. "I'm going to tell him it's me or her," she said, feeling the heavy weight removed from her chest.

Renee gasped. "With two babies on the way? Sasha, your hormones are making you insane. You're almost thirty. What better thing is out there do you suppose? You have a successful business. A beautiful home. A sexy, famous husband. All the money in the world. And two healthy babies on the way. I couldn't imagine raising Liam without Evan's financial support and love. You don't want to be a single mother. Children need their fathers. Peter will sue for custody. Wake up and stop acting like a spoiled brat."

As if she'd been slapped, Sasha's cheeks suddenly felt hot.

The handsome waiter placed a silver cone with hot fries sprinkled with parsley and parmesan in front of her. "Will there be anything else?" He smelled like pine and sandalwood. So familiar.

He smelled like Lynn. After a moment of uncomfortable silence, Sasha grabbed the paper cone out of the silver cup, ignoring the tears running down her cheeks. "I'll need these to go," she announced.

The waiter leaned to comfort her but quickly pulled back. "I-I'll just get you a container," he said, in a quiet voice. "And your check."

Renee's blue eyes softened. "I'm sorry, but someone had to say it. We have first world problems. You're not homeless, are you?"

Sasha tightened her jaw, swallowing back her tears. She reached for Renee's wine and downed the remaining sweetness. "I'm twenty-seven," she said. "And I'm tired of playing at happiness. I deserve better."

The waiter set a compostable container on the table. "Thank you," she managed, dumping in the fries and closing the lid.

She reached for her purse, but Renee interjected, "It's on me. Try and enjoy the holidays."

Sasha stood. "Renee, we have been starving ourselves for society expectations all of our lives." She straightened her shoulders. "My children won't have to live with that sickness. I also hope Liam will be spared."

Renee's stretched face blanched white.

Stepping out onto Rodeo, a cool breeze caressed Sasha's exposed legs. One step forward at a time, she coached herself. God!ess, help me find my car in the parking garage. God!ess, keep me from screaming in public. Thank God!ess, she spotted the BMW.

"Excuse me?" a young man's voice called out. "Excuse me?"

She turned to see the handsome waiter racing toward her with the box of fries. "It seemed like you really needed these," he said when he reached her. His green eyes were filled with warmth.

She took the box from his outstretched hand, noticing the peace symbol tattooed on his inner wrist. "That was very kind of you."

He nodded. He had an open face and curly waves of short chestnut hair. He looked like an outdoorsy kind of guy. She caught herself wondering if he gardened or hiked.

"It's just," she started, feeling the truth wanting to push out again. "It's almost Christmas, and my husband—"

"I'm a big fan of The Disasters," he interrupted.

Her heart dropped a little at the revelation—just another fan—and she quickly clicked the key to unlock the car.

"I have a demo, a few tracks, I've written . . . ."

"I write the songs," Sasha interjected. Anger rose in her throat. She opened the driver's door. "I get help on the melody from Enrique, the drummer. But *I* write the lyrics. *All* of them. Peter is a hack."

"You write them? Really? Wow, I had no idea. You're . . . ."

"An idiot." She awkwardly slid her belly behind the steering wheel.

"You're a seriously good songwriter." The waiter held onto her car door, leaning in slightly. There was that smell of sandalwood and pine again. "Did you even write La Brea Heartache? *Passing bars and bodega promises, nobody stops for miracles in the Miracle Mile,*" His voice captured her melancholy. "It's one of my favorites."

Sasha nodded, feeling her tensed muscles relax. "I wrote all of them except 'Crazy Boy, Crazy Girl, Love.' Dani, his ex, wrote that."

"Wow. But he gets all the credit?"

"Yep."

"You should start your own band," he said. "Stand back and let karma find him." He closed her car door and tapped on the roof like she was good to go.

It was as if the God!ess had spoken herself.

DANI

Christmas arrived. And it was a balmy seventy degrees. They made deli turkey cranberry sandwiches because it was too hot to cook and ate them, picnic style, in the backyard while opening presents.

Violet ripped away the red and green tissue paper and grinned, pulling out the cat harness and leash. "Thank you, Aunt D!"

"You're welcome, V. I'm sorry it wasn't a dog. Now, stop texting me cat training videos."

"Mission accomplished!"

"That's got to be the dumbest thing I've ever heard of," Jack said and mussed Violet's hair with an affectionate palm. "Don't come cryin' to me when you're dripping with blood."

"Don't be so pessimistic, Grandpa," she said. "It doesn't look good on you."

Doris stifled a laugh.

Jack shook his head. "Well, if anybody can train that cat, I guess you can, smarty pants."

"I am very good with animals." Violet puffed out her small chest. "And one day, when I'm grown up, I will get my own dog."

Doris opened the gift from Dani and Violet: tea towels embroidered with clichés like *April Showers Bring May Flowers* and *Birds of a Feather Flock Together*, cooing as if they'd given her a gold bracelet, as Jack had earlier in the morning, alone in her apartment. Was it the bloom of love, or did Doris look younger? Dani wondered if true love did that to people. Opened them up like flowers. Jack certainly smiled more than he had before moving to Pasadena.

It didn't hurt that Doris had given him the gift he coveted, the new Smith & Wesson, against Dani's pleas. He held the revolver up again, shoulder height, aiming it at the bare fig tree. "A Colt Cobra, 1959 38 Special. Jack Ruby used this gun to kill Lee Harvey Oswald. Bang! Bang!" Jack said.

"Grandpa, it's bad karma to talk about shooting people," Violet scolded. "And really bad to take a life."

"It's okay to shoot the bad guy. Tell 'em your grandpa says so."

"An eye for an eye until we all go blind," Violet quoted. "Charity's mom has that bumper sticker."

"Charity?" Doris sighed. "Her mother needs to open her own eyes. That girl is trouble waiting to happen."

Dani had begged, admonished, and instructed Doris not to purchase the gun. Doris had considered that point of view "too politically correct" (old people with dementia and guns, really?) and even added a box of ammunition for home protection.

Where could Dani hide the bullets?

Jack leaned over and gave Doris a smack on the lips. She pressed her hands against his freshly shaven cheeks.

"Gross," Violet protested. "Get a room."

Violet gave Dani a book of personalized coupons, with *I promise to's* for cleaning, changing the litter box, and even not cussing out Jack. Every gesture, sigh, breath, giggle of Violet's, felt precious. Dani couldn't stop staring at the way the light sparkled red on the ends of her hair. Just like Peter's.

"Jesus," Violet scowled. "Take a picture. It'll last longer."

Dani fought back tears, grateful for her sunglasses. She held up her phone and took a photo. "Christmas always makes me weepy," she reflected.

"Just Christmas?" Jack snorted.

Doris added, "Americans are so sentimental. It's really quite off-putting."

"Oh, yeah, you're totally calm, Doris," Violet said. "You had a full-on drama the other day when that bee flew into your apartment."

Color rose in Doris' overly rouged pink cheeks. "I will have you know, missy, that having never been stung by a bee—and it was a wasp, I'll mind you to remember—there's a chance I could be allergic. How would you have felt if I'd gone into anaphylactic shock?"

Jack clapped his hands and laughed. "I love it when my women fight."

"Grandpa, we're not your women. You don't own us."

"Nineteen fifty-two called, Jack," Dani sang. "It wants you back."

"I, for one, would love to go back to the days before all this equality crap. News flash: not everybody is equal. Men are physically stronger than women. And some people are born just dumb ass stupid, shit for brains . . ." Jack droned on.

Doris placed a hand on Jack's arm. "*I* am your woman," she said, which made Dani tear up again. He quieted. Was it all the sugar that made her feel like she was wading up to her ankles in a warm tide pool with the waters rising?

"Yuck. Can I please be excused now?" Violet asked.

"Of course."

"Thanks, everybody, for the great Christmas!" Scrambling to her feet, Violet grabbed the cat harness, yelling, "Dick!" and ran into the house.

Whenever Monica had complained about how hard it was to be Violet's mother, Dani had thought her sister meant that Violet was rough and difficult to love, like Monica. But she wasn't. Violet was witty, emotional, kind, and street smart. She was the most lovable girl in the world. Some days she wanted to be a marine biologist, others a Supreme Court Justice. Today, she was talking about karma and quoting Gandhi. As time passed, Dani's feelings only deepened. When Monica had asked Dani to take care of Violet that day at Vroman's, to keep her from Peter, Dani had resisted. Now, she understood what Monica couldn't explain. Loving Violet was bigger than a wave. It was a tsunami. If you weren't strong enough, it knocked you over. Love did that, loving someone more than yourself. Jack's edges were softened. Dani hadn't posted to the blog since. In giving her daughter to Dani, thinking her capable of such responsibility, Monica had revealed the best part of herself.

Monica was a good mother.

Goddamn it. Dani realized she would have to read the letter.

Tomorrow, after the high of Christmas passed.

RED

The snow blanketed the desert floor, temperatures down in the teens. Red snuggled deeper into the down bag and listened to the wind pick up through the canyon. Joshua Tree was best during winter months when the paw prints of rabbits, foxes, coyotes, and cougars dotted the white and brown expanse, and park vacationers were scarce. Only stationed marines and local artists remained tucked safely inside their warm homes, making dinners or writing short stories.

Since her last visit, Matt's boyfriend, Carlos, had finished building the skeleton of the A-Frame hacienda—no heat or running water—on his property and invited her to join them for the holiday weekend.

Over Christmas beer and tacos, the three had discussed Red's dilemma with Sasha, her job, home, love life, etcetera. She'd twisted off another bottle cap and aimed but missed the aluminum trash can. "I'm tired of my life," Red had said.

"You're burned out," Matt pronounced. Carlos nodded in agreement. Carlos nodded at everything Matt said; they were in that new lovers' phase.

"You need to take a lover," Carlos insisted.

Red needed a life that revolved around more than herself. She had nothing: no parents, no children, no partner. All she had was a small blue house in a rapidly gentrifying area with an unnamed cat. What did she want?

She wanted to stop drinking.

Red wasn't a person who made New Year's resolutions, but she was tired.

The truth was that she'd been ignoring what moved her for so long that it was hard to tell even herself the truth. The dream had light around it, she knew and not just photosynthesis.

Healthy greens! Verte santé! Vert frais! Sasha would *love* the French name. What else might Sasha suggest for a personal chef gardening business?

Red missed driving up to the house, the smell of jasmine, the quiet, white surroundings, even the fucking tea. She missed listening to Sasha work out the notes to a song. Even her fucking annoying high-pitched voice. Sasha was talented. Sharing her talent with others from the studio to music. She welcomed new people into her life. With generosity. Could Red develop that quality? What was the mantra?

She inhaled and held the breath. I am beautiful. I love myself. The God!ess created me perfectly, Red repeated the saying in her mind. Exhaling, Red imagined her breath as little bubbles of colorful light sending out love to Sasha wherever she was.

She remembered Sasha writing the new song. "Lynn? What do you think of this?" Sasha had asked.

Red had stood in the living room doorway. Sasha, healthy and round, was seated at the piano.

"Does it sound like this," she'd asked and played a few notes, simple and clean, "or more like this?" These notes were sadder, wandering, a melody. "It should feel like longing, missing him, but also, love. You know that feeling that's just abiding? Constant?"

Red had walked to the piano. "I don't," she'd confessed.

Sasha shook her head slightly, sad. "Would you sing it for me?"

She'd placed her slender fingers on the keys and started the slow, quiet intro Red knew from memory now. She sang the words that Sasha had written for Peter's birthday. Beautiful and haunting. Abiding.

Never traveling away from you.

Why couldn't they be that for themselves?

"Oh! You have the voice of an angel!" Sasha had clasped her hands to her heart.

Red had bent over and hugged her friend, the most compassionate person she had ever met.

Red missed Sasha. Now, she wondered how the woman was doing. Had Sasha made the deposit for the vegan taco truck? Did the mariachi band know where to set up? What about the margarita stand? The puppy? Secret meat deliveries? Would she ever forgive Red? She reached for her cell.

There were no bars; it was a dead zone this far into the desert. Just as well. It was never a good idea to drink and text.

DANI

*D*ear *Dani,*
     What I'm telling you, I've needed to tell you for a long time. But I didn't know how. I know you will be mad that I didn't, but please, for Violet and me, try not to do anything. Okay? I'm tired of lying and running and using and disappointing people. I have to tell the truth to stay sober.

     It happened the night of The Disasters' first big concert, at the Hollywood Bowl. Remember, it was in July? You and Peter were separated. Eddie was supposed to come with me, but he got high and passed out. I didn't want to go alone, so Peter sent a driver. The car was a big black SUV, an Escalade maybe? I felt special being driven by someone wearing a suit and a hat. I liked it. It was really selfish to go and not tell you, but I didn't think that at the time. Mostly, I was surprised that Peter had even invited me.

     My seat was in a box, I think they call it, with two couples. They were impressed that I was related to him. They poured me the best glass of white wine I'd ever tasted.

But I didn't drink much that night, Dani. I swear. I didn't want to embarrass you. And the show was amazing, outside, under the stars, but you know that from the reviews that you burned years later in the kitchen sink. Remember when we did that? You had no idea how good that made me feel.

Peter asked me to go with him to an after-party. He didn't want to go alone. You know how he hates to be alone. And it was exciting. The party was in Hollywood. There was a line of people waiting for autographs and taking pictures. We walked right in. Everyone seemed nice. We smoked some weed, but I didn't feel too high. Not so high that I wouldn't recognize the signs. You know? I mean, I was wearing jeans and a black t-shirt, a leather jacket, boots, not even heels. My hair was in a ponytail. I don't even know if I used mascara. A couple of times, I caught Peter staring at my breasts from across the club. And it felt a little weird. I mean, I'm your sister.

The party was lame, and I was getting tired, so I asked Peter to take me home. I didn't have money for a cab, and Eddie wasn't answering his phone. Peter told the driver to drop him at the hotel first. He'd booked a room at the Chateau Marmont to party. The famous hotel that looks like a castle above Sunset? Where John Belushi died? It's so beautiful sitting on the hilltop, Dani, like an enchanted land where only princesses can visit.

Peter had a small flask with him in the car, but I only had a couple of sips. It was vodka, no big deal. When we got to the hotel, Peter said I had to come in for a drink to check out the bar. That it was really cool. The place is so private that the valet didn't even look at my face in case I was Princess Diana. I mean, not Princess Diana, she dead, but Lady Gaga maybe. Maybe the valet thought I was famous, too? It was strange. But the bar was closed, so Peter asked me up to his room. One drink, he said. I like hanging with you, he said. I remember nodding but thinking that he never really wanted to be my friend. My brain wasn't working right. Like

I was foggy. The lights were glittering like I'd dropped acid or something. I followed him into the elevator up to his room. It was a big suite. I asked if I could use the bathroom. I felt like I might get sick. That's when I realized someone must have put something in my drink.

The bathroom was so small for such a fancy place, Dani. I left a voicemail for Eddie. I texted him, too. I flushed the toilet and ran the water in the sink so that Peter would think I was using the bathroom. My lips were numb. My legs didn't work right. When I came out, I lied and said Eddie was coming to get me. Peter poured us gin in these big glasses. I hate gin. But I took it. I sat down on the couch. It was red leather. I remember that it crackled, like a dry leather jacket. Peter sat down next to me. He told me I looked really good, that he'd always thought I was pretty, that he liked skinny women with flat chests. I said it didn't seem right that he should say that. I needed to get up for work. I had a shift. Remember, that's when I was opening Mimi's at seven. I asked him if his driver could take me now. He laughed and asked why I'd lied about Eddie.

Dani, everything slowed down, you know, like in a scary dream when you're trying to scream but can't get the words out? Like I was watching it happen outside of my body. From across the room? Everything felt weird and foggy. What had I done? My arms and legs didn't work right. I didn't want to hurt his feelings, but I said that I had to go. But I'm not sure he understood because my lips weren't working. That I was sorry if he'd gotten the wrong impression, but I didn't want to sleep with him. He was still married to you. I tried to stand, but he grabbed my arm a little too tightly. He laughed, said he was sorry. But it really hurt. But he was Peter, you know? I knew him. It was just Peter pulling down his jeans and underwear. Standing there naked in this hazy kind of dream where I was falling back, the earth crackling and cracking, the ceiling spinning in circles with Peter's face too close to mine saying words, I couldn't understand the words coming out of his mouth. They were slowed down, but I heard a sucking sound, slipping and sucking, and someone crying out in the dark. Everything was dark. Like I was dying in a suite in the Chateau Marmont like John Belushi.

I wish I had.

In the morning, Peter shook me awake. I had fallen asleep on the couch. I wasn't wearing pants. He was in a bathrobe. He said he needed a shower to rinse off the stink and that his driver would take me home. And then he went into the bathroom and turned on the shower. I took the elevator down. And his driver took me home.

And I never told anyone. Keep Violet safe. Keep her well. Do whatever you can to keep her far away from Peter. I know you will. You are the best person that I have ever known, Dani.

Love, Monica

Dani stared at her sister's horrifying revelation scribbled in blue ink until the handwriting blurred into the lined paper. Silent tears fell down her cheeks. Her mind was numb.

"Dick!" Violet's voice interrupted from the living room. "Come back here!"

Dani quickly refolded the letter in her shaking hands and stashed it behind Jack's box of ammunition, hidden behind the secret candy stash in her nightstand drawer.

She grabbed a small packet of Kit Kats and tore open the wrapper. Desperate, she snapped the milk chocolate wafer in two and shoved both halves into her mouth, chewing but not swallowing. She felt oozing sweetness, nauseated, but not tasting anything. Frantic, she unwrapped another wafer, snapped it in two, and shoved in both pieces. Waxy milk chocolate melted into the super sweet vanilla. She tossed the empty wrappers on the floor as she went, unwrapping, breaking, and shoving in candy until her cheeks were filled to capacity, and the Kit Kat box was empty.

Breathing through her nostrils, Dani waited for the cocoa, flour, and sugar to melt, sucking to form a soft, sweet mound on the roof of her mouth. Slowly, she released the chemicals down the back of her throat and waited for her anxiety, her ragged breath, to calm.

There was a knock at her door. She jumped.

"Aunt D?"

Dani quickly scrapped the stuck chocolate off the roof of her mouth with her fingernails. Wiping the goo from her teeth with her tongue.

Another knock. "Can you help? Dick won't sit still."

"Hang on!" Dani heard the shaking in her voice. A sickening rage rose in her stomach. She grabbed her bathrobe from the end of the bed and vomited into the blue terrycloth. Heaving up coffee, breakfast, and Kit Kats until there wasn't anything left but bile.

She wiped her face and hands with tissues, then pulled her cell out and sent a text:

> DANI: I'm sorry. I'm so sorry, Mon. Forgive me. Please come home. We need you. We'll right this together. I love you.

And then she texted Red.

> DANI: I need to see you. Now.

She waited, staring at the screen, watching the dots form, thank God, as Red texted back.

RED: Just got back home. Come on over.

DANI: Be there in twenty minutes.

Dani stood up from the bed, squared her shoulders, and opened the bedroom door. She found Violet standing in the middle of the living room, cat harness in hand, looking up at Dick, who eyed her warily from high on the bookshelf.

"I don't get it," her niece stated with frustration. "He liked walking in it *yesterday*." She looked over to Dani, and her brown eyes widened. "What's wrong?"

Dani swallowed hard, wracking her brain for an excuse to leave. "I need to get to a meeting," she lied.

Violet's cheeks reddened, the way they did when she got upset. "What about taking Charity and me to the movies? You promised."

Shit. Shit. This was Violet's Christmas present to Charity. The fucking movie. Her mom was dropping her off soon. "I didn't forget," Dani lied again. "The meeting's just at the Presbyterian Church. I won't be long. But you and Charity have to hang out with Jack at Doris's until I get back."

Violet rolled her eyes. "We don't need a babysitter."

"You do. They're playing checkers. You like checkers."

"Fine. But I *don't* like checkers."

Dani brushed a strand of hair from her niece's face, leaned in, and kissed her on the forehead. "I love you," she said, fighting back tears. "I'll be right back."

RED

"Here." Red held out a glass of Scotch. The amber liquid rippled against the sides with her shaking hand.

Dani downed the drink and set the glass on the wooden coffee table. She leaned forward on the couch, resting her head in her hands.

Red also desperately needed a drink, but she had to stay clear-headed, of sound mind, objective, not a participant. It was crucial. Don't get emotionally involved, she reminded herself, feeling her blood boil. Keep the distance. Don't fall down the rabbit hole. Maintain a calm, supportive voice with the client. Walk Dani through this traumatic experience step by step to a resolution. Resolution? What fucking resolution? Peter had raped Monica. Later, there would be time to spill rage. Fight, kick, punch him in the face. Not now. It was Red's professional expertise Dani needed, not her blind rage.

"We have to take the letter to the police," Dani said and rubbed her puffy, red eyes.

"Statute of limitations is ten years," Red replied and kept her tone flat. "Monica would have to press charges."

"I don't know where she is." Her friend's voice verged on hysteria. "She hasn't responded to my text." She stood abruptly. "Why didn't she tell me? I would have helped her. He would be in jail . . . ."

"He was your husband," Red gently interrupted. "She kept the secret out of loyalty to you." Peter wasn't just a narcissist, a liar, and a cheat; he was also a menace, truly dangerous. "Dani, what if your sister isn't the only one?"

A look of horror crossed Dani's face. "I will kill that son of a bitch." She pulled at her hair. "I'm not waiting for Monica. I will choke him to death with my bare hands."

Red wondered if Peter was still coming home for his birthday. "When do the DNA results get back?"

"Next week." Dani pounded her fists on her thighs. She desperately needed to punch something. "Is there a Winchell's or Dunkin' Donuts around here?"

Red stood, suggesting, "How about a walk around the lake? It would do us both some good." She needed to move, or she'd scream, drink herself into oblivion, do something dangerous like get on a plane to wherever the band was playing, jump onstage, and tell the whole audience.

"We have to figure out what to do about Violet." As if on cue, Dani's phone rang. "Jack?" she answered. "Doris, where's Jack?" Dani listened, nodding her head. "Oh my God." She quickly picked up her purse from where she'd dropped it on the floor. "Tell Charity's mom not to go anywhere!" She opened Red's front door. "Doris! Don't call the police! Don't go anywhere. I'll be right there." Dani hung up and turned to Red, panicked. "Violet's run away."

DANI

When they pulled up in front of her apartment, Dani saw Jack, still dressed in his pajama pants, t-shirt, and slippers, standing with a tall woman in a dress that resembled a burlap sack. Where was Doris? Charity sat on the front steps, her pale, thin arms crossed. Had the girls gotten into a fight? God, Violet, where were you? Anxiety rising, Dani's eyes scanned the empty sidewalk. She climbed from the car.

Red left another voicemail. "Violet, just let us know where you are." They'd been calling and texting with no reply the whole drive back. "Any chance she'd call Monica?" Red asked.

"No." Dani pointed down the street to the park. "She likes to swing on the swing set when she's upset."

Red nodded, taking Dani's arm. "Let's find out what happened first."

Doris stepped out of her apartment, pulling a long, yellow twisted phone cord, speaking in a firm voice into her landline. "No, I will not hold any longer, thank you. This is an emergency. My boyfriend's granddaughter is missing."

Dani raced toward her. "Goddamn it, Doris!"

Doris put her hand over the receiver, whispering, "Dani, we must file a missing person's report so that they will start investigations if Violet isn't home in the next twenty-four hours."

"Back off," Jack growled. "Doris watches *Law & Order*."

Dani gritted her teeth. "You were supposed to be watching her."

"Who?" Jack replied, confused.

"Dani." Doris held up her hand. "The girls only stepped into your apartment for a minute. We don't know what happened. They must have had an argument."

"Where's Violet?" Jack started searching the front yard.

The woman in the frumpy dress stepped forward, holding out a slender hand. "I'm Charity's mom, Marianne."

Dani ignored the formal greeting. "Do you know what happened?"

Marianne's hand fell to her side. "Thirty minutes after I dropped Charity off, she called and asked me to come back and get her. Charity is not yet ready to share. She's very upset." Marianne gestured to her daughter staring at them from her seat on the stairs.

"Not ready?" Dani turned away from the incompetent mother. Charity sat cross-legged, a patch of black underwear visible between her thighs. "What happened?"

Charity looked up at Dani. Her dark eyes were smudged in the smokey eye shadow she'd used on Violet. The girl shrugged.

"Charity Jane," Marianne cajoled. "Violet's aunt is also in distress. Don't we want to help her? Wouldn't it make you feel better?"

What sort of new agey mumbo jumbo bullshit is this, Dani thought. Get to the point. "Where did Violet go?" Dani demanded.

The girl slowly rose to her feet. She tilted her chin in defiance and glared.

Dani glared back, clenching her fists to keep herself from slapping the teen. She never should have allowed Violet to spend time with this horrible girl.

"Let's all go inside," Red said and began herding Jack and Doris and her long phone cord, still on hold with the police, toward Dani's front door. "We need to calm down. Regroup. Go over what happened. Make a plan." Red opened the screen door. Dick shot out between her legs, but no one chased after him. "Marianne?" Charity's mother reluctantly moved to the door, offering Dani an embarrassed smile, and stepped inside. The screen door slammed behind her.

"This isn't a game," Dani hissed to Violet's friend. "If anything happens to Violet, it's *your* fault."

"*My* fault? Oh, that's rich, D." Charity flipped her hair back with her hand. "Violet was so *worried* about *you* that she went your OA meeting."

Dani's heart stopped. "Oh, my God. Shit."

"Yeah, shit," Charity sneered. "That church doesn't even have OA meetings."

"Shit, shit, shit, shit. Okay. Where did she go?" Dani had screwed up. "Did she go to the park?"

"Where were you? Why did you lie?" Charity demanded. "You're just like her mom!"

Dani grabbed the girl's skinny arm and pulled hard. "Where did Violet go? Tell me! Tell me right now!"

"Let go!" The girl ripped her arm away. "Ow. Jesus!"

Dani quickly stepped back. "I'm sorry, sorry. Are you okay?"

"Psycho." Charity rubbed the red fingerprints on her arm. "I was here when

Violet got back. Man, she was freaking out. I told her we should look around to see what else you were lying about."

Please, dear God, no. Please don't tell me Violet looked in the nightstand, Dani thought.

In the living room, Doris was loudly scolding a police officer on the phone, while Jack tore the sofa apart, cursing, "Where in the hell is it?" He tossed a pillow across the room, where it almost hit Marianne, who was flattened in terror against the bookcase.

"Dani," Red said. "We may have a problem."

In her bedroom, Dani found the nightstand drawer open. The letter was gone. The box of bullets gone. Shit, shit, shit. No. No, no, no.

She ran back out into the living room.

"She found the letter," Dani announced, breathless. "And Jack's bullets are gone."

Jack was on his hands and knees, looking under the sofa. "I put the gun under the sofa cushions for easy access in case of an intruder. I'm positive. Ask Violet," he said.

Red turned, a look of panic on her face, just as Doris proclaimed, "The police are sending over a car," and hung up the phone.

"Charity," Red said and turned to the girl frozen in the doorway. "The police are on their way here. You could be in a lot of trouble unless you answer right now. Is Violet headed to Peter's?"

Everyone looked to the frightened girl who looked down at the chipped black polish on her toenails.

"Charity!" Marianne demanded. "Right now."

Charity nodded. "We found his address through Star Maps. He lives in the Hollywood Hills above Sunset Plaza. I called the Lyft. I told her to take the gun.

Make him confess." She burst into tears. "I'm sorry. I'm so sorry."

Marianne rushed toward her daughter.

"Shit." Red pulled out her phone. "I'm calling Sasha."

"Oh, dear. Oh, dear." Doris wrung her hands. "Violet's such a good girl. It seems very out of character." She turned to Marianne. "Is your daughter in a gang?"

"This isn't *my* daughter's fault," Marianne snapped, glaring at Dani.

Dani fought the anxiety taking over her body. "Shut up," she shouted. "Everyone just shut up." She took a deep breath and forced herself to hold it.

"Shit, voicemail." Red left a message. "Sasha, it's Red. Don't open the front door for anybody. We're on our way."

"Doris." Dani was quickly forming a plan. "You and Jack wait here for the police. Nobody mentions the gun. Got it? Apologize to the officers and say that we've found her and are going to pick her up. Send them away. Marianne, you got that?"

Marianne nodded, cradling her wailing daughter.

"Wait 'til I find my Smith & Wesson." Jack ran a worried hand back and forth across the stubble on his shaven head. "I'm gonna kill whoever kidnapped my beautiful granddaughter. Shoot them right between the eyes."

He wouldn't be able to keep the story straight. "On second thought, Doris," Dani said, "Red and I will take Jack. You three wait here." They could leave him in the car.

"Dear, why don't I just put him in front of the TV at my apartment?" Doris asked.

"Because he'll come looking for you." Dani grabbed Jack's hand. "Come on, Jack, let's go get Violet."

Jack acquiesced.

"All right," Doris said. "Have it your way. We won't mention the gun. It isn't registered."

Dani drove eighty miles an hour in the carpool lane on the 134 to the 101, taking the Laurel Canyon exit. Jack sat in the passenger seat cursing other drivers, and Red was in the back, dialing and texting Sasha and Violet to no avail.

"Where's Monica?" Jack asked.

"I don't know," Dani sighed. "I don't know."

Hitting bumper-to-bumper traffic in Studio City, Dani was breathing so fast she was afraid she might hyperventilate and pass out. "My divorce, my pain, my weight, my broken heart . . . my fucking addiction." She was gripping the wheel so hard that her forearms ached.

"You're a terrible driver," Jack grumbled from the passenger seat. "Next time, I'm calling a cab."

Dani felt sick to her stomach. Hating herself, she confessed, "When she reached out to me, I slapped my sister in the face. I'm a grade-A asshole."

"Here, here," Jack cheered. "Here's to assholes everywhere."

"Dani!" Red commanded. "Focus on the road."

"I sure hope we're not looking for Diane," Jack said. "That woman deserves the ground that's coming to her."

The light at Laurel and Ventura turned green. A bright red KIA in front of them didn't move. Dani honked. The driver, a pretty young woman, stuck her manicured middle finger out her window and then looked down at the phone in her lap.

"Is she texting?" Dani asked, exasperated. Turning on her blinker, she merged into the other lane.

As they passed the KIA, Red rolled down the back window and gave the young woman both middle fingers.

The woman didn't look.

"Buy American," Jack yelled. "You fuckin' traitor!"

Dani steered the curves, speeding up Laurel Canyon Boulevard, passing big, modern, homes with drives lined in palm trees and old brick houses with protected oaks and sycamore, the tires squealing toward the Mulholland intersection.

"Peter. Fucking Peter," Red muttered from the back seat.

"I hate that son of a bitch," Jack interrupted. "He used to be married to my daughter. Real piece of shit. I'd like to shoot him where the sun don't shine."

The light at Mulholland turned yellow. Dani slowed.

"Gun it, Dani," Jack bellowed. "Stop being such a fucking Girl Scout!"

"God!ess!" Red covered her eyes.

Dani pushed the gas pedal to the floor. They sailed through the red light. Brakes squealed, and horns honked, as drivers cursed, veering to miss them.

She maneuvered the car in silent concentration down the thin asphalt ribbon of road through the Hollywood Hills, passing ramshackle bungalows and concrete houses clinging to hillsides, their windows glinting in the bright sun. She breathed, kept deep breathing while driving downhill, taking the shortcut to Sunset, turning right at the liquor store. Taillights as far as they could see.

Please Violet, Dani silently begged. Wait. Wait. I'm coming for you. I'm coming.

RED

When Dani screeched to a stop near the stone statue fountain, Sasha's BMW was parked in front of the house. Thank God, Sasha hadn't yet changed the gate code. Red hoped it would be the same with the front door.

She took the front steps two at a time. She inserted the key. *God!ess, please tell me that locks haven't yet been changed.* She jiggled the key in the lock. It wouldn't turn. She jiggled the long handle back and forth. No luck. She was locked out.

"Sash!" Red banged on the front door. "Sasha! It's Red!" She pushed the intercom button, hearing the slow quiet doorbell echo. She rang the bell again, then pressed the intercom, hoping it was activated. "Sash, please open up. Is Violet inside? Are you guys okay?"

"Over here!" Dani called from around the side of the house.

Red raced around the corner to see Jack pointing up at an open guest bath window. "That's how you get murdered," he said. "Never leave a window open."

"Jack," Dani yelled. "Shut up."

Red shuddered. God, she hoped not.

"I think I can squeeze through," Dani said. "Give me a hand."

The window ledge was about six feet above their heads.

"I'm the tallest." Red stepped up.

Dani gently pushed her back. "She's my niece. I'm going in." She turned back to Jack. "Hoist me up."

Jack obliged, squatting a little, grunting. "My knees," he complained. Dani stepped into his interlaced fingers. "Jesus." Jack's face quickly reddened in effort. "You've got some heft."

"Not. Now. Jack," Dani said and gritted her teeth as she stretched her arms, reaching for the window ledge.

Had Violet climbed through this window? Was she inside? Not even the puppy was barking. Shit, what if? They hadn't talked about what if. "Dani," Red called out. "Wait. We really should call the police."

Jack fell back on his rear end with a grunt, leaving Dani swaying free. "Help!" Her fingers clutched the ledge, but she was unable to pull her body up. "Help!"

"Hang on!" Red quickly maneuvered under Dani's dangling body. "Put your feet on my shoulders."

Dani stepped her big feet onto Red's shoulders. She *was* heavier than she looked. Red sucked in her core, stabilized her knees, and gave a final push up. Dani's rear end wiggled, squeezing through the opened window. Suddenly, she fell out of sight with a thud.

"I'm in," she called out, voice echoing.

They hadn't had time to prepare for this. If Violet was inside, why wasn't anyone answering their phones? Or the door? Oh Jesus, she couldn't just stand there.

Red pushed aside the branches of a jasmine bush. "I'm heading up the hill," she told Jack. "Maybe she left a back door open."

"I never should have let Violet watch those murder shows," Jack said, his voice caught. He covered his eyes with his hand, clearing his throat.

Red placed a hand on Jack's bony shoulder and squeezed. "Jack, it isn't your fault. Trust me. How about you go and wait at the front door for Dani?"

Jack nodded, shuffling his slippers through dead leaves. It would take a fucking miracle for Dani's family to survive this.

SASHA

The heaviness gathered like a black cloud. It weighted her limbs to the sofa cushions, conquering her spirit. Sasha was tired of the pain, the lies, the mess. The carnivorous destruction Peter left in his wake. The sleeping girl breathed softly into the crook of Sasha's neck. The puppy was passed out on his back, fat pink belly exposed, paws chasing rabbits in the air. Sasha nestled her head deeper into the girl's thick locks. All cried out into surrendered slumber. Sleep, baby, sleep, Sasha thought breathing out, releasing the red-hot pain. They were winding toward each other to hold the truth, too big to hold alone.

Was there ever a time in history when it was safe for women to live?

After Violet offered the letter, Sasha had fallen to the floor, sobbing, twisting, and pulling her hair. She'd ripped at her gossamer shirt. She'd howled as if to wake the dead. Her cries had frightened Violet, made Violet cry harder, holding her hands up to her ears, begging, "Stop, stop, stop!" until Sasha had finally seen the terror in her young face.

Rape.

She had rushed to Violet's side and gathered the hysterical girl back in her arms.

The doorbell kept ringing, far away. A call to arms. Sasha wouldn't understand that language, didn't recognize the voices, the banging. Leave us alone, she thought. Somehow, the girl continued sleeping. The puppy, also. Sleeping beauty, such a beautiful face. Sasha stroke the girl's thick coarse locks; her hair was like Peter's, and Sasha felt the deepest surge of love.

Where was there a village, an island surrounded by a treacherous sea where a fortress could be built to protect her? And me and my babies!

Images of Peter broke through—his body, his smooth skin she had loved, the feel of the long, lean muscles of his arms and legs against hers. She couldn't push them away. They pressed harder into her brain the more she resisted. Peter's mass of curly dark chest hair, the dark line running from his belly into the nest around his thick long penis. The perfect space, the crook, the adductor, where the flank of his leg met his torso. She'd slept with her hand in that groove, so comforting, for years. She'd loved the nearness, the certainty of knowing a man. This man, troubled, moody, sensual, and strong, the only man she'd ever truly trusted. Ever truly loved.

This man was rotten to the core.

Nausea welled up at the thought of ever allowing him inside her temple. The hard cock she had once caressed and licked and sucked, a weapon of destruction.

Voices outside shouted repeatedly, trying to break through. Her cell phone rang. The girl's buzzed in the pocket of her jacket. The doorbell, a fog horn warning—danger, danger, danger. Don't wake the child, for God's sake, give the child a rest. Her poor mother. Allow the child to sleep and a brief moment to forget this awful truth.

She unfurled her wings, pulling the girl deeper inside her soft feathers. She cried out for the God!ess to fly them swiftly to safety.

"Sasha?" Dani stood in the doorway of the living room.

It was too late. Truth had let itself into her life.

RED

Jack put the unloaded gun and the box of bullets pulled from Violet's backpack on the center of the kitchen table. It could have been a crime scene. It could have been a goddamn bloodbath.

Sasha placed three mugs of green tea and a bottle of bourbon on the table. She sighed and squeezed her belly into the nook. Dani poured bourbon liberally into her mug. She took a sip. Red wanted a shot but resisted. It wasn't time for self-soothing. She had to push them forward.

They had to be ready for anything. She had to take charge.

Violet was tucked under a blanket on the couch down the hall in the library with the puppy. She hadn't wanted to be too far away from them. Jack, believing the girl had a cold, was watching over his granddaughter from a leather chair and laughing at *Some Like It Hot* on the big TV. Red worried that if he learned what Peter had done, Jack would hunt him down. If he could hold the memory that long.

"I'll give you the name of a good children's trauma therapist," she whispered to Dani. "She'll need to speak to someone right away. Thank God Peter wasn't here." Thank God Violet hadn't known how to load the gun.

Dani nodded, taking another sip of tea, wincing at the taste of bourbon.

"He's a monster." Sasha's quiet voice shook with fury.

Dani picked up the bottle of agave nectar and squeezed a liberal amount into her mug. She stirred slowly, staring at the spoon, mesmerized.

"We have to confront him," Red began. "Sash?"

"Don't call me that," Sasha snapped. "He calls me that." She looked out the window into the backyard.

"I'm sorry. Sorry." Red reached for the bourbon and took a swig against her better judgment, handing it to Dani, who did the same and winced. Red knew it was too soon, but she had to press. "We need a strategy."

"I need fresh air." Sasha wiggled back out of the nook. "I will confront Peter. He's still my husband."

"He raped my sister," Dani whispered. "Sasha, please."

She turned away from them and walked out into the sun of the yard.

Violet would be awake soon. Red needed to clear her own emotion and use her skills to mediate a truce. Red stood. "We all could use some fresh air," Red said. She turned to Dani. "I'll tell Jack where to find us and meet you out there."

A half an hour later, the three still sat in silence side by side on a marble bench facing the long lap pool, looking out over the smoggy skyline. Trouble seemed far away. Birds chirped, and a white butterfly flitted around and passed them on the breeze. Somewhere close, flowering jasmine offered a peaceful scent. Three women who had loved the same man, had been broken by the same man, were now brought together by him.

How could they set themselves free?

"We should confront him together," Red finally spoke, treading lightly. "I know you each want to, and I feel that. I honor it. But we each deserve to use our voice to stop him, to begin the healing. Can we put our differences temporarily aside?"

Sasha stared at the calm blue water. "I just want it over."

"I will try. For Violet," Dani said. "And Monica."

It's happening, Red thought, nodding slowly. "Thank you," Red replied. "When does he get into town?"

"Ten a.m., the morning of the birthday party. Which I am cancelling," Sasha said. "We will confront him some place public. He's not allowed here."

"I agree we should do it in public," Dani said. "Maybe a mall?"

"Or a restaurant?" Sasha added.

Suddenly, Red knew where it had to happen. "The party," she said. "We confront him at the party."

"I will not spend the day alone in this house with that monster so close to my babies."

"You'll be busy getting ready," Red insisted. "You won't be alone. There will be caterers, the planner, the florist. Stay out of his way."

"And when he wants to fuck me?" Sasha demanded, her high voice rising. "Does the beauty queen take one for the team?"

Dani's gaze darted to the house and back. "You've had plenty of practice."

Red said, "Dani, that's not fair."

"Didn't he make you do things, sexually, that you didn't want to do? Things that made you uncomfortable or ashamed?" Dani asked.

As if a nerve had been hit, Sasha's nostrils flared. "Could *you* could spend the day with him? Acting like nothing had happened? Knowing he raped your sister?"

"I would do anything to bring him down."

The two women stared at one another. Sasha pursed her lips. Dani bit hers. Once rivals, not yet on the same side. Deciding.

"Sasha, nobody is saying that you have to have sex with Peter," Red said. "Lie and say you don't feel well. Or run a fake errand and come to my house. But we have to do this. Peter's actions forced us." The intensity of her voice increased. "It doesn't matter that we're sickened, or scared, or wanting to hide. We can do this. We survived him. But Monica didn't. How many others do you think he's hurt? How many will he hurt in the future?"

Red felt a chill up her spine. The three of them were powerful. "We confront him in front of his label. His producer, agent, publicist, the band, the press . . . ."

"Before or after the cake?" Dani asked.

"I didn't order a cake," Sasha said. "Nobody eats dessert in public anymore."

Dani snorted. "So true."

"I want to be there," Violet said from the door.

They turned to look. The girl's eyes were red from crying.

"Why don't you come sit with us?" Red asked the girl. "The sunset is going to be beautiful."

"It's because of the smog." Violet crawled between Dani and Red on the bench. Red patted Violet's thigh. Dani wrapped an arm around her niece's shoulder, kissing the crown of her head.

The women looked out over the rooftops of Los Angeles glittering rose gold in the waning afternoon light, watching the sun make its way to the edge of the Pacific Ocean.

And then there were four, Red thought.

ALL TOGETHER

Twilight, magic hour, showtime.

The windows beckoned, ablaze in golden light. Mariachi music filtered down through the fragrant bushes covered in twinkling lights to welcome the well-connected, rich, and famous guests idling impatiently in their respective Teslas, Lamborghinis, and Range Rovers for the security guards to double-check invitations and wave them through.

Sasha, wearing a low-cut, gossamer white gown with flowing sleeves, leaned against the railing of the master bedroom balcony, watching the headlights slowly curve up the driveway to the valet station. Nervous energy tingled up and down her spine. Only the final gray-white of the day remained, turning the palm trees that lined the drive into dark silhouettes. God!ess!

In a guest room down the hall, Dani and Red waited to make their secret entrances. They'd snuck into the house late in the afternoon masquerading as florist staff, carrying large bouquets of colorful zinnias, salvia, and dahlias in bright Fiestaware pitchers. Violet, who hadn't needed a disguise, was already busy in the kitchen helping the chef prep for the catering staff.

Their presence steadied Sasha.

She looked down at the valet station and recognized Gary Cohn, the powerful gray-haired record executive who'd first brought Peter to the label, flanked by two languid, half-dressed, barely legal-aged models, remarkable in their beauty, and yet unremarkable, because Gary always traveled with at least two of the same type of girl hanging from his arms.

If Peter had real talent, he could have followed in Gary's producer footsteps—a well-established musician turned producer, discovering and developing new talent, starting his own label, or building an imprint. But Peter only had charm and charisma. His one skill was spotting talented women and charming them into offering up their skills for him. As if he were more important.

A bright yellow Porsche skidded to a stop. It was Terrell, a jovial neon artist with copious amounts of facial hair who normally traveled with a pack of up-and-coming actors. Tonight, he wasn't alone either. Sasha watched the passenger door open, and Renee placed one stiletto onto the driveway. She was gorgeous—decked to the nines in a silver pantsuit, her blonde hair teased into a sixties hive. It wasn't a surprise to see them together, especially since Renee's open-marriage reveal. Terrell had designed a neon installation for Renee's Aspen home remodel. The two had been as thick as thieves ever since. Terrell was a sweet enough guy trapped in a lucrative, pretentious art situation. Renee looked up, shielding her eyes as if the sun were still shining and spied Sasha on the balcony. She offered a friendly wave. Sasha held up her hand.

Would she lose this friendship? Truth came at a cost.

Earlier, while the gardener had trimmed hedges, and the pool man skimmed leaves, Sasha had made certain the housekeeping staff, the chef, and the caterer hired for the event had moved into their places, cleaning and prepping, filling up as many empty rooms in the house with strangers' bodies as possible. She'd pulled on a pair of baggy sweatpants and an oversized, sexless t-shirt and had gone into her office to meditate, to visualize locking the door of her heart against Peter for good.

She hadn't slept well, shifting positions all night with low back pain. The discomfort was from anger, she knew, breathing it away.

At ten a.m., Sasha heard a car pull up and stop on the graveled drive. She'd been constipated for two days. The front door opened, and Peter's deep, honey-sweet voice had called out, "Babe, I'm home."

The bad news didn't seem as real as his voice.

Waddling out of her office and down the hallway, she'd offered a nervous smile to the cleaning lady. When she reached the top of the stairs, heart pounding like a fist, she'd pasted on her best pageant smile and sung out, "Happy birthday!"

Peter had looked up the stairwell. "My love!" and clasped his big hands to his heart.

Sasha's heart had caught for real.

He was her husband. Her mate. The man of her dreams. The father of her babies. The love of her life.

"Babe, you're really pregnant." Peter's big brown eyes gave her body a quick up and down. "Get on down here!"

She'd started down the wide staircase, a clammy hand gripping the railing, knees unsteady, wanting to forget everything. His dark hair was pulled back into a short, thick ponytail, and the underside had been shaved close to his skull. There was a new green and blue tattoo she couldn't make out winding up around his neck. It was going to be harder than she'd thought. Be quiet! she'd ordered her monkey mind.

On the last step, Peter had come to her, wrapping his strong arms around her waist, and she'd leaned over awkwardly with her big belly, putting her arms around his warm neck. God!ess, he'd smelled like home—clean sandalwood and tea tree oil shampoo. She'd breathed him in while his hands had lowered to grope her ass. Her pelvis had immediately responded to his touch. Her eyes followed the trail of green, blue, and red ink that coiled up around his neck to the base of his skull. A warning, poisonous, a serpent with fangs.

God!ess!

She'd pulled away, breathless, saying, "Sorry, sorry! I forgot to tell the chef about Don Ebersole's dietary restrictions. He can't eat shrimp or scallops!" Her voice was too high, fast, and nervous.

A look of confusion had crossed Peter's face. "Babe," he'd laughed. "Slow down. Accountants are a dime a dozen. He probably carries an EpiPen." He'd gently grabbed her arm, raising one fuzzy eyebrow. "You know what I want for my birthday."

"Why don't you take your luggage up?" she'd suggested. "You're probably tired. Take a nap before your party." He'd tightened his grip.

"Baby." He'd stared at her breasts. "Your tits look amazing." He'd slipped a hand inside her shirt. "Look at your heart beating. Excited to see me?" He'd tweaked her nipple, and she'd cried out in pain.

"Don't!" Tears stinging in her eyes. Christ, it had hurt.

"Jesus, sorry," he said. "I'm sorry. I didn't know."

"Didn't you read any of the articles I sent?" she'd snapped. "It's what happens to your wife's body when she's pregnant." She'd swallowed hard, twice. What a selfish asshole she'd married. Had he always sounded like this? So sleazy and low-class? Why hadn't she noticed? "I need to talk to the chef," her voice hardened.

"Wow," Peter had grumbled. "Happy birthday to me."

Sasha had to bite down on her tongue to keep from apologizing like an obedient little beauty queen. Apologizing to Peter? Apologizing for hurting a rapist's feelings?

The entire day had been like that. Cat and mouse.

Peter had angled, cornering her when he could: in the hallway, the kitchen, once on the back patio in front of the shocked florist, grabbing a breast, touching between her legs, rubbing his hands on her ass. Sasha had finally escaped by car in the name of errands, driving down Sunset to the ocean, fighting tears, but she didn't dare give him any heads-up.

When she'd reached the ocean, Sasha had turned the BMW around and given herself a pep talk the whole drive home. You can do this. You are strong. You have to fight for others even when you're scared. Think of Violet, she thought. Her back hurt. No matter what, she and the babies would survive.

When she'd returned home, Peter had cornered her in the master bedroom and forced her back onto the bed. He'd pulled out his erect cock and made her hold it with both hands. When she'd pulled away, he'd finished the job himself, coming all over their freshly-made bed while she watched in horror.

That was her marriage. The truth of it. She saw him now for who he was. This man had drugged and raped a woman. This man ruined women's lives. God!ess, all day she'd felt like she was dying inside.

Meredith Blevins pulled up in a shiny Lincoln SUV. She jumped out, dressed in a dark business suit, brusquely handed her keys to the valet, and hurried up the steps, her pointy black shoes clicking as if she were late for an appointment. For her, a party *was* an appointment.

Peter wasn't the first famous man to rape a woman. Meredith would keep her publicity client until he could no longer pay the bill.

Could The Disasters go on without their lead singer? Would they?

The rest of the band arrived early, thank God!ess, to jam, drink, and get stoned with the birthday boy. All three guys now wore dreads, eyebrow rings, and tattoos whose meanings Sasha had long ago forgotten. Cory had brought a new girl with purple hair, but Enrique still loved Emiko with her easy laugh and good edibles, and Steady's wife of ten years, Maria, an earth-mama type elementary school teacher with salt and pepper hair, had baked Mexican chocolate cupcakes. God!ess, they had been her family. She had loved singing backup in The Disasters before the pregnancy and still felt connected to them. They were accomplices to his cheating by never disclosing it. Had they also known that he was a rapist?

Rock and roll would always be a boys' club.

A burst of cheers erupted downstairs. Sasha imagined guests gossiping and networking, grabbing Oaxacan canapes and Mezcal from the trays of passing waitstaff. Peter was either receiving a blowjob from a waitress in the guest bath or getting high with Enrique and Emiko out back. Annie, so far, hadn't made an entrance—which wasn't a concern one way or the other anymore.

Sasha felt the loss slipping from her body and stood up from the railing, catching an image of her reflection in the sliding glass doors. Suddenly, she looked more pregnant. "I love you, babies," she said.

She raised her arms over her head and began the Kundalini breath of fire, panting, her tongue hanging out. She punched the solar plexus upward with the breath to ignite the small flame of red in her pelvic region and to light the embers, building a fire that would ground her in strength and the certainty of her purpose. The breath of fire wasn't supposed to be done after the first three months of pregnancy, but Sasha needed to be calm and stable. The God!ess would protect the babies.

Warmed up, she unclenched her fists, rolled the tension from her shoulders, and walked back inside the house, pasting on a wide smile to greet her guests.

Behind a locked door in a guest room down the hallway, Dani lifted her long hair to let Red hook her macramé necklace.

"I know the necklace looks a little hippie with this dress," Dani observed and stared at her reflection in the full-length mirror in the guest room. Her hips didn't look as big as they felt. In fact, overall, she looked almost attractive. "It's Monica's."

Red locked the clasp and stepped back. "Then it's perfect." She appreciated the way Dani's black dress clung to her curvy figure without being too obvious, unlike the tight purple dress that Matt and Carlos had chosen from the back of Red's closet. "This color is too bright against my skin. Are you sure this is age appropriate?"

"You're gorgeous." Dani leaned into the mirror to reapply her lip gloss. "You look like sex on a stick."

"A glowing, white, naked stick," Red replied, feeling exposed and vulnerable. She was uncomfortable in high heels. "I'd feel better attacking wearing hiking boots and a backpack."

"Why do we care what we look like tonight?"

"You're right," Red said. Fuck him. "We really let Peter do a number on our heads."

"He just confirmed what I already believed about myself." Dani sat down on the bed, black heels in hand. "Now, what about these awful, uncomfortable shoes?"

Red stared at the pointed toes of Dani's kitten heels. Wasn't the night going to be uncomfortable enough without having to dress up? She wiped her sweaty palms on the satin fabric of her dress. Jesus. So much damage had already been done. Why had she pushed them to confront Peter at a birthday party? Because her rage demanded an audience? Why hadn't she contacted a journalist, or gone to the police instead? Once the truth was out, Red would no longer be anonymous. What an idiot. Rage had made her blind to self-care. Dani had been traumatized by bad press. Sasha lived in the limelight. But her quiet Echo Park life was still private. Once exposed, she would be just as vulnerable. There would be no more flying under the radar, hiding in the safety of invisibility. Reporters would find her front door. Whack jobs would torment on social media. Red would be subjected to the taunting and cruelty that happened to victims who stepped forward to accuse their perpetrators. Red shuddered, wrapping her thin arms tightly around her torso, thinking of what the media did to women who exposed rapists. They helped to destroy their lives even if they didn't intend it. Was Red about to destroy their lives?

From her years of counseling, she knew better than anyone that victims of sexual assault were always put on trial. It didn't matter if there were scars, bruises, pregnancies, police reports, a trail of evidence—outing a rapist rarely felt like a victory. The first question would either be, "How much had Monica had to drink that night?" or "What was Monica wearing?" And then, her sexual history would be brought to the light. Not his.

The final nail in their coffin would be the most asked question, "Why didn't she report? Have a rape kit done? Get tested for GHB and Rohypnol? Why a letter so many years later? Where was she?"

They had each been in love with him. The tables would get turned. Peter's life might falter briefly, but the public had a short attention span for holding horrible men accountable. Was it too late to cancel the plan?

"Hey," Dani said, interrupting Red's spiraling thoughts. "Stop pacing. It's making me nervous. Everything will be okay."

Red nodded, self-consciously touching the stiff bun on the back of her head. A "Chignon," as Carlos had called it. It felt sticky like a Cinnabon. She looked at her reflection in the mirror. She blinked; the extra false eyelashes felt too heavy on her upper lids. "I'm a stoned sixties casino waitress," Red said. The plans were already in motion. Sasha bravely leading the way. It was sink or swim.

"You're freaking out." Dani patted the hard mattress. "Let's do that stupid breathing exercise Sasha showed us."

Red sat down on the silk duvet beside her new friend. The bed gave a slight wheeze. She needed a drink. Just one drink. But she'd promised herself. No alcohol until after. She fidgeted, pulling her dress down over her exposed thighs. "I need wine," she confessed.

"Well, I need a six pack of donuts with a Kit Kat chaser, but too bad. Close your eyes," Dani instructed. "Let's at least try."

Red sighed and obeyed. They practiced the breath of fire as Sasha had taught them, side by side with Violet, earlier in the day. In out, in out, quick sips of air deep into the belly like punching the gut, feeling the heat rise up in their chests.

The breath of fire caught in Dani's thoughts. Where was Monica? She hadn't responded to any text messages. Dani remembered again that moment, that horrible moment, at the table outside of Vroman's when she'd reached across the table and slapped her sister across the face. The sound of the smack. The immediate beet red color that had risen to the surface. The way that Monica had sat perfectly still after, while tears spilled down her cheeks. As if she'd deserved punishment. There wasn't any way Dani could take that hit back. She'd never hit anyone in her life.

Where had Monica gone after that? Did she have anyone, a sponsor, maybe, to talk to? Had she started using again? Her sister could be anywhere. All Dani wished was that she were in the room with them. That Monica knew they were fighting for her. Should Violet know the DNA results? Did they even matter?

Dani opened her eyes and let out a long sigh. "I hate deep breathing," she complained. She nervously played with the macramé threads on the necklace. "Should I check on Violet?"

"Sasha said that Peter never goes in the kitchen. The odds of Violet running into him are low." Red tried to sound reassuring, but her pale, knitted brows betrayed concern.

Dani's phone buzzed. She startled, pulling it out of her small evening purse. Her heart sank. A text from Jack.

> JACK: Pizza number?
> DANI: Have Doris call them.
> JACK: Doris cooked dinner.
> DANI: Then eat Doris' food.
> JACK: It's green.
> DANI: Eat green. Thank Doris.
> JACK: middle finger emoji

"Time?" Red asked, breathless.

Dani shook her head, no. "Just Jack being Jack."

Red placed a hand on Dani's thigh. "Violet will move forward from this, Dani," she promised. "It will shape her, but not break her."

"When my mom left us for a *better* life," Dani said, because telling the truth was all she had left, "people told Jack, 'Don't worry, children are resilient,' as if being abandoned by our mother wasn't that big a deal. We were flexible. Like bendy straws or red licorice vines. Not whole people. We'd forget about it by summer and learn to swim in the neighborhood pool. But we didn't learn to swim after she left. We sat in the house watching cartoons and microwaving TV dinners. And we were never the same again. Every birthday, holiday, summer picnic. Every mother-daughter dance. Getting my period. Falling in love. Getting married. Divorced. Everything felt incomplete. Living without a mother is like phantom limb pain." Dani looked away. "I can't make this better for Violet."

"You're the right person for the job." Red wiped away the moisture under her eyes. "Is my mascara smudged? Do I look like a raccoon?"

"I don't know what we'd do without you."

"You won't have to find out." Red held out her hand and stood. "Let's get this party started." She wiggled her hips in the tight purple dress.

Dani took her friend's hand.

Outside the locked door, birthday party sounds—laughter, music, voices, footsteps, car doors echoed.

The women squared their shoulders, lifted their hearts, and took one last deep breath braced for Peter's night of reckoning.

Downstairs, Sasha was faking her role as an entertaining hostess. "Vegan street tacos are my favorite, too," she absentmindedly replied to the middle-aged music manager with a sagging gut openly ogling her breasts while he waited in line for the taco bar. She hated vegan tacos. The almond cheese tasted like wet napkins, tofu gave the babies gas, and she was craving brisket, but she was too constipated to try.

"Sasha, you are gorgeous!" Terrell interrupted her brisket daydream. He turned to the ogling guy beside her. "I just saw your wife doing shooters with the bartender. Might want to lock that shit down."

The guy sucked in his gut and walked away.

Sasha smiled. "Thanks," she said. "Your beard is longer."

Terrell gave a slow tug on his long, bristled beard. "Renee says it goes with my brand." He nodded his head in the direction of the patio corner. "But not her sensitive skin."

Renee leaned over a table, chatting up a young couple—a handsome boy and an even prettier girl. "New buyers?"

The artist shrugged. "Potential, or she wouldn't give them the time of day. What's going on between you two?" His blue eyes were genuine, intense.

Sasha felt the water at the edge, just behind her eyes. She put a hand on his broad shoulder and changed the topic. "I saw your show review in *The Calendar.* Congratulations."

He bowed his head.

"I keep meaning to get there, but everything right now," her voice broke.

"Hey, hey, Sasha." Terrell took her hand. "It's just art. You okay?"

"You might want to take Renee home early," she said, with all of the bravado she could muster.

Renee called Terrell over to meet the couple. He offered a quick kiss on Sasha's cheek. "Always pimping my wares, a blessing and a curse." Then, "Why, hello!" as he bounded toward the table.

Sasha scanned the crowd, mingling. No Peter. No one over the age of fifty, except for Meredith, who'd cornered someone from *Variety*, and Gary Cohn talking to a younger male suit, their ladies off lounging with drinks near the pool.

Where was Eric from *Rolling Stone*? They needed the big guns.

The mariachi band started to play, and Suz, the lead singer, took the mic, her strong alto voice bursting into a song familiar to Sasha, the one she had requested before everything: Si Nos Dejan. *"Si nos dejan. Nos vamos a querer toda la vida."* If allowed to, we will love each other for our whole lives.

People bopped their heads. Several couples started dancing. The movement of their bodies swaying against one another, the loud trumpet, Meredith, the waiter, the time for the toast growing closer—a heavy wave coursed through

Sasha's body. She looked around for salvation. A flash of purple fabric in the distance caught her eye. Thank God!ess!

Sasha and Red met behind the potted palm near the back door to the kitchen. With the catering staff quickly moving in and out, no one would notice.

"Everything okay?" Red asked. "You look faint."

"I just," Sasha shook her head. "It's almost time. Have you seen Peter?"

"No." Red shook her head. "And we need to get this show on the road. The writer from *Pitchfork* is playing games on her phone in the family room."

"Get her out here now, okay? Also, grab the photographer from *Complex*. Have you seen Eric?"

"Guy with the big beard and camera?" Red gestured toward a guy seated alone at an empty table dipping chips into salsa.

Sasha nodded. "*Rolling Stone*. Plant him at the foot of the stairs . . . ."

"Where's Dani?"

The kitchen door swung open, and Red pointed to Dani standing at the counter.

Unaware that she was being watched, Dani palmed a lemon sugar cookie from a silver tray, her mouth watering. She quickly put it back. The last thing she needed was an injection of sugar to add to her nerves. She quickly brushed her hands on her dress. "Shit." Now, she'd need a damp rag to remove the powder white fingerprints.

Violet reentered, carrying a large bundle of pungent bright cilantro, placing it on the counter. She was so young and eager. Such a beautiful person in spite of everything she'd endured.

In this moment, Dani realized, it was still a secret. Violet was safe, unexposed to the danger of Peter. Wasn't it her job to protect the young girl? It wasn't the right choice, confronting him in front of so many people. People were brutal and cruel. Dani pressed her palms on the cool marble countertop to steady herself. "Listen, Violet, we can still leave," she said. "It isn't too late."

Violet pushed her glasses back up her nose. The lenses were smudged in fingerprints. "No," her niece said. "We have to do it."

"People will say all kinds of things about us after tonight. It won't be easy."

Violet rolled her eyes, "Like I care what people think."

She was already a lot stronger than Dani. "All right then," Dani said, nodding. If Violet was ready, then she had to rally. She held out her hand. "First, glasses."

Violet obliged. Dani went to the sink, found the dish soap and cleaned the lenses. "I will never lie to you again. You have my word." She handed her niece back the frames and then grabbed a dishtowel to get to work removing the prints from her dress.

"When this is over," Violet asked, putting on her glasses. "Can I get a dog?"

Caught off guard, Dani snorted.

Her niece grinned. "Dick is an asshole."

"Agreed."

"On the asshole or the dog?"

"Both." They had no room for a dog, but at this point, Dani would have agreed to an orangutan. Dick would regret returning from his last escape. Anything for Violet. Everything. Take responsibility. Make amends.

A young waitress burst into the kitchen. "They're lining up for the toast! We need more glasses."

Dani's phone dinged! She grabbed it from the countertop.

SASHA: thumbs up emoji

Her stomach rolled. Jesus, Jesus, she needed more time. Time to catch her breath. The reality of what was about to happen was moving as quickly as a freight train. It wasn't going to stop.

"Ready?" her niece whispered.

This wasn't killing Peter on paper. Dani let out a heavy sigh. Real life had more repercussions than a blog.

A bright, white spotlight illuminated the wooden deck on the hill. The guests below turned their faces to the light, some shielding their eyes.

Above, Sasha materialized from the shadows on the deck, strutting like a runway model, to the microphone stand waiting in the center of the light.

The party went silent. Only the sound of a plane buzzing overhead, the gurgling of the pool filter, sound of dishes clanking in the kitchen.

No time for stage fright now, Sasha thought. She was the host of the show. "Thank you for coming tonight," she said, hearing her high vibrato reverberate over the speakers. She looked out over the sea of expectant faces. Where in the hell was Peter? "Hey," she joked. "Has anyone seen my husband?"

Laughter bounced around as heads swiveled, searching for the guest of honor.

Red's eyes darted across the patio looking for Peter. Less than four shoulders deep to her left stood Eddie, one arm slung around Emiko's shoulders. His eyes widened in recognition. Red steeled herself. Eddie nudged Emiko, who leaned forward curious, revealing—surprise—Peter standing on her other side.

Damn it, why did his chin have to be so chiseled, his jaw so strong and masculine? Those full lips. Why did Peter have to be so fucking beautiful? He wore light gray jeans and a white button-down shirt opened to reveal a colorful new tattoo coiling up from his chest and around his neck. His dark hair was pulled back into a thick, sexy ponytail. Emiko touched his shoulder and Peter leaned his ear to listen. Suddenly, he turned to look in Red's direction.

Shit, Red quickly darted behind two guests holding giant frosted margarita glasses. She held her breath, hearing the whoosh of blood pounding in her ears.

"Honey?" Sasha's voice called out in singsong. "Everyone's waiting . . . ." She shielded her eyes, scanning the people below bathed in blue pool light. There wasn't any time to waste. She was losing confidence by the second.

"I'm here," Peter's voice finally answered back in mimicked singsong. "I'm coming."

There was immediate applause as bodies parted to create a path. Cheerful greetings, the murmured "Happy birthday," could be heard as he made his way, smiling and nodding.

When he reached the cement path to the staircase, Peter stopped. "Get ready," he called out. Dramatically, he crouched down to one knee like a track star at the start of a meet. "Get set!"

"Go!" the party people called out with great cheer.

Peter raced up the cement path to the cries of "Woo-hoo" and "Time!"

What a fucking asshole, Dani thought. She squeezed her knees together to avoid peeing her pants. She was that nervous. Violet stood on her tiptoes, trying to get a better view of Peter over some poser's top hat. Who wore a top hat to a birthday party? Who wore a top hat?

Dani tapped the guy's shoulder. "Hey, can you please take off your hat?"

"Oh." The guy quickly removed the top hat as Peter lunged up the stairs taking them two at a time.

When he reached Sasha, he was out of breath, and the whites of his eyes were deep red from smoking weed. "Hey, baby." His speech was slightly slurred. He gripped her by the shoulders to steady himself. "How was your day?"

Everyone laughed. So enamored with his bullshit. Sasha shrugged off his pressing fingertips. It was all she could do not to smash his recently whitened teeth with the microphone.

That's when it hit her like a fresh breeze. She didn't have to mask her rage and hatred. She didn't have to hide the darkness that had been brewing since she'd read Monica's letter. For Monica, for Violet. For the girls and boys everywhere, whose *no's* had gone unheard. For those who weren't allowed to say no. For the anger from the little girl whose mother had paraded and prodded and ignored the leering coaches and judges. And other contestants' fathers.

"Happy birthday, asshole," Sasha hissed. The words hanging between them felt strong and true.

Peter's mouth gaped open in surprise.

She leaned back into the microphone. "So nice of you to finally join me, Peter," Sasha turned back to the gathered guests. "Tonight, I was going to sing a surprise song, 'Traveling Away from You.' I spent months writing it. But, naughty Peter." She forced herself to look over to him. "You ruined my surprise."

"Oh, babe." Peter offered a weak, embarrassed smile. "Man. I had no idea."

"I know, I know," Sasha said, brightly. "He just can't help himself. Don't worry, I found another song. A better one." And then, mustering all of her professional pageant training, Sasha announced, "Happy birthday, Peter. May you get everything you deserve."

The leader of the mariachi band stepped into the spotlight. He pushed his sombrero back off his bald head, letting it rest on the string around his neck, leaned forward, and began strumming a soft, familiar melody on his guitar.

Sasha looked out beyond the roof of the house, breathing, focusing on the city lights twinkling in the distance. This wasn't her first time singing under duress, but it would be her last. She breathed deeply into her diaphragm and began sweetly singing that old 1970s syrupy Karen Carpenter song, "*Why do birds suddenly appear, every time, you are near? Just like me, they long to be close to you.*"

There were a few *ahs* and *oohs* as couples moved closer. A woman rested her head on her date's shoulder. A man took his boyfriend's hand. "They're so in love," a catering waitress whispered to Red.

Red wanted to puke. She took a champagne class from the waitress's tray.

Sasha continued singing in her piercing, clear voice. "*Why do stars fall down from the sky? Every time, you walk by? Just like me, they long to be close to you.*"

Red lifted the champagne glass in a toast to finally taking action. To women who didn't back down. Women who got things done. The Carpenters' classic was perfect for this narcissist. Sasha had thought of everything in such a short amount of time. She was smarter, braver, a whole world of human better than him.

"*On the day that you were born, the angels got together and decided to create a dream come true.*" Sasha prayed the song would pierce the darkness of the night with the light from within. God!ess! God!ess, be with us.

Dani grabbed the handheld mic hidden near the planter. "Violet," she whispered. "It's time."

Violet's eyes were pools of tears.

Goddamn it, Dani thought, anger burning in her chest. Peter, you piece of shit. I will kick you to death. "It's going to be okay. Just wait here, okay?" she said. "I love you."

Violet wiped her nose with the back of her hand. She pushed up her heavy frames. "I love you, too," the girl said.

Sasha watched Peter's eyes darting across the crowd. "*So they sprinkled moon dust in your hair of gold and starlight in your eyes of blue.*"

From opposite ends of the backyard, Red and Dani pushed through the bodies, joining each other at the bottom of the path near the stairs. Red offered her a nervous, encouraging smile. Dani took another deep inhale, switching on the mic and held it out between them, her hand shaking. *"That is why, all the girls in town, follow you, all around,"* Red sang out in her lyrical voice.

"Just like me, they long to be close to you," Dani joined in, her low voice unsteady but loud. With the anxiety jittering inside of her body, she was surprised that she had any breath at all.

There was a smattering of applause. "Beautiful," a man's voice uttered.

Red looked up the wooden slatted stairs. There were maybe twelve steps, but they felt like one hundred. She grabbed the railing with one hand and started to climb beside Dani as they sang.

Peter's eyes were wide. He looked at Sasha, confused, clearly sobering up fast.

Sasha felt her confidence building as Dani and Red climbed closer. *"So they sprinkled moon dust in your hair of gold."* The adrenaline pumped through their veins.

When Dani reached the top step, just ahead of Red, she moved to stand beside Sasha. She dared herself to look straight into her ex-husband's face.

The panic in Peter's big brown eyes was exciting.

"Just like me," they finished singing. *"They long to be close to you."*

Dani, Red, and Sasha quickly formed a semi-circle in front of Peter as the crowd applauded. The mariachi leader grabbed the neck of his guitar and hustled down the steps of the deck disappearing into the garden.

Peter looked to Sasha. "What's going on?" he demanded, voice panicked.

"Karma," Sasha replied, feeling her lips spread in a wicked smile.

Red hissed. "Hey, dickface. Happy birthday." It felt so good to say it.

Peter grimaced. "I don't know what the fuck this is." He gritted his teeth.

"But I'm not playing." He made a move for the stairs, a purple vein of anger pulsing in his right temple.

Red blocked his exit.

He puffed up his chest, coming closer.

She sneered. "What are you going to do? Huh?" She gripped both sides of the rail for support, heart pumping with flight or fight against her sternum. "Push me down the stairs in front of a hundred witnesses?"

"No." Peter took a step back. "Don't be ridiculous."

Dani felt the soft cover of the mic tickling against her lips. It was time for her to speak. That was the plan. Dani was to tell the truth. To seek revenge for Monica. She tasted vomit in the back of her throat and swallowed. Her legs were shaking. Her mouth was too dry. She couldn't get it out, her body was rigid. Helpless, she looked to Sasha.

Sasha saw Dani frozen in stage fright. She quickly moved back to the mic in the stand. "Eric?" she called out. "Can you get up here?"

Rolling Stone Eric, with the bushy beard, bounded up the steps, camera swinging from a strap around his neck.

"I'll triple whatever they offered," Peter told the photographer.

Eric sighed. "For the last time, I'm a journalist, dude." He held the camera up to his eye, adjusting the aperture. "Ready," he told Sasha.

Sasha looked to Dani and then Red. We can do this, her eyes told the women. She took a deep breath and began, "This evening we ask you to bear witness." The power in her voice reverberated over the crowd. "To be the eyes and ears that record our story. The true story of Peter."

Murmurs rippled through the audience.

"First, Peter lied to you all. He lies to everyone. He can't read or write music. Dani and I wrote all of The Disasters' songs."

A few heads nodded, but Red noted with distress that most of the faces looked bored, while bodies shifted restlessly. She felt a growing panic in her chest. A few people slinked back to the bar. They didn't care who wrote what. What male artist hadn't stolen from a more talented woman? Red's ideas, her lifeblood. Speed it up! she wanted to yell. Sasha, get to the rotten core of him more quickly! This is Hollywood, they have short attention spans. Red moved to grab the mic from Sasha, but Peter pushed a firm hand on her chest and wrenched it away from his wife.

"Stay put," he growled under his breath.

Red twisted away from his grip. "Don't touch me."

Peter looked out over the throng of familiar faces. "Ladies and gentlemen, friends and colleagues, welcome!" Peter's voice boomed out of the speakers. "Tonight really is a surprise party."

Party goers laughed.

Red felt her hands tremble and clasped them tightly together.

"First, let me introduce the women sharing the stage with me." Peter turned to Dani. "Most of you know my ex-wife, Dani." He gave a sarcastic wink. "She writes a blog about killing me? It's actually pretty entertaining!"

"Truth!" some idiot shouted back.

"Remember, she lost that lawsuit. Didn't you, Dani?"

Dani tried to maintain eye contact, but Peter's steady gaze was a terrifying black. She caved in shame, looking down at the wooden platform. Her eyes stopped on his bare feet, toes curling and uncurling in an unconscious nervous motion against the wood. What the fuck was happening?

"And this is Red." Peter whistled, gesturing up and down Red's frame as if she were cattle. "We had a fling for a while. I didn't recognize her wearing makeup!" He snickered. "That dress would've kept me around longer."

The crowd tittered.

Red glared daggers, pulling down on the hem of her short dress. Embarrassed, she felt her shoulders slump, back to the ugly duckling, while the birthday guests enjoyed Peter's casual sexist mocking. He had always been good with an audience.

"And my gorgeous, sexy pregnant wife." Peter sighed, putting a hand to his heart. "The only woman who loves me exactly as I am."

Red watched Sasha's expression soften. He was getting to them. He was getting to her.

"Sasha is so close to delivery. We're having twins! You'll excuse the hormonal outburst?" He flashed his biggest snake charmer smile.

"My pregnant wife tried to run *me* over at seven months!" a guy laughed.

Unbelievably, people cheered.

The audience sounded miles away. Dani watched the rhythm of Peter's pinky toes curling on the wood. Such ugly, ugly feet. He believed he was better than them. He thought he was untouchable. The edge of her anger flared up again. It started a fire, an urgency to hit, to wound, maim, to fucking punch Peter right in his sanctimonious face. "Shut up," she shrieked. "Shut up." Hysteria echoed off the hillside.

Shocked, Peter turned to her.

Dani pointed an accusing finger. "You raped my sister!" she screamed, the emotion making her voice violently shake. "You raped Monica!"

The crowd gasped.

Peter's face fell.

Red and Sasha exhaled in unison.

It was done.

Crickets chirped.

A horn honked.

A siren wailed.

A coyote yipped; another howled back.

The women's gaze narrowed on Peter. His expression was impossible to read. Eric held his camera steady, poised for the kill shot.

At first, Peter only shook his head in disbelief. Then a quiet rumble grew in his chest, until he burst into wild laughter and doubled-over as if it were a comedy. He put his hands on his knees, gulping for air. When he'd composed himself, he stood upright again. "All right, ladies," he said, holding up hands as if he were jokingly under arrest. "You got me. Everybody, I don't write the songs."

Sasha's knees wobbled. A surge of nausea coursed through her body. She fought it back. "We have a signed letter from the woman he drugged and raped!" She implored the audience. "Peter invited his wife's sister to his concert, and then he drugged her . . . ."

"The woman was a drug addict, Sasha," Peter interjected. "A drunk. It's a very sad story." His voice turned harsh. ""But Dani got it wrong. Her sister passed out in my hotel room. Did she tell you I paid for a cab to get her home?" He turned to Dani, who silently shook her head in disbelief. "Your sister was a white hot mess."

Red couldn't take one more minute of his lies. Blind with rage, she lunged toward Peter, her fists raised. "Liar!" she screamed. "Liar!"

She beat her fists against his chest.

Peter quickly restrained Red's arms pressing himself against her body. "Stop it," he warned through gritted teeth. "Stop it." His breath was hot in her face.

Terrified, Red wriggled, desperate to free herself from his rough grasp. "Let me go," she said, grunting in effort.

The fight quickly escalated.

Horrified, Sasha clawed at Peter's arms. "Let her go, you monster!"

Peter easily shrugged off Sasha. "Back off." Sasha tripped, and Dani grabbed her just before she fell.

"You all right?" Dani quickly asked.

Sasha nodded, biting her lip to stop from crying. She tasted blood.

Furious, Dani whipped around and jumped onto Peter's back. She roared, feeling the heat of emotion rush to her face.

Below, the spellbound crowd watched Peter fighting the three women in anticipation, uncertain if the action had been planned. They were on the edge of their seats eager for the climax.

Dani's hands went around Peter's neck. She felt his soft skin, the ropey muscles. The urge to squeeze, to choke the life of him, for Monica felt natural. She wanted to kill him with her bare hands. She gripped her legs around his torso, adrenaline coursing through her body, as she rode her ex-husband. This was how it had to end.

Peter dropped Red. She quickly scooted away toward Sasha, cowered against the railing. "Okay?" she asked. Peter's wife nodded, wiping tears from her cheeks.

Dani tried to hold on, choking and squeezing, Peter's face turning purple. It felt so good to hurt him. Suddenly, Peter pivoted, twisting his shoulders, and dropped Dani on her ass.

She landed with a hard thud against the deck, hearing a small crack in her tail bone. Feeling a quick, sharp pain.

Peter towered over her. "You really want to murder me, don't you, Dani? How pathetic." He shook his head in disgust, turned, and walked to the railing. Rubbing his reddened sore neck, he scanned the silenced crowd. Finally, he said, "I hope there's cake!"

A smatter of uncomfortable laughter arose. Several people clapped and then more joined in. Peter bowed to a round of applause.

The three women's bodies shook. Red looked at her friends in dismay. Did the party goers actually think this was a play? Why didn't anyone see the truth?

Sasha understood that this was the nature of delusion, the devilish function of people's minds. People were invested; they needed to believe the mirage story of a famous man. They were personally invested. That image they had attached themselves to wouldn't be easily shaken. Suddenly, her uterus was seized by a small contraction, and her hands rushed to her belly. God!ess!

In the middle of the melee, no one had noticed the small, solitary figure climbing the stairs until she spoke, "My mother's name is Monica!" Violet's voice rang clear in the night.

Peter's eyes darted to the dark-haired teenage girl standing with her small fists clenched in defiance.

"Violet, no." The three women swiftly closed in to protect the girl. A tribunal, a women's court, Red grabbed Sasha's hand. Everything now was up to Violet.

Peter's expression remained calm, but his eyes widened as the recognition of Violet's similar features set in.

"You raped my mom." Violet's small body shook with fury.

Another collective gasp from the crowd was followed by murmurs. Eric clicked away.

"Tell them," the young girl demanded, pointing to the people below. "Tell the truth! You raped my mom!"

Dani put an arm around Violet's shaking shoulders. "I have the DNA results, you piece of shit," Dani announced. "The truth will come out."

Peter's gaze intensified on Violet. "What did you say your name was?" he asked in a quiet voice.

"Violet." Her young voice held less bravado in closer proximity.

"Violet," he slowly repeated, nodding his head as if formulating a plan. "I promise that the situation with your mom was consensual." His words were evenly measured. "She may not remember it that way. Because, you know, Monica had . . . a few problems."

Violet didn't move a muscle, but Dani could tell that her niece was listening. Once again, Dani felt her confidence in Monica's story slipping. Was her sister's recollection of the story marred by alcohol and drug consumption that night? How could she think that Monica would lie about rape?

Say something, Dani, Red thought, feeling the mood of the evening shift toward Peter again. "No, no, no," Red said under her breath.

Unhindered, Peter continued. "I'm so sorry, Violet," he said. "What a terrible thing to think happened to your mom. God, how horrible. Violet, it isn't true. I promise." As he spoke, Peter slowly moved toward the girl in small unhurried steps, gauging his target's energy as if he were tracking and hunting a small rabbit, his gaze never leaving her face.

Dani pulled Violet in closer to her body.

Red felt the fight leaving her body.

Suddenly, Sasha was hit with another wave of cramps. Stronger this time. The pressure on her lower back was almost unbearable. She took in a deep breath and held it. She needed to lie down. No, no babies, not now. Not now!

Peter lowered on his haunches to meet Violet at eye level. His big brown eyes emitted that love he was so good at playing. "Violet," he said. "It's so nice to meet you."

Violet let out a long, slow exhale. Her glasses had slid to the bottom of her nose, but she didn't push them up.

"Peter," Dani began, watching the little girl taken in by Peter's charisma. "Monica wrote me a letter about what you did."

"Violet," Peter continued, ignoring Dani. "Your aunt Dani, she's always had to take care of your mom. You know, it was hard on your aunt. We all cared about Monica." Peter adopted a loving, parental voice. "I didn't hurt her. I would never, could never, do something like that to a woman."

Violet sobbed. She gently freed herself from Dani's grasp.

"No!" Dani cried out. What had she done? Fallen down the rabbit hole and taken Violet with them.

Unnoticed by the others, Sasha gripped the wooden railing with both hands for support as another cramp seized her pelvic region. She lowered onto her haunches. Just hold on, she prayed, oh God!ess, just hold on, babies.

"Show's over, everybody." Peter waved to the party. He held his hand out to Violet. "What do you say we go down to the house and properly meet over some chocolate ice cream?"

Violet looked to Dani; the poor girl's thoughts were so mixed-up. Dani's heart tore in pieces. You hate ice cream, she wanted to remind her niece. No, this can't be how it ends. It must end in ruin, not ice cream. Please, please, Dani silently prayed, we need some fucking help.

Suddenly, a woman's voice answered her plea. "Liar!"

Heads turned, searching the backyard.

"Rapist!" she shrieked.

Red looked to Dani. Was it?

Startled, Dani shook her head. No. It wasn't Monica's voice.

Sasha spotted a twenty-something brunette in a white pantsuit standing on the concrete bench near the pool.

The young woman waved her arms. "Remember me, Peter? It's Yasmine?" she yelled. "Meredith Blevin's assistant?"

Cornered, Peter's eyes frantically searched the deck for an escape route.

"You gave me a ride home from the Peppermint Club? After the Grammy's last year?"

A look of real terror crossed Peter's face.

"He raped me," the young woman told the horrified crowd. "And threatened to have me fired if I told anybody."

"Yasmine?" Meredith Blevin called out, striding, heels clicking, toward her assistant.

"Fuck off, Meredith. I quit," the young woman wept. "You people are horrible!"

The audience moved closer to the bottom of the deck, craning their necks to get a better look at Peter's reaction.

He was crumbling. Dani moved closer to him. He backed away, afraid. Of her!

Red looked at the man she'd let ruin the last year of her life. He was shrinking before them.

Sasha gripped the rail with both hands, breathing deeply, praying the contractions were still far enough apart. God!ess, hold off the babies until this reached its end.

"Hey," Violet laughed, catching their attention. She pointed down at Peter's crotch.

A wet stain bloomed in the center of Peter's gray pants.

He looked down in horror.

"Oh, man." Eric clicked away. "Dude, you pissed yourself."

The images of Peter's wetting himself would soon be plastered across social media as evidence of his guilt.

"Rapist!" Violet pointed her finger at him.

"Rapist!" Dani spat.

"Rapist!" Sasha's and Red's voices echoed in unison.

Convicted, trapped like an animal, Peter scrambled up onto the deck railing. His body teetered back and forth like a man trying to walk a tightrope, his panicked gaze darting up and down the hillside.

"Admit it," Dani said. "Tell the truth for once in your miserable fucking life."

A collective shout rose up. "Get him!" A mob started up the stairs.

With nowhere left to go, Peter lunged into the open air.

Everyone gasped.

The women raced to the edge of the deck and peered out.

Miraculously, Peter landed on his feet on the rocky soil, stable for a moment. He starting running downhill, but the momentum of his fall caught up to him, and he slipped and slid onto his knees, tumbling into a painful somersault over the bramble and cactus. It was thrilling for Dani to hear his cries of pain as his body slammed against the ground, breaking twigs of sage and mazanita, until he flew out over the small, rocky ledge.

Peter's lean frame plummeted in free fall toward the concrete.

Red heard her sharp intake of breath, caught herself praying that the death would be instant.

Instead, Peter's body hit the surface of the pool—splat—in a giant belly flop. A plume of water rose up, splashing the bystanders and crashed down plunging him underwater.

Gasps of horror rose up.

The searing pain, dropped Sasha down to her knees. Each contraction was stronger than the last as her body made way to deliver the babies. She prayed that this night of revelations hadn't hurt them. That they wouldn't hold onto this energy. "I'm sorry, babies," she whimpered, alone in her suffering.

All eyes remained steady on the pool's surface.

Peter's body bobbed back up, face down. He floated unmoving, arms outstretched, illuminated by the lights shining from the bottom of the indigo pool. Dark hair flowing out like a fan.

The contraction subsided and Sasha caught her breath. She peered through the railing and saw Peter's lifeless body floating on the water. "He can't swim," she commented.

Dani heard her. "That's right," she remembered. "Peter can't swim." She looked over to Red, trying to gauge the reaction on her friend's face. Wouldn't it be all right if they let him drown? Red shrugged, thinking, I'm not running down those stairs and jumping in to save him.

It was Violet who rescued Peter. "He can't swim," the girl cried out, sprinting down the wooden stairs. "He can't swim!" Dani scrambled after her niece.

People sprang to action. A man pulled off his jacket and shoes and dove into the pool. Several others rushed to help drag Peter's heavy motionless frame up onto the concrete. A small woman with short, dark hair knelt over him. She quickly swiped the wet hair away from his face and leaned in to offer a breath of life into his mouth.

Above, Red watched thinking that the woman knew what she was doing. Maybe she was a doctor or a nurse. But it didn't look right, a woman saving that wretch's life. Suddenly, Red wished that the three of them had pushed him off the deck. Watched him plummet to his death. Why hadn't she brought a knife, or that gun, or even a two-by-four to smash his skull to bits? How was this ending satisfying in her gut? Exactly what revenge had they enacted? Was telling the truth enough to stop a rapist these days?

By the time Violet and Dani had pushed through people and reached the edge of the pool, Peter was violently coughing up water. "Roll him on his side," someone cried. Her ex-husband looked like a pathetic drowned rat. Curled in a fetal position, that wet mop of dripping hair, white shirt plastered to his muscular frame. Eddie and Emiko knelt beside him. Emiko looked up at Dani, her big eyes pleading. For what? You want mercy? Dani wanted to scream at her. To save The fucking Disasters? Well, she hadn't killed him. But she wasn't happy to see him resuscitated. She looked hard into Emiko's eyes. It was the women who kept the horrible secrets. The women who did nothing to stop a terrible man that made it possible for men to be terrible in the world. Emiko had sold t-shirts for the band, drank with the band, traveled and slept with the band; Emiko had always known who Peter was. Boys will be boys, Dani thought, as long as women let them.

Fuck you, she silently mouthed. Emiko's eyes widened. Dani gave the girlfriend her middle finger, and then she grabbed Violet's hand and led her niece away, toward the empty garden. Would people feel sorry for Peter now that he'd almost died? Maybe Sasha should have planned a Run with the Bulls themed birthday party with a guaranteed bloody goring happy ending?

Once in the quiet garden, Violet turned her face into Dani's breasts, shoulders heaving in jagged sobs, tears streaming down her round cheeks. Maybe, Dani realized, this ending was traumatic enough for them.

Sasha gripped the wooden rails as another contraction hit. The splinters would need to be pulled tomorrow, but for now, they were nothing compared to the pain, ripping up her insides. She gasped as another cramp, so severe, squeezed her pelvic region. Liquid trickled down the inside of her legs. She grabbed her belly. "Guys?" she cried. "Help!"

Sasha's cries jolted Red back to the present. Sasha was on her knees. "Jesus," Red exclaimed.

"The babies are coming," Sasha announced. "The babies are coming!"

The wail of sirens reached the house.

DANI

"Whoever the hell this is," Jack growled into the phone, "it better be important. Calling in the middle of the night."

The sound of Jack's voice was so normal, so crabby, so Jack, that Dani almost started to cry. She was tired, relieved, and overwhelmed. "It's Dani. I'm sorry I woke you up. I didn't want you to worry. Violet and I won't be home tonight."

"I'm not home either. I'm at Doris's."

Sasha's howls from the master bedroom echoed down the hallway.

"What in the hell is that? Sounds like a cat fight."

"My friend, Sasha, is having her babies."

"Poor woman. Having a baby is painful. Your mother screamed her fool head off with you. You were big even then."

Dani ignored the dig. "You could hear Diane yelling from the hospital waiting room?"

"Waiting room?" Jack bristled. "I was in the goddamned room for both of my girls. I cut your cord, Danielle Desi Smith. I held you before your mother did."

She was amazed, shocked, by this discovery. "Wow. I guess I always imagined you in the waiting room. Handing out cigars."

"And leave Diane alone to do the heavy lifting? Miss out on the births of my girls? Who in the hell do you think I am?" he demanded.

Jack, Dani wanted to say, I think you're Jack, but maybe she didn't know everything about her dad. Had she ever asked?

Sasha wailed again.

"Dani?" Jack's voice softened. "My poor sweet daughter."

"Yes?"

"Go help your friend!" And the phone went dead.

A small, warm sensation, almost like blossoming love, spread through her chest. Dani rushed back into the master bathroom.

Sasha's naked body was lit by candlelight. She was squatting on her haunches, leaned back against Red, who cradled her below the breasts. Soft classical music played under Sasha's well-practiced breathwork and guttural effort to birth the twins. Dani watched, mesmerized.

Dr. Simone sat cross-legged in front of them waiting to catch the little squids. "That's it, Mommy," she coached in a soothing tone. "Everyone is right on schedule."

Sasha got to have the home birth she wanted, Dani thought. With Peter in the hospital, he would soon be transferred to jail to await bail. Bail Meredith would probably pay, but none of that mattered.

Sasha squatted deeper. She gritted her teeth. "Thank God!ess for yoga. Red, are your feet asleep?"

"I'm fine. I'm fine," Red said. "You're doing great."

Dani moved to Violet sitting on the bathroom countertop, timing contractions on the doctor's wristwatch. "All good?"

As if on cue, Sasha hollered, "Oh my God!"

The girl nodded, eyes wide. "Seven minutes," she reported in a serious voice to the doctor.

Dr. Simone nodded. "Thank you, Violet."

Dani hoped that witnessing the miracle of birth would diminish the darkness of the evening for Violet. "From poison, make medicine," she remembered the Buddhist saying. Was it past midnight yet?

Dr. Simone leaned forward and gently massaged Sasha, feeling around the rim of her cervix. "You're slowly getting ready," she encouraged her patient.

None of them wanted the babies born on Peter's birthday.

"Violet! What time it is?" Sasha called out.

Violet checked the wristwatch in her hand. "Almost eleven thirty."

"Thirty-one minutes until their own birthday!" Tears squeezed out from the corners of Sasha's eyes. "I want to push. The babies want me to push."

Red whispered into her ear. "You're doing great, Mama."

"Sasha, let's take a deep breath," Dr. Simone gently encouraged. "It's not time yet to push."

Sasha yelped as another contraction hit. "God!ess, fuck!" Sasha cried. "I'm sorry. I'm sorry. But it hurts. It really hurts."

Dani felt helpless and slightly faint. She grabbed a hold of the doorframe.

"One deep breath, Sasha." Red demonstrated, sipping in air.

Dr. Simone gently caressed Sasha's calves. "Almost, almost, Sasha. Hang in there."

"No! I have to push!"

"Sasha!" Dani quickly moved to her side. "You are the queen of deep breathing."

"Fuck you, Dani." Sasha's cheeks were bright red with effort. "Have you ever shoved a basketball out of your ass?"

Red bit her lip, trying not to laugh.

"No," Dani said. "You're right. I'm sorry. I hate deep breathing."

"Ow, ow! Jesus fucking H Christ!" Sasha screamed as contractions tore through her abdominal wall. "Stop it! Make it stop!"

Dr. Simone motioned to Violet. "Maybe you could get Mommy some fresh ice cubes? And hot tea for me?"

Violet solemnly nodded. Dani followed her out the door.

In the kitchen, Dani put the kettle on the stove. "If you need a timer break, I can take over."

Violet grabbed an orange from the bowl on the nook and started peeling. "Can I get the puppy out of its crate?"

"In the morning, okay?"

Violet nibbled on an orange slice.

Dani's stomach rumbled. "Do you want me to make you some toast or eggs? There's probably some kind of fancy cheese in the refrigerator."

Violet opened the refrigerator and searched. "Just that plastic vegan stuff. There's peanut butter!" She pulled out a jar and brought it to the counter.

Dani grabbed two big spoons from a drawer.

"Sometimes," Violet said, running the tip of her tongue over the thick paste on the roof of her mouth. "My mom would leave a loaf of white bread and a jar of chunky peanut butter when she went out. I don't know why chunky. I like smooth."

"Creamy is my favorite, too." Dani licked the last of the peanut butter from her spoon. "With grape jelly."

"I wish there was bread and jam now."

"In Sasha's kitchen?" Dani cracked a smile.

They looked around, admiring the shiny appliances. The bigness of everything.

"It's like a chef's dream on TV."

"Violet." Dani put the spoon on the counter and looked at her niece. The girl's eyes were puffy from crying. "Before I read your mom's letter, I imagined you living here. With your own ensuite and a pool."

Violet pushed up her glasses. "Didn't you want me to live with you?"

"Oh my God, no." Dani reached out and touched Violet's arm. "I can't even give you a nice house with a bathroom of your own."

Violet shook her head. "That's insane. Grandpa and I are sharing fine. And Dick doesn't live here, or Doris. It isn't anywhere near my school." She raised an eyebrow. "Plus, I like us being smooshed together on our couch."

Dani felt herself choking up. "I like snuggling on our couch, too." She cleared her throat. Ready, but not, for this conversation. "I haven't read your DNA test results."

Violet pursed her lips, thinking for several moments. "Do I have to?"

"They're yours. To do with what you want."

"I want to go watch babies being born," her niece said. "I think I am the only person in my whole school who's ever gotten to see it in person. Charity will flip. Do you think we could have Sasha's puppy?"

RED

Red slept for two blissful days after the birth. A boy and a girl. After twelve hours of labor, their beautiful, shining and intense heads had emerged, a dark-haired girl first, followed by a bald-headed boy five minutes later. Sasha had finished delivery like the warrior goddess she was, with dignity, fits of vulgar language, and all of the love in her heart.

The day *after* Peter's birthday.

Red stretched her arms over her head, took a deep breath, and eagerly padded out into the garden barefoot with her hot coffee. She put the coffee on the deck chair and got down on her hands and knees in the clumpy, dry dirt, crawling down the row, pulling up dead plants, weeds, breaking clumps of hard earth apart in her hands, dust to dust. She apologized, forgive me forgive me, knowing the apology would release the dead to regenerate the soil to begin again with one small seed.

It felt fucking good.

When she was done, she lay back on the hard earth, feeling the pebbles pricking into her, an ant tickling her leg, imagining rebirth after the death. Visualizing, like Sasha had taught her, she saw shoots of green, a promise she had made to herself to choose again.

I will be reborn. I will give myself what I need, she thought.

She was learning to understand the anger, to work with the anger. A way to create inner happiness out of a bright red seed, a way to grow it into something beautiful and fiery, that could nurture and generate instead of destroy.

"Take poison, make medicine," Dani had reminded her.

Later, Dani was bringing Violet over to learn a little bit about how to grow their own food. It was the beginning, the seed of her decision to start her business.

The Daily Plant would be Red's personal chef gardening business, cultivated from a hard-won victory. She would teach victims of trauma to rebuild their inner happiness by sticking their hands in the soil and growing food.

Plant one seed, Violet, Red would tell the girl. Plant it well. Tend it carefully. Taking care of one's self is an act of political defiance, like Audre Lorde said. Be kind to thy self, Violet. Let not the men nor any woman take away your magnificence. Make a life for yourself. Become strong so that nothing can defeat you. Take this one seed and make a strawberry to feed your soul. To feed the people who will become your people. May our experiences nurture your soil into a tall tree, wide with deep roots, arms leafy green, bursting with colorful fruit.

Violet would get to witness green shoots, pull root vegetables, and learn to eat something besides carrots and butter lettuce because she would come to appreciate and love the gifts from Mother Earth. And her own power to create them.

In loving Peter, they had found each other. In finding them, Red had found the courage to be herself.

SASHA

A soft afternoon breeze lifted the white curtains from the screen, tinkling the seashell chimes in the corner of the twins' room. Peace. Perfect peace. Sasha took a deep breath, smelling the salty air and felt appreciation again fill the center of her chest.

Venice, California was the perfect place to raise Azur and Asha.

Their little three-bedroom cottage was bright and happy and would give them space, but also keep them connected to each other and to nature, with the garden Red and Violet had helped her plant.

Plus, she loved the newly relocated and rebranded God!ess studio: wisdom is listening to your soul's needs in all things—food, movement, and love. Eat meat if you must! The interior wasn't stark, or white. It was purple and gold and green. Absolutely fecund (Red's word, she'd had to look it up—fruitful, luxurious, and alive). Plus, the new studio was in walking distance to their future preschool and grade school. And home.

Home. She was home.

Keep swimming, she thought. Nemo was the perfect theme for Azur and Asha's bedroom. Sky and water, boy and girl. Trust, confidence, and power. Together, we three are one.

The salt air would be better for the babies and clients.

All of them would benefit.

Except Peter.

Peter's life was ruined. Peter had ruined his own life.

He was no longer free to play stadiums with Annie or the band. His passport had been revoked. The Disasters' international tour, dates from Paris to Buenos Aires to Lisbon, had all been cancelled while he awaited trial. Six credible women had come forward.

But not Monica.

Maybe one day, Sasha prayed, Monica would return, ready to receive the love and support that she, like all of them, so deserved.

Her heart absorbed a stab of loss and let it pass. She knew that it would take time to let go of the memory of Peter, real time that she needed, plus a wave of forgiveness she didn't yet feel.

While the babies slept, she closed her eyes, repeating her new mantra:

I am a wave on the ocean remembering that I am the ocean. I am a wave on the ocean remembering that I am the ocean. Nam Myoho Renge Kyo.

She was blue, the blue waves of eternal creativity and healing.

My body is my body. It is not yours to own. I will tell the truth of my body. I will tell the stories of my body. I will look at my body from the feeling of inside to out. I will no longer look at my body from the male gaze or your gaze. I will create my own way, my own way of looking at myself, in such a way that my esteem will rise in magnificence. I will be beautiful because I am.

For what is beauty but acting toward oneself with kindness and compassion? And in offering herself this, Sasha would heal. She would raise children who loved themselves and would, in turn, love others well.

Loving would never again be mistaken for giving herself away. That wasn't love.

That was a disaster.

JUST-DESERTS.COM

Lovers don't start out hating each other. Of course they don't. Love begins, a small thrill, a tickle, or a tingle down the back. Eyes meet, pulses race, your breath catches at first sight. Love is fast, hard and quick! Or three months of slow dates, long talks, making love until the wee hours followed by more wine and maybe a pizza delivery or Chinese takeout. The first blush of Steve and me was a dream, a haze of hormones where nothing existed but us, and the time in-between touches felt like an eternity. Everything was brighter and deeper. Ordinary life was richer, seeing the world through each other's eyes.

The Perseids meteor shower was expected in early August. We'd been married four years. The intensity of our love wasn't the same, but I kept telling myself not to worry. Men changed after marriage. Every relationship book I'd checked out at the library had advised not to make a big deal of a husband's muted ardor. The conquest was over; now it was real love, real time to learn intimacy, love in the daily routine.

Instead of crying alone at night while he was rehearsing or at a gig, I planned romantic dates, sent him a love note in the mail, a message in a bottle, gave a blowjob in the shower, covered my body in chocolate, and did as the books advised: keep yourself looking sexy and good. I'd been starving myself since I'd met him. But none of these recommendations had increased his appetite. In fact, even the massage (with a happy ending) had left Steve cross. What was happening? I felt powerless over his lack of interest. Desperate to get it back. Steve had a crush, a fresh, new thing occupying his mind, time, and desire. The Calamities, a band name I'd suggested after an especially bad gig, was Steve's new love. And my competition.

When I read the *LA Times* article about the Perseids meteor shower saying it was "a reliable celestial shower with spectacular trails expected as the Perseids sped through the constellations of Cygnus, Capricornus and Aquarius at over 140,000 miles per hour after midnight this weekend," I'd begged Steve to come home Saturday night straight from his gig. "We need this."

Around eleven p.m., Steve staggered through the door, tipsy but feigning exhaustion. I was ready with a thermos of hot coffee, sleeping bags, and warm jackets already packed in my car.

"Really?" he whined. "You still want to?"

"You told me you loved camping under the stars."

"But it's so cold. I had such a long night."

"That's why I'm driving," I cajoled and encouraged.

Soon, he was in the passenger seat, Paul McCartney crooning, *"I need you,"* on the radio, as I drove us up, winding into the hills of Burbank, city lights falling behind, a faint trace of marine layer, but the stars above still visible.

I pulled into a turnout, dark hills on either side and grabbed the flashlight. Steve took the thermos and blanket, and we slid quietly down a small hill, discovering an open patch with a full view of the city in the distance, facing north. Spreading the scratchy flannel blanket out on the hard ground, I felt us coming back together again, no one around to disturb the energy, shoes scuffling, a far-off cry of a coyote and a response. We were just two people, a husband and wife, thighs lightly touching, chilly but not cold, staring up at the stars. I curled my head into the curve of his neck, a smell of sandalwood and vanilla and sweat and something else? Did Steve wear body lotion now? It was sweet, a trace of a feminine scent. Had he hugged a friend?

"Look!" Steve pointed up at the sky.

A sparkling trail of white shot through the night and then another, followed by several arcs in its wake. We were up on our feet. "Oh my God," I heard myself yell. "Holy shit." Steve grabbed my hand. "It's amazing, honey. Amazing!" I felt the warmth of his body. He turned and kissed me as meteors showered us with love from the heavens.

It was beautiful; life was beautiful. When it was over, we laid on the blanket, hands still intertwined and stared at the stars.

"What a memory. Our memory." He rolled over to kiss me again. I felt the hardness growing in his pants. I kissed his neck and inhaled the spicy-sweet scent. Patchouli—which had always given me a headache.

Finally, my aching broken heart knew for certain that no matter how hard I would try, no matter how hard I beat my breast with that relentless passion, no matter how full my love was for him, Steve was incapable of loving anyone.

And I would have to learn to love myself.

DANI

Satisfied, Dani hit "publish," took a swig of Diet Coke, and typed:

The End.

Acknowledgements:

I was working on *All the Girls in Town* just before the #MeToo movement broke us all wide open. The courage of the women who spoke out against powerful abusive men inspired me to finish this book.

Thank you to my creatives Lisa Sheppard, Linda Hill, and Debbi Wisher for reading the first wonky draft. Pat Verducci, for her creative wisdom. Victoria Barrett, for helping me separate the wheat from the chaff. Besties Jodi Barmash, Joe Gironda, Charity James, and Marianne Kopie Liggett, who always have my back. My loving parents, Bob and Marilyn, my sister, Julz, and my niece Willow, who cheer me on. I married into a big family while writing this novel and Larry and his Shores have been nothing short of amazing. Ryan, Destin, Levi, Sevy, and, especially Cameron and Samara who taught me the day-to-day of real love – y'all are everything.

Working with Touch Point Press has been effortless – publisher Sheri Williams, associate publisher Ashley Carlson, media Jennifer Bond, fabulous cover designer, David Ter-Avanesyan, and especially, Kelly Esparza, my editor. You made this book better.

To my extraordinary publicist who became a good friend, Sheryl Johnston. And my amazing agent, Katie Salvo, for not giving up until we got this story into the right hands. Love abounds.

In life, it's important to have good mentors. Thank you to my first writing teacher, the generous and talented Jim Krusoe, who validated my choice and reminded me that a writer reads. Gratitude to my spiritual mentor, Daisaku Ikeda, a living example of a walking Buddha. And appreciation for my supportive friends in the SGI Buddhist community who helped me to never give up!

For my wonderful, patient, kind, sexy, and smart husband, Larry, without your love, wisdom, and support, this book wouldn't have happened. I can't imagine a better person to share life's adventures. How truly grateful I am.

Lastly, I am forever indebted to courageous survivors who share their stories. The courage, love, and light of community helped set me free. You are never alone. Every person's story matters. Nothing can stop the power of people united for good.

CPSIA information can be obtained
at www.ICGtesting.com
Printed in the USA
BVHW040239210522
637574BV00002B/14